## PRAISE FOR ALEJO CARPENTIER
### AND *REASONS OF STATE*

"Alejo Carpentier transformed the Latin American novel . . . He took the language of the Spanish baroque and made it imagine a world where literature does not imitate reality but, rather, adds to reality . . . We are all his descendants." —CARLOS FUENTES

"[Carpentier is] one of the great novelists of the Spanish language." —MARIO VARGAS LLOSA

" 'Magical realism,' made famous by García Márquez's *One Hundred Years of Solitude*, was primarily Carpentier's invention . . . Carpentier, except for Borges, is clearly the genius of Latin American fiction in its great period, during the second half of the twentieth century." —HAROLD BLOOM

"Mr. Carpentier's writing has the power and range of a cathedral organ on the eve of the Resurrection." —*THE NEW YORKER*

"[*Reasons of State* is] a jocular view of imaginative idealism, repressive power and burgeoning revolution, all done with breezy panache. Once again, Carpentier has shown how canny and adept a practitioner he can be in mediating between the many realms which his own life has touched upon. I wonder what Fidel thinks of his emissary's *Reasons of State*." —*THE NEW YORK TIMES*

"The question asked by both of these remarkable novels [Carpentier's *Reasons of State* and Gabriel García Márquez's *The Autumn of the Patriarch*] is, how were these men able to make themselves so needed, and more important, how is a country to do without them, and to keep their future avatars from coming back? They are the malign royalty of a whole culture, clarifiers of countless fears and hopes and hatreds: hence their fascination even for those who detest them." —MICHAEL WOOD,
*THE NEW YORK REVIEW OF BOOKS*

"*Reasons of State* is the slow, sarcastic exploration of the exercise of power—a power inevitably bastardized, secondary, illusory—in a misdeveloped continent." —ARIEL DORFMAN

"Carpentier's energy is gigantic and pell-mell, sweeping colossi on top of each other with ruthless, contemptuous daring." —*THE YALE REVIEW*

# REASONS OF STATE

**ALEJO CARPENTIER** (1904–1980) was born in Lausanne, Switzerland, the son of a French architect and a Russian-language teacher. When he was eight years old, the family moved to Cuba. Carpentier studied architecture at the University of Havana, but he left school and began to work as a political and cultural critic to support his mother after his parents' marriage broke up. He soon became a founding member of *Revista de Avance*, a magazine devoted to the avant-garde, and his involvement in leftist groups that resisted the dictatorship of Gerardo Machado y Morales led to his arrest in 1927. After his release, he escaped to Paris and spent the next eleven years there, immersing himself in the Surrealist movement and writing his first novel, *Écue-Yamba-O*, an exploration of Afro-Cuban traditions among the poor. He also pursued his interests in music and anthropology, which resulted in 1946 in a magisterial ethnomusicological study, *La Música en Cuba*, the first history of the mixed origins of Cuban music. He spent time in Venezuela and Haiti, the inspiration for his novel *The Kingdom of This World*, in whose introduction he laid out his theory of *lo real maravilloso*, the origins of "magical realism." In 1959, after the Cuban Revolution, Carpentier moved back to his home country to serve in a number of official positions, including Director of the Cuban State Publishing House and Professor of the History of Culture at the University of Havana. In 1966, Carpentier returned to Paris as the Cuban cultural attaché and remained there until his death.

**FRANCES PARTRIDGE** (1900–2004) was a member of the Bloomsbury group, a writer, and a translator from French and Spanish.

**STANLEY CROUCH** is a novelist, essayist, and jazz critic whose books include *Don't the Moon Look Lonesome: A Novel in Blues and Swing* and *Kansas City Lightning: The Rise and Times of Charlie Parker*.

## THE NEVERSINK LIBRARY

*I was by no means the only reader of books on board the Neversink. Several other sailors were diligent readers, though their studies did not lie in the way of belles-lettres. Their favourite authors were such as you may find at the book-stalls around Fulton Market; they were slightly physiological in their nature. My book experiences on board of the frigate proved an example of a fact which every book-lover must have experienced before me, namely, that though public libraries have an imposing air, and doubtless contain invaluable volumes, yet, somehow, the books that prove most agreeable, grateful, and companionable, are those we pick up by chance here and there; those which seem put into our hands by Providence; those which pretend to little, but abound in much.* —HERMAN MELVILLE, *WHITE JACKET*

# REASONS OF STATE

## ALEJO CARPENTIER

TRANSLATED BY FRANCES PARTRIDGE

INTRODUCTION BY STANLEY CROUCH

MELVILLE HOUSE PUBLISHING
BROOKLYN · LONDON

REASONS OF STATE

First published under the title *El Recurso del Metodo* by
siglo veintiuno editores, s.a. Mexico, Madrid, and Buenos Aires
Copyright © 1974 by siglo XXI editores, s.a.
Copyright © 1974 by siglo XII argentina editores, s.a
Translation copyright © 1976 by Victor Gollanez Ltd
Introduction copyright © 2013 by Stanley Crouch

First Melville House printing: October 2013

Melville House Publishing          8 Blackstock Mews
        145 Plymouth Street    and    Islington
        Brooklyn, NY 11201             London N4 2BT

mhpbooks.com    facebook.com/mhpbooks    @melvillehouse

Library of Congress Cataloging-in-Publication Data

Carpentier, Alejo, 1904–1980.
  [Recurso del método. English]
  Reasons of state : a novel / Alejo Carpentier ; translated by
Frances Partridge.
      pages cm. — (The Neversink Library)
  ISBN 978-1-61219-279-6 (pbk.)
  1. Dictators—Fiction.   I. Partridge, Francis, translator.   II. Title.
PQ7389.C263R3813 2013
863.6—dc23
                                                        2013033421

Design by Christopher King

Printed in the United States of America
1 3 5 7 9 10 8 6 4 2

To Lilia

# GRAND ALLUSION
## BY STANLEY CROUCH

*Alejo Carpentier transformed the Latin American novel. He transcended naturalism and invented magical realism. He took the language of Spanish baroque and made it imagine a world where literature does not imitate reality but, rather, adds to reality ... We owe him the heritage of a language and an imagination. We are all his descendants.* —CARLOS FUENTES

*The novelist makes no great issue of his ideas. He is an explorer feeling his way in an effort to reveal some unknown aspect of existence. He is fascinated not by his voice but by a form he is seeking, and only those forms that meet the demands of his dream become part of his work ...*

*The writer inscribes himself on the spiritual map of his time, of his country, on the map of the history of ideas.* —MILAN KUNDERA

*Reasons of State* is a magisterial novel that raises ideas and passions about time, seamlessly converting them into mythic fact. I first had my coat pulled about it by Enrique Fernandez, a low-keyed critic and writer who was then either in possession of or working on a doctorate. We met at *The Village*

*Voice*, headquartered in Manhattan, back during the time now thought of as the *Voice*'s good years, roughly three decades from the middle 1950s to its final period of occasional depth and quality, the 1980s. Even so, that is as dubious a description of a "counterculture" newspaper as "the good years" is of the Third Reich that Borges was not impressed by—long before the removed literary sect that this grand inquisitor of a world-class librarian *supposedly* represented, because Borges stood apart through his accurate awareness, his tendency to ongoing study, his rejection of simplemindedness. Way down yonder in Argentina, this was a man who clearly saw the blood on that tragically warlike and naive German entity led by an imperial Austrian who loved to savagely flash his pure white Aryan teeth.

Fernandez was not taken in by much of the *Voice* because he was not opposed to adulthood or growing up, but he was as responsible for this essay as any that I was lucky enough to hear as well as I could, during an influential and heated learning time, one in which intelligence, discernment, and any attempt to understand life through reading the best books was in a photo-finish with the adolescent drives that seem to permanently have a good chance to stand in the United States, either in its academy or in a homemade lynch mob, because of a confusion between overly or underrespecting the aristocracy and the common people.

This confusion is usually undisputed as a *version* of freedom. It can be defended as such while throwing eggs and rocks over the barricades, missiles that are supposed to be taken as the released birds of the revered leaders who had risen from the mud, purportedly glistening with blood and scars from their ennobling wounds: they were then floating, willy-nilly, atop the surge of hypnotic chaos indifferently threatening us all, worldwide. Call it what you would, those years were like a return to the mad years following the fall of Louis and Marie Antoinette. Deep blues turned her hair gray, that last mile soiled by eruptions from her terrified stomach as she rolled in a cart on the Parisian thoroughfare not far from the guillotine. But the former immigrant queen was permitted, by her guards—obviously sympathetic servants of the people, and easily appreciated in the era of the Weather Underground and the Black Panthers—to relieve herself against a wall.

This was a period when heresy became a profession, a religion, an ideology that worked for pursuing an updated Never Never Land; rebellion had become a reduced kitsch, resulting from a starvation diet of loud and shallow entertainment, what Kundera describes thusly: "the need to gaze into the mirror of the beautifying lie and to be moved to tears of gratification at one's own reflection."

So there was plenty of darkness to go around, and plenty of muddy water to swim through, no shortage of hollow logs to sleep a mind inside.

Decisively as a burst of sustained wind or light or water, Enrique told me about *Reasons of State* and recommended getting with Carpentier. This man was, he said, the most formidable writer since Borges. This was uttered with a startling confidence that did not condescend to any others from wherever in the Latin World they grew up or moved. Carpentier was beyond the Latin or Spanish-speaking universe. Rendering his range and ability, Enrique made sure that the Cuban writer I had never heard of was introduced as a world force.

I was told he seemed a mythological figure in his sense of order, where everyone had to be evaluated by a couple of things—all that had been done and was known—as well as by what was *most* important—how much an original creator could make anew when he stepped into the heavyweight boxing ring of the literary world, in which one did not defeat other careers while pummeling to the top. At the very best place, one established what all writers sought, recognition distinguished by the fire, the subtlety, and the grace of the individual talent. Lord help us.

I was intrigued because I had never heard of this Cuban. García Márquez was the one considered above all others, so I wondered. But I had to step up because I was now in New York and trying to make my way through new information and newer circumstances. For too many years, I had been longing for Manhattan, its filth, its overcrowding, its sublime intelligence, its buried and hidden soul.

Back in Los Angeles, my hometown, I'd spent some time, after graduating from high school, as an outsider teaching English for the Poverty Program in East L.A. There I wandered and wondered how all of that American Latin world went together, so much of it a penetrable synthesis that made life seem a bit bigger, part of it from here and part of it from somewhere *over there*, as Carpentier loves to say, pulling a popular song's lyric into the narrative of *Reasons of State*. *Over there* could be in Southern Europe or the Caribbean or South America. It could also be Africa, the Dark Continent, or the City of Light, where the deposed dictator with a smutty soul dies a pariah at the end of the novel, disgraced for shouting the downstairs blues so recognizably upstairs and showing no class at all.

After moving up as a teacher and serving seven years in the academy, I left Los Angeles and moved to New York at almost thirty years old in the fall of 1975.

I soon found myself writing for *The Village Voice*, for which I penned reviews of music, theater, and film, believing I had made it to the *big time*. But I discovered I had to travel either in or out of the country in order to learn what I had to say about a subject. Subjects were perhaps serial murders and the attendant inner complexities of ethnic politics in Atlanta, Georgia; or a jazz festival superbly backdropped by the vibrancy of Perugia, Italy, and hovered over by Rome itself.

As far removed as those faces and places were, one by one they became essential to understanding or comprehending the massive girth of Carpentier's talent. His work was beyond everything popular in American literary trends. Synthesis and the grand *allusion* were his goals, and he paraded them as completely in *Reasons of State* as he ever did, except, perhaps, for the feeling and music delivered in his late novel *Baroque Concerto*.

Almost exactly like Borges, the unconvinced blind man in the porno house, Carpentier had not been duped into a limited sense of personal identity or irresistible appetites. He too could smell something more rotten than anything that had flipped out the great Dane. The Cuban did not step into and break the legs of his literary imagination with reductive nationalism, or let a ring be ideologically inserted into his nose and pretend to sing sorrow songs as it was pulled and forced him into motion, with the wondrous horror of great pain radiating from a tender part of the head.

## INEBRIATED BY THE WESTERN HEMISPHERE

Around those early 1980s, I became an acquaintance of Enrique at the big office of the paper on Thirteenth Street and Broadway, where an unknown man once wheeled a cart with an old phonograph onto the cold and barren first floor downstairs. He played both sides of Caruso singing, then continued down Broadway going from place to place, never insulted for making noise because the tenor sound did certain things

it might have done in *Reasons of State*. That horned phonograph player melted all hostility with the beautiful made
audible from the hissing surfaces of frail shellac discs. One
could understand why Louis Armstrong, the titan who had
risen on the banks of the Mississippi, remembered being
moved by Caruso recordings floating from windows in the
New Orleans slum where he grew up.

I had many conversations with Enrique about Latin
American literature and Spanish writing in general. He was
more than ready to teach me. Bilingual, he became an important influence on me and a guide who introduced me to
the depths of Borges. Fernandez possessed the calm common
to many so gifted with large, well-informed minds. They do
not become too activated when explaining things they had
concluded were either profound *already* or on the way there.
He did not think that all of Borges or Carpentier was great,
but he was firm in seeing all their material, failures or not,
as creation that never slumped under the trivial, or drew an
academic chalk line around a version of bragging on having absorbed so much gargantuan data it was hard to keep in
check, too hard and valuable to lose itself in the simple ways
of the dregs. He chose not to be one of the slick, self-assured
academic rodents running from the belly of a dead horse that
had rotted in the street, turned into an instrument of percussion as it was beaten by the newest regime. When I first
read *Reasons of State*, I was in the midst of many independent
studies, undertaken because I was impatient with the academy and had little respect for degrees. This was why it became
one of my favorite novels from the moment I finished it and
sat happily furled by a state of wonderment that occupied my
loft apartment on the derelict-ridden Bowery.

*Reasons of State* proves that vast knowledge is cold com-
fort in a time of preferred hogwash, particularly if the living

presence exits in smoke; we can see it leaving the bucket as flaming swords are dipped by blacksmiths wanting razor smoothness. Carpentier constructed a double-edged tool as broad as a sword on one side, as slim and shining as a shaver ready for all wet soap or mayonnaise on the other. He decided to make a style or approach that was direct and simple-seeming, because all his variations were based on popular art, clichéd stances, and stories that were so familiar they might result in being a version of the aesthetic and mythic fact that *Moby-Dick*, after all the huffing and puffing, is no more than a fish story; but one told like those tales Jack Johnson used to befuddle reporters, because he lived in a dream world where freedom could be realized only if the dreamer was as big as the dream.

The magnum dream drunk by Carpentier was the New World, sensibly in need of new ways to match new forms, sights, and the distance of deep thoughts, safe in the mind, if not in the air or on the earth. Fuentes writes that Carpentier called it " 'the marvelous reality' of a land where 'the unusual is a daily occurrence' ... The men and women said, America *is*, and the world has to be ceaselessly re-imagined from now on. Carpentier in his fiction made this marvelously explicit."

## MODERN FREEDOMWAYS

Carpentier was, in other words, alienated from nothing, having taken seriously the modern freedom of utilizing all things that could be connected to one another. Choosing that route makes him a descendent of the first great and internationally effective writer from the Americas, Walt Whitman, who swallowed all the fish in the bowl of life and spat them out as fire and brimstone, ready for war against separation, garbed in the audible mufti of celebration, that commonplace lyric sung with open arms in the graveyard, its strongest song. The man Carlos Fuentes says is the father of a vision abandoned all religion or nationalism or ideology, stationary in air-tight dictates, instead favoring recurring myth, tweaked, as they say, by the specifics—time and period, geography, the animal kingdom, tradition, and functional intelligence, none completely devoid of poetic explanation, terror, ambivalence, or affirmation.

We know no freedom is that big, but in the universe of what seems true, or accurate, it is not at all hard to believe in extensive perception. This was Carpentier's take on the freedom that came with and through world exploration and straight-up conquest, all inevitably destined to submission through miscegenation one way or another. Missionaries, sailors, conquistadors, naturalists, and villainous roustabouts, each type giving the close listener access to something close to thematic infinity in every direction given prelude by fanciful tales. But in this case, the Carpentier Case, much more unifies, since this writer's knowledge, interests, and imagination were apparently liberated by masterful creation itself, juices brought through characters always contrapuntal in their relationships to one another. This foamed into the great getting-up morning of the New World. A varied bush where colonized women learned what all princesses knew the world over: they possessed lush boxes as magnetic as any opened by Pandora, come one, come all.

## NOTES OF THE GHOSTS

Walt Whitman, along with Herman Melville, is a father of free form in American and world literature, developed along with what Rousseau, Baudelaire, Flaubert, and the European gang threw into the boxing ring of art; both the wandering poet and the novelist seem to foreshadow the ambition at the crux of Carpentier's fiction. The sloppily made huts, some rather neat caves, the indignant whirlpools, and his magnificent cathedrals of intellect, his branches and crevices of feeling, and all that is there, living, dead, or ghostly, appears in the introduction to the 1855 edition of *Leaves Of Grass*, Whitman coming right out of the box and leaving the stadium with the stains of new paint on his breeches: "Who knows the curious mystery of the eyesight? The other senses corroborate themselves, but this is removed from any proof but its own and foreruns the identities of the spiritual world. A single glance of it mocks all the investigations of man and books of the earth and all reasoning."

Carpentier's Cuban-born art was prefigured in his youth by an obsession and scholarly leap into Afro-Cuban music, which he was one of the first to study seriously. A sincere grasp of music actually pulls him away from most writers who are tone-deaf enough to write either telephone lists of names and numbers or advertising copy. But the Cuban work came to loom over its time because Carpentier's inner strength increased until it was aged wisdom, a condition known everywhere but perhaps most significant in the aesthetic context, and always aided by a sense of human recognition that escapes all of those snares, the intricate heaps of holes made by academics and meant for the capturing of imagination, its wind and breath, itself an Edenic force like the line in geometry that has no beginning and no end. Carpentier knew we have access to the part of the line that we pretend, together, has a start and a finish. Nothing not only comes from nothing, as the Greek said, but life emerges from and continues into oblivion, moving from mist to mist, impenetrably.

The relationship between time and space always follows the rules of quicksilver on a board beneath feet that is also a floor through which we see moments disappear—now you see it; now you don't.

Bessie Jones speculated to a college audience that the only meaning clearly said by life was this: *Being born meant that one was going to die.* A perfect grasp of existentialism by a Georgia Sea Island singer at an age carved into later space by wisdom. Whitman, Melville, Twain, and Joyce were open to such a scope of communication between the learned and the not-too-literate, since the poetic was always available to take the giant steps necessitated by democracy and its central thoughts, with recognition of the grand mystery of personal importance or group significance seeming to rise from nowhere and going somewhere on engines of vitality.

That is the roller coaster of international mulatto life, an inevitable that all human closeness brands as invincible. Alejo Carpentier believed and lived and danced and sang by it, if not to it. Happiness, sadness, or any variations on either are secondary to the vitality, the affirmation, of the breath itself, and to the wind that blows along or reveals the prints and footprints of the past.

> I was forlornly born in a bucket of butcher knives
> I been shot in the ass with two ice-cold Colt .45s
> So you got to be mighty goddam ignorant to
>      mess with me
> When asked, I say, Whatever will be,
> *already* happened.
> Ice freezes red, you hear me?

# REASONS OF STATE

# ONE

*... it is not my design to teach the method that everyone must follow in order to use his reason properly, but only to show the way in which I have tried to use my own.*

—DESCARTES, *DISCOURSE ON METHOD*

# 1

... BUT I'VE ONLY JUST GONE TO BED. AND THE alarm has gone off already. Half past six. It's impossible. Quarter past seven, perhaps. More likely. Quarter past eight. This alarm clock would be a marvel of Swiss watchmaking, but its hands are so slim that one can hardly see them. Quarter past nine. That's not right, either. My spectacles. Quarter past ten. That's it. Besides, daylight is already shining through the yellow curtains with morning brilliance. And it's always the same when I come back to this house: I open my eyes with the feeling of being *there*, because this same hammock accompanies me everywhere—house, hotel, English castle, our palace—because I've never been able to sleep in a rigid bed with a mattress and bolster. I have to curl up inside a rocking hammock, to be cradled in its corded network. Another swing and a yawn, and with another swing I get my legs out and hunt about with my feet for my slippers, which I have lost in the pattern of the Persian carpet. (*There*, always thoughtful for my moments of waking, the Mayorala Elmira, my housekeeper, would already have put on my shoes for me; she must be asleep in her camp bed—she has her fads too—with her breasts uncovered and petticoats over her thighs, in the darkness of the other hemisphere.)

A few steps towards the light. Pull the cord on the right, and with a rattle of curtain rings above, the scenario of the window is revealed. But instead of a volcano—the

snow-covered majestic, remote, ancient Home of the Gods—
in front of me stands the Arc de Triomphe, and behind it the
house of my great friend Limantour, who was Don Porfirio's
minister, and with whom I have such profitable talks about
economics and our problems. A slight sound at the door. And
in comes Sylvestre in his striped jacket, carrying aloft the silver tray—thick, beautiful silver from my mines: "*Le café de
Monsieur. Bien fort comme il l'aime. À la façon de là-bas ...
Monsieur a bien dormi?*"

The three brocade curtains have been pulled back, one
after the other, showing a fine sunny day for the races, and
Rude's sculptures. The boy hero with his little balls exposed
to view, being carried off to war by a tough, dishevelled chief-
tain, one of those—make no mistake—who utters yells of victory but will hurry from the van to the rear if things turn out
badly. Now *Le Journal*. The *Excelsior*, with so many photos
in its pages that it's practically a cinema of real life. *L'Action
Française*, with Pampille's gastronomic recipes, which my
daughter outlines in red pencil every day for the attention
of our excellent cook, and Léon Daudet's abusive editorial,
whose inspired and apocalyptic insults—supreme expression
of the liberty of the press—could promote duels, kidnapping,
assassinations, and shooting daily in our countries. *Le Petit
Parisien*: the rebellion in Ulster is still going on, with its concerto for machine guns and Irish harps; universal indignation
has been aroused by the second round-up of dogs from Constantinople, condemned to eat one another on a desert island;
more rioting in the Balkans, that eternal wasps' nest and powder magazine, but very like our provinces in the Andes. I still
remember—on my last journey—the ceremonious reception
of the King of Bulgaria. He came on a visit here with President Fallières, exhibiting his plumed and braided majesty
(for a moment he looked to me like Colonel Hoffmann) in a

superb state coach, while the band of the Republican Guard, stationed at the foot of Napoleon's monument, played "Platcha Divitza, Chuma Maritza," with a profusion of trumpets, clarinets, and tubas, enhanced by a zarzuela-like combination of flute and triangle. "*Vive le Roi! Vive le Roi!*" shouted the republican crowd, pining at heart for thrones, crowns, sceptres, and maces, very inadequately replaced as a spectacle by presidents in frock coats with red ribbons across their waistcoats, who moved their top hats from head to knee in a gesture of salutation very like that of blind men asking for alms after trying to extract the singsong tune of "La jambe en bois" from the black depths of an ocarina. Twenty to eleven.

Happiness due to an empty agenda tray, on the night table beside the hammock, instead of a whole timetable of interviews, official visits, presentation of credentials, or ostentatious entry of soldiers, suddenly bursting in on one without warning, to the rhythm of boots and spurs. But I've slept longer than usual and that's because last night, yes, last night—and very late—I fucked a nun of Saint Vincent de Paul, dressed in indigo blue, with a starched, winged headdress, a scapular between her tits, and a whip made of Russian leather at her belt. The cell was perfect, with its cardboard missal made to look like calf, lying on the rough wooden table beside the plated candlestick and the too-grey skull—the truth is I never touched it—which was probably made of wax or perhaps rubber. The bed, however, in spite of its conventual and penitentiary appearance, was extremely comfortable, with its pillows of false serge (down-filled slips looking as if made of austere sackcloth) and that bedstead whose elastic springs collaborated so obligingly with the movements of the elbows and knees working away on them. The bed was as comfortable as the divan in the caliph's room or the velvet seat of the Wagons-Lits-Cook sleeping compartment

(Paris-Lyon-Méditerranée) eternally at a standstill, with two wheels and a little ladder leading up to it, in a passage that always smelled—I don't know by means of what ingenious device—of the breath of locomotives. I didn't have time to try all the possible combinations of cushions and mats in the Japanese house; nor the cabin on the *Titanic*, realistically reconstructed from documents, and seeming as if branded with the imminence of the drama. (*Vas-y vite, mon chéri, avant que n'arrive l'ice-berg ... Le voilà ... Le voilà ... Vite, mon chéri ... C'est le naufrage ... Nous coulons. Nous coulons ... Vas-y ...*) The rustic attic of a Norman farm, smelling of apples, with bottles of cider within reach; and the Bridal Suite, where Gaby, dressed in white and crowned with orange blossom, was deflowered four or five times a night if she wasn't on the day shift—"on duty," it was called—because one or two friends of the house, in spite of their grey hairs and the Legion of Honour, still enjoyed from time to time the glory of Victor Hugo's triumphant awakenings. As for the Palace of Mirrors, it had so often subjected my image to lengthenings and foreshortenings, distortions and grimaces, that all my physical proportions were imprinted on my memory, just as an album of family photographs catalogues the gestures, attitudes, and clothes of the best days of one's life. I understood very well why King Edward VII had kept a private bath for himself there, and even an armchair—today a historic object, put in a place of honour—made by a skilful and discreet cabinetmaker, so that it allowed him to submit to delicate caresses which might be hindered by his capacious abdomen. Last night's spree had been very good fun. However—because of the amount I'd drunk—I was left with a sort of fear lest my sacrilegious amusements with the little Sister of Saint Vincent de Paul (another time, Paulette had presented herself to me as an English schoolgirl, armed with tennis rackets and riding whips; yet another time, very much made up like a sailor's whore, in black stockings, red garters, and high leather boots) might have brought me bad luck. (Besides, that skull, now I came to think about it, was pretty sinister, whether it was made of rubber or wax . . .) The Divine Shepherdess of Nueva Córdoba, Miraculous Protectress of my own country, might have known of my deviations from the mountain fastness where her ancient sanctuary stood, between crags and quarries. But I calmed myself by reflecting that they hadn't gone so far in their zeal for authenticity as to provide a crucifix in the false convent of my guilty adventure. The truth was that Madame Yvonne, dressed in black with a string of pearls, exquisite manners and a way of speaking that passed from Port Royal to the argot of Bruant, according to circumstances and the condition of the client—much like my French, which was part Montesquieu, part *Nini-peau-de-chien*—understood each person's whims perfectly, and yet always knew exactly where to stop. There was no portrait of Queen Victoria in the Room of the English Schoolboy, any more than there was an icon in the Room of the Great Boyar, nor a too-ostentatious Priapus in the Room of the Pompeian Fantasies. And when certain clients visited her she took care that "*ces dames*" should take up their position, as actors say: that they should concentrate on interpreting their parts—whether that of impatient girlfriend, satanic nun, provincial girl full of perverse curiosity, aristocrat concealing her identity, grand lady come down in the world, foreigner-passing-through-and-avid-for-new-sensations, etc., etc.; in short that they should behave like well-trained actresses, and they were forbidden to snatch coins off the corner of the table with their sexual labia, as other girls of a very different style did in the Salon of Performances down below—"*au choix, Mesdames*"—wearing nothing at all except a bolero made of Spanish sequins, a Tahitian necklace, or the hint of a Scottish kilt with a fox's tail in the belt buckle.

Now Sylvestre brings in the barber. While he shaves me he tells me news of the latest exploits of the apaches, who are now using motor cars and guns. Just as he is powdering my cheeks he shows me a recent photograph of his son, looking very martial—as I tell him—with cassowary plumes in his shako. I praise the organisation and discipline of a nation where a young man of modest origins can by his own virtue and industry rise to the same military rank as soldiers who, before they ever fire a gun, have to know by calculus and logarithms what will be the trajectory and distance of a shell. (My artillery, for the most part, decide on the sighting and angle of a gun by the empirical method—although marvellously effective in a few cases, one must admit—of: "Three hands up and two to the right, with a finger and a half of rectification, towards that house with the red roof . . . Fire!" And the best of it is that they hit the target.) From beneath the portrait of the cadet from Saint-Cyr the barber brings out a recent photo of a young woman swathed in transparent veils, who is so tremendously excited by the interest at 6.4 per cent on the new Russian loan that it seems she would be ready—very discreetly, of course—to acquire shares and so restore a fortune once supported by escutcheons covered in gules and ermine, which was now on the point of shipwreck; this young woman—and it was easy to see that her "know-how," as they say, was not to be sneezed at—in short, this young woman . . . (I must first send for Peralta to have a look at me, palpate me, and say . . .)

Through the window panes summer announces its presence, as if new, just arrived, in the splendid foliage of the chestnut trees. Now the tailor comes and measures and remeasures me, covering me with segments of sports coats, jackets, frock coats, adjusting, tightening, joining together, drawing theoretical figures in white chalk on pieces of a dark woollen garment. I turn around, like a mannequin, stopping at angles where my figure appears in a favourable light. And according to the orientation thus imposed on my eyes, I look at the pictures or sculptures surrounding me, which seem to be reborn as I turn, since I've seen them so often that I hardly ever look at them now. Here, as always, is Jean-Paul Laurens' Saint Radegonde, Merovingian and ecstatic, receiving the relic brought from Jerusalem, a piece of the Cross of Our Lord, offered to her in a beautiful marble casket by hooded emissaries. Over there, a spirited sculpture of some gladiators by Gérome, with the retiarius defeated, tangled in his own net, and twisting his body under the victorious foot of a he-man in a helmet and mask, who seems to be awaiting Caesar's verdict, with his sword ready. ("*Macte*," I always say when I look at this work, turning down my right thumb . . .) A quarter turn on my own axis, and I am looking at Elstir's fine seascape, exposing its restless blues between a confusion of foam and clouds, with sailing boats in the foreground, not far from the pink marble of the *Little Faun*, winner of the Gold Medal in the latest Salon of French artists.

"A little more to the right," says the tailor. And now it is the voluptuous nudity of the *Sleeping Nymph* by Gervex.

"Now the sleeve," says the tailor. And here I am in front of Luc-Olivier Merson's *Wolf of Gubbio*, in which the wild beast is tamed by Poverello's ineffable preaching, has become holy and good, and is playing with some mischievous children who are pulling its ears. A quarter turn more and it's Dumont's *Cardinals at Supper* (and what expressions of enjoyment they all have, and how lifelike! You can even see the veins on the forehead of that one on the left!), next to which is *The Little Chimney-Sweep* by Chocarne-Moreau and Béraud's

*Fashionable Reception*, where the red background marvellously sets off the pale low-necked dresses of the women amongst black tailcoats, green palms, and glittering glass.

And now, almost facing the light, my eyes rest on the *View of Nueva Córdoba*, a work by one of our own painters, obviously influenced by some Toledan landscape by Ignacio Zuloaga—the same orange-yellows, the houses similarly terraced, with the Puente del Mapuche transformed into the Puente de Alcántara. And now I am facing the window, and the tailor is telling me about some of his clients whose names add to his professional prestige—just as happens in England when a biscuit or jam manufacturer labels his goods "By appointment to His Majesty." Thus he informed me that Gabriele D'Annunzio, who was extravagant and grand in his ideas but always absent-minded and slow about paying, ordered twelve fancy waistcoats and other garments to the details of which I hardly listened, because the mere name of Gabriele D'Annunzio immediately called up to my mind that mysterious paved and aristocratic courtyard, hidden behind the façade of a wretched-looking house in the Rue Geoffroy L'Asnier, where, at the end of a passage smelling of leek soup, there appeared like some incredible opera set the pavilion with its classical façade, masks, and grilles, in which I had more than once had the honour to dine alone with the great poet. That luxurious yet secret hiding place had its own legends and mythology; it was said that when Gabriele was alone he was served by beautiful waitresses with fantastic names, and while his numerous creditors were kept at bay by a concierge hardened in such duties, inside that mansion filled with alabasters and ancient marbles, mediaeval parchments and chasubles, amongst steaming censers, the fresh voices of a choir of child acolytes, alternating antiphonally with plainsong, could be heard through curtains concealing the

naked bodies of women, a lot of women—and some of them
great, famous, and aristocratic—who were submitting to the
mood of the Archangel of the Annunciation. ("I don't know
what they see in him," Peralta used to say: "he's ugly, bald and
squat." "Go and see," I said, reflecting that, for the great man
in question, it was probably a good deal more interesting than
frequenting the de Chabanais brothel, however haunted that
might be by the shade of Edward VII.)

And at this very moment in came Peralta himself, carrying a pile of books on top of which was a yellow copy of
*L'enfant de volupté*—the French version of *Il piacere*—wherein
my secretary had certainly not found, to his disappointment,
the ribaldries promised by the title.

"They were in my room, half read." And he puts them
down on the library table, while the tailor carries off his materials, after stripping me of expensive coatings, shapeless evening dress, and trousers badly cut in the fork.

"Give me a drink." Doctor Peralta opens my little boule
writing desk and takes out a bottle of Santa Inés rum, with its
label of gothic letters on a canefield.

"This is a life saver."

"Especially after last night."

"You seemed to have taken a shine to nuns."

"And you to negresses."

"You know, my friend, I'm an incendiary."

"All of us from *over there* are incendiaries," I said, laughing, but just then Ofelia, hearing I was awake, began playing
"Für Elise" upstairs.

"She gets better every day," said my secretary, with his
glass in mid-air.

"Such smoothness and feeling . . ."

Today "Für Elise," coming so sweetly from my daughter's rooms, although she always made a mistake in the same

bar, reminded me of how it had always been played by Doña Hermenegilda, her unselfish and devoted mother—who always made the same mistake in the same bar—and how, *over there*, in those days at Surgidero de la Verónica—days of youthful hopes and torment, sturm und drang, escapades and brawls—after treating me to some waltz by Juventino Rosas or Lerdo de Tejada, she would move on to her classical repertory by the Deaf Master ("Für Elise" and the beginning—she never got past the beginning—of the *Moonlight Sonata*), Theodore Lack's *Idilio*, and various pieces by Godard and Chaminade included in the album called *Music for the Home*. I sighed to think that it was now three years ago that we gave her a queen's funeral, with her urn under a canopy, and a procession of ministers, generals, ambassadors, and grandees, with a military band reinforced by three others brought from the provinces—a hundred and forty performers in all—playing the Funeral March from the *Eroica* symphony, and—inevitably—Chopin's. Our archbishop had delivered a funeral oration (considerably inspired, at my suggestion, by what Bossuet said in memory of Henriette de France: "She who reigns in heaven ..." etc., etc.), adding that the merits of the dead woman were so exceptional and outstanding that her canonisation could well be contemplated. Doña Hermenegilda was married and the mother of children, of course— Ofelia, Ariel, Marcus Antonius, and Radames—but the Archbishop reminded his listeners of the blessed conjugal virtues of Saint Elizabeth, mother of John the Baptist, and of Monica, mother of Augustine. Naturally, the appropriate words having been said, I didn't think it vital to send up any prayers to the high authority of the Vatican, especially since my wife and I had lived in concubinage for many years before the unforeseeable and agitating vagaries of politics led me to where I now am. The important thing was that my Hermenegilda's portrait, made at Dresden in full colour by the initiative of our minister of education, was an object of worship throughout the length and breadth of the land. It was said that the flesh of the dead woman had defied the onslaught of worms, and that her face had retained the serene and kindly smile of her last moments. Women used to say that her portrait miraculously cured colic and the pains of childbirth, and that promises made to her by girls who wanted a husband were more effective than the hitherto common practice of putting the bust of Saint Anthony upside down in a well.

I have just finished putting a gardenia in my buttonhole when Sylvestre announces that the Distinguished Academician has come to see me—a recently elected academician, I do not know how he got himself received under the Dome, since a few years ago he decribed the Forty Immortals as "green-clad mummies in cocked hats, the anachronistic midwives of a dictionary intended to increase our understanding of the evolution of the language—a sort of *Petit Larousse* for domestic use." (Once elected, however—"*J'ai accepté pour m'amuser*"—he took the trouble to have the hilt of his sword designed by his famous friend Maxence, who had abandoned pictorial creation for silversmith's work, and succeeded in incorporating the spirit of the Bible and mediaeval legends with a style combining the aesthetics of the scenic railway at the Magic City with a subtle flavour of Pre-Raphaelitism—too much for my taste.)

Peralta hid the bottle of Santa Inés and we greeted this witty and polished man, who is now sitting in a ray of sunlight, full of ascending motes of dust, which picks out the red ribbon of his Legion of Honour. Upstairs, Ofelia is trying hard to remove those inconvenient flats from the passage of "Für Elise" that she always gets wrong.

"Beethoven," says the Distinguished Academician,

pointing upwards as if giving us an important piece of news. Then, with the indiscreet hand of someone who always treats my house as his own, he turns over the books my secretary brought back a little while ago. *Atheism* by Le Dantec. Good. Solid reading. Bourget's *The Disciple*. Not bad, but don't let's imitate the German *emmerdeurs* with their mania for mixing philosophy into their novels. Anatole France: undoubted talent, but overestimated outside France. Besides, his systematic scepticism doesn't lead anywhere. *Chanticleer*: a strange thing. A success and a failure. Audacity that is both brilliant and unsuccessful but the only attempt of its kind in theatrical history. And he declaims:

> *O Soleil! toi sans qui les choses*
> *Ne seraient pas ce qu'elles sont . . .*

(The Academician is unaware that for some years past ten thousand bars and whorehouses in America have been called Chanticleer.) He grunts ironically but acquiescently at the sight of an anticlerical pamphlet by Leo Taxil, but makes a face of disgust, of open disapproval, over *Monsieur de Phocas* by Jean Lorrain, without perhaps knowing that his own publisher, Ollendorf, has swamped the bookshops of our continent with a Spanish translation of this novel, presented as an incomparable example of French genius, with a coloured frontispiece of a naked Astarte by Géo Dupuy, which at least gives our schoolboys dreams. Now he's laughing, slyly, indulgently, as he comes across *Les cent milles verges*, *The sexual life of Robinson Crusoe*, and *Les fastes de Lesbos*, by unknown authors (three asterisks), profusely illustrated and bought by me yesterday in a specialist shop in the Rue de la Lune.

"*Ce sont des lectures de Monsieur Peralta*," I say, coward that I am.

But our friend suddenly becomes serious and starts talking about literature in the deliberate and magisterial way Peralta and I know so well, trying to prove to us that the true, the best, the greatest literature *from here* is unknown in our countries. We all agree in admiring Baudelaire—sadly buried under a sad stone in the cemetery of Montparnasse—but we ought also to read Léon Dierx, Albert Samain, Henri de Régnier, Maurice Rollinat, Renée Vivien. And we must read Moréas, above all Moréas. (I remain silent rather than tell him how, when I was introduced to Moréas some years ago in the Café Vachetti, he accused me of having shot Maximilian, although I tried to prove that, on grounds of age alone, it would have been impossible for me to be in the Cerro de las Campanas on that day. "*Vous êtes tous des sauvages!*" the poet had replied with the fire of absinthe in his voice.) Our friend laments the fact that Hugo, old Hugo, still enjoys enormous popularity in our countries. It's known that *over there* workers in cigar factories—who subscribe to public readings to relieve the monotony of their work—are especially fond of *Les Misérables* and *Notre Dame de Paris*, while *Oration pour tous* ("*naïve connerie*," he says) is still often recited at poetical soirées. And, according to him, this is through our lack of the Cartesian spirit (that's true: no carnivorous plants grow, no toucans fly, nor do you find cyclones in the *Discourse on Method*); we are too partial to unbridled eloquence, pathos, platform pomposity, resounding with romantic braggadocio.

Feeling slightly irritated—though he couldn't have guessed the fact—by an evaluation that directly wounded my concept of what oratory should be (to be more effective among us it must be luxuriant, sonorous, baroque, Ciceronian, original in imagery, implacable in epithets, sweeping in its crescendos), I try to change the subject by laying my hand on an extremely rare edition-de-luxe of Renan's *Prayer on the Acropolis*, illustrated by Cabanel.

"*Quelle horreur!*" exclaims the Distinguished Academician with a gesture of condemnation. I point out to him that this fragment figures in many manuals of literature for students of French.

"An abomination, due to secular education," says our visitor, qualifying the prose as amphigoric—pretentious, vocative, blown up with erudition and pedantic hellenisms. No. The people of our countries ought to look for the genius of the French language in other books, in other texts. Then they would discover the elegance of style, the distinction, the sovereign intelligence with which in *L'ennemi des lois* Maurice Barrès can show us in three lucid pages the fallacies and errors of Marxism—which are centred in the cult of the stomach— or give us a marvellous picture of Ludwig of Bavaria's castles, in the phraseology of a true artist, very different from the professorial logomachy of a Renan. Or if we want to go back to the past century, let us read and reread Gobineau, that aristocrat of expression, master of the carefully constructed and unique phrase, who had exalted in his work the Super-Man, the Men of the Pléiade, sovereign spirits (according to him there were about three thousand in all Europe), proclaiming his inability to be interested in "the mass of those who are called men," whom he saw as a swarm of despicable, irresponsible, and destructive insects, without Souls.

At this point I decide to remain silent and not join in the discussion, because the question would bring to light an explanation that would be better avoided: during the fiestas for the Centenary of Mexican Independence, the authorities made arrangements for the wearers of sandals and shawls (*rebozos*), native musicians and cripples, to be kept away from the places where the main ceremonies took place, because it

was better that foreign tourists and guests of the government
shouldn't see the individuals our friend Yves Limantour called
"the Kaffirs." But in my country, where there are many—too
many!—Indians, negroes, half-breeds, and mulattos, it would
be difficult to hide away our "Kaffirs." And I couldn't see the
Kaffirs belonging to our intelligentsia—who are extremely
numerous—being exactly pleased by reading the *Essay on the
Inequality of Human Races* by Count Gobineau. It would be a
good moment to change the conversation.

Luckily, "Für Elise" starts up again upstairs. And the Academician pounces on this fact to deplore the extravagances
of modern music—or what is called "modern"—a cerebral,
dehumanised art, an algebra of notes, alien to any form of
feeling (just listen to the Schola Cantorum group in the Rue
Saint-Jacques), which betrays the eternal principles of *me-
los*. There are exceptions, however: Saint-Saëns, Fauré, Vinteuil, and above all our beloved Reynaldo Hahn—born in
Puerto Cabello, Venezuela, which is not unlike Surgidero
de la Verónica. I know that my *"paisano"* (he always calls
me *"paisano"* in his smooth creole Spanish when we meet
anywhere), before writing his sublime choruses for Racine's
*Esther*, had begun work many years ago on a very beautiful
opera full of nostalgia for his native tropics, the action taking place in picturesque surroundings in every way reminiscent of the Venezuelan coast he knew as a child, although
the programme described it as a "Polynesian idyll": *L'île du
rêve*, inspired by *Le mariage de Loti*—and *"Loti, Loti, voici
ton nom,"* sang Rarahú in this history of an exotic love affair,
whose plot, according to certain mischievous critics fond of
demolishing everything, was too much like that of *Lakmé*.
But, come to that, one could say the same of *Madame Butterfly*, a later work then Reynaldo's. And just as in the old days
his *Chansons Grises* were heard at one of the regular musical

evenings of the Quai Conti, we used to talk about people like
the Belgian Chargé d'Affaires, the Comte d'Argencourt, who
surrounded himself with sodomites although he wasn't one,
because he didn't want to expose his too youthful mistress to
the desires of manly men; or about Legrandin, who had the
brilliant idea of endowing himself with the non-existent title
of "Comte de Mes Eglises" or something of the sort—("If he
had been born in Cholula he could have called himself Count
of the three hundred sixty-five churches," broke in Peralta)—
and was beginning to boast of being a snob in a world where
snobbishness was taken as a sign of being enthusiastic for the
"latest" in everything.

Paris, so the Distinguished Academician went on to say,
was getting like the Rome of Heliogabalus, opening its doors
to everything strange, out of joint, exotic, barbarous, primitive. Modern sculptors, instead of being inspired by the great
periods of the past, marvelled at Mycenaean, pre-Hellenic,
Scythian art, the art of the steppes. There were people these
days who collected horrible African masks, figures bristling
with votive nails, zoomorphic idols—the work of cannibals.
Negro musicians were arriving from the United States. A
scandalous Italian poet had gone so far as to publish a manifesto declaring that it was necessary to destroy Venice and
burn down the Louvre. That way could only lead us to exalt-
ing Attila, Erostratus, the Iconoclasts, the cakewalk, English
cooking, anarchist outrages, and the reign of new Circes calling themselves Lyane de Pougy, Emilienne d'Alençon, or Cleo
de Mérode.

("I'd willingly be transformed into a swine for them,"
murmured Peralta.)

But now, to cheer up our visitor, I said that every big city
suffered from temporary fevers, foolish enthusiasms, fashions, affectations, and extravagances, which lasted only one

day and made no impact on the genius of a nation. Juvenal was already complaining of the habits of dress, perfumes, cults, and superstitions of a Roman society fascinated by everything that came from outside. Snobbishness was nothing new. After all, Molière's Précieuses were merely snobs "*avant la lettre*." You either have a great capital or you don't have a great capital. And in spite of so many novelties, Paris was still the Holy of Holies of good taste, moderation, order, and proportion, and dictated the rules of polite behaviour, elegance, and savoir vivre to the whole world. And, as for cosmopolitanism, which was also a feature of Athens, it in no way harmed the authentic French genius. "*Ce qui n'est pas clair n'est pas français*," I say, proud of still being able to quote a certain Rivarol whom the Marist Brothers of Surgidero de la Verónica made me read in my schooldays.

"Certainly," agreed the Academician: but our politics, our abject politics, with its rioting, and conflict between parties and fierce parliamentary battles, was introducing confusion and disorder into this essentially rational country. The Panama scandal or the Dreyfus Affair would have been inconceivable in the time of Louis XIV. Not to mention the "socialist mire," which, as our friend Gabriele D'Annunzio said, "is invading everything," befouling all that was beautiful and pleasant in our ancient civilisations. Socialism (he sighed, looking at the toes of his patent-leather shoes). Forty kings had made France great. Look at England. Look at the Scandinavian countries, models of order and progress, where stevedores wear waistcoats at work and every bricklayer has a watch and chain under his overalls. Brazil was great when it had an emperor, like Pedro II, who was the friend, fellow diner, and admirer of that same Victor Hugo you all think so well of. Mexico was great when it had Porfirio Díaz as its almost permanent president. And if my country enjoyed peace and prosperity, it was because my fellow countrymen, more intelligent perhaps than others on the Continent, had re-elected me three, four—how many times? Knowing that the continuity of power is a guarantee of material well-being and political equilibrium. Thanks to my government.

I interrupted him with a gesture of defence against the expected encomium, which would have relegated our countries of volcanoes, earthquakes, and hurricanes to the peaceful latitude of Flemish lace makers or the aurora borealis.

"*Il me reste beaucoup à faire*," I said. Nevertheless I was proud—very proud—of the fact that, after a whole century of tumult and uprisings, my own country had brought the cycle of revolutions to an end—revolutions that in America were counted merely as adolescent crises, the scarlatinas and measles of young, impetuous, passionate hot-blooded races, who had to be subjected to discipline sometimes. *Dura lex, sed lex . . .*

There were cases when severity was necessary, the Academician thought. Besides, as Descartes put it so well: "Sovereigns have the right to modify customs to some extent."

Ofelia had finished her very long session with "Für Elise"—we hadn't noticed that the piano had been silent for some while—and she now came into the library, looking dazzling but strange, dressed in light-coloured muslin, a feather boa around her neck, a hat wreathed in flowers and with a hummingbird nesting among its roses, embroidered gloves, and a parasol whose handle was made of finely carved ivory; perfumed, and with a suggestion of hidden lingerie wafting through her clothes, her hair waved, her figure enhanced by bows and tight lacing. She advanced with a lively air, like a ship before the wind, a fully rigged model of Boldini's.

"It's the day of the Drags," she said, reminding me that while I was talking to the Distinguished Academician a few

moments before, I had in fact seen crossing the Place de la
Concorde some of those old-fashioned English carriages with
double doors and high box seats, drawn by four horses, which
would shortly drive off amid a great turmoil of sunshades,
whip-cracking, and postillions' bugles, to where the President
of the Society of Steeplechasers was awaiting them, flanked by
two huntsmen in scarlet livery.

"*Jamais je ne vous avais vu si belle*," said the Distinguished
Academician, weaving thereupon an elaborate compliment
comparing my daughter to some sort of beautiful Gauguin
rising from the foamy waves of a summer dawn.

"We *are* having fun," murmured Peralta.

My face became serious: all this about Gauguin stressed
our being foreigners—but Ofelia took it all in good part. "*Oh!
Tout au plus la Noa-Noa du Seizième Arrondissement!*"

The truth is that her smooth complexion, derived from
her Indian ancestry, was a feature of my daughter's beauty.
She had inherited none of the roundness of face, thickness
of thighs, and width of hips of her sainted mother, who was
much more of a peasant in complexion and figure. Ofelia was
long-legged with small breasts, and slenderly built—a woman
of the new race springing up *over there*—nor did her straight
hair, artificially waved to suit the fashion, possess any of the
natural fuzziness that many of our countrywomen coun-
teracted by using the famous Walker Lotion, invented by a
chemist of New Orleans.

Covering me in exaggerated caresses, Ofelia asked my
permission to go away that same night, after the dinner at the
Polo de Bagatelle to which she was invited. She wanted to be
present at the Wagner Festival at Bayreuth, which was opening on the following Tuesday with *Tristan und Isolde*.

"*Œuvre sublime!*" exclaimed the Academician, starting to
hum the theme of the Vorspiel with the gestures of someone

conducting an invisible orchestra. Then he spoke of the superhuman voluptuousness of the second act, of the great solo for cor anglais in the third, of the paroxysmal chromatic progression, almost cruel in its intensity, of the "Liebestod," and went on to ask my daughter whether she would enjoy visiting the Villa Wahnfried. Gratified by Ofelia's dramatic emotion, as she declared that the mere thought of the Famous Mansion was to her so moving and sacred that she would never dare to enter it, the Academician went to the little boule Santa Inés writing table and took a sheet of paper. Would she take these lines of introduction to his friend Siegfried, a noted composer, although his works were seldom performed? But ... how could one compose music if one was the son of Richard Wagner? And now his pen stopped its calligraphic career, adorned with Greek "e"s and tall "l"s: "*Voici, Mademoiselle.*" Would she greet Cosima affectionately from him? He warned her that the seats in the Festspielhaus were rather uncomfortable. But the pilgrimage to Bayreuth was something that every cultivated person must experience, even if only once in a lifetime—just as the Mohammedans went to Mecca or the Japanese climbed Fujiyama.

Taking the letter he had embellished with a Renaissance flourish composed of very carefully drawn capital letters, Ofelia left us, with renewed demonstrations of affection for such a kind father, who indulged her in everything—although to tell the truth I hadn't given the smallest sign of pleasure at the idea of this sudden journey, which in fact thwarted my plan for her to act as hostess to a reception shortly to be given here in honour of the editor of the *Revue des Deux Mondes*, who was very much interested in publishing a long article on the splendid prosperity and stability of my country. Her kisses on my forehead had been pure humbug and play-acting for the benefit of our visitor, because in fact she never needed my advice or consent to do whatever she fancied. She used and abused the terror inspired in me by her appalling rages, sudden losses of control whenever I tried to oppose her wishes— rages expressed in frantic stamping, obscene gestures, and such foul and insulting language that it seemed to come from a brothel or low nightclub. At such moments the "cunts" and "pricks" of the Infanta—as my secretary called her—reached as high as the allegoric figures on the Arc de Triomphe. But when the storm had passed, and she had got what she wanted, Ofelia used to return to her usual delicate language full of such subtle nuances that sometimes, after listening to her, I had to go to the dictionary to discover the exact significance of some adjective or adverb, possibly destined in the future to fill the sails of my own oratory.

When we were alone again, the Academician suddenly seemed depressed, remembering the years of poverty Richard Wagner had gone through, and the contempt that was felt for true artists in this horrible epoch. There was no Maecenas, no Lorenzo the Magnificent, no cultured Borgias, no Louis XIV, no Ludwig of Bavaria. Perhaps some Louis of the card table? He himself, in spite of his successful literary career, was not immune from want—so very far from immune, in fact—that under pressure from emissaries of the Law in cocked hats who might be knocking on the door of his house tomorrow with their symbolic ivory sticks (would such a thing have been conceivable in the Grand Siècle?) he had sorrowfully made up his mind to sell the manuscripts of two plays: *Robert Guiscard* (a historical pageant, whose chief characters were the Norman condottiere, his brother Rogerio, and the unfortunate Judith d'Evreux, which in spite of a masterly interpretation by Le Bargy, was a resounding flop) and *L'absent* (a drama of conscience: David and Bathsheba, whose nights of love were poisoned by the ghost of Uriah, etc.) which had been performed more than two hundred times at the Théâtre de la Porte Saint-Martin, to the great fury of that swine of a Jew Bernstein, who had thought of writing a piece on the same theme ... But the bookshop around here hadn't any funds available, and lawsuits couldn't be postponed: tomorrow those men in cocked hats with their ivory-handled sticks ... But perhaps the National Library of my country ...?

He had no need to say more. I quickly wrote him out a cheque, which he received with the distrait air of a nobleman, without even looking to see what sum was written on it, although I suspect he knew from having watched the way my hand moved as I traced the numerals.

"*Ils sont très beaux,*" he said: large pages of art paper, enclosed in leather cases stamped with his ex-libris. "*Vous verrez.*"

The package, left downstairs, was brought up by Sylvestre. I untied the string, fondled the covers with their calligraphy in two different inks and drawings illustrating the text; I turned the pages with respectful slowness and felt grateful to the distinguished friend who had thought of the Library of my country to save these invaluable writings—a library that, modest though it was, possessed some extremely valuable incunables, Florentine maps, and a few codices from the Conquest. And noticing that his movements were being orchestrated into an ambiguous ceremony of departure, I stood up, as though to look towards the Arc de Triomphe, declaiming:

> *Toi dont la courbe au loin*
> *s'emplit d'azur, arche démesurée ...*

Feeling obliged to show me some gratitude, the Distinguished Academician picked up his top hat and his white gloves and—knowing that it would please me—said that Hugo wasn't such a bad poet after all, and it was understandable that we, who were so generous with our admiration for French culture, should continue to appreciate his great virtues as a lyric poet. But we must also get to know Gobineau; we *must* read Gobineau.

I went with him down the red-carpeted stairs as far as the front door. And I was just going to suggest to Doctor Peralta that we should go to the Rue des Acacias and visit Monsieur Musard's *Bois-Charbons*, when a taxi drew up in front of us and out got the cholo* Mendoza in a remarkably agitated state. Something serious had happened to my ambassador, because he was sweating—he always looked sweaty, but not so much as this—his parting was crooked, his tie carelessly knotted, and his grey felt boot tops badly laced. I was about to make a joke about his disappearances of several days—whether to Passy, Auteuil, or who could say where?— with the blonde of the moment, when with an agonised expression he handed me a deciphered cablegram of several pages: it was from Colonel Walter Hoffmann, President of my Cabinet:

"Read it . . . Read it."

IT IS MY DUTY TO INFORM YOU THAT GENERAL ATAÚLFO GALVÁN HAS REBELLED SAN FELIPE DEL PALMAR WITH INFANTRY BATTALIONS 4.7.9.11.13 (FOREMOST IN THE COUNTRY) AND THREE CAVALRY REGIMENTS INCLUDING "INDEPENDENCE OR DEATH" SQUADRON, AND FIVE ARTILLERY UNITS, TO CRIES OF "LONG LIVE THE CONSTITUTION, LONG LIVE THE LAW."

---

* In Latin America a "Cholo" is usually an educated and civilized Indian. It can also mean a cross between an Indian and a European.

"The cunt! The son of a bitch!" yelled the Head of State, hurling the cables to the ground. "I've not finished reading it," said the cholo Mendoza, picking up the papers. The movement had spread to three provinces of the north and threatened the Pacific zone. But the garrisons and officials of the Centre remained faithful to the government, so Hoffmann assured me. Nueva Córdoba was unaffected. Troops were patrolling the streets of Puerto Araguato. Curfew had been imposed, presumably pending guarantees of constitutional behaviour. The newspaper *Progreso* had been suppressed. The morale of government troops was good, but there was a shortage of armaments, especially light artillery and Maxim machine guns. His Excellency knew how loyal to him the capital was. They awaited instructions. "The cunt! The son of a bitch!" repeated the Head of State, as if his vocabulary was limited to these sordid phrases when thinking of the treachery of the man whom he had dragged from the squalor of a provincial barracks, the rubbishy, third-rate soldier whom he had helped, made rich, taught to use a fork and pull the lavatory chain, and converted into a gentleman, giving him braid and epaulettes, and finally appointing him Minister for War, and who now took advantage of his absence to ... The man who, when in his cups at receptions at the palace, had so often called him his benefactor, providence, more than a father, a friend, godfather to my children, flesh of my flesh, to be rebelling thus, in the Bolivian style or that of the sudden risings of a past era, clamouring for respect for a constitution that had never been observed by any government since the Wars of Independence, because as we say *over there*: "theory is always buggered by practice" and "a leader with any spunk pays no attention to documents."

"The cunt! The son of a bitch!" repeated the Head of State, who had now returned to the large drawing room and

was pouring himself great swigs of Santa Inés rum—a rum
that no longer seemed merely the nostalgic breath of patriotic feelings in *laissez-vivre* Paris, but had suddenly become
the wine of battle, hot and strong, foretelling hard, rough
marches and counter-marches in the near future, the smell
of horses, soldiers' armpits, and gunpowder. And all at once,
blotting out Jean-Paul Laurens' blessed Radegonde, Elstir's
seascape, and Gérome's gladiators, they were in the middle
of a council of war. Forgotten was the adolescent hero of the
Arc de Triomphe, although it was true that on its walls was
inscribed the name of Miranda, precursor of American independence, who had refused to imitate the treachery of the
infamous Dumouriez—another version of Ataúlfo Galván;
forgotten was Monsieur Musard's *Bois-Charbons*, where the
Prime Minister and Doctor Peralta were so fond of taking a
glass of Muscadet in the mornings, an aperitif at noon, and
a Pernod in the evening, because that establishment with its
aroma of charcoal, its modest counter set parallel to a wall
covered with out-of-date almanacks, its allegorical picture
of the Ascent and Descent of the Ages, its advertisements for
Géraudel pastilles and Vino Mariani, reminded them of the
bars and taverns of *over there*—with the same ambience, and
decorative posters, and the cheerful sallies of clients fuddled
on red wine, but always ready to discuss questions to do
with cycling, recent films, women, politics, boxing, the passing of a comet, the conquest of the South Pole, or whatever
they liked . . .

Council of war. Three silhouettes thrown on the walls
and pictures by the lamp on the writing desk: as in a cinema,
the cholo Mendoza's restlessly revolving shadow, the slender form of Doctor Peralta, busy with papers and ink; the
thickset, broad-shouldered, slow and choleric figure of the
Head of State, gesticulating as he sat in his armchair dictating

letters and plans. To Peralta: cable to his son Ariel, Ambassador in Washington, ordering the immediate purchase of armaments, gun emplacements, logistic supplies, and observation balloons like those recently adopted by the French Army (they would have a tremendous effect over there, where they had never been seen before); proceeding, since all wars cost money and the National Treasury was in a bad way, to hand over the banana zone on the Pacific to the United Fruit Company—a transaction that had been too long delayed because of the doubts, arguments, and objections of professors and intellectuals who talked a lot of foolishness and denounced the greed—inevitable, good God, inevitable, fated, whether we like it or not, for geographical reasons and historical necessities—of Yankee imperialism. To the cholo Mendoza: cable to Hoffmann, ordering him to defend the communications between Puerto Araguato and the capital at all costs. Shoot whoever must be shot. To Peralta, again: cable a Message-to-the-Nation declaring our insuperable determination to defend Liberty following the example of the Founders of Our Country, that ("well, you know the sort of thing . . .").

And the cholo Mendoza had already telephoned Cook's agency: a fairly fast ship, the *Yorktown*, would leave Saint-Nazaire at midnight. They would have to take the five o'clock train. Another cable to Ariel, announcing their arrival time so that he should find means of getting them *there* as early as possible: cargo boat, tanker, whatever was available.

"Tell Sylvestre to pack my bags." He swallowed a large drink, already mounted on the horse of great decisions.

"Tell Ofelia not to worry. We've plenty of money in Switzerland. Let her go to Bayreuth as if nothing had happened and have a good time with her Niebelungen. For me it's a question of a few weeks. I've thrashed people with more guts than that shit of a general."

And when Sylvestre began carrying down the luggage the Prime Minister thought that probably that affair last night with the little nun of Saint Vincent de Paul had brought him bad luck after all. That starched headdress. And the scapulary. And that rubber skull, certainly bought in the shop called Farces et Attrapes in the Boulevard des Capucines—another unfortunate coincidence—that couldn't have helped. But, once again, the Divine Shepherdess of Nueva Córdoba would accept his sincere repentance. He would add a few emeralds to her crown; a lot of silver to her cloak. And there would be ceremonies. Candles. A great many candles. The Flag of Her Divinity between wax tapers and the ambos. The cadets on their knees. The ceremony of the accolades. The Cathedral would be lit up and freshly decorated . . .

Outside, Rude's Marseillaise kept up her imaginary noise—sounding soundlessly—from a deep stone mouth which was only one hole more in the monument where the names of 652 generals of the Empire, consecrated by Glory, were inscribed.

"Only six hundred and fifty-two generals?" murmured the Dictator, reviewing his army in his imagination. "Baedeker must have made a mistake."

# TWO

*. . . each man is so fixed in his own judgement that we could find as many reformers as there are heads.*

—DESCARTES

# 2

TWO HOURS AFTER THE TRAVELLERS HAD ARRIVED
in their suite at the Waldorf-Astoria, they were proceeding
to sign the final papers of their negotiations with the United
Fruit Company, rapidly carried through by Ariel while his
father and Doctor Peralta were on the high seas. The documents were incontrovertible, provided that the signatory was
by act and right—and he would continue to be so for a long
time according to forecasters specializing in the politics of
this hemisphere—the Constitutional President of the Republic. Besides, the Company ran no risk, whatever happened,
because at the start of his rebellion General Ataúlfo Galván
had the intelligence and forethought to tell the agencies of the
press that now as always, today and tomorrow, *hic et nunc*,
both during the progress of the armed struggle and after
the "certain victory"—what a nerve, brother!—of the movement to seize the leadership, all the wealth, property, concessions, and monopolies of North American businesses would
be safeguarded. It was known by cablegram that the revolutionaries had consolidated their positions on the Atlantic
coast—up till now they held four provinces out of nine, that
was the dramatic fact—but a stubborn resistance was frus-
trating their present attempts to advance towards Puerto Araguato and cut the communications between the capital and
the ocean. One squadron of warships was awaiting the Head

of State off a little Caribbean island, at which a Dutch cargo ship would drop anchor next day on her way to Recife. As for arms, bought from an agent of Sir Basil Zaharoff, they were to be despatched from Florida on board a boat registered in Greece, by a freebooter accustomed to hoisting a Panama or Salvador flag once outside the United States' three-mile limit when it returned to its usual business—transporting men, arms, slave labour, anything that was wanted in South America, whose creeks, inlets, and bays he knew as well as did the most travelled of local coastal steamers.

And since there was nothing urgently needing to be done that night, the Head of State, who was a great opera fan, wanted to hear *Pelléas et Mélisande*, which was on at the Metropolitan Opera House, with the famous Mary Garden in the leading rôle. His friend the Academician had talked a lot about this score, which was said to be very good and, although much discussed at first, had fanatical admirers in Paris, whom that eccentric homosexual Jean Lorrain described as "Pelléasts."

They seated themselves in the front row, the conductor raised his baton, and the huge orchestra spread at his feet began to play, soundlessly. It made no sound, but emitted a murmur, a quivering, a whispering of a note here and a note there which didn't amount to music ...

"And is there no Overture?" asked the Head of State.

"It's coming, it's coming," said Peralta, hoping that the sound would grow, rise, become definite and swell into a fortissimo. "*Faust* and *Aida* begin like this, almost in silence (I think they call it *a la sordina*), so as to prepare one all the more for what is to come next." But now the curtain was going up and it was still the same. The musicians were all there, numbers of them, intent, with their eyes on their music— yet they had achieved nothing. They were testing their reeds, shaking the saliva from their horns, giving a half-turn to their instruments, making a string vibrate, sweeping their harps with their fingertips without succeeding in producing anything like a definite melody. A little stress here, an imperceptible plaint there, themes sketched, impulses still-born, and on the stage two characters gassing away but unable to make up their minds to sing. And now—a change of scene—here is a mediaeval lady reading a letter aloud in an accent from Kansas City. An old man is listening. Shaking his head like someone who didn't want to hear, who was bored; and then came the interval.

The sight of the galleries and corridors now aroused some amusing and pungent reflections in the President's mind, about the artificiality of the aristocracy of New York, and how pompously they showed off, compared with that of Paris. However well-cut a tailcoat might be, on the back of a Yankee it made him look like a conjurer. When he bowed in his white tie and shirtfront one expected a rabbit or a pigeon to emerge from his top hat. The matrons of the Four Hundred wore too much ermine, too many tiaras, too many of Tiffany's wares. Behind them one glimpsed luxurious houses, with gothic fireplaces bought in Flanders, columns from Cluniac monasteries transhipped in the holds of transatlantic liners, pictures by Rubens or Rosa Bonheur and some authentic Tanagras, whose dancing movements were out of rhythm with the beat of "Alexander's Ragtime Band" pouring in through the renaissance windows. Although some surnames from the former Dutch or British ascendancy went back to the seventeenth century, when they were heard in proximity to Central Park they absorbed an indefinable quality of being imported products—at the same time false and exotic, like those vague titles of Marqueses de la Real Proclamacion or del Merito or del Premio Real that we have in Latin America.

That aristocracy was as fictitious as the atmosphere of the opera they were putting on this evening, with its floating Mediaevalism, its ogival arches all over the place, its vaguely dynastic furniture, its battlements of no special date emerging from a perpetual mist to suit the taste of the designer.

The curtain went up again and other scenes and another interval followed; the curtain went up yet again and more scenes followed, all submerged in evanescent pearly haze, with caves, shadows, serenades, an invisible chorus, doves that didn't fly, three dead beggars, distant flocks of sheep, things seen by others but not visible to us ... And when at last the final interval was reached the Head of State broke out: "No one is really singing here; there is no baritone, tenor, or bass ... there are no arias ... no ballet ... not a single ensemble ... and what a little squit that fat-arsed American girl is, dressed as a boy, looking through the window to see what's going on in the room where, needless to say, the handsome young man and the long-haired blonde are hard at it. And the cuckold in despair downstairs. And that old man with a face like Charles Darwin, who says that if he was God he would be sorry for human heartache. The fact is that although our friend the Academician, and that other chap, D'Annunzio, tell me that this is a masterpiece, I'd rather have *Manon*, *Traviata*, and *Carmen*. And talking of whores, take me to a brothel."

And, in no time, the three of them found themselves in an apartment on Forty-second Street where some blondes, with faces made up and hair combed to look like cinema stars, served them with mixed drinks—it was the fashion at this time to mix drinks—after which they amused themselves by comparing what was provided here with the Veracruzan *minyules* of the Hotel Diligencias, pink punches of the Antilles and Cuban *mojos* with their iced mint leaves, *rocios de gallo* (made of gin and angostura) and *zamuritas* of cress or

lemon, pineapple or agave juice with salt, from our Torrid
Zone. The women were amazed that in spite of his obvious
age the Head of State could swallow so many drinks—always
with a regal and deliberate gesture—without getting tangled
up in stories that never ended, or losing his aristocratic air. It
was unusual for his son Ariel to see him drink like this—"It's
a special occasion," said Peralta—because when the Dictator
was moving in palace circles he was—with his famous drinking of healths in mineral water, and his praise of Peregrino,
whose bottling establishment he had bought—a model of
sobriety. At fiestas and celebrations he never exceeded one
or two glasses of champagne, and his tone became emphatic
and his brow furrowed when he broached the serious theme
of the constant proliferation of bars and taverns, one of the
great social problems of the nation, a defect we owed to the
vicious nature of the Indians and the Spanish colony's ancient
monopoly of aguardiente. But people didn't know that inside
a case invariably carried by Doctor Peralta—which looked as
if it contained papers of transcendental importance—there
were in fact ten flasks, very flat and curved to slip easily into
a pocket, such as are made in England, which, being covered
in pigskin—and bought at the smart Parisian shop Hermès—
never clinked when they were thrown together. So it was that
in the presidential study, in the dressing room attached to
the Council Chamber, in his bedroom—and of course the
Mayorala Elmira was in on the secret—in the train, in the
pauses of any journey by road, it was enough for the Head
of State to put a thumb to his left ear for one of the flasks instantly to appear out of the secretary's bureaucratic briefcase.
In other respects, the always serious, frowning drinker—a
"before-breakfast man" for whom the good Elmira prepared
lots of tamarind juice quite early to refresh "his livers" (she
always used the plural)—took the greatest possible care to

hide a long-standing addiction to Santa Inés rum, which—
it must be admitted—in no way affected the rhythm of his
movements, nor the balance of his judgement when faced
with some unexpected predicament, nor the almost natural
flow of his perspiration: he always talked to people—his head
slightly on one side so that his breath would be diverted—
across a table, or keeping a definite distance, thus increasing
the respect due to his patriarchal figure. To these precautions
he added constant use of toothpaste, peppermint lozenges,
cachous, and a suspicion of liquorice, flavouring the halo of
eau de Cologne or lavender water that always clung to his
under-garments and stiff shirts, all most suitable to the dignity of the Head of the State.

Seeing his father drinking that night, Ariel was amazed
to find he had a power of absorption greater than his own.

"It's because he has a virgin organism," said Doctor Peralta. "He's not like us, who carry the 'mother liquor' about
inside us and can never get rid of it."

Next day, after purchasing from Brentano's an exquisite
edition of Sarmiento's *Facundo*—which gave rise to some bitter
thoughts about the dramatic fate of Latin American peoples,
always engaged in a Manichaean struggle between civilisation
and barbarism, between progress and dictatorship—the Head
of State went on board the Dutch cargo ship which was to
make a short call at Havana. And the sea was becoming less
grey, and the broad yellow Caribbean moons were shining on
a recurring baroque pattern of sargasso and flying fish.

"The air already smells different," said the Head of State,
absorbing a breeze laden with the unmistakable scent of
mangroves.

Arrived in Havana, the Consul told them that, in spite of
his present lack of light arms, Colonel Hoffmann was maintaining his defensive position, although the revolutionaries had made no futher progress. Everything was the same

as when the cable was sent to Paris. As the news was good and carnival was in progress, the Head of State watched the fancy-dress procession and masquerades, and threw paper streamers down on them from above. Then he hired a black domino and went to the Shoemakers' Ball, where a mulatto girl dressed as a marquise of the period of Louis XV or XVI—in a red crinoline, with powdered hair, a beauty spot on her rouged cheek, a red-and-green fan, and a tortoise-shell lorgnette—taught him how to dance without dancing, all on one tile; to jig up and down, almost without moving, in smaller and smaller, slower circles, ending up in mutual immobility, breathing the perfume of satin so drenched with sweat that it was more like skin than skin itself—all this in a din of cornets, clarinets, and kettle drums, produced by Valenzuela and Corbacho's orchestra. When the masqueraders began to disperse, the lights of the theatre to go out, tier by tier, the mulatto invited the Head of State to sleep with her in a room she had near the Arco de Belén, in a "modest but respectable house"—so she said—with a patio planted with pomegranates, basil, and ferns. They took a cab, drawn by a scraggy horse whose driver urged it forward—it was practically asleep—with a spur fastened to the end of a stick, and passed between tall sleeping houses smelling of dried beef, molasses, and the steam of roasting, blown this way and that, as they entered the orbit of the breeze from the port, the effluvium of brown sugar, hot furnaces and green coffee, within a widespread reek of stables, saddlers, and mildewed old walls still cool with night dew, saltpetre, and mosses.

"Watch while I sleep, my friend," said the Head of State to me.

"Don't worry, my friend, I've got the needful here," I said, taking my Browning out of my breast pocket. And while the Head of State and the mulatto disappeared for I don't know how long behind a blue door, I installed myself on a cowhide stool, with my weapon across my thighs. However, no one knew that my president was in the city. He had disembarked with a false passport, to avoid the news of his journey reaching the place where he wanted to arrive entirely unexpectedly.

The cocks crowed, the awnings were brought down, and in a few minutes the normal everyday noises increased; lorries and vans went by, with their crescendo and decrescendo of bells; blinds were pulled; shutters creaked; trays and buckets fell over: "Flooo-wers, flowers; brooo-brooms; lottery tickets; a lucky number?" Hawkers of fruit, avocados, and tamales cried their wares with a sound like Gregorian chant; others offered to exchange bottles for toffee apples, and the morning news was shouted by paper sellers: a Cuban airman, Rosillo, had beaten the Frenchman, Pegoud, at looping the loop at the Bien Aparecida airfield yesterday; a suicide by fire; cattle rustlers captured in Camagüey; a cold spell—13 degrees according to the Observatory—on the heights of Placetas; confused situation in Mexico—where there actually was a revolution going on, as we know by the terrifying accounts of Don Porfirio; and in our own country, yes, in our own country, the crier's voice had named it, there had been a victory for Ataúlfo Galván (yes, "a victory," I think he said) in the region of Nueva Córdoba.

The shock of this awoke the Head of State, who had been asleep with one huge thick thigh thrown over the just as fleshy but longer thigh of the mulatto, and composed and dignified, we now walked together to San Francisco Quay, where the cargo boat was waiting to weigh anchor. A barrel organ decked out in tassels and portraits of La Chelito and La Bella Camelia suddenly struck up the piercing din of a bull-fighting *pasodoble.*

"What a noisy town!" remarked the President. "Our capital is a monastery in comparison."

And here we are now, in Puerto Araguato, where Colonel Hoffmann is waiting for us, standing stiffly to attention, wearing his best monocle, and with the good news that nothing has changed. The rebellion has been supported only in the northern provinces, whose population has a long tradition of hostility to the Central Power, believing themselves slighted, belittled, treated like a poor relation, although they possess the richest and most productive land in the country. Of the fifty-three risings in the last century, more than forty were led by caudillos from the north. Nobody yet knew, except the ministers and highest officers of the army, that the Chief of State was to arrive today. This should make the most of the surprise. (Feeling sadder now than before at the treachery of the man I had most trusted, I had been gazing at the view of the port from the deck of the cutter that was conveying me and was suddenly moved to sentimental but irrepressible tears by the sight of the rows of cottages and farms heaped up against the hill, like fragile cards in a house of cards. With my anger dissolving at this reunion with my own country, I noticed from the quivering of the lamplight that this air was the air of my air; that some water brought me to quench my thirst, though it was water like any other, suddenly reminded me of forgotten tastes, linked to faces from the past, to things seen by my eyes and stored away in my mind. Breathe deeply. Drink slowly. Go back. Paramnesia. And now that the train is going up and up, in endless curves and tunnels, making short stops now and again between cliffs and the scrubby woods of the Torrid Zone, I see, with the eyes of smell, the outline of leaves growing inside chapels of shadow; I depict for myself the architecture of a tree by the plaintive creaking of a bough; and know what fungi grow on the bark of the amaranth by the permanence of its remembered aroma.

As though naked and unarmed, mollified, disposed to

indulgence, settlement, possible accommodation—things derived from an *over there* that from hour to hour was being
left further behind at the foot of its Arc de Triomphe—as I
climbed towards the seat of the presidency and regained an
aggressiveness possibly due to the surrounding vegetation
and its uninterrupted battle to reconquer the open space of
the railway line along which our locomotive was winding, I
considered recent events with greater animosity and passion.
Every two hundred metres climbed by the engine added to
my authority and stature, strengthened also by the thin air
from the high peaks. I must be hard, implacable; this was de-
manded by the implacable, pitiless Powers that still made up
the dark and all-powerful reason of existence—the visceral
peristalsis—of the world in gestation, though problematic as
to shapes, desires, impulses, and limits. Because *over there*—
now the over there of *over there*—the seaport of Basilia still
continued to exist and carry on its Rhenish occupations of
the year 1000, and the Seine with its *bâteau-mouches* was still
cut up by the changeless cross-bars of the Pont Neuf with its
booths and pseudo-renaissance tabarins; while here and now,
jungle scrambled over jungle, estuaries twisted and turned,
rivers changed course and left their beds between night and
morning, so that twenty towns built in a single day out of
anything from plastered dung to marble, from pigsties to
castles, from gaucho guitar music to the voice of Enrico Caruso, suddenly fell into ruins, disreputable and abandoned,
until even the saltpetre had ceased being of interest to the
world, even the seabirds' excrement—the guano, such as covers the rocks with milky slime—was no longer quoted on
the Stock Exchange, with shouting and scribbling on slates,
bidding and overbidding, now that its place had been taken
by some chemical substance manufactured in German test
tubes. As I filled my lungs with the breath of my native air,

I became more and more a president.) And I really was the President, standing erect and stiff on the platform of the train, my expression hard, whip in hand, my attitude grim, when we arrived at the capital through the familiar landscape of the suburbs; here was the soap factory, the sawmill, the powerhouse; on the right, the rambling country house with caryatids and telamons, and its ruined mosaic-covered minaret; on the left, the huge advertisement for Scott's Emulsion and the other for Pompeian Lotion. Sloan's Liniment, useful for everything; Lydia Pinkham's Vegetable Mixture—a portrait with bare throat and cameos—sovereign cure for all menstrual disorders. And above all—above all—Aunt Jemima's Flour—be sure to remember the brand—a universal favourite in suburbs, tenements, and smallholdings because the label had on it the figure of a negress from the south, with a checked handkerchief on her head such as is worn by the people of the lowlands hereabouts. ("She's almost exactly like the grandmother of that Prussian, Hoffmann," people used to say jokingly, remembering that the old woman had been relegated to the furthest outbuildings of his house, and was never present at the Colonel's dinners and parties; she was seen in the street only when going to six o'clock communion, or she would take to haggling at the top of her voice over the price of marjoram or lettuce at the stalls of market gardeners, who used to drive their heavily burdened donkeys from the surrounding mountains in the early mornings, before the daily awakening in sunlight of the Tutelary Volcano.)

Railway lines crossing, signals rushing to meet us, and at two o'clock in the morning we entered the deserted station of the Great Eastern Railway, all made of iron and frosted glass—much of it broken—built some time ago by the Frenchman Baltard. The United States military attaché was waiting for us on the platform, along with members of the Cabinet. And in several motor cars we crossed the silent town, as silent as if uninhabited, because of the curfew, which had been put forward from eight o'clock in the evening to six, and (starting today) to half past four. Grey, ochre and yellow houses with doors and windows closed and rusty pipes spouting water from their roofs slept on raised sidewalks. The equestrian statue of the Founder of the Nation loomed in melancholy solitude, in spite of the presence of the bronze heroes standing beneath him in the Plaza Municipal. The Grand Theatre, with its classical columns, looked like some sumptuous cenotaph in the absence of any human figures. All the lights of the Government Palace were lit, in honour of the Extraordinary Council, which had lasted ever since breakfast time. And at ten o'clock, in response to a very sensational special edition of the morning newspaper, an enormous crowd had assembled in front of the façade of tiles and volcanic stone built in the days of the Conquest by an inspired Jewish architect, a fugitive from the Holy Inquisition, to whom we owe the most beautiful colonial churches in the country—the finest of all being the National Sanctuary of the Divine Shepherdess in Nueva Córdoba.

When the Head of State appeared on the balcony of honour, he was greeted with acclamations that sent a great cloud of pigeons over the roofs and terraces that chequered the valley with red and white, between thirty-two more or less aspiring belfries. After the cheering had died down, the President slowly and with marked pauses, as was his custom, began to make a clearly articulated speech in his resonant tenor voice, exact in its purpose, though embellished, so thought some, with too many expressions such as "nomadic," "myrobalantic," "rocambolesque," "eristic," "apodeictic"; before this he had already elevated the tone by a glittering mobilisation of

"acting against the grain," "swords of Damocles," "crossing
the Rubicon," trumpets of Jericho, Cyranos, Tartarins, and
Clavileños, all mixed up together with lofty palm trees, solitary condors, and white pelicans; he then set about reproach-
ing the "janissaries of nepotism," the "imitative demagogues,"
the "condottieri of fastidiousness," who were always ready to
break their swords in some wild undertaking: creators of dis-
cord, whereas industry and a patriarchal view of life should
make us all members of one great family—but of a Great
Family, which although reasonable and united was always
severe and inexorable to its Prodigal Sons—who, instead of
repenting of their errors as in the biblical parable, tried to set
fire to and destroy the Homestead where they had grown to
Man's estate and been heaped with honours and degrees. The
Head of State was often a good deal jeered at for the affected
turns and twists of his oratory. But—or so Peralta believed—
he didn't use them out of love of pure verbal baroque; he
knew that such artificial language had created a style that was
part of his image, and that the use of words, adjectives and
unusual epithets seldom understood by his hearers, far from
being prejudicial, flattered some atavistic taste of theirs for
what was precious and flowery, and thus gained him fame as
a master of language, whose tone was in strong contrast to the
monotonous, badly constructed military pronouncements of
his adversary.

The speech ended with an emotional call to all citizens of
good will to be calm, peaceful, and united, worthy heirs of the
Founders of the Nation and Fathers of the Country, whose
revered tombs were lined up in the aisles of the pantheon
close by ("... turn your heads and contemplate with the eyes
of your mind the tall Babylonian tower that ..." etc., etc.).

Hearing an end to the cheering, the orator retired into
the Council Chamber, where several maps were spread out on

a large mahogany table. With little flags on pins—one sort for the nationalists, another for the reds—Colonel Walter Hoffmann, President of the Council and now Minister for War, traced a compact and clear picture of the military situation. On this line were the bastards and sons of bitches; here, here, and here, the defenders of the national honour. The bastards and sons of bitches had been joined by other bastards and sons of bitches during the last few weeks: this was obvious. But now that the Pacific zone had been handed over to United Fruit, the possibility of their landing munitions in the Bay of the Negro had been nullified. The loyalists had contained the advance of the revolutionaries to the north-east.

"But if we had had more arms we could have done more."

"Within a week we shall have everything we need," said the Head of State, checking the invoices of the cargo put aboard in Florida. Meanwhile he must strengthen the morale and combativeness of the constitutional troops. He would set off himself that same night for the zone of operations. The general aspect of the situation, although serious, could be considered optimistically.

"And Nueva Córdoba?" he asked, however, thinking of that extraordinary city of ruined palaces, so rich in mines, possibly too Indian, always leaving a disconcerting aftertaste, alarmingly prone to produce unexpected surprises, which had been such a centre of tough resistance in former revolutions.

"Nothing," replied Hoffmann. "Ataúlfo isn't popular there. So he's left it untouched. Besides, he promised to respect English and North American interests, and there are a lot there, and he wants to show he's as good as his word by keeping the war away from that region."

The Head of State was sleepy. He asked the Mayorala Elmira to get his battle uniform ready, polish his boots, and shammy-leather his peaked hat; then, moved by a sudden caprice, he seized her without warning, pulled up her skirts while she stood with her elbows on a marble sideboard, amazed at the "good condition" the Señor had arrived in from Paris—that stupendous Paris, where men lose their very souls ... after which he curled up in his hammock and slept for a few hours.

When he awoke he was confronted by the face of Doctor Peralta, but frowning and preoccupied this time. The students of the ancient University of San Lucas had had the temerity to circulate an insolent, inadmissible manifesto, which the President read with growing rage. They remembered that he had gained power by a coup d'état; that he had been confirmed in it by fraudulent elections; that his powers had been extended during an arbitrary reform of the Constitution; that his re-elections ... in other words, it had been as usual in such matters. The time had come to put an end to an authority without trend or doctrine, expressed in ukases and edicts by a president proconsul guided in governmental affairs by messages in cypher from his son Ariel. But the gravity of the present situation—and its new feature—lay in the fact that the students had proclaimed that at the present time there was no difference between a uniform and a frock coat, and that the government cause was every bit as uninteresting as that of the so-called revolutionaries. The players had changed places around the same board, but an interminable game, begun more than a hundred years ago, was still going on.

And to aid the return to a constitutional and democratic order, the figure of Doctor Luis Leoncio Martínez had come forward, an austere professor of philosophy and translator of Plotinus, well known to Peralta, who had been a pupil of his. He was a man with a high, narrow, balding forehead with prominent veins, dry and short in speech, abstemious and an

early riser, a militant vegetarian, father of nine, admirer of
Proudhon, Bakunin, and Kropotkin, who had corresponded
with Francisco Ferrer, the great Barcelonese anarchist, and
started a demonstration in the city when the news was received that he had been shot at Monjuich. The Head of State
winked at this demonstration because indignation was universal, and because in fact, now that Ferrer was done for
and couldn't rouse any rebels, a procession starting at dusk
and ending in the nine o'clock evening breeze (three hours
of shouting that had nothing to do with opposing the government) would show our respect for liberty, our tolerance
of ideas, etc., etc. Doctor Luis Leoncio Martínez combined
his libertarian convictions with a form of theosophy, nur-
tured on the Upanishads, the Bhagavad Gita, Annie Besant,
Madame Blavtsky, and Camille Flammarion, was interested
in metaphysical phenomena, and attended very intimate se-
ances for table turning, hypnotism, knocks, and levitation,
demonstrating the presence of the spirits of Swedenborg, the
Comte de Saint Germain, and Katie King, or of the still-alive
but far-distant Eusapia Paladino.

And now this dreamer, this pale utopian, had appeared
unexpectedly in Nueva Córdoba, and was inciting the workers in the copper and tin mines to rebel, with the help of half
a dozen student leaders. It seemed a bold undertaking, all the
more so when one reflected that he was an academic from
the university, admired by some local inhabitants but without
political following in the rest of the country. The President's
calm was restored by a drink served him most opportunely,
and analysing the situation from the tactical point of view, he
decided that in fact an attack by a common enemy on General Ataúlfo Galván's rear was in his favour, because it limited
rebel action to two provinces of the north-east. And if this
affair of Nueva Córdoba really came to something, he could

in the last resort count on the help of the United States, since
the White House was now more than ever opposed to the
smallest germ of an anarchistic or socialistic movement in
that other America, which was already so revolutionary and
Latin. And now the Head of State was beginning to discuss
the situation with Colonel Hoffmann when a second news
sheet, written in a satirical and mocking tone, was brought in
and revived his subsiding anger—and this time to a more violent degree than before. It made fun of his oratory in markedly Creole prose, describing him mockingly as a "Musical
Comedy Tiberius," "the Satrap of the Torrid Zone," "Moloch
of the Public Treasure," and "Upstart Monte-Cristo," who always travelled about Europe with a million in his wallet. His
ascent to power had been the "Gangsters' 18th Brumaire." His
Ministry was a "Gold Rush," "Court of Miracles," and "Council of Buddies." No one was spared: Colonel Hoffmann was "a
Prussian with a black grandmother in the back yard"; General
Ataúlfo Galván a "jabbering street hawker, an Ostrogoth with
sword and buckler," just as a great many functionaries and
police chiefs were cast in the mould either of the Inquisition
or farce, according to whether they were assumed to be tragic
or grotesque. But the worst of all was that his daughter, Ofelia,
was dubbed the "Infanta of King Midas," as a reminder that,
while the barefoot women of this country had no hospital to
give birth in, the favoured Creole, collector of antique cameos, exquisite musical boxes and racehorses, had given thousands of the national pesos (at an exchange of 2.27 against
the dollar) to enterprises and organisations such as "Mission-
ary Work in China," the "Society for the Protection of Gothic
Art," and the "Drop of Milk Foundation," this last having a
European duchess for president. So they passed from joke to
joke and the President didn't care for jokes. Moreover, Colonel Hoffmann now arrived with the news that the students

had shut themselves inside the University and were holding a meeting to oppose the government.

"Send the mounted police into the building," said the President.

"But ... what about their ancient privileges? Their self-government charter?"

"I can't be bothered with such swine. They've caused quite enough trouble with that bloody self-government of theirs. We're in a state of emergency."

"And what if they resist, if they throw tiles from the roofs, if they hamstring the horses as they did in 1908?"

"In that case ... shoot them! I repeat: we're in a state of emergency and this disorderly behaviour can't be tolerated."

Half an hour later shooting was going on in the courtyards of the University of San Lucas. "And if some are killed," said the Head of State, as he buttoned his tunic, "none of those solemn funerals, with coffins carried on shoulders and speeches in the cemetery, which are merely demonstrations sheltering under the guise of mourning. Just give the stiff to the family and let them bury it without weeping and wailing, because if they do otherwise the whole family, mother, grandparents, and their brats too, will go to prison."

Outside, the firing went on. Eight killed and more than twenty wounded.

"Much good their education has done them," said the Head of State, getting into the long black Renault that was to take him to the railway station. "Have any soldiers been killed?"

"Two, because one student and a janitor were armed."

"See that they have national funerals with gun carriages, funeral marches, and places in the Pantheon of Heroes, since they fell in the performance of their duty."

And the armed forces gathered on the pavements with a

great display of helmets, leather belts, chin straps and spurs, binoculars and riding whips, and with much to-ing and fro-ing of sergeants looking like German *Feldwebels* and piling the troops into coaches, cattle trucks, and luggage vans. They began with the élite: the chasseurs and hussars, with shining boots and soldierly spit and polish; they were to go in the presidential convoy. Then, in other trains, came shabbier infantry, in stained tunics and unpolished boots, and after that third-class infantry, with machetes, cartridge belts, old rifles, and odd pairs of shoes. And slipping in everywhere among the groups of soldiers, sneaking through the carriage windows, climbing onto the roofs, were the camp followers carrying stores and kitchen utensils, wrapped up in bedding and bags. Two Krupp cannons had been set up on platform wagons on a turntable, with its complicated machinery of cog wheels, levers, and handlebars.

"And is all this going to be needed?" asked the Head of State.

"It's been proved by experience," said Hoffmann, "that water conduits and four yoke of oxen can be carried in railway wagons."

"Very practical for quick action," said the President, who had been put in a good humour by all these preparations.

In the end, after a delay of three hours spent intercalating trucks, moving trucks, interpolating trucks, extrapolating trucks, finding this wouldn't do but that would do, that the one farther up was blocking the brakes, that the cistern wagon was full of putrid water, and that the cement mixer didn't work, and after two more hours occupied in pulling up bogies from disused lines, breaking up strings of trucks to make others, moving forwards, backing, while locomotives whistled and the bugles of the military bands sounded, the army started off, to the accompaniment of the indispensable song:

*Goodbye, goodbye.*
*Light of my life,*
*Said a soldier,*
*Underneath a window.*

The Head of State withdrew early with Peralta into his comfortable presidential compartment, to drink what had been brought in the Hermès case, out of sight of the captains and colonels who were celebrating their departure to the front in the Pullman car around bottles bearing good labels. Sitting on the edge of his bed, he gazed gloomily at the toes of his shining boots, his Sam Browne belt hanging from a peg, his pistol in its holster—heavier and of larger bore than the light Browning for his own personal use.

"General" ... "My General" ... "Señor General" ...

And the sleepers under the railway lines repeated with obsessional regularity as the wheels passed over them: "Gen-ral ... Gen-ral ... Gen-ral ... Gen-ral ... Gen-ral." Possibly he was the only general in the whole world to whom the title of general gave no pleasure, and he accepted it only when he was with soldiers, or when he had, as now, to direct some operation. Because the truth was that he had conferred that title on himself a great many years ago, in an early incarnation of his political life, when he had placed himself at the head of an armed contingent back in Surgidero de la Verónica, and led about seventy men to attack a small fort occupied by some rebels against the government to which at that time he was loyal—though he was to overthrow it later on (but then with the help of real generals) and instal himself in the Presidential Palace. Now, for a while—as long as the operations lasted—he would once again become "General," "My General," "Señor General." And again he looked at the toes of his boots, his spurs and belt. And he thought mockingly of himself as being like the character in Molière's comedy who was a cook when he wore a cap and a coachman when he put on livery.

"Give me a drink," he said to Peralta, "and reach me that book."

And while waiting for sleep to come, he turned the pages till he came to a certain Sixth Volume that he had been interrupted when reading weeks before. *Chapter XI*: "Since I have arrived at this point, it would seem to be not inappropriate to set forth the customs of Gaul and of Germany and the difference between these nations. In Gaul, not only in every state, and every canton and district, but almost in each several household, there are parties ... *There are parties ...*" "That's why they were able to blast them to blazes as they did blast them," commented the Head of State between two yawns ... Outside, the singing went on:

> *The night they killed Rosita,*
> *Oh what luck she had!*
> *Out of the six that hit her*
> *Just one shot left her dead.*

# 3

WHEN GENERAL ATAÚLFO GALVÁN HAD BEEN
beaten in the first pitched battle and crossed the Rio Verde
behind his wretched, broken troops, leaving on the bank his
two camp followers, Misia Olalla and Jacinta the Negress—
who had stayed behind to load up with parcels of blouses,
worn blankets, and ribbons stolen from the shops of a recently
sacked village—the first of the lightning flashes that seemed
to crack the sky from top to bottom was seen and two endless
claps of thunder resounded, forming the overture to months
of hard, inexorable, exasperating rain; persistent, sustained
rain such as is seen only in these forests. The forested lands
lay on the flanks of mountains that were always haze-covered,
veiled in mists that cleared in one place only to thicken in another, letting the sun filter through a gap of sky—a few minutes here, a few minutes there—to illuminate the unknown
splendour of nameless flowers, scrambling over the tops of
hidden trees, or to magnify uselessly, since there was no one
to see them, some superb efflorescence of orchids on the roof
of the jungle; these were the rain forests, where the mahogany
trees, júcaros, cedars, and quebrachos, and species so numerous and so rare as to confound traditional classifications—
they had even confounded Humboldt himself—were bathed
in rains so profuse that when men realised their proximity by smelling them from afar, they had the impression of

embarking on a year seven months long occupying its special place within the twelve-month year, or of abandoning the four seasons to keep to only two: one short, moss-covered, a time for hard work, and the other long and wet, of interminable boredom. When the storms had died away a new life began—a new stage, a new stride forwards—surrounded by vegetation so damp and so entangled in its own dampness that it seemed to have been engendered by the lagoons and marshes below, always croaking with frogs, covered with toads, iridescent with wandering bubbles arising from submerged decay . . .

The army commanders had ordered a number of tents to be set up. The President's was in the middle, its ropes attached to posts supporting a tall canvas pediment crowned by the republican flag. After supper of sardines, corned beef, baked bananas, *dulce de leche*, and Rhine wine, the victor of the day's expedition, thinking his officers might be exhausted after this fierce battle, invited them to take a well-deserved rest until the meeting of the General Staff next day. Colonel Hoffmann, Doctor Peralta, and the Head of State were left alone, playing a half-hearted game of dominoes by the yellow kerosene glow of the street lamps. But at that point five, ten, twenty streaks of lightning plunged into the forest, followed by thunderclaps, each echoing for so long that they were blended one with another, bringing in their train the wind that heralded the downpour—the *"gira-gira"* as the locals called it—which in the twinkling of an eye had carried away the whole encampment. While the soldiers did their best to deal with the situation, Colonel Hoffmann and the Head of State, guided by Doctor Peralta, made for a hill, where they had that morning glimpsed the dark opening of a cave. And there they arrived, slipping, stumbling, soaked, shivering with cold, by the light of lanterns. There was a fluttering of terrified bats, which quickly subsided, and then the solid shelter of damp walls, beneath an argillaceous vault festooned with stalactites, under which the rain only made its presence felt like the sound of a distant waterfall. But it was cold; the cold of clay in shadow, onto which water from the deep fissures of the mountain was ceaselessly dripping. The Head of State, sitting on his military cloak, had an unappeasable craving for a drink. (A need that clutched his stomach and his entrails, that made his body seem empty, without viscera, contracted by an urgent obsession which rose towards his throat and his mouth, which concentrated memory in his lips and sense of smell ...) Doctor Peralta understood what was happening, and with a sly expression produced the Hermès case, and announced that as a precaution against possible chills during the campaign he had loaded it with brandy, to which—why deny it?—he was a confirmed addict.

"Everyone knows you were the Prior of Santa Inés," said Colonel Hoffmann, suddenly cheering up and unbuttoning his overcoat. And joining his entreaties to the secretary's, he persuaded the Head of State to take some alcohol to preserve his health—more vital now than ever before—from harm from the stormy weather.

"Just this once," said the Head of State, raising the first flask, the smell of whose thick and porous pigskin cover at once brought back the Parisian shop where Ofelia used to buy picador's saddles, reins, bits, and bridles.

"Don't hesitate, Señor President; go right ahead; this is a special occasion. A glorious day, too."

"A glorious day, indeed," echoed Doctor Peralta. They were answered by a peal of thunder, which increased their pleasant sense of safety here within. The sweet yet vegetable aroma of the strong liquor drunk in the cave harmonised with the moisture of mud and mosses to call up a remote image of the classical vintners' bodegas where new wine sleeps under deep vaults. His spirits revived, the Head of State remembered a text he had humorously quoted in the Cabinet Council— where he often boastfully referred to books read, quoted poems, appropriate phrases, and proverbs suiting the case— during some passing political squabble wrapped up in military jargon. "Blow, winds, and crack your cheeks ... And you thought-executing fires, vaunt couriers of oak-cleaving thunderbolts, singe my white head .." To which Doctor Peralta, who was more of a Zorrillean than a Shakespearean, replied with some sparks from *Puñal del Godo*, so often launched in our National Theatre by the Spanish tragedian Ricardo Calvo, whose too pure diction he imitated in a comic manner:

> *Oh what a threatening storm!*
> *What a night; may heaven preserve us!*
> *Is the terrible voice blind,*
> *and the light that flashes*
> *when the wind blows and rages*
> *and lightning strikes the zenith?*

Once more the case of flasks was opened, to celebrate the "terrible voice" of the poem, and the owner of the "terrible voice" that was roaring. And now that they were sufficiently warmed up, with their uniform tunics somewhat unbuttoned, Colonel Hoffmann began to describe the campaign: until yesterday there had only been slight armed clashes, skirmishes, sharpshooting by guerrillas, collision between patrols; on our side the worst had been the blowing up of a train at the exit of the Roquero tunnel, with a loss of horses and equipment, seventeen men killed and fifty-two put out of action with more or less serious wounds. But the enemy—and he directed the light of his lantern onto a map spread on the undulant surface of bats' guano covering the ground—had steadily retreated towards the Rio Verde, without ever taking the initiative. Today, on the other hand, we had met them in a pitched battle, such as had not been seen since the Wars of Independence. Of course, thorough preparations had been necessary. The enemy had got too much help from the partisans, mounts, cattle, sacks of maize, information passed from village to village with incredible speed by these filthy mountaineers, always sympathetic with rioters and pronunciamentos. It was not a modern battle. Half a century ago these Andeans had come, driving us all crazy with their marches on the capital and their caudillos, and (on arriving at the Presidential Palace) had been amazed to find kitchens worked by gas, sanitation, taps running hot water, and telephones from room to room. This was why it had been necessary to carry out a huge "mopping-up" operation before the battle: burning of houses and villages, summary execution of all suspects, shooting at random into groups of dancers, birthday or baptism parties, which were merely pretexts for whispered propaganda, passing on of information and revolutionary plotting—not to mention certain wakes when, strange to say, there was no corpse in the coffin.

"But in Santo Tomás del Ancón you had no choice," said the Head of State. Sad, very sad, of course, but one couldn't make war with kid gloves on. You had always to follow Von Moltke's two incontrovertible principles: "The best thing that can happen in a war is a quick ending . . . But to end it quickly all means are good, not excepting the most iniquitous." A text of basic importance published by the German General Staff in 1902 stated: "If a war is waged energetically it cannot be directed solely against the combatant enemy; it must also aim at destroying his material and moral resources. Humanitarian considerations can be taken into account only if they do not

affect the result of the war itself." Besides which, Von Schlieffen had said . . .

"Stop buggering about with your German classics," said
the Head of State. Von Schlieffen wanted battles to be fought
on the chessboards of maps, from a distance, with communications by telephone, cars and motorcycles. But in this
damned country without proper roads, and with so many forests, swamps, and mountain ranges, communications had to
be maintained on the back of a mule or donkey—even horses
were no use in some densely wooded mountains—or by mes-
sengers who could run till they dropped like the Indians of
Atahualpa. Those theoretical battles fought by telescopes and
field glasses, with squared maps and precision instruments,
made one think at once of certain generals with moustaches
like the Kaiser and a bottle of cognac within reach, not at all
disposed—although there were a few exceptions—to rely on
shooting and hanging. Our battles, on the other hand, had
to be fought with our guts—like today's—forgetting all the
theories taught in military academies. And here the old gun-
ners with their "three hands higher and two to the right, and a
finger and a half of rectification," who could wedge a gun with
a millstone, were much more use than these raw lieutenants,
stuffed with algebraic and ballistic gibberish that their subor-
dinates didn't understand, and who had to make calculations
in an exercise book before letting off a shell, which in the end
generally missed the target on one side or another. "In Latin
America," went on the Head of State, "in spite of artillery,
machine guns, and all modern ironmongery bought from
the Yankees, nature makes us go on fighting as in the times
of the Punic Wars. If we had elephants, we'd make them cross
the Andes."

"All the same, Von Schlieffen . . ."

"Your Von Schlieffen based his entire strategy of war on

the battle of Cannae, won by Hannibal." And the President, who had directed the day's operations, surprised the others by revealing—or perhaps wanting to make them believe—that he had been guided in his conduct of the action by Julius Caesar's Commentaries. Three ranks of infantry in the centre; two to attack, the third entrenched as reserve. Two troops of cavalry: on the right, under Hoffmann; on the left, his own. Objective: to break up the enemy's wings, agglomerating and concentrating him in such a way that his rearguard was useless, and to cut off his retreat to the river. Realizing that he was practically surrounded, Ataúlfo Galván had taken refuge on the farther bank, leaving on this side his two sleeping companions, Misia Olalla and Jacinta the Negress, who by this time must have submitted to the lust of half a battalion of the nation's Hussars, taking turns between their thighs, one after another. The battle had in fact been like Caesar's against Ariovistus, beginning by the infantry harassing the ill-armed Indians and negroes who had joined the revolutionaries—in Caesar's case they were Veneti, Marcomani, Heruli; to us they are Guahibos, Guachinangos, and Mandingos—until the leader, finding his men virtually surrounded, put the Rio Verde between them. So Ataúlfo Galván became our Ariovistus, who fled abandoning his two camp followers, the Suevian and the Norican. And don't let us forget that Caesar, too, had to fight against certain *Andes*, who seem to me, I don't know why, rather like our damned Andeans.

"Bravo, my President!" exclaimed Doctor Peralta, full of admiration for his knowledge of the wars of antiquity.

"What I do know is that we gave Ariovistus Galván a thorough thrashing today," said Hoffmann, somewhat pained by the Head of State's lack of admiration for Von Moltke and Von Schlieffen.

They began passing the flasks around again. Now and

again, the flash from a streak of lightning came in at the mouth
of the cave. The President thought of that boring opera they
had seen in New York, where one scene had taken place in a
mysterious underground grotto, with its vaulted roof covered
in a greenish phosphorescence. Colonel Hoffmann, who had
a powerful voice and considered himself something of a *Hel-
dentenor*, was reminded of the caverns of Mime and Alberich,
and tried to sing a few bars from Wagner, emphasizing the
libretto in hoarse German, without finding the exact words
that in fact accompany Siegfried's leitmotiv. Vexed by this
failure of memory, which he put down to drink, he picked up
a large stone and threw it into the depths of the cave. But the
response he received was not the sound of stone on stone, nor
yet of a stone falling into mud or water, but the breaking of a
large earthen jar, struck in the belly and shattered to pieces.
The soldier raised his lantern. On top of fragments of clay a
horrible piece of human architecture was sitting erect—yet
it was barely human now, consisting of bones wrapped in
torn pieces of stuff, of dried worm-eaten skin full of holes,
supporting a skull bound by an embroidered fillet; a skull
whose hollow eyes were endowed with a terrifying expression, whose hollow nose looked angry in spite of its absence,
and with an enormous mouth battlemented with yellow
teeth, as if immobilised for ever in a silent howl, at the pain
in its dislocated joints and crossed shinbones, to which there
still adhered fragments of rope-soled shoes a thousand years
old—yet seeming new because of the permanence of their
red, black, and yellow threads. It was like some gigantic fleshless foetus that had gone through all the stages of growth, maturity, decrepitude, and death—and returned to its foetal state
in the course of time—sitting there, beyond and yet closer
to its own death, a thing that hardly was a thing, a ruined
skeleton looking out through two hollow sockets beneath a

repulsive mass of dark hair that fell in dusty locks on either side of the dried-up cheeks. And this king, judge, priest, or general was gazing angrily from across countless centuries at the men who had broken his former earthenware covering. On the right, on the left, stood six more great jars, close to the walls, glistening with water that had filtered through the mountain. Snatching up several large stones, Hoffmann broke them, one by one. And now six mummies came into view, squatting with crossed arms—more or less flayed, their femurs and joints more or less shattered, with more or less accusing expressions in their blackened faces—making up a terrifying conclave of violation, a Tribunal of Desecration.

"The devil! The devil! Keep away!" all three shouted, disturbing a cloud of bats that went whirling overhead. And still pursued by the vision they had left behind them, they went out into the night, into the rain, making for the camp, where the ruined canvas of their tents was floating in muddy water. Wrapping themselves in these, sodden as they were, they sat down at the foot of a large tree to await the first light of dawn. And as it grew colder, the last flasks in the Hermès case were emptied. Regaining the surprising serenity that heavy drinking gave him, the Head of State told his secretary to draw up a report to the National College of Science describing the discovery of the mummies, with indications of the position of the cave and the orientation of its entrance in relation to the rising sun, exact arrangement of the funeral jars, etc., as archaeologists do nowadays. Besides which, the chief mummy in the centre was to be presented to the Museum of the Trocadero Palace in Paris, where it would make a splendid show in a glass case, on a wooden plinth, with a brass plate: *Precolumbian Civilisation. Culture of the Rio Verde*, etc., etc. As for dating it, their experts could see to that—they were more cautious in this respect than ours, but eager to prove, every time they came across the handle of some ancient pitcher or clay amulet, that this was an earlier example of the techniques of pottery than the oldest Egyptian or Sumerian specimens.

In any case, the more centuries ago the brass plate was dated, the greater the prestige of his country, which would thus possess remains comparable in antiquity to finds in Mexico and Peru, whose pyramids, temples, and necropolises represented as it were the heraldry of our civilisations and proved that we were in no sense a new world, nor the New World, since our emperors wore magnificent gold crowns, jewels, and quetzal feathers when Colonel Hoffmann's presumed ancestors were wandering in dark jungles dressed in bearskins with cows' horns on their heads, and when the Gateway of the Sun of Tihuanaco was already old, the French had not got any further than erecting a few menhirs—piles of stones without art or charm—on the coast of Brittany.

# 4

*By a body I understand everything that can fill a space,*
*in such a way that any other body is excluded from it.*

—DESCARTES

ALTHOUGH, AFTER THE VICTORY, THE HEAD OF STATE
would have liked to give the troops a rest, proceeding meanwhile to evacuate the many casualties wounded by bullets,
bayonets, machetes, or peasants' knives, he realised that the
Rio Verde must be crossed today, because last night's rain—
and it was still falling—was raising its level hour by hour. It
was still possible for the cavalry to take advantage of a ford
nearby; but the infantry had to use barges, scows, and any
boats available, such as a mould-covered ferry boat, abandoned among the rushes, which was speedily repaired and
used to take across impedimenta—some Krupp cannon, six
pieces of light artillery, the artillery park, blacksmith's equipment, tinned foods and cases of gin and brandy for the officers, as well as pots and pans and portable stoves for the
troops—to which, to the great joy of the Head of State, General Hoffmann gave the pompous inclusive name of "logis-
tics," when according to Doctor Peralta it deserved only the
title of "swill, kettles, and aguardiente."

But now operations were going ahead with speed, though
there was no enemy to fight, because the rebel forces were
retreating towards the sea with the obvious intention of
entrenching themselves among the low hills surrounding

Surgidero de la Verónica, base of the Atlantic Fleet, with its
two small cruisers of old-fashioned design and cannons of
limited range, as well as several coastguard vessels of a more
modern type now laid up for careening behind the Naval Arsenal. Although all villages and hamlets had been despoiled
in their retreat by Ataúlfo Galván's men, the sutlers and camp
followers always managed to find pigs, young bulls, and hens
hidden in caves, cellars, and even the vaults of cemeteries,
or bottles of rum, flasks and earthenware jars of strong cane
liquor and plum spirit buried in domestic patios, sacristy gardens, and even in the dust of graveyards. And so there followed carousing, uproar, and revelry throughout the night
watch, quarrels and music from guitars, gourd rattles, drums,
and maracas, while mulattos and half-breeds of all descrip-
tions stamped their feet with a will to the rhythm of the
*bamba, jarabe,* and *marinera,* before leaving the campfire and
going with their men into some thicket nearby to give them
bodily pleasure.

In April the first attacks were made on the advance positions of Surgidero de la Verónica, obliging the enemy forces
to dig themselves in, in the city suburbs.

"Foch's wise remark is relevant now," said the Head of
State, quoting a French authority in order to pique Hoffmann: "When one of two adversaries gives up an offensive,
he digs trenches and buries himself underground." And from
the summit of one of the three hills dominating the town, he
studied its domes and cupolas, its baroque bell towers, its old
walls built in the colonial period, with tender emotion. There
he had been born and given his first lessons by the Marist
Brothers (in that two-storey building with ogival windows
between cement pilasters), from charming illustrated books
that told him about the Nile floods, the breaking-in of Bu-
cephalus, Androcles' lion, the invention of printing, how Fray

Bartolomé de las Casas was lawyer to the Indians, how the Eskimoes made igloos out of ice, and how the monk Alcuin, creator of Carlovingian colleges, used to prefer studious boys, even of humble birth, to the lazy and careless sons of the nobility. Later on he had received an intelligent education in history and French combined, using texts in which more space was occupied—naturally enough—by the Soissons Vase than the Battle of Ayacucho, and by Cardinal Balue's cage than the Conquest of Peru, and which necessarily laid more stress on Saint Louis of the Crusades than on Simón Bolivar of Carabobo—although they informed us of the interesting fact that his name had been used to designate a tall hat favoured by Parisian dandies of the last century . . .

So the boy grew up on lesson books—he understood little mathematics but remembered some classics—and the Head of State was reminded of his adolescent escapades in the streets around the port, noisy with sailors, fishermen, hawkers, and tarts, with their lively taverns with such names as The Triumphs of the Venus de Milo, Wise Men Without Learning, The Staggering Monkeys, The Ship on Land, or My Workshop; with its trade in fish hooks, baskets, and nets, its rope makers, its trucks carrying oysters, octopuses, and jurels along pavements where the smell of tar, brine, and troughs full of anchovies mingled with the jasmine and tuberose scents worn by prostitutes.

There at his feet lay the town of La Verónica, still so like the copperplate engraving made of it by an English artist a hundred years ago, with the figures of slaves and their masters on horseback in the foreground; there it was, with the massive bulk of its Palace of the Inquisition, on whose terrace some Indians and negroes accused of witchcraft had been flogged, mocked by the crowd, and covered with excrement and filth a long while ago.

There was the town of La Verónica, with that big house
and its three wings and two roofs—lightning conductor, sky-
blue dovecote, and squeaking weathercock—where his children had been born while he was still leading the miserable
existence of a provincial journalist and could provide them
with only cane syrup one day and brown sugar the next, to
sweeten the stew of bananas and crusts, which was their in-
variable supper dish. There, in that whitewashed patio, he and
his family had taken the first jump in that game of hopscotch
which, following in his father's bold political footsteps, had
taken them jump by jump, from square to square, from number to number, up the spiral path in the game of royal goose.
From Surgidero they had gone to the capital, always ascending
from the tiny area of our port life to the great world outside,
the old world, for them the New World, although there was to
be sadness among the pleasures and bright lights of that climax of good fortune. Ofelia was who she was—*sum qui sum*
ever since a child—and would never be otherwise; she still
had the character and appearance of the tempestuous, determined little girl, both stubborn and unstable, who had discovered the universe through blind man's buff, "Frère Jacques,"
ring-a-ring-of-roses, skittles, forfeits, and "Malbrough s'en
va-t-en guerre." Nothing could be said against Ariel: a born
diplomat, he tricked the priests as a small boy, answered questions with other questions, lied when he wanted to, kept in
with both parties, wore a row of decorations, and (when under pressure to explain some awkward incident) had instant
recourse to a manual of ambiguities, just as Chateaubriand
would have done with ministries in a similar predicament.
Radames, amongst many successes, had been struck by cruel
and sudden disaster and the evidence could still be seen in
newspapers all over the world: having entered himself in a
motor race against Ralph De Palma at Indianapolis, he shot

to heaven from the burning hot asphalt of the sixth mile, as a result of adding too much ether to his petrol so as to make it lighter, more explosive and dynamic. He had tried to forget the blow of being ploughed in an exam at West Point Military Academy in the intoxication of speed ...

And there, limping among the hopscotch squares, he saw his youngest son, Marcus Antonius, in short pants, the most evasive and invisible of the clan, lost amongst the branches of trees that did not belong to this earth, but to some genealogical forest where he had taken refuge—perhaps because he was the least precocious of the family and the most exotic-looking, both as to profile and eyes. Much given to fantasizing—mad, we should say now—carried away by the impulse of the moment, he had experienced an adolescent mystical crisis on discovering one day, as he stood before the looking-glass on his cupboard, that his penis had become twisted into a corkscrew by the clap. Absurdly enough, he decided to go to Rome and kiss the Pope's sandal, and cure himself with cardinal's permanganate; but he had got no farther than the Cardinal's antechambers, where, happening to run into a dealer in armorial bearings, he convinced himself that he was descended, by a rather crooked, collateral, indirect, and tangled line, from the Byzantine emperors, the last of whom, Palaeologus, died in Barbados, leaving descendants who came to our country. His mystical aspirations forgotten, he spent a great many pesos on acquiring the title of *Limitrophe* [*sic*: see Justinian's Code], Count of Dalmatia, as it happened; he paraded his brand-new nobility throughout Europe, a Title among Titles, jealous of other Titles, expert in Titles, going to bed with women of Title, and many comments on his virility went the rounds among those who had experienced the virtues, well known amongst us, of a "stallion liana" often used by our ardent old men. With such talents, his life took him from

Andalusian estates to the farms of Peñaranda, from antique
Venetian palaces to Scottish grouse moors, from the hunting
parties of Kolodje to the Alfonsine regattas of San Sebastian,
travelling according to a map of somewhat tarnished nobility
that had seen better days, among whom credit and prestige
was given to the North American coats of arms of Armour
and Swift, the ketchup aristocracy of Libby, who promoted
their advance to grandeur by studying, learning, and anno-
tating the Almanack de Gotha (the entry of their names was
always postponed to the next edition) with the close attention
of a rabbi interpreting the Talmud, or a Saint-Cyran translat-
ing the Bible three times, the better to master the subtleties
of its vocabulary and the complications of its hermeneutics.
Marcus Antonius was both brilliant and useless; excitable
and ambitious like his father, whose anxieties, however, were
unknown to him; flesh of a flesh to which he felt alien, he
declared himself to be a luxury product, the herald of our culture, a necessary factor in our international prestige, a lunatic,
dandy, collector of gloves and sticks, refusing to put on shirts
that hadn't been ironed in London, a harsh critic of famous
artists, pursuer of Woolworth heiresses (he dreamed about
Anna Gould, who had presented Boni de Castellane with a
pink marble palace), five times divorced, occasional aviator,
friend of Santos-Dumont, champion polo player, skier at
Chamonix, critic of duelling along with Athos de San-Malato
and the Cuban Laberdesque, brilliant *rejoncador** in the mak
ing, believer in miracles at roulette and baccarat, although
somewhat absent-minded and Hamlet-like at times and given
to signing dud cheques, which found their way by way of legal
proceedings to our discreet embassies.

And there lay, at the feet of the Head of State, that same

* A bullfighter on horseback with the *rejón*, a form of spear.

Surgidero de la Verónica where a plaque set up by one of the doors was engraved with the date of his birth, and where Doña Hermenegilda had groaned as she gave birth to her four children under a mosquito net as blue as the dovecote outside.

And that was the town that fell into the hands of the government troops, intact and undamaged by shells, because almost all the disloyal officers surrendered, on a historic April 14.

Finding himself abandoned by his most trusted men, and with no one owning a boat or schooner ready to take him on board, General Ataúlfo Galván shut himself into the old castle of San Lorenzo, built by order of Philip II on a pinnacle of rock that narrowed the entrance to the port. And there, in the middle of the afternoon of the day of surrender, the Head of State disembarked, followed by Colonel Hoffmann, Doctor Peralta, and a dozen soldiers. The defeated man was waiting in silence in the main courtyard. His lips moved strangely, without any accompaniment from his voice, as if wanting to emit words that refused to be uttered. He was trying, with a checked handkerchief, to mop the sweat coming from under his kepi so copiously that it was making dark drops on the cloth of his military tunic. The President stood still and gazed at him for a long time as if measuring his height. Then suddenly, in a sharp, cutting tone: "Shoot him!"

Ataúlfo Galván fell on his knees: "No, no ... Not that. Not a bullet ... For your dear mother's sake, no ... For the sake of that sainted Doña Hermenegilda, who loved me so much ... you can't do that to me ... you were like a father to me ... More than a father ... Let me explain ... You'll understand ... I was misled ... Listen to me ... For the sake of your dear mother ..."

"Shoot him!" He was dragged, groaning, weeping, and

imploring, towards the farther wall. Hoffmann arranged the firing squad. Unable to stand upright, the defeated man fell against the wall, his spine slipping slowly down the stonework till he was sitting with his boots in front of him, the toes turned in. The barrels of the rifles followed his descent and stopped at the correct angle.

"Aim!" The order reaffirmed the position they had already taken up.

"No ... No ... A priest ... Confession. I'm a Christian ..."

"Fire!" Rifle butts on the ground. Coup de grâce, because that was the drill. Crying of seagulls. A very short silence.

"Throw him into the sea," said the Head of State. "The sharks will finish the job."

This business was finished and done with. But there was still another, perhaps more serious: Doctor Luis Leoncio Martínez, whose potential as a leader and fighter had been scorned and disregarded by us during the urgent emergency of military action, was free and active in Nueva Córdoba, from whose town hall he was sending out manifesto after manifesto attacking the government. He had built up a strong, a very strong position in the city, where he had gathered around him students, journalists, ex-politicians, provincial lawyers, those with socialist views, besides a few young officers, fresh from the School of Cavalry at Saumur, who constituted the army's intelligentsia—an intelligentsia opposed to such men as Walter Hoffmann, but who, like him, had been formed by German instructors and were devotees of the pointed helmet. United there in permanent session, sleepless and with shirts undone, smoking cigarettes by the gross, drunk on black coffee and bad cigars, arguing, discussing, rounding on one another, cursing, their purity of aims worthy of a Committee of Public Safety, the rebels were drawing up a plan of reform that became ever more radical as the hours passed, and which having settled the matter of trials to investigate peculation and illicit gains, embarked on the risky project of reducing large estates and dividing them up as common land. The Head of State had learned from letters received that same morning that events which at first he had viewed with a certain irony were really happening: "Utopian vegetarian notions," he had said. Yet now, in Nueva Córdoba—among meetings, rallies, proclamations, and factions—intensive military instruction for students and workers was going on, under the leadership of an obscure Captain Becerra—a spare-time entomologist—who had been named Military Chief of the town. And, observing that the movement was gaining strength, with signs of syndicalism inspired by foreign, anti-patriotic doctrines, inadmissible in our country, the United States Ambassador offered a speedy intervention by North American troops, to safeguard democratic institutions. Some battleships happened to be manœuvring in the Caribbean.

"It would be humiliating for our sovereignty," observed the Head of State. "This operation won't be difficult. And we must show these filthy gringos that we can manage our own problems by ourselves. Besides which, they are the sort who come for three weeks and stay two years, carrying out huge business deals. They arrive dressed in khaki and go away laden with gold. Look what General Wood did in Cuba."

Three days passed in inspecting and preparing the East Railway, and after a grand campaigning Mass, at which they begged the Divine Shepherdess to grant triumph to the national forces, several convoys set off towards the new front, with a great noise of cheering and laughter under their regimental flags. It was almost midnight when the last train left, with a whistle and hiss of escaping steam. On the roofs of wagons and trucks men in ponchos and women in rebozos were singing hymns and songs together, while bottles of white rum circulated by the light of lanterns, from the coal tender at the front to the rear lights on the guard's van: "If Adelita sleeps with another, I'll follow her by land and sea, by sea in a warship, by land in a troop train."

Night lay behind them, and frogs croaked in the black marshes of Surgidero, now restored to the peace of its slow provincial activities, with gatherings in the barbers' shops, a huddle of old women in the doorways, and—for the young— lotteries and games of forfeit, after telling their beads among the family with their minds focused on the fifteen mysteries of the Virgin Mary.

# 5

*Sovereigns have the right to modify customs to some extent.* —DESCARTES

FOUNDED IN 1544 BY GOVERNOR SANCHO DE Almeyda, the city of Nueva Córdoba stood out against the surrounding wasteland—saffron-coloured deserts, anaemic patches of grass, cactuses, thorn bushes, and sponge trees smelling of the sweat of illness—as blindingly white as a Moroccan settlement, on the banks of a river (dry ten months of the year) whose sinuous course was hollowed out between stony tracts bristling with the bones, antlers, skulls, and claws of animals dead from thirst. Under the cloudless sky, from the rapid sunrise to crimson dusk, vultures and turkey buzzards flew over the hills at the mouths of mines, which were so divided up, and cut into steps with picks, shovels, and sledgehammers, that their original rotundities had been transformed into geometric shapes by the men who had for the last two centuries been extracting the slag hidden in their entrails. Like giants' chairs and sofas, they were sculptures created by the rough, calloused, blackened hands of the peons of the Du Pont Mining Company, who had made of these euclidean shapes resulting from their labours a formless panorama of scree, ridges, and hills of rubbish, mineral waste, gravel, and pebbles, all adding their desolation to the sterility of the desert. And there, in the most barren region of the country, hedged around by prickly pears, stood the rebellious, tendentious, combative city of Nueva Córdoba, defying the Head of State's troops, already victorious in the east. Thousands of enemies of the regime had surrounded a dry university professor and made themselves into a Sacred Legion. And to defend the immediate neighbourhood of the city, the troops of General Becerra (as he now was) had had more than enough time to organise a strong line of defence, with a whole network of trenches and blockhouses surrounded by walls and palisades made from wooden sleepers destined for railway lines. Studying these military preparations through his field glasses, the Head of State murmured in a joking tone that ill concealed his annoyance: "Just as I've always said. In these countries strategy is the only thing that works—either Julius Caesar's or Buffalo Bill's." And in a Grand Meeting of the General Staff it was decided that the most adequate way of dealing with the present situation was to prepare for a classical siege, cutting off all lines of communication with the small towns of the north—also disaffected—which were providing them with food and ammunition: "Even their drinking water has to be brought from elsewhere! The climate is on our side here ..."

And, having pitched their tents at a reasonable distance from the defence lines, from which few shots were coming since the enemy couldn't afford to waste ammunition on useless firing, they settled to wait. For lack of any other reading matter the Head of State had begun leafing through some of the classical works on military tactics that Colonel Hoffmann always carried in his luggage. And, to mortify the "Prussian with a black grandmother in the back yard," as the wits of the opposition used to call him, he quoted the most glaring idiocies he came across with significant shouts of laughter.

"Listen to this, listen!" he said. And in a portentously

deep voice: "Victory resulted from the fact that the battle had been won" (Scharnhorst). "He who is on the defensive can pass to the offensive" (Lassau). "A battle is the only thing that can produce a result" (Lassau). "It's essential for the head to be in command, because it controls the reason" (Clausewitz). "A leader must understand war and its hazards" (Von Moltke). "It is necessary for the leader to know what he wants and have a firm wish to conquer" (Von Schlieffen). "The general theatre of operations contains only three zones: one on the right; one on the left; one in the centre" (Jomini).

"Where there is no centre there is neither left nor right," observed the Head of State, exploding with laughter. "And was this rubbish what they taught you in the military school?"

The days passed in an inactivity made exasperating by heat and flies, until one morning, dressed in an explorer's pith helmet with a gauze veil over the neck, and shorts—in the style of Stanley in search of Livingstone—the United States Ambassador appeared in the camp. The news was serious. Several armed bands, under orders from agents of the so-called Caudillo of Nueva Córdoba, had violated the banana zone on the Pacific and taken possession of $200,000 kept in one of the offices of the United Fruit Company. All work at the Dupont Mining Company had been paralysed, with disastrous immobilisation of ships in Puerto Negro. It had become necessary to put an end to the socialist mysticism of Doctor Luis Leoncio Martínez. We couldn't tolerate the encumbrance of a second Madero in South America. If the country didn't quickly return to a regime of calm and respect for foreign property, North American intervention would be inevitable. Under this pressure, the Head of State gave a definite undertaking that decisive operations would begin within the next forty-eight hours. And next day, employing all desirable guarantees for a military parley, he invited young General

Becerra to come to the camp, where, without any noise or
action that might cast a slight on his honour, he bombarded
him with 100,000 pesos, and a little something too—a bonus
with several noughts—for the two lieutenants accompany-
ing him. And, as dusk fell, white flags were hoisted over the
trenches and blockhouses, to proclaim to the inhabitants of
Nueva Córdoba that their capitulation had been accepted—in
consideration of the superiority of government troops, with
the humanitarian aim of avoiding unnecessary bloodshed.

But at this moment there suddenly appeared the gigantic, frightening, vociferous figure of Miguel Estatua, so-called
because he worked and moved impassively, was strong and
enormously tall, with broad shoulders widening sharply
above a waist so slender that he always had to make extra
holes in his leather belts to ensure that the silver buckle decorated with initials—his sole piece of finery—should stay
firmly fastened in the centre of his stomach. A master driller
and borer, thoroughly understanding the use of dynamite,
and nearly always carrying cartridges of it in his mouth when
he was going to blow up part of a quarry, the negro had made
a name for himself throughout the country by his discovery
that he could carve animals out of stone. Yes. That was how
it was. He knew, of course, that the mountain trees are living
creatures to whom one can talk, and that when one says the
appropriate words they answer by the creaking and movements of their branches. But one day, up there on that ridge,
he came across a great stone that apparently had two eyes and
indications of nostrils as well as the outline of a mouth.

"Get me out of here," it seemed to be saying. And Miguel
seized his drill and his hammer and began to lower the level
here and smooth the surface there, freeing front feet, and
then back feet, a spine slightly convex in the middle, even-
tually finding himself confronted by an enormous frog, the

result of his handiwork, which appeared to be thanking him. Excited by his discovery, Miguel began looking at loose rocks and schist, the hard substances surrounding him, with fresh eyes. That fallen rock over there contained a bat; he could see the tips of its wings. Over there was a pelican with its beak gloomily sunk on its breast. From that outcrop of rock a deer was trying to escape, having lain there for eternity, hoping for freedom.

"The mountain is a prison confining the animals," said Miguel. "The animals are inside it; the thing is that they can't get out until someone opens the door for them." And so he began to use all his drills—he had them ending in points, blades, screws, and bits—to extract enormous doves, owls, wild boars, pregnant she-goats, and even a tapir, which stood in front of him in lifelike proportions. And Miguel looked at all this, the dove, the owl, the wild boar, the she-goat, and the tapir, and saw that it was good, and as he was tired with so much work, on the seventh day he rested.

He lined up all his pieces in an abandoned shed belonging to the Nueva Córdoba Railroad Company, which was no longer any use for mending coaches and trucks, and here people came on Sunday to see the exhibition of animals. His fame spread. One of the capital's newspapers published an article on him, describing him as a "spontaneous genius." But when members of the Spanish Chamber of Commerce came to him with a proposal that he should make a statue of the Head of State, Miguel had replied: "He doesn't inspire me. I don't do portraits of people like him." Ever since, he was without further reason assumed to be against the regime. But others—members of the Literary Club—defended him: "It's because he doesn't dare attack a human figure. It's nothing to do with politics, just fear of failure." And any priests who came near him were commissioned to ask him to do the Four

Evangelists, to be set up around the extension of the garden of the canons of the Divine Shepherdess.

"I can't make men out of stone," Miguel had answered. But when he learned that Marcos was starting on a lion (he had recently seen one in the circus that was giving performances in the villages nearby), that Lucas was working on a bull (a bull is a bull everywhere), and Juan on an eagle (there are no eagles here but everyone knows what eagles are like), he accepted the work and began by sculpting the symbolic animals attributed to the Survivors of the Apocalypse, leaving for later on a Matthew whose youthful face he couldn't succeed in imagining. However, he worked, worked, and worked, digging out of the stone for the first time some human faces crowned with haloes, putting the finishing touches not with drills but with chisels as thin as knives, brought from the capital.

And he was busy on this task when he heard the news of the base capitulation. He instantly threw down his tools and rushed into the street. All at once the dreamer, reinventor of animals and people, the absent-minded eccentric, raised his voice at the crossroads, drew himself up to his full height, and created himself tribune, leader and caudillo of the people. Such was his authority that he was listened to and obeyed. He ordered the white flags to be hauled down and the white flags were hauled down, and Miguel Estatua saw that it was good to haul down the white flags, and also good to resume the battle. With a cartridge of dynamite in each hand and blazing tinder on his shoulder, he declared that it was necessary to resist until they had by fighting converted daily bread into Daily Bread, earned today and eaten today, and not owed to the stores run by Yankee, national, or "associated" companies, who ruled the mines and paid wages in vouchers for goods. There and then, calling on everyone who would listen, he organised one company of dynamiters and another of sappers. And, roused by a speech couched in sincere if crude and ill-expressed terms—eloquence from the heart, clamorous and rough, but more convincing than an elaborate harangue—the students, members of the intelligentsia, workers in mines and olive fields, makers of rope-soled shoes and sandals (who had lost faith in the cowardly Luis Leoncio Martínez, although he was still issuing proclamations to the country, asking help from people barely aware of his existence and declaring that he counted on aid from provinces which had never been involved in the movement) announced their decision to fight as long as their means lasted.

However, it was not enough for adolescents, young women and brave boys to mobilise themselves, while old women made lint bandages and old men worked in the forges transforming belaying pins into spears: all this in an open city, with no old walls—such as some other towns possessed—nor buildings that could be used as defences, and with streets ending in scattered adobe houses encroaching on the surrounding desert. And in spite of mined roads, sending shattered bodies flying into the air, shedding arms and legs in the roar of an explosion; in spite of a bloody battle from patio to patio, from rooftop to rooftop, waged by the defenders with old Winchesters, sporting rifles, blunderbusses from the armoury, Colt pistols, guns with ramrods, and three or four Maxim machine guns, which had to be cooled by urine for lack of water, the government troops captured the plaza around the cathedral, inside which some hundred desperate men had shut themselves with what was left of the ammunition, and were shooting out of windows, loopholes, and gateways. Most danger came from the bell ringers who took aim at everyone advancing along the streets that debouched into the Plaza Mayor. So the hours passed and there they still were, eating a snack and taking a drink now and again; but not succeeding in occupying the now-deserted municipal buildings, whose façades and galleries were in the line of fire from that handful of buggers who must still have had enough bullets or food for a short while longer. Hoffmann kept his Krupp cannon in readiness; he had brought them in bullock carts to a point whence they could be trained on the tower. A number of these animals, conspicuously coloured and slow in their movements, had been wounded from above; but even so, bleeding, with the second of the third yoke fallen and the first of the second yoke vomiting spittle, they had dragged their burdens to their destinations. Yet the Head of State for once appeared to hesitate: this was the National Sanctuary of the Divine Shepherdess, patron saint of the country and the army. An object of devotion, the goal of pilgrimages, a jewel of colonial architecture.

"Hell and damnation!" said Colonel Hoffmann, who was a Lutheran. "One can't make war with sacred images." When all was said and done, every building could be restored. And every restoration involved improvements in solidity and permanence for the future.

"And what if the Holy Image should be damaged?" enquired the Head of State.

"They sell some very pretty ones in Saint Sulpice in Paris," remarked Doctor Peralta.

"What are you waiting for, to finish off those sons of bitches?" asked the North American Military Attaché. "Our marines would have liquidated them by now. They aren't sentimental like you."

"I see there's no help for it," said the Head of State at last. "If Pilate washed his hands, I shall stop my ears."

"A strategic necessity," said Hoffmann. The Krupp guns were tilted to the firing angle. The old artillerymen aimed it by "three hands up, two to the right, and a finger and a half of rectification," etc., and the first shot was fired. Hit in the centre, the tower loosed its bells over the roof of the Sanctuary, with a thunder of falling stones and statues. A second shot was fired—by calculation and logarithms this time—and sneaked in at the main door and across the altar without touching the statue of the Divine Shepherdess, who remained there, intact, indifferent, standing on her pedestal without even wobbling—a portent that was thenceforth recorded as "The Miracle of Nueva Córdoba."

"The Virgin was on our side!" shouted the victors.

"The Virgin," said the Head of State, much relieved, "couldn't possibly be on the side of an atheist, a believer in talking tables and gods with six arms ..."

And then all hell was let loose; free and uncontrollable, the troops abandoned themselves to hunting men and women, with bayonet, machete, or knife, throwing corpses into the streets, pierced through, cut open, beheaded, and mutilated, to warn the rest. And the last to put up a fight—some thirty or forty of them—were carried off to the Municipal Slaughterhouse, where, among hides of oxen, animals' viscera and tripes, or pools of coagulated blood, they were battered and kicked, and hanged from hooks and beams, by the armpits, the knees, around the ribs, or by the chin.

"Who wants a skewerful of meat? Who wants a skewerful of meat?" shouted the executioners, imitating the town crier and giving another jab with a bayonet to a dying man, before posing in front of the camera of a French photographer, Monsieur Garcin, who had been living in the town for some time (scandalmongers said he had escaped from Cayenne), taking family groups and photographs of weddings, christenings, first communions, and "little angels" lying in their small white coffins.

"Look pleasant!" he said to the soldiers, changing a plate, about to press the rubber bulb. "Two pesos fifty for half a dozen, postcard size, with one hand-coloured enlargement as a souvenir ... Don't move. That's it ... Now another ... With the four strung up over there ... Another with these danglers ... Pull down the woman's skirt so as not to show her cunt ... Another, with that chap with a trident in his guts ... There's a reduction for anyone taking a dozen."

Already the turkey buzzards and vultures were flying over the patios of the Municipal Slaughterhouse. From the post office, from the poplars in the park, from the balconies of the Town Hall, hanged men were suspended in clusters. A few who tried to escape were lassoed like young steers in a rodeo, and dragged by horsemen over paving stones and bare pebbly ground. Some fifty miners, standing with their hands up, were run through in the baseball stadium, opened only a few months before by the Du Pont Mining Company. At the feet of the Divine Shepherdess, standing erect on her scorched altar in the ruins of her sacred dwelling, there was a confused heap of human bodies, from which emerged, like things broken off and out of context, a leg, a hand, a head frozen in its last grimace. Rifle fire was still to be heard from the miners' quarter, where soldiers carrying drums of paraffin were setting fire to houses full of cries and entreaties.

And at midnight there was a huge explosion in the forgotten hangar of the Nueva Córdoba Railroad Company. Miguel Estatua had just destroyed himself and all his stone creatures with dynamite. A few fragments of the Evangelists flew over the crowd, killing three soldiers by slicing them with haloes filed as sharp as an axe by the chisel of the inspired driller and borer.

Now that the chief focus of resistance had been destroyed, the Head of State returned to the capital, entrusting

to Hoffmann (raised to the rank of general for services ren-
dered) the now-easy task of punishing those surrounding
villages that had helped the rebels. Doctor Luis Leoncio Martínez had fled towards the northern frontier by way of a dry
ravine that lost itself in the inhospitable sierras of Yatitlán.
Here and there he proclaimed himself Leader of a Government in Exile or of the National Legalist Party, etc., etc.,
building up an inefficient nucleus of political exiles, soon to
be destroyed—the President knew all about this—by rivalry,
defections, schisms, mutual accusations, and litigation, fed by
periodicals printing three hundred copies, tracts, and news
sheets with fifty readers. And the Apostle of Nueva Córdoba,
deep in theories and wool gathering, ended up, like so many
others, a forgotten man in some Los Angeles boarding house
or squalid hotel in the Caribbean, writing letters and pamphlets quite without interest for those who knew only too well
that what counts in politics is success.

When he returned to the seat of government, the Head of
State was received with flags, triumphal arches, fireworks, and
the march *Sambre-et-Meuse*, which he liked particularly. But
in his first press conference he looked sad and was frowning,
and declared that he felt overcome with grief at the thought—
no doubt based on recent events—that the nation didn't trust
his honesty and disinterested patriotism. For this reason he
had decided to relinquish the power and entrust his respon-
sibilities to the President of the Senate, in the hope that elections would be held and some outstanding man, some good
citizen, more capable than he was of controlling the fate of
the nation, might be raised to the presidency, unless—unless,
I say—a plebiscite should produce a contrary result. So the
plebiscite was quickly organised, while the Head of State
carried on his ordinary business with the noble and serene
melancholy—not to mention pain endured with dignity—of

someone who believes in nothing and nobody, and who has been wounded to the quick after having done everything possible for the good of other people. The misery of power! The classical drama of crown and purple! Bitter old age of princes!

As 40 per cent of the population could neither read nor write, coloured cards were prepared—white for "yes" and black for "no"—with a view to simplifying the mechanism of voting. But mysterious voices, sly voices, insidious voices began whispering in towns and countryside, in mountains and plains, from north to south and from east to west, that every vote, although secret, would be known to the rural or municipal authorities. There were new techniques today to make this possible. Cameras concealed in the curtains of the polling booths that functioned every time a citizen stretched out his hand to a ballot box. Where this arrangement didn't exist, there were men hidden behind those same curtains. Then—without any doubt—they would examine the fingerprints left on the cards, not forgetting that in small villages everyone knows his neighbour's political views, and twenty negative votes in such places would mean twenty individuals identified without possibility of error. A growing sense of alarm was taking hold of public servants—of whom there were many. On the other hand, the mysterious voices were now insinuating, more openly, in taverns, food stores, and bars, that the great mining and banana companies, manufacturers, etc., would sack anyone who opposed the Head of State's remaining in power. The disaffected peasants had to look out for the machetes of the rural police. The schoolmasters would be thrown out of their classrooms. The tax returns of some traders—it was understood—would be severely checked, since they always managed to trick the tax collectors. It was remembered in time that any recently naturalised foreigner could have his citizenship card taken away and be sent back to his own country, if he fell into the ugly category of undesirable or anarchist.

As a result of all this, the plebiscite produced an enormous and massive "yes," so enormous and massive that the Head of State felt obliged to accept 4,781 negative votes—a figure arrived at by dice thrown by Doctor Peralta—to show the complete impartiality with which the inspectors of the returns had worked.

There were more speeches, triumphal marches, fireworks, and Bengal lights. But the President was tired. Besides which, his right arm remained out of action day after day, because of some strange and unpleasant sluggishness, heaviness or disobedience of the muscles, and he had a sharp pain in the shoulder which neither massage nor medicine relieved, nor even the herbs prepared by the Mayorala Elmira, who, as the daughter of a herbalist, knew a lot about plants and roots, nearly always more effective than some of the concoctions of eminent chemists, advertised in the press by beautiful illustrations of Convalescence and Recovered Health. A North American doctor came specially from Boston and diagnosed arthritis—or something of the sort with one of the new names proliferating on the covers of medical magazines, causing great panic and confusion among the sick—indicating that this country didn't possess a certain electric apparatus that was the only means of curing the trouble. The government unanimously begged the Head of State to go to the United States and recover his very important health. During his absence the President of the Cabinet would be responsible for governing, with the close collaboration of General Hoffmann, in charge of National Defence, and the President of the Senate.

So it was that the Head of State embarked on a voyage in a luxury ship of the Cunard Line. But once arrived in

New York, he was aware of sudden, irrational, almost child-
ish fear—perhaps he was tired; his nerves had been affected
by recent events—when confronted by Yankee doctors, who
spoke a foreign language, were cold in their manner, too
ready to use a scalpel, to cut without great cause, addicted
to rough new methods whose consequences weren't fully
understood, very different from the gentle, bearable, and
intelligent therapeutics of the French or Swiss specialists,
who were undoubtedly—he was thinking of Doyen, of Roux,
of Vincent—at the top of the tree over there. To the asep-
tic, white, impersonal surgeries full of forceps, probes, saw-
edged scissors, and other cruel objects on view in the glass
cases of these Yankee doctors, the President much preferred
the consulting rooms hung with pictures by Harpignies or
Carolus-Durand—the Persian carpets, antique furniture,
books with eighteenth-century bindings, an almost imperceptible smell of ether or iodine—of the doctors with imperi-
als, frock coats, and the Legion of Honour, who officiated,
paternally and elegantly, in the Avenue Victor Hugo or the
Boulevard Malherbes.

"Very well," said Peralta. "But ... do you think it's wise
to go so far away? And supposing there's another coup,
my President?"

"Ah, my friend ... Everything is possible in our countries.
But I don't think it's likely. We'll be away only a few weeks.
And my health comes first. I wasn't born to be a cripple. And
to become a cripple without having ever been to Lepanto
would be stupid. Besides, with no right hand I can't depend on
my best friend. Because even when I'm in my country, where
so many people love me, I feel calm, firm, and in control of
myself only during audiences and visits, when I know that's
with me." And he pointed with his chin at the place where he
kept his Browning, there, under his left armpit, praising the

lightness of its trigger and the style of its butt, with the tender accents in which a man boasts of the beauty of the woman he loves: it was faithful, docile, safe, beautifully shaped, of perfect proportions, pleasant to touch, slim and elegant right up to the mouth, well bored though invisibly, and with the National Arms engraved on the back of the butt. It was looked after with maternal affection by the Mayorala Elmira, who cleaned it every day when he removed it before he took a long bath, returning it to him recharged and ready for use, just as he was drying himself with a large plushy towel, one of those Ofelia bought for her father in La Maison de Blanc.

And so, leaving behind the electric apparatus, progressive inventions, and torture tables of North American clinics, which seemed to him like huge prisons, the Head of State embarked one morning on *La France* to take refuge, after so many trials and tribulations, in the charms of a Parisian summer—so sunny and warm that year, the newspapers reported, that nothing like it had been seen since the middle of the last century.

# THREE

*All truths can be perceived distinctly, but not by every-one, because of their prejudices.* —DESCARTES

# 6

THE TRAVELLERS WERE MET AT THE GARE DU NORD
by the cholo Mendoza—yellow gloves, gardenia in buttonhole, and grey spats as usual, although it was summer; he
had been notified by aerogram sent off on the high seas, and
had hastily returned from Vichy, where he was combining
the water cure in the daytime with nocturnal cures in the bar,
and this intelligent alternation of spring water with bourbon
had given him the appearance of a twenty-year-old. The other
embassy officials were on holiday with their children, at Trou-
ville or Arcachon. And Ofelia was in Salzburg, where the Mozart Festival was opening that very day with *Così fan Tutte*.
The diplomat's expression showed his alarm when he saw that
the Head of State had his inert right arm in a sling made from
a cashmere shawl. A tiresome affliction, but not serious, Doctor Peralta explained. The doctors over here would put it right
with their up-to-date scientific methods. Besides, the atmosphere, movement, gaiety, and civilised way of life ...

Merely by breathing the air here—thus: breathe in,
breathe out, expand the chest—one felt better. And it was
well known that morale affects the physical state, since pain
gets so much worse when we concentrate on the idea of pain,
because, in fact, modern psychologists had agreed with Epi-
curus that etc., etc.; but one couldn't talk in all this noise from
trains, whistling engines, bustling porters, and perhaps you'd
better go on ahead with the luggage, Cholo, while Peralta

and I take a little walk, as our legs are numb with sitting for
so long.

And the Head of State, followed by his secretary, entered
a well-known bistro, rather Flemish in style, with a dartboard
and a statuette of the Manneken-Pis, where one could drink
Hoegaarde bitter, or another beer the colour of cherry juice,
or strong Lambic—"branded" with a red-hot nail dipped
in the froth—all of them good to start off a day that should
be full of health-giving savour. Everything seemed pleasant
today—people sitting outside cafés, soldiers' red trousers, the
zouaves' skullcaps, the burning carrot advertising Le Brazza,
the buses with their placards advertising the Opéra, Répub-
lique, Bastille, Parc Monceau, and tours of the Napoleonic
sights. The returned travellers renewed their old habits of taking idle strolls according to whim, from the Chope du Panthéon to the tulip bulbs of the Quai de la Mégisserie; from
Chaponac's occult and Rosicrucian bookshop (fortune-telling
cards, initiatory leaflets, the works of Estanislao de Guaite) to
a gymnasium where they still practised the noble art of all-
in wrestling; from the sky-blue shop selling religious objects
close to Notre-Dame-des-Victoires to Aux Glaces, at 25 Rue
Sainte-Apolline, where in the mornings an ample blonde was
often on duty who was particularly skilled at manipulation à
la Duc d'Aumale—which gave an air of somewhat aristocratic
raffishness to the cavalry barracks nearby. Everything above
and behind the zinc bar counters spoke the language of smells
and taste: brioches in their paper cases; madeleines, fluted
like scallop shells from Compostela, in square glass contain-
ers; Dubonnet's cat, the *bersagliere* on the Cinzano bottles, the
gleaming pottery of the flasks of Dutch gin, the wooden lad-
ders enclosed in bottles of marc brandy; the aroma of Amer
Picón—something between orange peel and tar.

"We're better off here than in the Mummies' Cave,"

murmured the Head of State. And finally they hailed an open car and were driven to the Rue de Tilsitt.

"Paris will always be Paris," opined the secretary when, between the horses of Marly, the Arc de Triomphe appeared in the distance, useless and magnificent.

And now, installing himself, sinking into his leather armchair, the Head of State felt something approaching an organic need to re-establish relations with the city. He put through a telephone call to the house on the Quai Conti where delightful concerts often took place: Madame was not at home. He rang up the violinist Morel, who congratulated him on his return in the hasty and evasive tone of someone who wants to end the conversation quickly. Next he telephoned Louisa de Mornand, whose housekeeper kept him waiting longer than she should and then told him that the beautiful lady was away for a few days. He rang Brichot, professor at the Sorbonne.

"I'm almost blind," he answered, "*but I have the newspapers read aloud to me.*" And he hung up. "As irritable as ever," thought the Head of State, rather surprised by this strange response and looking up another number in his diary. He rang, rang, rang, first one friend then another, always— except when it was his tailor or hairdresser—being answered by voices that had apparently changed their tone and style. Then he thought of D'Annunzio; perhaps he would be in Paris. After a maid had told him that her master had just left for Italy, he heard the poet's own voice giving the lie to what she said, and launching a terrific invective against the creditors who were literally besieging him in his house. Yes, *besieging* was the word: suggesting a tribe of Erinyes, of Eumenides, of Furies; of Hecate's hellhounds, there at all hours, stationed in the bistro opposite, in the *tabac* at the corner, in the neighbouring bakeries, with their eyes on his door, waiting for him to go out so that they could hurl themselves on him, destroy and tear him with their savage demands for money.

"Ah, what wouldn't I do to have the power of a Latin American tyrant, and be able to cleanse the Rue Geoffroy l'Asnier of rogues and scoundrels as our brave friend who was talking just now did in Nueva Córdoba."

Realizing that the blow was about to fall—and it wouldn't be the first—the Head of State struck the mouthpiece with his fountain pen, saying: "*Ne coupez pas, Mademoiselle! ... Ne coupez pas,*" and then hung up the receiver in the middle of a sentence from his interlocutor, to make him think they had been cut off. But he felt uneasy and disconcerted. He didn't know how to take this talk of a "tyrant" even though the poet habitually used "imaginific" and ambiguous language, but as to Nueva Córdoba, he wasn't aware that D'Annunzio even knew the name of the town. Something was up. Perhaps it would be a good idea to ring up Reynaldo Hahn, his amiable and pleasant "compatriot" from Puerto Cabello. The composer came to the telephone, speaking in his agreeable Spanish with a Venezuelan accent, curiously interspersed—a habit he couldn't explain himself—with occasional turns of speech obviously coming from the River Plate. After the usual greetings, Reynaldo informed him, in his characteristically mild, slow, and rather lazy tones, as if he were talking about something different, that *Le Matin* had published a series of savage reports on the events *over there* in which his "compatriot" was described as "The Butcher of Nueva Córdoba." All of Monsieur Garcin's photographs had appeared, occupying three or four columns, and showing corpses lying in the streets, mutilated corpses, corpses being dragged along, corpses hanging by their armpits, by their chins, by their ribs, from the meat hooks in the Municipal Slaughterhouse, and pierced with pikes, tridents, and knives. And female defenders of the town being forced to run naked through the streets of with bayonets in their backs. And others raped after taking refuge in the church. And other women thrown into cattle pens. And the miners shot down with machine guns *en masse* in front of the cemetery wall with military bands and cheerful bugles playing. All this, accompanied by portraits of the Head of State in battle dress, in profile, half-face, or sometimes back view, but always identifiable by his corpulent frame giving the order for the artillery to fire on the National Sanctuary of the Divine Shepherdess ("It wasn't me, it was Hoffmann," he protested), that marvel of baroque architecture—*la Notre-Dame du Nouveau Monde* as the newspaper called it. And the unkindest cut of all perhaps was that when his son Marcus Antonius was questioned by a reporter two days ago on the beach at the Lido, where he was staying with an Arsinoe from the Comédie Française, instead of defending his father, he declared: "*Je n'ai que faire de ces embrouillements sudamericains.*"

At last, the appalled listener understood the reason for so many excuses and ancillary rebuffs; now Louisa de Mornand's fictitious absence and Brichot's strange reply were explained.

"I know there's a lot of exaggeration in it all, compatriot. They do extraordinary things nowadays in the way of trick photography ... You wouldn't be capable ... Of course it's all false." But he couldn't dine with him at Larue that night. Nor tomorrow, as he had a date with Gabriel Fauré. A lot of work on hand, also. a project for an opera on Moratin's *El si las niñas*, a concerto for piano and orchestra. He was extremely sorry...

Overwhelmed, the Head of State fell into the hammock, swinging diagonally from the rings that he had ordered to be fixed to two corners of his bedroom, months ago. He wasn't even cross with the cholo Mendoza, who could well have warned him. But he knew very well that the only French papers his diplomats read were *Le Rire*, *Fantasio*, and *La Vie Parisienne*, and they were always the last to know what was being written about their country. He gazed at the moulded plaster on the ceiling with the bitterest feelings he had perhaps ever known. It would have upset him very little to be treated as a "butcher," a barbarian, a savage, or whatever else, in places he had never been attached to, and which he had for that reason spoken about slightingly. In his view, Berlin was a city that had every right to its primitive name of "place of bears," with the architectonic heaviness of the Brandenburg Gate, like some granite locomotive, its walled-in temple of Pergamum and Unter-den-Linden: Vienna, in spite of its reputation for elegance and voluptuousness derived from its operettas and waltzes, was really terribly provincial, with its little officials from the dyeworks, its ten or twelve restaurants anxious to be like those of this city, besides its café-au-lait-coloured Danube, which looked blue only on an occasional February 29 of leap year; Berne was a boring town with its heraldic statues in the middle of streets that were one vast shop window of watches and barometers; in Rome, every square, every street corner was a scene from an opera, and whatever the passers-by wore or talked about, they always had the air of the chorus in *La forza del destino* or *Un ballo in maschera*, whereas there was a certain smallness about Madrid, with its kiosks selling mineral water, sweets and aguardiente, its night watchmen with key rings at their belts, and its social gatherings in cafés where the dawn rose on a provincial panorama of last night's cups of chocolate and yesterday's toast, some people just going off to bed while others were starting the day early with fritters and tobacco. On the other hand, Paris was an Earthly Paradise, the Promised Land, the Shrine of Intelligence, the Metropolis of *Savoir-vivre*, the Source of All Culture, and anyone fortunate enough to live *here* found that its

dailies, weeklies, reviews, and books, year after year, praised
Rubén Dario, Gómez Carrillo, Amado Nervo, and many
other Latin American writers who had, each in his own way,
contributed to make the Great City into a City of the Gods.

Slowly, overcoming reserve, observing strict rules of polite behaviour, always carefully dressed according to hours,
days, and seasons, giving valuable but never ostentatious
presents, sending flowers at odd times, showing generosity
to charity sales and tombolas for good causes, befriending
artists and writers who were not eccentric bohemians, and
attending important concerts, fashionable meetings, and theatrical and musical first nights—thereby showing that our
countries *also* knew how to live—he had opened a way for
himself, which without elevating him to the peaks of Gotha
had nevertheless three times admitted him to Madame Verdurin's musical evenings—not such a bad beginning. When
he was tired of all the agitations and crowds of *over there*,
he intended to retire and await death in the house that every
journey made more pleasant to him. But now everything had
collapsed. Forever shut against him would be the doors of the
great houses he had dreamed of entering when as a provincial
journalist he had walked the steep streets of Surgidero de la
Verónica, reciting poems in which Rubén Dario sang of "the
times of King Louis of France, a sun with a court of stars on a
blue field, when the splendid and majestic Pompadour filled
his palaces with fragrance." Or when, sitting in some tavern
in the port, in the steam of prawns on the grill, his nose buried in reviews from *over there*, he used to come across works
by the most famous painters in the world, showing him the
gold and crimson of the foyer of the Opéra, the whiteness
of sylphides and wilies, the aristocratic confidence of horse-
women at a gymkhana, the greyness of cathedrals in the rain
("*il pleut dans mon coeur / comme il pleut sur la ville*"), and

the iridescence of women whose portraits showed them as
birds of paradise, symphonies of jewels, unimaginable beings,
suddenly blazing out from the pages of *L'Illustration*—as he
sat there, between the siren of a Danish cargo boat and the
squeaking of the crane as it loosed a torrent of coal on to a
dirty quay close by.

Now he thought he read scorn and mute accusation in
the eyes of everyone who looked at him: his manservant Sylvestre was rather evasive; the cook, whose gesture of wip-
ing her hands on her apron when she saw him could have
various different interpretations; the concierge, reserved and
cold, seemingly uninterested in his arm in its sling—or else
not thinking it discreet to allude to it; the familiar old Bois-
Charbons, where he had the half-fearful curiosity to go that
same evening to drink a bottle of Beaujolais with Doctor Peralta. Monsieur Musard seemed to be in a bad mood. His wife
didn't come out to greet him. And, to judge by their glances,
those two men in caps at the other end of the bar were talking
about him. In all the cafés the waiters had strange expressions
on their faces. In the end, in order to soothe his nerves and
after taking Peralta's advice, he turned up without warning
at the house of the Distinguished Academician, who owed
him so many favours. There, in an apartment full of shadows and with views over the Seine, surrounded by old books,
Hokusai prints, portraits of Sainte-Beuve, Verlaine, Leconte-
de-L'Isle, and Léon Dierx, the President received an affec-
tionate welcome, understanding, and lucidity, which touched
him. Power entailed terrible obligations, his friend declared.
"When kings carry out their promises it is terrible, and when
they don't carry them out it's just as terrible," he said, perhaps
quoting Oscar Wilde. No leader of men, no great monarch
or captain, had had clean hands. Dramatic and comforting
pictures passed before the President's eyes, pictures of the

destruction of Carthage, of the siege of Numantia, of the fall
of Byzantium. Sudden images arose, confusedly shuffled at
random by his memory, of Philip and the Duke of Alba, Sala-
din, and Peter the Great obliged by reasons of state to extermi-
nate the Naryshkins in a courtyard of the Kremlin. Besides . . .
who had ever been able to control the frenzied excesses and
cruelties—lamentable but repeated throughout history—of a
brutal soldiery, drunk with victory? And worse still when a
rebellion of Indians and negroes had to be crushed. In fact,
to speak frankly, that affair had been the result of a mob of
Indians and negroes running amok.

His strength of mind restored, and his mood made more
aggressive by the conversation, the Head of State suddenly
discarded his rather careful French, with its attention to pronunciation and choice of the right word, and impetuously
triggered a deluge of Creole insults, which his astonished
friend received like a verbal invasion of ideograms outside
the scope of his understanding. Indians and negroes, yes; but
"*zambos, cholos, pelados, atorrantes, rotos, guajiros, léperos,
jijos de la chingada, chusma, y morralla*" (Doctor Peralta tried
to translate this into a language learnt at Monsieur Musard's
Bois-Charbons, as *propres-à-rien, pignoufs, galvadeux, jean-
foutre, salopards, poivrots, caves, voyous, escarpes, racaille,
pègre, merde*) and above all—now the President returned to
French—*socialists*, socialists affiliated with the Second International, anarchists, men who foretold an impossible levelling
of classes, who fomented hatred in the illiterate masses, who
exploited for their own advantage the conceit of uneducated
people who had refused the schooling offered them, people
crazed by practising witchcraft and unimaginable superstitions, and devoted to saints somewhat like our saints but
who were not our saints, since these illiterate people, hostile
to the three Rs, called the Beautiful God of Amiens Elegná,

Velásquez's *Crucified Christ Obatalá*, and Michelangelo's *Pietà Ochum*. They didn't understand that *over here*.

"More than you think," observed the Distinguished Academician, growing more indulgent and convinced all the time. Everything could be explained (and he returned to Philip II and the Duke of Alba, passing on to the America of Cortés and Pizarro) by Spanish blood, the inheritance of the Spanish temperament, the Spanish Inquisition, bullfights, banderillas, cape and sword, horses being disembowelled among sequins and *pasodobles*. "*L'Afrique commence aux Pyrénées.*" We had been born with that blood in our veins; it was fate. Men of *over there* were not like those *over here*, although of course they didn't lack certain qualities, because there had been, after all, Cervantes, El Greco—who had, by the way, been revealed to the world by the genius of Théophile Gautier.

At this moment, that schoolteacher Doctor Peralta sprang up from his chair in a rage and shouted: "*Je vous emmerde avec le sang espagnol.*" And, in an irreverent outburst, he paraded before the amazed eyes of the Distinguished Academician, as in pictures from a magic lantern, Simon de Montfort's crimes and the Crusade against the Albigenses; Robert Guiscard (the hero of his own play, the manuscript of which, bought by our National Library, told how the Norman *condottiere* had gone through the middle of Rome knife in hand); the massacre of Saint Bartholomew, that universal synonym of horror; the pursuit of the camisards, the massacres of Lyons, the *noyades* of Nantes, the White Terror after Thermidor, and above all, above all (by skilful handling of analogies), the last days of the Commune. Then, the most intelligent and civilised men in the world hadn't hesitated to conquer revolutionary resistance by exterminating more than 16,000 men. The ambulance of the Seminary of Saint-Sulpice—"*Oh! fuyez, douce image!*"—had become a scaffold in the hands of the people of

Versailles. And Monsieur Thiers, after his first walk through Paris in the days of punitive measures, had said, in the most ordinary way: "The streets are full of corpses; this horrible spectacle will be a lesson." The periodicals of that time—those of Versailles, of course—were preaching the holy bourgeois crusade of murder and extermination. And recently ... what about the victims of the Fourmies strike? And more recently still? Did the great Clemenceau show any mercy to the strikers of Draveil or of Villeneuve-Saint-Georges? Eh?

Under this frontal attack the Academician turned to look at the Head of State: "*Tout cela est vrai. Tristement vrai. Mais il y a un nuance, Messieurs.*"

And then, after a rather solemn introductory pause, raising his voice with each name, he reminded his listeners that France had given the world Montaigne, Descartes, Louis XIV, Molière, Rousseau, and Pasteur. The President had a mind to reply that though it had had a shorter history, his own continent had already produced great men and saints, heroes and martyrs, thinkers and even poets, who had transformed the literary language of Spain, but he reflected that the names he wanted to mention would fall into the void of a culture that knew nothing of them. Meanwhile, Peralta was encircling the Academician with awkward questions: just because it was here that Racine's alexandrines were first heard and the *Discourse on Method* was so famous, certain barbarities were all the more inexcusable. It was deplorable that Monsieur Thiers, first president of the Third Republic, illustrious historian of the Revolution, Consulate, and Empire, should have given orders for the massacres of the Commune, the shootings at Père Lachaise, and the deportations to New Caledonia; it was less grievous that Walter Hoffmann, grandson of a half-breed and an emigrant from Hamburg, a bogus Prussian and tenor of military messrooms, should have carried out—since he had been responsible for the whole thing—the repressive action at Nueva Córdoba.

*"La culture oblige, autant que la noblesse, Monsieur l'Académicien."*

Seeing that his eminent friend's forehead was dark and frowning, the President silenced his secretary with an expression of fatigue and buried himself between the arms of his chair in an attitude of mute despair. He looked at objects in the room without seeing them—the portraits, the old books, an engraving by Granville. The Academician, on the other hand, behaved as if unaware of Peralta's presence, blundering into him as he passed—"Pardon!" (treading on one of his feet) "I didn't hurt you, I hope?"—and walked from one end of the room to the other with the expression of someone reflecting deeply. *"On peut essayer! Peut-être?"*

He put through a telephone call to the editor in chief of *Le Matin*. Monsieur Garcin's photos—that damned Frenchman of Nueva Córdoba—had been carried off by some students, refugees from *over there*, who were now in Paris, talking and agitating in the cafés of the Latin Quarter—all of them followers of Doctor Luis Leoncio Martínez. The newspaper couldn't recant, nor yet cancel publication of forthcoming articles already announced. People would say that it had sold itself to someone known to possess enormous wealth. The best it could do was suppress from tomorrow's issue a photo of the Head of State standing beside a corpse placed on a bodega counter, under a calendar advertising Phosphatine Fallière, whereon the date of the massacre could be clearly read. "That's completely buggered us," said the President, overwhelmed. And if only there had been—goodness knows what—something to distract the attention of the public: a big liner sunk like the *Titanic*, the appearance of Halley's Comet announcing the End of the World, another eruption of Mont-Pelée, an earthquake in San Francisco, some lovely murder like that of Gaston Calmette by Madame Caillaux ... But there was nothing. In this bastard of a summer nothing happened. And in the sole place in the universe where other people's opinion had some importance to him, everyone was giving him the cold shoulder. Seeing him sunk into a state of despair expressed by his hunched back and vacant gaze, the Distinguished Academician offered him the warmth of his friendship with a long press of his left hand, and began talking in a low and, as it were, confidential voice about a possible counter-offensive. The French press—sad though he felt to have to admit it—was tremendously venal. Of course he wasn't referring to *Le Temps*, connected as it was with the Quai d'Orsay, nor was its editor, Adrien Hébrard, a man who would entertain a certain sort of transaction. No more could one think of *L'Echo de Paris*, to which his friend Maurice Barrès contributed, nor that splenetic Arthur Meyer's *Le Gaulois*. But behind these leading papers were others, which on condition there were funds available (the Head of State nodded) would—well, you understand. Everything depended on doing things diplomatically.

So it was that, three days later, *Le Journal* published the first of a series of articles under the general title of *L'Amérique Latine, cette inconnue*, wherein, passing from the universal to the local, from general to particular, from Christopher Columbus to Porfirio Díaz (and showing, *en passant*, how a great country like Mexico had been overtaken by the most atrocious anarchy through not having suppressed a revolution in time), it then turned to our own country, praising its cataracts and volcanoes, its flutes and guitars, the clothes and huts of the Indians, its typical dishes such as tamales and chili stews, with references to the great moments in its history—a history that necessarily led to the period of progress, agricultural development, public works, encouragement of education, good relations with France, etc., etc., due to the Head of State's wise conduct of affairs. While other young nations of the continent were shipwrecked in disorder, that little country was setting an example, etc., etc., not forgetting that having to deal with populations that were often uncivilised and rebellious and easily seduced by destructive and subversive ideologies (here came opportune references to Ravachol, to Caserio, who killed President Carnot, to Czolgosz, assassin of McKinley, and Mateo Moral, who threw a bomb at the wedding coach of Victoria of Battenberg and Alphonso XIII); having to deal with an infiltration of libertarian and anarchist ideas, an energetic government was obliged to take energetic decisions, without always being able to prevent the much-provoked, angry, and sorely tried soldiery giving way on occasion to deplorable excesses, but, however, nevertheless, as soon as . . .

"You see? My President!" exclaimed Doctor Peralta, reading and re-reading the articles. "That ought to settle the hash of those filthy students who kick up rows in the Latin Quarter with their meetings without any audience and their leaflets that no one reads."

Just then a cable arrived telling the Head of State that a case, a prodigiously large case, a magic case, a providential case had been dispatched a short while ago from Puerto Araguato: a case that contained, with all his ornaments, bits of cloth and bones, the Mummy—the Mummy of *that night*—destined for the Trocadero Museum. Skilfully strengthened with glue and invisible wires, sitting in a new funeral jar open in front—just enough for one to see the whole skeleton—invisibly restored by a Swiss taxidermist, more of a specialist in reptiles and birds, but who had done a masterly job in this case, the Mummy was on its way, was crossing the ocean, and arriving, actually arriving in time to give material to a certain element of the press whose greed and absence of scruples were revealing themselves, and astonishing the President, day by day. For the house in the Rue de Tilsitt was now subjected to a perfect invasion from early morning to night. There were journalists, gossip columnists, editors of periodicals never seen on stalls or kiosks, reporters, *échotiers*, men in frock coats, in shabby suits, in bowler hats, in caps, with sword sticks and monocles—would-be specialists in foreign politics, who knew nothing about America except the condor of General Grant's sons, the last of the Mohicans, La Perichole, and an Argentine tango called "El Choclo" that was the rage of the moment. They came at all hours "in search of information," vaguely menacing, declaring that they were still receiving terrible news from *over there*, that it was known that students and journalists were being ruthlessly persecuted, many European interests threatened, and above all, above all, there was the extraordinary suicide of Monsieur Garcin—a former inmate of Cayenne it was true, but a Frenchman after all— whose body had been found a little while ago, hanging from a disused excavating machine a few kilometres from Nueva Córdoba. Behind *Le Petit Journal*, whose sales were diminishing seriously at that time, there loomed representatives of *L'Excelsior*, insidiously suggesting that pictorial matter was reproduced in its pages unusually clearly; behind *Le Cri de Paris* stood *La Libre Parole*, and so from greater to less, from blackmailing dailies to scandalmongering reviews, finally reaching the provincial papers—*Basses Pyrénées*, *Alpes Maritimes*, Echoes of the North, Armorican beacons, Marseillaise lampoons—forming a daily procession of treacherous cadgers, who had to be kept quiet by the language of figures, with the splendid help of the Mummy. There it was, photographed from every angle; there was the Ancestor of America, two,

three, or four thousand years old, according to the whim of
the writer, but in any case the most ancient exhibit from the
continent whose history had been sent rocketing vertigi-
nously backwards by the discovery. There was promise for
our scientific institutions, and for the Head of State, author of
this sensational find; thanks for having made such a valuable
present to a Parisian museum. But the Mummy didn't arrive.
Put on board a Swedish cargo boat, to be unloaded at Cherbourg, by some mistake it had got to Gothenburg, whither the
cholo Mendoza had been sent to look for it.

And meanwhile, ever insatiable, ever-threatening reporters kept on arriving at the Rue de Tilsitt "in search of news."

"I can't take any more; I can't take any more," the Head of
State groaned, after receiving a visit from a woman journalist
from *Lisez-moi Bleu.* "These shits will fleece me utterly! They
may say what they like, I won't give them a centime more!"
However, he went on handing out and handing out, although
now that the Mummy had been photographed, described,
and compared with other mummies—in the Louvre and the
British Museum—it provided no material for any more articles. Searching for a new approach, Peralta studied cases
of the Virgin's appearance on earth, in order to relate them
to our cult of the Divine Shepherdess—perhaps this theme
might interest readers of Catholic papers.

And in the middle of all this confusion the pistol shot at
Sarajevo rang out, followed by the shots that killed Jaurès in
the Café du Croissant.

"Thank God something has happened at last on this
bloody continent!" said the Head of State. On August 2 there
was general mobilisation, and on August 4 the war began.

"Don't let another journalist into this house," said the
President to Sylvestre. And to Doctor Peralta, "Now we can
have a rest!"

That same night the Head of State began doing his former rounds. He and his secretary went to Monsieur Musard's Bois-Charbons, to Aux Glaces at 25 Rue Sainte-Apolline; to the house of the English schoolgirls and the little Sisters of Saint Vincent de Paul. Everywhere the talk was the same. Some said that the war would be short and French armies would soon arrive in Berlin: others said it would be a long, agonizing, dreadful war.

"Nonsense," said the President. "The last war, because it was the last classical war, was the Franco-Prussian in '70." An eminent English economist had recently shown ("and you can find his book in Nelson's Edition") that no civilised nation was in a position to stand the expense of a prolonged conflict. Modern arms were too dear, no country could face the cost of maintaining armies that now added up to millions of men. Moreover, as the French General Staff had already proclaimed: "Three months, three battles, three victories."

At this moment Ofelia arrived from Salzburg by way of Switzerland, pregnant by the Papageno in *The Magic Flute*. They had foolishly embraced one night, when she had drunk so much that she had forgotten to use the diaphragm she always carried in her bag for unforeseen circumstances—and idiotically let herself be fucked in a little house surrounded by pines on the Kapuzinnersberg. She arrived in a fury; furious at having to get rid of *it* elsewhere, because the stupid doctors here wouldn't undertake this form of intervention, whatever one paid them; furious at the article in *Le Matin*, which had been echoed in Germany and Austria, and at a caricature in Munich's *Simplississimus* showing the Head of State in a wide Mexican hat, cartridge belt across his chest, with a millionaire's paunch and a cigar between his fangs, shooting a kneeling peasant woman.

"You've ballsed up everything as usual!" cried the

Infanta. "The monkey's frock coat doesn't hide its tail! If you killed so many people you might at least have included the photographer!"

"They've seen to that already!"

"Fine goings-on! When everything was past praying for! They did better when they shot that archduke! Perhaps as things are now they'll forget your imbecilities! Because everyone is giving us the cold shoulder. We're sunk. Up to here in shit" (putting a finger on her forehead).

The Head of State took his right arm out of its silk sling. The power to move it was coming back; already the elbow joint had stopped hurting. He could almost feel the butt of his pistol. Leaving Ofelia shouting and stamping (she must have had a few more whiskies than usual in the dining-car), he went out to dinner with Doctor Peralta in a basement near the Gare Saint-Lazare where, sitting at a table covered with pitchers of wine, one could taste eighty varieties of cheese— among them a goat cheese marbled with aromatic herbs whose strong flavour reminded him of the cream cheese of the Andes.

# 7

*. . . when we are particularly pleased with ourselves our injuries seem to us all the greater.* —DESCARTES

THAT SUMMER WAS THE MOST BEAUTIFUL AND THE sunniest recorded by European meteorologists. The monks in all the German hygroscopes had their hoods permanently thrown back on their necks; the peasant with the umbrella of Swiss hygroscopes remained hidden in his rustic alpine chalet, while that personification of fine weather, the girl with a red apron, was out all the time. The chestnuts bloomed gaily and the birds sang often among the statues in the gardens of the Tuileries and Luxembourg, ignoring the perpetual warlike preparations invading the life of the capital; but there was considerable dismay at a succession of events which took many people by surprise, notwithstanding a succession of dramatically premonitory signs, and reminded those who had experienced it in a disquieting way of the chaotic epic of '70. The Head of State assumed that the very costly campaign of praise of his country and government in the newspapers could now come to an end, since the public was interested only in news of the furies unleashed upon Europe. His campaign had been doubly useless, because of what was now happening and because (to tell the truth) it had not re-established his prestige in quarters where he had been most anxious to have it restored. Or, anyway, he could see no signs that it had. No one had rung him on the telephone to make favourable comments about any article—except his tailor and his barber, of course. The people he was interested in were all on holiday—holidays that had been wisely prolonged in expectation of developments. Reynaldo Hahn, whose opinion he had been brave enough to ask, gave a short, inconsistent, and slippery reply: "Yes, I saw ... Yes, I saw ... All very good ... I congratulate you, compatriot." It was obvious that at the end of the year, when he was *over there* again, he wouldn't receive all those cards covered in bells and mistletoe from Paris, those cards on filigree paper, with signatures (far more soothing to his spirit than the praise handed out to him daily by the local press) written by highly esteemed and admired hands in response to his own carefully thought-out Christmas wishes, always accompanied by some charming object made by our country's craftsmen. He had therefore to give up cultivating those persons whose company and friendship he counted on for the days when, having resigned from office—out of boredom, fatigue, or anything else—he could pass the last days of his life in this always agreeable and comfortable mansion in the Rue de Tilsitt. He had no intention of leaving Paris at the moment—and in fact there wasn't much danger here— provided that the treatment of his arm was soon completed; it had already nearly been cured by the skill of Doctor Fournier, obliged by his duties as a house surgeon to remain in the city. Accompanied by his secretary, the President took long, aimless walks, waiting for the evening papers; sometimes, when he felt a desire for fresh verdure, getting as far as the Bois de Boulogne, whose Sentier de la Vertu was now deserted, while the swans on the lake stretched their necks interrogatively, vainly hoping for pieces of biscuit that passers-by and

children would have thrown them, even a few days ago. They
sat together in front of the Pré-Catalan, feeling nostalgic for
the charming frivolities of other days, although the Head of
State, passing from intimate monologue to semi-confession,
suddenly began considering this war from the viewpoint of
a somewhat bitter and stern moralist, to Peralta's increasing
surprise. Nations given over to luxury and indolence—he
said—grew soft and lost their fundamental virtues. Aestheti-
cism was all very well, but to recover the use of muscles grown
feeble in the contemplation of Beauty, man felt a need—after
his long period of dreaming—for hand-to-hand fighting,
*agon*. The romantic figure of Ludwig of Bavaria, celebrated
by our Rubén Dario and even by Verlaine, was all very fine,
but for the unity and greatness of a divided and dormant Germany, a solid, rough character like Bismarck, always ready for
war, could do much more than the musical prince, builder of
castles as poetic as they were remote from all reality. This contest would not last long ("three months, three battles, three
victories," said the generals themselves) nor would it be so
bloody as the war of '70, because people had learned from
the remembered experience and wouldn't allow it to be prolonged as it was in the horrors of the Commune. And France
would soon be subjected to a jolt, a therapeutic emergency, a
shock to shake her out of her self-sufficient lethargy. She was
too stuck up, she needed a lesson. She still believed she ruled
the world, whereas in fact her great resources were exhausted,
she had entered on a phase of obvious decadence. The Reign
of the Giants—Hugo, Balzac, Renan, Michelet, Zola—was
over. Minds of such universal brilliance were no longer being
produced here, and that was why France was beginning to
pay for the grave sin of proudly underestimating, in this mul-
tiform century, what lay outside her frontiers. Nothing foreign to his own country interested a Frenchman, convinced

as he was that he was born to delight humanity. But today he was confronted by a new man, thunderously declaring what he wanted, a man who might make himself master of this age: Nietzschean man, motivated by an implacable Will to Power, the tragic and aggressive protagonist of an everlasting reward, repeated today in actions that disturbed the world.

Peralta was well aware of the modest standard of his friend's powers of thought; he was convinced that the Head of State had never read Nietzsche, and that if he was quoting him so authoritatively today it was because in some article read yesterday he had come across some of his views, duly placed between inverted commas. Besides, he was accustomed to follow the ups and downs of his character, and understood that behind these general reflections the President concealed a bitter spite against the people who had humiliated and offended him, closing the road to his chosen abode. When he uttered the names of Bismarck or Nietzsche, he was aiming the mental batteries of his resentment at Brichot the Sorbonne professor, the insolent Couvoisier, the Forchevilles, and the Comte d'Argencourt, the unsuccessful diplomat who, on meeting him casually in a bookshop where they were both buying pornography disguised as the *Compendium of Hindu Erotism* or *The Licentious Writers of the Eighteenth Century* but illustrated with actual photographs, had ignored him with haughty disdain, leaving his outstretched hand in the air. And Peralta, maliciously observing him, stirred the fire of this growing aggressiveness by trying to find weighty arguments in his casual and unmethodical reading of the previous days about miraculous appearances of the Virgin all over the world, to support articles about "the miracle of Nueva Córdoba," though they hadn't yet been published—or paid for.

One morning he gave the Head of State enormous

pleasure by showing him an essay by a famous Catholic writer, celebrated for his irascibility, the outcries and imprecations of an ungrateful beggar ("ungrateful beggar" was his own name for himself), wherein he stated that after the Chosen People of Israel, France was the nation most beloved by God. Without France "God would not be entirely God," he said. Besides, everything went to prove it: the *considerate lilia agri* of the Scriptures announced the Fleur de Lys of French Royalty, the *Gallo* of the Last Supper was a plain allusion to the *Coq Gaulois*. France of the Lily, France of the Cock, France of the Good Bread and Good Wine of the Communion Service, whose position as home of the Chosen Race had been confirmed in modern times—added the writer—by three appearances of the Virgin in thirty-three years; at Pontmain, Lourdes, and La Salette.

These prodigies can never have aroused such hearty laughter: "So France is the land of the Paraclete? And what place does this gentleman allow to Spain, which spread the Catholic faith through a portion of the planet stretching from the Rio Grande in Mexico to the snows of the South Pole? And as for Virgins!" The radiant Virgin of Guadalupe, on her sacred rock of Tepeyac; the Virgin of Cobré in Cuba, whose image appeared floating miraculously, robed in sargasso beside the boat manned by Juan Odio, Juan the Indian, and Juan the Slave; the Virgin of Regla, patron saint of sailors and fishermen everywhere, standing in her star-spangled cloak on the Globe of the World; the Virgin of the Valley in Costa Rica; our own Divine Shepherdess; the Virgin of Chiquinquirá, with her proud bearing and beautiful breasts, very much the woman and the lady too, with her castellated crown; the Virgin of Coromotos, who had left her portrait—after an ineffable appearance—in an Indian's hut; the Virgin of the Amazon fighters of la Fe, clad in fiery armour beneath her protective cloak; the Virgin of Quinche, who led the Army of Ecuador; and the Virgin of Indulgences, patron of the army, and military leader of Peru, always accompanied by Saint Pedro Claver, patron of slaves, and the negro Saint Benito—"as black as the nails in the Cross"—and Saint Rose of Lima, dazzling Queen of the Continent, who owned the greatest forests, the longest mountain ranges, the Greatest River in the World. These Virgins advanced in a formidable Squadron of Splendour, Our Lady of Regla somewhat blackened, the Virgin of Coromotos with almond eyes; strong and full of pity, beautiful and gentle, carrying the Seven Dolours of their Seven Swords, prodigies, succour, good fortune, and miracles, ready to come to the aid of anyone who called them, seen a hundred times, heard a hundred times, diligent and magnificent, omnipresent and ubiquitous, able to appear—like God to Saint Teresa—in the depths of a stewpot or on the summit of an ivory tower; mothers, above all, the Mothers of a prodigious Offspring wounded in the side, who one day (seated on the right hand of Our Lord) would distribute punishment and rewards and submit us all to a judgement against which there is no appeal.

"Let that ungrateful beggar, or whatever he calls himself, come here and talk to me about his three French Virgins; the authenticity of one of them, Our Lady of La Salette, has been questioned by the Vatican itself!" We had Virgins, real Virgins, and it was high time to rid these people here of their conceit and suicidal ignorance of everything that didn't belong to them. They would soon realise what was meant by a strong, well-organised, disciplined, progressive race.

And Germany, where he had spent very little time, suddenly appeared to him as an illuminated tapestry of Black Forests, Master Singers, Soldier Kings, and cathedrals from whose Gothic windows apostles and trumpeters emerged

on the stroke of twelve, beside the Rhine—that great Rhine
with its incredible castles, sung about and sketched by Victor
Hugo—and its water nymphs who caught young men in the
nets of their hair, and its beer festivals attended by cheerful
men with solid calves to their legs, who combined yodelling
and playing the accordion with a taste for philosophy of the
contorted Heidelberg variety, a genius for mathematics, a cult
of obedience, and love of marching ten abreast—to sum up:
everything that those dirty Latins of the Second Decadence
lacked. But now they would see who was best, when Generals
Moltke, Kluck, Bülow, and Falkenhayn paraded through the
Arc de Triomphe (he would be watching the spectacle, standing stiffly erect at his window, although perhaps moved by
what others might be suffering, but resolved in the Cartesian
manner to take as proved everything whose truth was evident
to him), mounted on magnificent sorrel horses, escorting the
Crown Prince at the head of an impressive procession, with
the black dolmans of hussars, frogged Brandenburgs, and helmets with a point, to the rhythm of the great march from
*Tannhäuser*, taken at a military tempo, faster than is usual
at the opera. On that day Germany would finally carry out
the role of "regenerative ferment" prophetically assigned to
her by Fichte in a historic manifesto—a manifesto that had
not been read by the Head of State either, thought Peralta,
although he had to recognise his infallible instinct for acquiring information at second hand.

Agitated by the threat creeping towards Paris (though
in the streets people went on shouting, "*À Berlin! À Berlin!
À Berlin!*") and asking themselves if it wouldn't be advisable to move their offices to Bordeaux, Marseilles, or Lyons,
the consuls and high officials of Latin American embassies
used to meet together at the times of the morning aperitif,
the evening aperitif, and a great many late-night drinks in

a café on the Champs-Elysées, and discuss the day's events. Ever attentive to what was said at these gatherings, noting the opinions of each of them, the cholo Mendoza carried back information that confirmed the Head of State's intuitions. The President had received from his friend Juan Vicente Gómez, one of those generals much addicted to a Kaiser moustache and a monocle wedged in one eye (by confidential word of mouth, because the Venezuelan dictator was afraid they would jeer at his handwriting), the wise advice to remain on the margin of the whole affair (because "the little fellow who gets into a row between big chaps always gets crushed"). Although nearly all these Latin Americans sympathised with France for cultural or sentimental reasons—some loved her literature, others her women, and their duties involved very little work and amounted to long and pleasant holidays while their governments lasted, in the place it was most enjoyable to spend them—there were quite a few who agreed that the war was already lost to this side. One had only to observe the confusion, the fruitless agitation, the *pagaille* they were living in, although it was not reflected in the newspapers, which confined themselves to half-truths or disguised news items, as even Doctor Fournier admitted in the daily sessions of massage and ray treatment he gave to the Head of State's arm, which was every day becoming freer and more mobile. In the streets very different opinions were expressed from those filling the articles of Barrès, Déroulède, and other writers who were, like Tyrtaeus, stimulating the national energy: they spoke of whole regiments left without officers, or taken to sectors where nothing was happening and not knowing whether to stay there, advance, or retreat. In some units only half the men had proper uniforms, kepis alternated with police helmets, and puttees were supplanted by bandages from the chemist or waxed paper. Later came dramatic tales of rifles without bullets, shells without guns, ambulances losing their way, and field hospitals without surgical instruments. And next came rumours spread by romancers and alarmists and generally accepted in small cafés, porters' lodges, and among groups of street-corner strategists: about Uhlans seen only a few kilometres from Paris; a highly secret German plan of penetrating the city through the tunnels of the Métro; the activity of spies, who were everywhere, looking, listening, transmitting messages by a system of curtains shut or drawn at night in attic rooms, according to a code of lights invented by a Prussian cryptographer.

Already the first papers referring to the "European War" were arriving from our countries—a fresh, good, and exciting subject in these monotonous times—full of sensationalism and emotion. Once again people were confronted by huge headlines, or "stop-press telegrams" printed in twelve-point type, as they had been in more interesting times—with some important "news flash" enclosed in a frame of its own. Many people, accustomed to suppress their thoughts about local happenings for fear of persecution, felt free, elevated and relieved, as it were cathartically, by these great but far-away events, suddenly brought into the forefront of reality. At last they could discuss, argue, conjecture, protest (insult Von Tirpitz, censure Italian neutrality, laugh at the Turks) in accordance with similar tendencies in all the countries of the continent. *Over there* the clergy were pro-German, because impious France promoted lay education and had separated Church from State, while the Spanish bankers, the many descendants of German emigrants, and the relations and friends of the little clan of officials who were jokingly called "Little Fredericks" were already applauding the Kaiser's certain victory. But all the intelligentsia, writers, academics, readers of Rubén Dario or Gomez Carrillo were pro-Allies (no one understood about the *Entente*), as were all those who had been, or dreamed of one day becoming, schoolteachers, along with free thinkers, doctors trained in Paris, and a large section of the middle classes—above all those who, at social gatherings, sometimes talked French as affectedly and badly as the characters in *War and Peace*. Generally speaking, this was true of the whole nation, because the French came to our countries more for commercial than other reasons, and had never gone in for tiresome competition with the natives, but treated everyone alike amiably, and often allied themselves with zambas* and cholas, in this respect being very different from those who shut themselves up in "German Clubs," or "German Cafés," which admitted only those of pure white blood, and where the appearance of a negro or Indian would have been greeted by a Fafner-like baring of teeth.

And now they were entering the month of September, amidst doubts and anxieties, although the Head of State surveyed the daily prospect with almost enjoyable expectation. To judge from the speed of their operations, Von Moltke's armies would soon reach the Arc de Triomphe without much difficulty, since France now possessed no generals of the stature of those whose names were inscribed on Napoleon's monument. And this proud, perverted metropolis was to experience a purification by fire, which more than one French Catholic writer would have compared to Sodom and Gomorrah—or even to the whore of Babylon, after the erection (a word that should be used only in reference to statues or architectural works, according to Flaubert) of its Eiffel Tower, Tower of Babel, modern ziggurat, lighthouse of cosmopolitanism, symbol of the Confusion of Tongues, happily balanced by other pinnacles such as the white cupolas—though its architect had wanted

---

* Zambo (m.) and Zamba (f.) is the offspring of a negro and an Indian.

them to be gold—of Sacré-Coeur. But the Head of State, who was a dispenser of indulgences when other people's actions didn't force him to be Distributor of Punishments, was not thinking about fire in terms of conflagrations and collapsing ceilings, but about a psychological fire, a moral chastisement that would force the Arrogant and Self-sufficient to humble themselves and ask for peace. That fire must not of course damage the frescoes of the Panthéon, the pink stone of the Place des Vosges, the windows of Notre-Dame, nor yet the chastity belts in the Abbaye de Cluny, the wax figures and illusions in the Musée Grévin, or the leafy chestnut trees of the avenue where the Comtesse de Noailles lived (although she was one of those who were cutting him) and still less the Trocadero, where as soon as the war was over our Mummy (now being fetched from Gothenburg by the cholo Mendoza) would be displayed in a glass case. And it could need only a few days, surely, for the war to be over. Doctor Fournier, as he discharged his patient—whose hand now went to his pistol easily and quickly, without his forefinger going numb on the trigger—broke into lamentations about the lack of preparation on the part of the Supreme Command, the improvidence, negligence, muddle—*c'est encore la débâcle*—that were carrying us towards inevitable defeat.

"*Vous faites bien de repartir chez vous, cher Monsieur. Au moins, là -bas, c'est le soleil, c'est le rhum, c'est les mulâtresses.*"

But on the afternoon of September 7 the Battle of the Marne began. ("A war is not won by taxi drivers," the Head of State had remarked ironically.) It was soon apparent that in opposition to Jomini's tactics and strategy, the French front line had no centre, this being occupied solely by a weak contingent of cavalry. On the eighth it looked as if they had lost. But on the afternoon of the ninth victory was theirs. That evening, the Latin American diplomats gathered together in their café on the Champs-Elysées and celebrated this triumph by inviting every prostitute who passed to have a drink, while the Head of State—who had joined them for once—looking imposing in his frock coat, and with a patriarchal wisdom recognised by all, muttered: "Certainly . . . certainly . . . However, this doesn't settle anything."

Next day he got up very early, in an embittered frame of mind, and stood contemplating the Arc de Triomphe, whose size seemed to increase or dwindle according to whether his defeatist desires were satisfied or frustrated. Now that his arm was cured, he must think about returning *over there*—he had no reason to stay on here—moreover, he must renounce for the present his hopes of a triumphal procession with deafening yet comic military bands marching like automatons, trombones and trumpets with blown-out cheeks, and all the musicians conducted by an enormous drum major. He was just going to telephone Peralta to suggest a stroll to Monsieur Musard's Bois-Charbons when the secretary came into the room, looking disturbed and holding a long message on blue paper:

"Read this . . . read this."

The cable was from Roque García, President of the Senate: HAVE TO INFORM YOU GENERAL WALTER HOFFMANN REBELLED IN CIUDAD MORENO WITH INFANTRY BATTALIONS 3, 8, 9, 11. ALSO FOUR REGIMENTS INCLUDING HUSSARS, ALSO FOUR UNITS ARTILLERY TO CRY OF LONG LIVE THE CONSTITUTION, LONG LIVE LIBERTY.

"The cunt! The son of a bitch!" yelled the Head of State. But this was not all: three of the "Little Fredericks"—Breker, the blond "good chap," always favoured by notes and instructions from above; González, who had trained as a soldier in Germany; and Martorell, a Catalan artilleryman become a Creole out of hatred of the Spanish monarchy—these three young soldiers, flattered, privileged, and rapidly advancing in the hierarchy, were all taking part in the coup.

"Sons of bitches! Sons of bitches!"

And suddenly giving way to paroxysms of rage, the Head of State shouted, raged, and stormed, and then sank into the depths of despair, groaning, wounded, seeming as if pierced to the heart, stammering out the most damaging adjectives he could find to describe treachery, felony, ingratitude, deceit, and fraud. His monologue reached a climax of exasperation, only to relapse once more into lamentations near to tears, as if he were unable to find words to express his disillusion; then, quickly recovering himself and again growing excited, he exploded into a fresh outburst of oaths and terrible threats.

("I've heard that Mounet-Sully is a great tragedian," thought Peralta, "but there can't be another like my President.")

And the Head of State was still shouting and raging, overturning furniture, throwing books on the floor, aiming at Gérome's gladiators with his Belgian pistol, and making such a furious commotion that Sylvestre came hurrying from the pantry in alarm.

"*Monsieur est malade? ... Un médecin peut-être?*"

Suddenly controlling himself—or pretending to do so—the enraged man turned to his servant: "*Ce n'est rien, Sylvestre ... Rien ... Un mouvement d'humeur ... Merci.*"

And unfastening his tie, still red in the face, sweating, and with words of reproof ringing in his ears, the President began to walk from end to end of the room, giving orders and instructions to Doctor Peralta. Go to the nearest travel agency—the one near the Opéra would still be open—and do everything necessary to get them *there* as soon as possible. Ask Roque García for details of garrisons loyal to the government. Cable to Ariel; cable to our newspapers with a proclamation to go on the front page ("Once again, the blind ambition of a man unworthy of the rank he possesses, etc., etc. Good: you know what is wanted .. ."); cable to him, cable to the other, cables and more cables ...

Just then the cries of the newspaper boys announced a mid-day edition, with the latest war news.

"As if I cared a damn for all that!"

And out of pure rage he kicked over a picture brought him a few hours before by a pupil of Jean-Paul Laurens, and a protégé of Ofelia's, which was standing on the floor in front of him, waiting to be hung up: *The Execution of Ganelon.*

"The cunt! Son of a bitch!" repeated the Head of State, stamping on the canvas as if in the figure of the most famous traitor of mediaeval times he saw some similarity to the renegade, infamous, obscene soul of General Walter Hoffmann.

## 8

*It is better to modify our desires than the organisation of
the world.* —DESCARTES

SO NEXT MORNING THEY WOULD CATCH THE
train to Saint-Nazaire, whence a ship was leaving for New
York, full of Americans who, having seen the Germans approach too close to the Seine and knowing that the war was
by no means over, with its inconveniences and rationing, preferred to return to the opposite side of the ocean. After the
crossing, there would be several days of enforced idleness—
as before, at the Waldorf-Astoria. There was a possibility of
seeing a performance of Umberto Giordano's *Madame Sans-
Gêne*, sung by Geraldine Farrar (for the Metropolitan Opera
House had announced its world première), and although his
daughter took him for an ignoramus where music was concerned, merely because he had on occasion been so bewildered and bored by the telluric entanglements of *Rhinegold*
with its confusion of dwarfs, giants, and water nymphs as to
fall asleep in his box, the President was very appreciative of
Maria Barrientos' coloratura, Titta Ruffo's significant lyrical
energy, the pure timbre of Caruso's long, incredibly sustained
high notes and his magic voice, so prodigiously enclosed in
the body of a Neapolitan innkeeper.

After having got rid of *it* somewhere in Switzerland, Ofelia had left for London, to escape from this tiresome war, now making itself felt, according to her, in the lack of Russian ballets, tango orchestras, and elegant parties in full evening dress. In England, on the other hand, recruitment was voluntary, and life was fairly normal: so she would go to Stratford-on-Avon with a view to completing her Shakespearean education.

"I wonder if some Fortinbras or Rosenkranz will make her pregnant?" thought her father, well knowing that nothing that happened *over there* in their native land mattered to his daughter, who had decided some time ago to live forever in Europe, far away—as she said—from "that country of filth and sweat," with no amusements except municipal concerts, family parties where everyone danced the polka, mazurka, and redowa, and palace soirées where the wives of ministers and generals clustered together at the farther end of the room from a group of men telling dirty stories, to talk about births and miscarriages, children, illnesses, deceitful servants, and deaths of grandmothers, interspersed with exchanging recipes for crême caramel, egg flip, babas, marzipan, and cream cake.

That night the Head of State and Doctor Peralta paid a farewell visit to Monsieur Musard at the Bois-Charbons, and drank heavily. Afterwards they took two girls picked up on the street to a luxury brothel in the Rue Sainte-Beuve, whose entrance hall, decorated with ceramics by Léon-Paul Fargue's father, led to a rickety lift, worked by a piston rod and got up in traditional style so that it looked rather like the corner of a Norman dining room moving vertically. It was late when he got back to the Rue de Tilsitt, to find the corridors and rooms heaped with suitcases and trunks packed by Sylvestre. Doctor Peralta showed him some stereoscopic pornographic photographs—the *Verascope Richard*—he had bought the evening before, and which with their double images gave a surprisingly three-dimensional effect.

"Look. Do look at this. You'd think that man was alive. And you can see every hair on those two women. And what do you think of that combination of five in a row?"

In spite of having drunk so much, the Head of State, though intoxicated, was lucid and sad. He was invaded by a feeling of enormous fatigue when he thought of the efforts he had had to exert four times since he took on the government. Now there would be his arrival in Puerto Araguato. The train of old coaches climbing up to the capital through forests whose trees mingled—it was impossible to know which branches grew from the trunks and which had been cut by machetes—with those that roofed the huts in villages so melancholy and overshadowed by the universal vegetation that a laugh in one of them would have sounded like some obscene explosion of animality. Afterwards, the obligatory speech from the balcony of the palace. His battle dress, probably smelling of camphor, ironed by the Mayorala Elmira, his irreplaceable housekeeper, a woman of excellent judgement and (when he felt like it) a docile and complacent source of consolation; the journey to the battle front would be towards the south this time—a few months ago it was to the north, on other occasions it had been to the east or west. Now it led to the region of the Quaking Bogs, with their purplish lagoons constantly bubbling and pullulating with the animals and reptiles hidden beneath the deceptive peace of Victoria water lilies. Marching along flooded paths, with one's face plastered with revolting ointment that for barely an hour kept off the stings of a hundred species of mosquito. It was a world of sweating hibiscus, false carnations—traps for insects—scum that tangled and disentangled its convolutions from sunset to sunrise, fungi smelling of vinegar, oily flowers growing from rotten trunks, greenish dust and tendrils, collapsed anthills, deceptive turf that ate into boot leather. And it was through such country that he must pursue General Hoffmann, find him, surround him, corner him, and finally put him up against the wall of a convent, church, or cemetery and shoot him. "Fire!" There was nothing else to be done. Those were the rules of the game. Recourse to Method.

But something else was perturbing the Head of State this time. And it was a problem of words. When he returned *over there*, before he again put on the general's uniform that everyone knew was phoney—that was the truth, since he himself had assumed it, gold braid and all, on a day of youthful ragging, and kept it afterwards because one general more or one general less in his country . . . now, before increasing his stature by getting on horseback, before girding the cowboy spurs he usually wore during a campaign, he would have to make a speech, to utter words. And those words refused to come to mind, because the classical, fluent, serviceable words he had always used on former and similar occasions had been so often rehashed in different registers with corresponding pantomimic gestures as to have become worn out, old, and ineffective in the present contingency. Contradicted innumerable times by his actions, these words had passed from the marketplace to the dictionary, from fiery tirade to rhetorical repertory, from useful eloquence to an attic full of rubbish—devoid of meaning, dry, arid, useless. For years the pillars supporting his political speeches had been such expressions as *Liberty, Loyalty, Independence, Sovereignty, National Honour, Sacred Principles, Legitimate Rights, Civic Conscience, Fidelity to Our Traditions, Historic Mission, Duty to the Country*, etc., etc. But now these words (he was always a severe self-critic) had acquired such a ring of false money, of lead dipped in gold, that he felt tired of the twists and turns of his own verbal labyrinth, and began wondering how he would fill the audible gaps, the written spaces in the proclamations and admonitions inevitably involved in a military—and primitive—operation such as the one he must shortly embark on. Accepted formerly by most of his compatriots as a man of action, able to direct the fate of the country at a time of crisis or lawlessness, he had seen his prestige diminish and an alarming deterioration in his authority, in spite of every device he had invented to remain in power. He knew that he was hated, abhorred by the mass of the people, and this knowledge made him react against the external world, and at the same time increased the satisfaction and pleasure he found in the servility, solicitude, and adulation of his dependants, who had consolidated his interests and prosperity and extended to the utmost a sovereignty quite unsupported by legality and constitution. But he couldn't fail to know that his enemies were in the right when they accused him of giving more and more concessions to the gringos, and it would have been foolish to deny that the gringos were universally detested on the continent. We all knew that they called us "Latins" and that, to them, this was as good as saying rabble, small fry, and negro rebels. (They had even invented the euphemism "Latin colour" to justify the admission of important persons whose complexion was a trifle exotic into New York and Washington hotels.)

And the Head of State went on thinking about the speech he had to make, without being able to imagine it in a favourable light. Words, words, words. Always the same words. But above all, nothing about *Liberty*—with the jails full of political prisoners ... Nothing about *National Honour* or *Duty to the Country*—because these were the concepts always used by top-ranking military men. No *Historic Mission* nor *Heroes'*

*Ashes* for the same reason. No *Independence*, which in his case rhymed with *dependence*. No *Virtues*—when he was known to be the owner of the richest businesses in the country. No *Legitimate Rights*—since he ignored them whenever they conflicted with his own personal jurisprudence. His vocabulary was decidedly narrowing. And he had a formidable adversary: a regiment of the rebellious army; he would have to speak, yet the exasperated orator felt aphonic, without a language, as if he no longer had useful, dynamic, stimulating words at his disposal, because he had squandered them, blunted their edge, prostituted them in despicable skirmishes unworthy of such extravagance. As our countrymen would say: "He had wasted gunpowder on vultures."

"I'm getting old," he thought. But he had to make up something. Something.

He emptied one of the leather-covered flasks in a series of short but continuous gulps, and to pass the time of waiting for ideas that didn't come he picked up one of the morning papers—*Le Figaro*—that lay folded on his writing table. There, in the first column of the front page, and printed in a special frame, was an article by the Distinguished Academician. Drawing conclusions from the Battle of the Marne, our friend affirmed that that military miracle—more than a victory of arms: a victory for intelligence—signified, above all, the triumph of the Latin over the German spirit. Heirs to the Great Mediterranean Culture, descendants of Plato, Virgil, Montaigne, Racine, and the magnificent sansculottes of Valmy—appropriate to the present situation although their memory was detested by the whole Faubourg Saint-Germain—they had opposed the Genius of their Race, made up of sanity, balance, and moderation, to the pathological aggressiveness of the Teutons. The Gallic Cock against dragons, cave-dwelling blacksmiths, and Niebelungen. The nervous, active, thoroughbred charger of the already almost sainted Maid of Orleans—she was in fact about to be canonised—against Brunnhilde's fierce steed. Olympus against Valhalla. Apollo against Hagen. Versailles against Potsdam. Pascal's essential wisdom against Hegel's philosophical gigantism—expressed in that obscure Heidelberg jargon that our minds, addicted to lucidity and transparency in argument, have instinctively rejected. The battle of the marshes of Saint-Gond had been a victory for Descartes, rather than for the '75 cannon. And the writer closed with a forcible, implacable, unanswerable denunciation of German culture—or *Kultur*, as he called it—of Wagner's music, the bad taste of Berliners, the pedantic scientism of Haeckel, and the ideas of petulant dwarfs who (believing themselves to be superhuman and disguising themselves as Zarathustra, with swords at their belts and skulls on their shakos) had unleashed the present catastrophe, like modern sorcerers' apprentices. It was war, more than war, it was a Holy Crusade against Prussian neo-barbarism.

When he had finished reading the article, the Head of State began to walk up and down his room. He suddenly understood his mistake: the pro-German attitude of a resentful "metic," an alien in a foreign land—and he remembered that the Greeks didn't use the word in a denigratory sense—was neither useful nor profitable to him. In these crucial moments in his political career, Von Kluck's Uhlans and Von Tirpitz's submarines could not help him. The Valkyrie's cause was a bad cause for him—a cause that "didn't pay." He was forced to admit that in Latin America everyone sided with France—better to say: with Paris. And *over there*, to transfer the problem to our own country, pro-Germans were often Jesuits, pastors of a chosen flock, confessors to rich women and not very friendly to the humble French Marists who had

educated them; pro-Germans were found among rich Spaniards, gentlemen of the *Import-Export*—when they weren't
grocers or pawnbrokers—with large balances in banks in Cat-
alonia or Bilbao, antipathetic to the Creole by tradition and
custom; and also—but this was a special case—amongst the
population of the colony of Olmedo, descendants of Bavarian
or Pomeranian workmen who had no importance in public
life. Moreover—Good God! I've just realised!—all the Virgins
of our countries were Latins. Because Christ's Mother was a
Latin, doubly Latin, now that those disgusting Lutherans—
like Hoffmann and the "Little Fredericks" who sided with
him—have thrown her out of their chapels. The Divine Shepherdess of Nueva Córdoba, the Virgins of Chiquinquirá,
Coromotos, Guadalupe, La Caridad del Cobre, and all those
who made up the Ineffable Legion of Intercessors, were the
ubiquitous manifestations of the one and eternal Presence
enthroned in the nave of Notre-Dame by Louis XIII, when he
consecrated his reign to the worship of the Virgin Mary. The
Virgins must therefore be reckoned on our side—on mine in
this conflict, and her image erected on the labarum—since it
was the duty of a ruler confronted by hostile forces to make
use of anything that might advance his cause. A Leader of his
People, a Director of Men, must be adaptable and never obsti-
nate, although he might have to renounce his most personal
desires at any given moment, in order to remain in power. The
ideological basis—tactics—of his immediate struggle with
the traitor Hoffmann thus became clear. One had only to consider his name; remember his German training; his eagerness
to proclaim his pure Aryan blood, although he had relegated
his somewhat negroid grandmother to the remotest buildings
in his huge colonial domain. Suddenly Aunt Jemima—as the
foolish people *over there* called her—would have to be converted into a symbol of Latinity. (Worried and depressed a

few moments before, the Dictator recovered his spirits, drew himself up, banged on tables, and began to behave like an orator again.) After all, being a Latin did not mean having "pure blood" or "clean blood"—as the out-of-date phraseology of the Inquisition used to put it. All races of the ancient world had been mixed together in the great Mediterranean basin, mother of our culture. In that tremendous round bed Romans had lain with Egyptian women, Trojans with Carthaginians, the famous Helen with people of dull complexion. The wolf who suckled Romulus and Remus had several teats—and it was known that Italy would one of these days attack the Central Powers—and any cholo or zamba might have fed from them. To say *Latinity* was to say mixed blood, and in Latin America we are all mestizos; all of us have some negro or Indian, Phoenician, Moorish, Celtiberian blood, or the blood of Cádiz—and there's always Walker Lotion, or something of the sort, to smooth our hair, hidden away in the family medicine chest. We are all mestizos, and should be honoured that it is so!

And now the Head of State's mind began producing ideas; words returned to him and he was suddenly in command of a new vocabulary. Resplendent words, high-sounding, pleasant to the ear, which must be well received *over there* by those half-hearted, undecided, potential enemies, more or less dedicated to a pro-Ally outlook, who had all become strategists and showed their predilections by moving little tricolor flags on maps spread on café tables, far beyond the point where the army's advance had been halted by the General Staff itself. People felt passionately, and it was intelligent to capitalise their passion for his own advantage. *Alea jacta est.* His mind was made up: he would be a modern Knight Templar joining the Holy Crusade of Latinity. A victory for Walter Hoffmann and his party would mean the Germanisation of our culture.

It would be easy to ridicule him in the eyes of the public. With his personality, the books he read: the portraits of Frederick II, Bismarck, and Von Moltke that adorned his study; the fact that he treated the poor old woman to whom he owed his existence as a far from decorative ancestress—although she was a true incarnation of our race, flesh of our flesh—concealing her under the tamarind trees, close to the yard where the pig was being fattened for Christmas Eve. The rebel was a living mirror of the Prussian barbarism that had not only been loosed over Europe but would also soon be threatening these Lands of the Future, since the Germans believed they were predestined to govern the whole globe in virtue of a mystique about being a *superior race*, clearly expressed recently in an arrogant and xenophobic "Manifesto for Intellectuals" that had already appeared in our press. So he must raise the Crown of Saint Rose of Lima against the Shield of the Valkyries. Cuauhtémoc against Alaric. The Redeemer's Cross against Wotan's spear. The sword of all the liberators of the continent against the Technological Vandals of the Twentieth Century.

"Come here, Peralta."

And for the next two hours, always finding striking adjectives and illuminating images—although this time his style was not too ornate—he dictated articles for his country's newspapers, sketching the broad outline of the campaign as he believed it would develop before his arrival.

"Hurry along and take all this to Western Union."

And now, his energies spent, perhaps tired by so much dictation, and with a delayed feeling of sadness, he gazed around the room at the friendly furniture, pictures, sculptures. Within a few hours he would have to leave this peaceful maternal lap, this period of repose among silks, satins, and velvets, and plunge his horse's hooves for days, weeks, months maybe, in the mire of the southern Torrid Zone—lianas, mangrove swamps with their stagnant waters, murky streams, and tendrils lashing one's face—far from everything that made him happy. He thought about his country *over there*, and felt in advance the boredom of returning to the point of departure after constantly moving forwards with passing years. It would soon be November—our November with All Saints' Day, when the cemeteries were transformed into fairgrounds, with lanterns strung from tomb to tomb, barrel organs making a deafening din, guitars playing among the graves, maracas and clarinets close to the chapels of the dead, and girls being deflowered amongst the faded wreaths of a recent burial. Skulls made of sugar candy or pink icing, skulls made of toffee, marzipan, sesame-flavoured paste, amongst the sextons' spades and straps, coffins, urns, a fine show of bronzes and portraits of grandfathers, soldiers, and children in their Sunday best seen through oval glass dimmed by dew and rain. And then would come the vendors of little skeletons wearing crowns, mitres, top hats, kepis, dancing their Dance of Death from cenotaph to cross, with their cries of "A skeleton for your little boy," which on this day of all days was a summons to gaiety, aguardiente, and molasses. And what conversations were embarked on, what jokes and what quarrels flew between cross and cross, angel and angel, epitaph and epitaph!

"Ah, my friend! You're happy with your little dead son!"

"Ah, my friend, and what a bastard and rogue yours was!"

"So they say, my friend! Yours wasn't such a saint either!"

"That's because he took after his grandmother, my friend!"

"Come now, my friend, how can one say who takes after whom?"

Remembering all this, the Head of State saw himself as someone who had been enclosed in a magic circle made by

the sword of the Prince of Darkness. History, which was his
because he played a part in it, was something that repeated
itself, swallowed its own tail, and never moved forwards—it
made very little difference whether the pages of the calendar
were printed with 185(?), 189(?), 190(?) or 190(6?): it was the
same procession of uniforms and frock coats, high English
top hats alternating with plumed Bolivian helmets, as one saw
in second-rate theatres, where triumphal marches of thirty
men passed and re-passed in front of the same drop curtain,
running when they were behind it, so as to be in time to re-
enter the stage, shouting for the fifth time: "Victory! Victory!
Long live the Regime! Long live Liberty!" It was the classic
example of the knife given a new handle when the old one
wears out, and a new blade when that wears out in its turn, so
that after many years it is still the same knife—immobilised in
time—although handle and blade have so often been changed
that their mutations can't be counted. Time at a standstill,
curfew, suspension of constitutional guarantees, restoration
of normality, and words, words, words, to be or not to be, to
go up or not to go up, stand up or not stand up, fall or not fall,
just as a watch returns to the time it indicated yesterday when
yesterday it told today's time . . .

He looked at the silks, satins, and velvets, the defeated
gladiator, the sleeping nymph, the Wolf of Gubbio, Saint
Radegonde. He longed to stay here, to get out of the magic
circle, but just as if it really enclosed him, he could not. His
willpower was held firm by the roots of instinct, of what he
perceived and understood when he opened his eyes onto the
world. He knew there were many *over there* who detested
him; he knew there were many, very many, too many who
were hoping that someone, sometime would be brave enough
to assassinate him (if his death could be caused by pressing
the mythical button of the Mandarin in the story, thousands

of men and women would press that button). All the same, he *would go back*. To show that even though he stood on the threshold of old age, although his body's architecture was in decline, he was still tough, strong, and energetic, full of masculinity, very much a man. He would go on destroying his enemies while strength remained to him. He wouldn't copy the sad end of the tyrant Rosas, who died in obscurity at Swaythling, forgotten by everyone—even his daughter Manuelita. Nor did he want to be like Porfirio Díaz in Mexico, pursuing a living death, promenading his corpse in frock coat, gloves, and solemn hat through the avenues of the Bois de Boulogne, sitting sunk in the mournful black leather seats of a phaeton drawn by horses whose slow ambling pace already heralded his funeral . . .

And now he remembered a certain Holy Week when the people of his home town had organised a great display of the Mystery of the Passion, from a seventeenth-century manuscript preserved in the archives of the parish church. For months and months women and children had saved the silver paper from their sweets and toffees to cover the helmets and shields of centurions, and collected hair from horses, mules, and donkeys to make them into crests. A purple velvet curtain had served for the Redeemer's tunic; his belt was a sisal cord soaked in an infusion of acacia flowers; his crown of thorns came from the branch of a shrub known as "snakebite," which grew on a hill nearby. The Judgement scene had taken place on the patio of the Town Hall, where the Head of State (he was Chief of Police at the time) had consented to take the part of Pilate, sitting in a red armchair in the Chapter House. He had handed the Son of God over to the Pharisees and washed his hands in a Japanese basin lent by the Suárez brothers' china shop. And the ascent to Calvary had begun amidst the tears and lamentations of the crowd. A young and

simple-minded beggar woman, who believed she was witnessing the real events she had seen in twenty altarpieces in
village churches, had gone up to Miguel the shoemaker, who
was playing the Son of God, and tried to take on her own
shoulders the heavy wooden cross he was carrying, stumbling as he went, staggering, falling, and getting up again,
covered in sweat, half dead, and uttering desperate groans—
an amazingly theatrical martyr—as he advanced towards the
hill where he was to pretend to be crucified. Pushing away the
intruder who was threatening to spoil his splendid performance, Christ pointed his left hand at her and said:

"And if you take this from me, what shall I be? What
will remain to me?" And then went on his way up the hill
by the Way of the Cross, while the crowd sang an old tune,
whose origins had been forgotten, with the slow inflexions
of plainsong:

> *And if I have to die to tomorrow*
> *Let them kill me outright.*

Just at this moment Peralta returned from the Western
Union office, and finding me still up and somewhat pensive,
asked me:

"Why not let all this go to the devil, and stay here, enjoying what you've got? You're not short of cash. What a lot of
bottles we could drink! What a lot of women we could fuck!"

"And suppose I did get rid of *all that*, what should I be?
What would remain to me?" I said. Yes, I remember saying it
and thinking about the people who had turned against me because of that business at Nueva Córdoba, so that my personality had dwindled and become too small and helpless to play
a part in this apocalyptic world. I was taking on the Crusade
for Latinity in order to reinstate my image. And if it pleased

the Ineffable One to whom my requests were addressed to grant me victory within the next few weeks, I pledged myself, yes, I promised that immediately after my triumph I would bow my head and go as a pilgrim to her Sanctuary as Divine Shepherdess, mixing with the people (but also with those pretending to belong to "the people"), as an act of gratitude and rejoicing for favours received, and sorrow for many sins committed. I would go with those who dragged along their wounded legs, or wept in the night with eyes rolled upwards or with noses eaten away and the stumps of their arms joined in an impossible attitude of prayer; amongst women with closed wombs and breasts of gravel; amongst those long past adolescence, who could only cry like babies and sidle rather than walk, with withered arms and twisted hands; amongst those whose voices were forever dead inside their deformed throats; with the purulent and the paralysed. I would cross the wide tiled floor on my knees and, rejecting the red carpet laid down for the priests, I would drag myself over the stones to the feet of the Mother of God, to express my gratitude in the prose of the liturgy—I don't remember whether I learnt it from Renan or the Marist Brothers: Mystical Rose, Ivory Tower, Golden Mansion, Morning Star, *Ave Maris Stella*.

I look at my watch. Now I must rest a little. I'll have to leave early tomorrow. Already in my nightshirt, for a joke, I put on my English cap with earflaps, and the checked Inverness cape I have bought for the journey.

"I look like Sherlock Holmes," I say, admiring myself in the Empire looking-glass mounted on gilt sphinxes.

"You only need a magnifying glass," says Peralta, slipping into my pocket one of the brandy flasks encased in pigskin ... and the alarm already. Quarter past ten. It's impossible. Quarter past nine. More likely. Quarter past eight. This alarm clock would be a marvel of Swiss watchmaking, but its hands are so slim that one can hardly see them. Quarter past seven. My spectacles. Quarter past six. That's it. Daylight is beginning to show clearly through the yellow curtains. My foot can't find the other slipper, which always gets lost among the colours of the Persian carpet. And in comes Sylvestre in his striped jacket carrying aloft the silver tray—made of silver from my mines:

"*Le Café de Monsieur. Bien fort comme il l'aime. Monsieur a bien dormi?*"

"*Mal, très mal,*" I reply. "*J'ai bien de soucis, mon bon Sylvestre.*"

"*Les revers attristent / les grands de ce monde,*" he murmurs, in an alexandrine whose classical scansion brings an echo of the Comédie Française into this house where, in an atmosphere of confusion, far from the scenes to which destiny was taking me, a new chapter in my history was opening early this morning.

# FOUR

*What do I see from this window except hats and coats that might be worn by spectres or well-made imitations of men, moving by means of springs?* —DESCARTES

# 9

IT WASN'T NECESSARY TO SHOOT WALTER HOFFMANN. Every conflict has a way of developing in unforeseen ways, and the treacherous general came to an end that could be seen as having a certain Wagnerian dramatic power: like the death throes of Fafner in a considerably more dangerous forest than Siegfried's, which was almost municipal, a Tiergarten or Unter-den-Linden compared with the terrifying forest covering the region of Las Tembladeras—the Quagmires. We had pursued the rebel into a region of quicksand, where he was forced to withdraw, all the time being deserted by his men, who were so oppressed by defeat that they ignored all speeches and admonitions, proclamations and brandy rations, and admitted—with anxiety that increased from day to day—that they had played a rotten card, and that we were the ones who held the royal flush. It was useless for General Hoffmann, having discovered the remains of an Indian pyramid in the densest part of a thicket, to shout to his men:

"Soldiers ... fifty centuries are looking down at you from the top of this pyramid" (adding ten to the Napoleonic speech, out of patriotism).

"It could be seventy-five for all I care," thought the soldiers, whose "old women"—the rebel camp followers—declared that a lot of stones piled up like that, and full of holes, were useless for anything except a breeding ground for the most deadly snakes in the world, centipedes, tarantulas, spiders, and scorpions "about as long as this" (not bothering to illustrate how long) ... And after the "Little Fredericks" had fled in the direction of the southern frontier, mass desertion and fraternisations began, to an occasional shout of "they deceived us, they made us believe, we were sent," until the general and his few remaining faithful followers decided to cross one of the dreaded plains—the only means of reaching the sea—which by the abundance of its quaking bogs had given the region its name. As their advance grew more and more difficult and dangerous, and men kept deserting (first two artillerymen and a lieutenant, then fifteen private soldiers and a corporal, and sixty or so men with a captain), the rebel at last found himself practically alone with his few remaining supporters—and it's easy to imagine what was going on in their minds—on the brink of a yellowish waste, streaked with creeping plants, and dotted with ponds—or rather large potholes—of viscid slush, perhaps clay, looking like a thin coating of stagnant mud on top of firmer ground. General Hoffmann landed in one of these holes, as a result of inopportunely urging on his horse with a sharp tug on the reins, so as to avoid a thorny branch that crossed his path. And without warning the horse, feeling its feet sink more and more deeply into the deceptive clay, as if drawn in by some implacable suction from the entrails of the earth, began to neigh desperately for help, exhausting itself in useless rearing, while its frantic struggles and plunges did nothing to free it from slow but inevitable submergence. With the terrible mud now up to his knees, trying to get out of his boots, which were becoming heavy as lead, tugging again and again on the reins without response, and seeing that the floundering movements of his horse only hastened his inevitable submersion, the general shouted:

"A rope ... a strap ... a belt ... Get me out of here ... Quickly ... A rope ... a strap."

But the men standing around the pool in frowning silence calmly watched their leader slowly, terribly slowly, drowning.

"Die, you bastard!" muttered a corporal whom Hoffmann had struck, years before, to punish him for a disrespectful reply.

"Die, you bastard!" said in a louder voice a sergeant whom Hoffmann had refused to promote some time back.

"Die, you bastard!" said a lieutenant, fortissimo, who had begged without success for the Silver Star.

"No, God damn you, no! You can't let me die like this!" yelled their leader, clutching the ears of his horse, whose teeth were now just above the quagmire.

"Die, you bastard!" replied the Greek chorus.

The quicksand had risen to the general's neck, chin, and mouth, though he still emitted confused cries from a throat choking with mud—bubbling death rattles, inaudible shouts, last efforts at agonizing cries . . .

When only his kepi remained floating, one of the spectators threw a small crucifix onto it, but it was soon sucked in by the quagmire, now once more green and placid.

Delivered of his enemy, the Head of State returned to the capital, entered it under triumphal arches put up the day before and decorated with flags and garlands, and received the titles of "Peacemaker" and "National Hero" from both chambers, the representatives of Industry and Commerce, the Metropolitan Bishop in his pulpit, lesser dignitaries in lower pulpits, and the Press, whose pages described the details of a military campaign conducted in a masterly manner, illustrated with maps covered in black arrows showing the phases of offence and defence, penetration, encirclement, and breaking of the enemy lines in the decisive Battle of Four Roads—a drawn-out, bloody, difficult battle, finally won for the government forces by tactical judgement and occasional improvisation. This diagrammatic technique had been popularised by *L'Illustration* to explain the action of the Battle of the Marne.

In a speech full of elevated ideas, the President modestly declared that he didn't deserve the praise so generously heaped on him by his compatriots, since God himself, so great in mercy but terrible in anger, had been responsible for punishing the traitor. Properly considered, Hoffmann's death had been a sort of trial by ordeal, wherein a superior will whose designs were beyond our understanding had spared the victor the pain of shedding the blood of an old companion in arms, blinded by senseless ambition.

This was no time for Shakespeare's cry of "My kingdom for a horse," seeing that the guilty man, perhaps burdened by his own remorse and pursued by the Furies of our arms, actually entered the Kingdom of Shadows on his galloping steed. But the important thing was not that the Enemy of Order had been swallowed up in the quagmire of Las Tembladeras. The important thing was that by so doing he had fortified our Consciousness of Latinity in the face of the conflict now terrifying the world; because we *were* Latin, profoundly Latin, intimately Latin, trustees of the great tradition of the Roman pandects, foundation of our law, and of Virgil, Dante, Don Quixote, Michelangelo, Copernicus, etc., etc. (a long paragraph, ended by a long ovation). Aunt Jemima, who had exchanged her usual checked cotton handkerchief for a black one in token of mourning, climbed painfully up to the platform to give the Head of State a message of regret from the Hoffmann family, whispering in his ear at the same time that the general's wife deplored her husband's misdeeds and begged the favour of receiving the pension due to her as the widow of a soldier with more than twenty years' service, in accordance with the Law of June 18, 1901.

Tired out by a war that had taken him to the most un-
healthy jungles in the country, the President went for a
holiday to his house at Marbella. There was a beautiful long
beach, although its black sands were too often invaded by an
abundance of bladdery dead jellyfish lying amongst patches
of tar and oil washed up from the port close by. The sharks
and giant rays were kept at bay by a quadruple barbed-wire
fence, festooned with ragged seaweed. And if there were still
a few morays in the hollows of a little rocky promontory, it
was a great many years since a man had been emasculated
by a barracuda in this resort. When the winds blew from
the north—"*yelitos*" they were called—the sea darkened to
shades of deep blue while gentle waves moved in slow, majestic rhythm to cast their foam at the very feet of the coconut and soursop trees. But there were mornings, too—in
summer—when the water appeared singularly smooth and
transparent, without any of its usual light turbulence; a bather
diving into it at once had the strange sensation of falling into
a lake of gelatine. And then he would find that he wasn't
swimming, but *gliding* in a mass of transparent and almost
invisible molluscs, as big and as round as coins, which had
arrived on the beach during the night at the end of some long
and mysterious migration. To make the resort more attractive, the municipality had constructed a cement pier with a
casino at the end supported on piles, the whole affair cop-
ied from Nice   metal framework, orange tiles, iron dome,
green with saltpetre. Roulette, baccarat, and chemin-de-fer
were played there, and the few croupiers in dinner jackets,
counting in *louis* and *centens*—out-of-date gamblers' coins—
had given up saying "Don't be afraid to stake" and "Not another cent," as at Creole gaming tables, and taken to "*Faites
vos jeux*" and "*Rien ne va plus*," carefully if always peculiarly
pronounced.

The Head of State's "Residencia Hermenegilda" dominated the beach from a neighbouring hill. It was built in a
style somewhere between Balkan and the Rue de la Faisande-
rie, with caryatids reminiscent of 1900, dressed like Sarah
Bernhardt and magically supporting on their plumed hats—
better indeed than the Atlases of some Berlin palaces—a wide
terrace-balcony, enclosed by banisters shaped like seahorses.
A tower-belvedere-lighthouse overtopped the roofs, and displayed the eternal brilliance of variegated majolica. The vast,
cool, high rooms were furnished with rocking chairs of New
Córdoban make, hammocks suspended from rings, and a few
red lacquer chairs, a gift from the old Empress of China in
gratitude for a consignment of toys—a cable railway, some
kaleidoscopes, whistling spinning tops, a music box full of
Bernese bears, and a battleship the size of a water lily for the
pond at the Winter Palace—which the Head of State had sent
her years before, knowing her tastes. In the dining room was
a copy—reduced in size, of course—of *The Raft of Medusa*,
opposite two charming seascapes by Elstir, which were somewhat overpowered, truth to tell, by the dramatic weight of
the Géricault. The house was surrounded by a vast garden
tended by Japanese gardeners, where among the box hedges
stood a white marble Venus, disfigured by a greenish herpes
of fungi hanging from her stomach. A little farther on under
the pines one could see the chapel consecrated to the Divine
Shepherdess by the devout Doña Hermenegilda—a chapel
the sight of which now caused the President increasing remorse, as he remembered that the promise he had made her
at an extremely painful moment in Paris, of ascending the
steps of her basilica with a candle in each hand, still remained
unfulfilled. (But at the same time he reflected that the Virgin
was as intelligent in matters of policy as in everything; the
Virgin, who had just given him eloquent proof of her Divine

Protection with Trumpets of Victory, would understand that at such a moment the fulfilment of his promise in the sight of everyone, an ostentatious proof of Catholic fervour, would bring down on him—who already had so many enemies—a whole world of freemasons, Rosicrucians, spiritualists, Theosophists, and those who clamoured against the clergy, not to mention many atheists and free thinkers—a blaspheming legion of priest haters, all of them devotees of France, where the clergy were not allowed to teach in schools, theological students were subject to military service, and where the only religion possible in this portentous twentieth century had germinated and grown: *The Religion of Science*.)

Behind the house a little grove of pomegranates shaded the discreet path along which, when night fell, Doctor Peralta used to lead some cloaked woman to the Head of State's bedroom. ("Don't go and die as President Félix Faure did," the secretary used invariably to remark as he left his charge with his master. "Attila and Félix Faure were the two men who most enjoyed their deaths," the Head of State replied, also invariably.)

Early every morning the locomotive of the Little German Train used to whistle. And the President would go out onto the balcony, with a cup of coffee in his hand, to watch it pass. The little engine shone like polished enamel in those green mornings, with its gleaming copper connecting rods and rivets, climbing the mountain by its narrow track with a cheerful funicular snorting, as it dragged its small red awning-covered carriages behind it up to the Olmedo Colony; it was, in every way, like the cable railway the Head of State had sent to the old Empress of China to enrich her collection of automatic and mechanical devices. As soon as the little convoy left Puerto Araguato, everything it passed through seemed to diminish in size—intermediate stations, bridges over torrents,

level crossings and their gates, signals—yet it was with a great
clamour that it entered the minuscule terminal above, with its
load of ten passengers, a few parcels, several barrels, the post,
the newspapers, and a calf poking its head out of the window
of the only cattle truck. As if it had just come out of a Nurem-
berg toy shop, gleaming, repainted, and varnished, the little
train rested at the end of its journey in a strange exotic world,
quite different from that below, with its Black Forest houses
built between palms and coffee trees, its beer shop displaying
the sign of King Stag, its women in Tyrolese dress, its men in
leather breeches, braces, and hats with a feather in the band.
In spite of being excellent citizens of the republic for more
than a century, they could hardly speak Spanish. Ever since
they had been brought here by a certain Count Olmedo, a
rich man of Creole ancestry, a landowner obsessed by the idea
of "keeping the race white," the immigrants had been careful
not to mix with women from *here*, who were all suspected of
being zambas, cholas, or quadroons—one because her hair
was frizzy; another because her eyes were blacker than usual;
another because her nose was rather flattened, even though
her complexion was pale. So, from father to son, they wrote
to Bavaria or Pomerania to ask for women, and generation by
generation they had increased and multiplied, singing the Lutheran chorale, playing on the accordion, growing rhubarb,
making beer soup, and dancing an old-fashioned landler, and
now plump shepherdesses with Aryan pubic hair were to be
seen bathing in the mountain streams, and their names might
be Woglinde, Wellgunde, or Flosshilde. The Head of State
had bothered very little about these peaceable, law-abiding
folk, who never got involved in politics, and when elections
came along always voted for the government, on condition
that their customs weren't interfered with. But now his daily
reading of the French papers made him regard these people

with some irritation. Although their houses were tradition-
ally adorned with coloured plates of snow-covered landscapes, the banks of the Elbe, the Festival of Wartburg, or
the mythical maiden in a winged helmet who carried the
bodies of young athletes killed in battle up to heaven, there
hung beside these pictures a portrait of Wilhelm II. And
Wilhelm II was materializing in the Press as Antichrist. His
armies, his gang of supporters, his terrifying Uhlans had
penetrated into harmless little Belgium, into the Flanders of
Velazquez's lances—the forerunners of our own plainsmen's
pikes—razing everything to the ground. They had advanced
as conquerors between ruined cathedrals, stately homes laid
low and scattered, and after burning the Library of Louvain
had marched sacrilegiously over a pavement of incunables
hurled on the ground. *Eins ... Zwei ... Eins ... Zwei.* And
with barbarian tread, trampling on unique bindings, price-
less manuscripts, parchments with rich capitals and superb
lettering, they had marched on, not attacking men so much
as the distinguished figures in the Testaments, displayed for
centuries, like the pages of open books, on the tympana
and over the porticos of cathedrals. *Eins ... Zwei ... Eins ...
Zwei.* German cannon had thundered against Isaiah and
Jeremiah, Ezekiel and Esdras, against Solomon and the Shula-
mite, and David, who with Bathsheba—this was the theme
of the manuscript play we had bought from our friend the
Distinguished Academician   plotted the destruction of the
old cuckolded general (every general in a campaign was
probably a cuckold, reflected the President, and especially if
he was old), before relentlessly hurling themselves against the
Beau Dieu at Amiens, or the ineffable figure—now broken
and pulverised in an irreversible twilight—of the most beautiful of the Smiling Angels. But perhaps even this was less
horrible than the appalling chronicle of rape. *L'Illustration*

included some grey pages, not to be read by children, de-scribing how when the German troops took a village or town they dragged innocent girls, schoolchildren and ado-lescents, to the back of a shoemaker's shop or undertaker's, and violated them—there were nine, ten, eleven such cases, said *L'Illustration*; probably fifteen, said Louis Dumur, who specialised in these atrocities—an operation carried out with servile German discipline, while the *Feldwebels*, who con-trolled proceedings, said: "Now it's your turn ... Get ready, next man." But all this, the destruction of cathedrals, ruin of hagiography, altarpieces split in half, decapitated sibyls, burning, dynamite, rape, crime, were as nothing before the unprecedented tragedy of *the children without hands*. A Ger-man soldier had found them wandering amongst the ruins searching for their lost or dead mother, and hearing them weeping had gone closer as if to help them, but instead with an unexpected blow of his sabre (Did the infantry really carry sabres? asked Peralta) cut off two soft little hands: "So that they can never hold weapons against us." On the title page of a supplement to *L'Illustration* there was a sketched portrait of one of the victims of this atrocious ablation, holding up his stumps against an apocalyptic background of the ruins of Ypres.

The Head of State absorbed this literature daily, marking in red pencil anything that seemed to him worth reproducing in the national press, to cause confusion and shame among certain officers, ex-associates of Hoffmann, or "Little Fred-ericks" in the making, who were known to be disgusted—though they didn't show it openly—by the recent suppression of the pointed helmet with full dress uniform in the National Army. These readers must be de-Germanised, and the arti-cles he destined particularly for them were those about the sacking of famous castles, theft of clocks—this had begun in '70—melting down of bells six hundred years old, using cathedrals as latrines, profanation of the host, and shooting matches by intoxicated captains with Memlings or Rembrandts as targets.

The Head of State looked towards the cloudy heights of the Olmedo Colony—black rocks, between mulberry trees, an occasional naturalised silver fir, light northerly breezes in the mornings—and thought that those bastards up there, in spite of the shouts of "Loooooong live our cooooountry!" from girls with fair plaits wearing national dress, who received him with bunches of violets when he paid a visit to their chief village, were at heart in sympathy with the men who cut off children's hands in Artois or Champagne, whose cataclysmic landscapes—eroded, defoliated, mutilated by shells—were shown us in the pictures of Georges Scott and Lucien Simon, offered for sale complete with passe-partout, their muddy colours accentuating in a masterly fashion the tragic desolation of village squares, ruined town halls, and mediaeval houses reduced to the skeletons of their beams, while like some accusation proffered by the earth itself, the bare trunk of an ancient oak seemed to speak in the middle of all this desolation through the hundred mouths of its lacerated bark.

Every morning the Head of State stopped reading this painful material to watch from his window as the Little German Train started to ascend the mountain, sometimes braking with furious whistling to drive away a goat capering in the young grass between the rails. And after his usual breakfast of maize tortillas, curds, and meat pancakes, he used to sit at his Welte-Mignon pianola, a present from the Spanish colony of Nueva Córdoba. Pedalling hard and manipulating the regulators so as to extract "Für Elise" from the perforated roll, and the beginning—he never got beyond the beginning—of the *Moonlight Sonata*, he reflected that working this

musical machine must be a little like the activity of the engine driver who was now taking the Little German Train up
to the woods, where imported squirrels were frisking, and
in the opinion of a trouble-making journalist—an unfair
opponent—threatening to cause an epidemic of psittacosis
among the country's cattle, already ailing and in a state of decline, it was quite true, since experience showed that the cows
of the region suffered from weak legs and narrow haunches
and couldn't support the weight on their hindquarters of the
stock bulls, brought from Charolais to improve the breed,
when they mounted them.

"Ah, what a war this is, my President," groaned Doctor
Peralta every morning between a cup of very black coffee and
the first cigar of the day.

"Terrible, terrible," the Head of State would reply, thinking about the Little German Train: "And how long it's lasting."

But then they heard that those who discussed strategy in
the capital over brandy and grilled steak had been celebrating
the news, received by cablegram, that *Le Matin* had just published a really sensational headline covering eight columns:
"Cossacks only five days' march from Berlin."

"So now the Cossacks are the new defenders of Latinity,
along with the Sepoys and Senegalese we already had on our
side," remarked Peralta slyly.

"Let's hope they get held up on the way!" murmured his
friend, thinking that, thanks to the expectations and enthusiasms provoked by this amazing war, many people had had
their attention diverted to remote events. The Head of State
was at last enjoying peace and quiet in the shade of a flower-
ing tree.

# 10

*Many things that may appear to us supremely extrava-*
*gant and ridiculous are generally accepted and approved*
*by other great nations.* —DESCARTES

THE HEAD OF STATE PROLONGED HIS STAY IN
Marbella from week to week, carrying out the business of
government from a somewhat Pompeian pergola in the middle of a labyrinth of orange trees at the far end of the garden.
He took an early-morning ride along the shore on his horse
Holofernes, a powerful sorrel with a glistening coat, wild and
uncontrollable with most people but hypocritically submis-
sive to a master who brought him a pail of the best English
beer in his stable every afternoon, which he always received
with delighted whinnying. The President had reasons for feeling contented during these months, for he had never known
such a prosperous and happy period for the nation. This European war  which really, though it was better not to say so,
was turning out a blessing—was raising the prices of sugar,
bananas, coffee, and gutta-percha to unheard-of heights,
swelling the funds in the banks, making fortunes, bringing
the country luxuries and refinements that until yesterday had
seemed to belong to worldly novels or films centred around
the almost mythological figures of Gabrielle Robinne, Pina
Menichelli, Francesca Bertini, or Lydia Borelli. Surrounded

by age-old forests, the capital had itself become a modern forest of scaffolding, wooden beams pointing to the sky, cranes in action, and mechanical scoops, accompanied by a perpetual clanking of pulleys, hammer blows of iron on steel, pouring of cement, rivetting and percussion, interspersed with shouts between workmen up aloft and workmen on the ground, whistles, sirens, trucks carrying sand, and snorting of engines. Shops enlarged their premises overnight, and dawn showed them with new windows where a few wax figures—another novelty—were celebrating their first communion, showing off wedding dresses, the latest fashions, and even officers' uniforms, well cut and finished in English gabardine. Toffee-making machines, installed in the entrance to the old Royal Granary, astonished passers-by with the concerted movements of their metal arms, mixing, stretching, and compressing white substances streaked with red, and smelling of vanilla and marshmallow. Offices, banks, insurance companies, chain stores, and brokers proliferated. Theodolites and other surveying instruments transformed flooded regions, wasteland, and goat pastures, dividing them into a number of marked-out squares, which having been since remote times "The Lazar's small-holding," "Mexican farm," or "Misia Petra's ranch," suddenly adopted the names of "Bagatelle," "West Side," or "Armenonville," and were divided into plots to be selected from a plan but hardly ever built on, since their price increased every time they were bought and sold (sometimes several times in one day) in offices with many Underwood typewriters, gilt ventilators, relief maps, attractive maquettes, and brandy and gin in the safe, with much haggling and discussing between drinks and Havanas, and telephone calls from women—this was quite new—who offered their services by telephone in foreign accents, promising refinements that were refused—and it was the worse for them—by our own too-modest tarts, with whom "the business" had to be performed in the classic manner, with nothing baroque, perverse, or fantastic such as went on in other countries. Pianolas had invaded the capital, rolling and unrolling cylinders of "La Madelon," "Roses of Picardy," "It's a Long Way to Tipperary" from dawn to midnight. In the bars where cards and dominoes were played, or where Santa Inés rum gave way to White Horse whisky, the only subject of conversation was the profits, due to the war, which had made them forget the war itself, although everyone—whites, cholos, zambos, Indians, and those of swarthy complexion—had become Frenchified, protricolor, avengers, cockade wearers, Joan-of-Arcists and Barrèsians, declaring that we should soon get our own back for the disaster of Sedan, and the storks of Hansi would come back to the steeples of Alsace and Lorraine. At the same time the first skyscraper arose—five stories and an attic— immediately followed by the Edificio Titán close by, with eight. And the old city with its two-storey houses was very quickly transformed into an Invisible City. Invisible because, changing from horizontal to vertical, there were no eyes now that could see it and know it. Each architect, engaged in the task of making his buildings higher than those that went up before, thought only of the particular aesthetic qualities of *his* façade, as if it could be seen from a hundred yards off, whereas the streets were made to take only one car at a time—one mule train, one cart—and were only six or seven yards wide. Thus, with his back to an infinitely tall column, the passer-by tried in vain to admire the elegant decoration lost in the sky among vultures and turkey buzzards. It was *known* that up aloft there were garlands, cornucopias, and caducei, or there might even be a Greek temple perched on the fifth floor with Phidias' horses and everything; but this was only *known*, because those citadels, domes, and entablatures existed—city

upon city—in a kingdom that could not be seen. And higher
still were solitary, unknown, banished statues, of Mercury—
on the Chamber of Commerce—or of Minerva, whose lance
attracted August lightning, of charioteers, winged spirits,
Christian saints, isolated from one another and unknown to
men, who yet lorded it over intricate gradations of terraces,
slate-covered roofs, water tanks, chimneys, lightning conductors, and huts containing lift machinery. Without realizing it,
people were living in unsuspected Ninevehs, vertiginous
Westminsters, and flying Trianons, with gargoyles and bronze
figures who would become old without ever having had contact with the people below, busy among the porticos, arcades,
and colonnades that carried the great weight of invisible con-
structions. And as everyone was eager to have what was new,
those who had inhabited colonial mansions for two centuries
hastily left them and moved into new, modern houses in the
Roman, Chambord, or Stanford White style. So the huge palaces of the old town with their plateresque façades and coats
of arms carved in stone were taken over by the rabble, the
poor and diseased—the fictitious blind man with a paid
guide, the drunk whose hands trembled in the mornings, the
wooden-legged accordion player or the poor paralytic, begging alms for the love of God. The beautiful rooms were full
of dishevelled women, ragged children, whores, and tramps,
living in the fumes from stoves and clothes hung up to dry,
while the patios were given over to boxing, cock fights, and
conjurors with pickpocket partners. Hundreds of Ford cars—
like those in Mack Sennett films—streamed along the badly
paved streets, avoiding the potholes, running onto the pavements, knocking over baskets of fruit, breaking shop windows, in a mania for speed never before known in these
latitudes. It was all urgency, haste, rush, and impatience. In a
few months of war, oil lamps had been supplanted by electric

bulbs, gourds by bidets, pineapple juice by Coca-Cola, lotto by roulette, Rocambole by Pearl White, the messenger boy's donkey by the telegraphist's bicycle, the mule cart with its tassels and bells by a smart Renault, which had to go forwards and reverse ten or twelve times to get around a narrow corner and enter an alley recently christened "Boulevard," causing a frenzied flight among the goats which still abounded in some quarters where the grass growing between the paving stones was good. The Ursuline nuns instituted a Grotto of Lourdes with wonderful effects of electric light; the first dance hall was opened, with a jazz band from New Orleans; horses and jockeys were brought from Tijuana to race in a gaily decorated hippodrome made on the site of the swamp, and one morning the Old Town, described as "Very Loyal and Very Illustrious" in the deed of its foundation in 1553, awoke to the full realisation that it had become a leading twentieth-century capital. The last reptiles—rattlesnakes and elaps—vanished from the building sites, the goldfinches were silent, and phonographs opened their mouths. And there were bridge championships, fashion parades, Turkish baths, money changers, and exclusive brothels, admitting no one with darker skin than the Minister for Public Works, who was taken as a yardstick because although not perhaps the black sheep of the Cabinet he was indubitably its brownest sheep. The police exchanged their worn slippers for regulation boots, and their white-gloved hands controlled a traffic whose noise was enriched by klaxons with several rubber bulbs, so that they could play "The Merry Widow Waltz" or the first bars of the National Anthem.

As he watched the metropolis grow and grow, the Head of State was sometimes worried by the changes in the view from the palace windows. He was himself involved in a real-estate business managed by Doctor Peralta, whose buildings were

destroying the panorama for so long part of his life, so that
when his attention was suddenly drawn to some alteration in
it by the Mayorala Elmira—"just look at that," "look at that"—
he started as if at some evil omen. The factory chimneys he
had had erected broke up and destroyed a natural scene until
recently innocent of the ugly cross-trees of telegraph poles.
The Volcano, the Grandfather Volcano, the Tutelary Volcano,
abode of the Ancient Gods, symbol and emblem, whose cone
figured on the National Coat of Arms, was less a volcano—
less even the abode of the Ancient Gods—when on misty
mornings its majestic presence seemed to insinuate itself,
with the modesty of a humiliated king, a monarch without
a court, above the dense clouds of smoke sent up by four tall
chimneys from the recently inaugurated Central Electricity
Company. By becoming more vertical and geometric, and
by dividing up the verdant background of mountains, hills,
and distant valleys, the city was shutting the President in. The
population was being augmented by an ever-increasing in-
flux of peasants, labourers, day workers, artisans from the
provinces, attracted by the wealth of the metropolis, all bringing their dependants with them: grandfathers with bilharzia
or weak from years of malaria, scrofulous children, suffer-
ers from amoebic dysentery—easy preys to the periodical
epidemics of virulent influenza coming from no one knew
where—and it was a common sight to see a funeral procession tightening its circle of black clothes and coffins around
the Presidential Palace.

"Here comes the Whore!" the Mayorala Elmira would
exclaim when a hearse appeared in the Plaza Mayor on its
way to the cemetery.

"Be off!" replied the Head of State, joining the first and
little fingers of both hands to ward off the Evil Eye.

"Even Napoleon couldn't lick you," concluded the

Mayorala, giving actual existence to someone whose name she took to represent the greatest power God had ever given to a human being, because coming from nothing, born in the manger as one might say, he had finally conquered the whole world—while still remaining a good son and brother, a good friend (even of his laundress, it was said when he became a great man!), and always the lover of fine women, like that one from the Caribbean, who had got hold of him you know where, because mulattos and cholas are born with the Devil between their legs ... (There were some men who would throw up everything, disappear and leave home at the summons of Women of Great Power, who held their lamps in the doorway, repeating as often as there are beads on a rosary: "Let him come after me like a mad dog. Amen.")

After a great deal of thought the Head of State devoted himself with renewed energy—energy that was diminishing with age in some directions—to the project of a great building, the material symbol in stone of his government: he would give the country a national capitol.

Once the decision was made, he planned to promote a great international concourse, open to all architects, so that they could compare ideas, projects, and plans. But hardly was the news spread around than the nation's own architects, who had recently formed themselves into a college, protested that there were quite enough of them for such an undertaking. And then began a tiresome process of criticisms, changes, arguments, producing a succession of metamorphoses in the appearance, style, and proportions of the future building. First it was a Greek Temple with Doric columns without bases, thirty metres high—a copy of Paestum with the dimensions of the Vatican. But the Head of State thought he remembered that Kaiser Wilhelm, incarnation of Prussian barbarism, was addicted to such Hellenisms, going so far as to possess an

Achilleion, reminiscent of the Parthenon, in Corfu. Besides, the Greeks had no domes, and a capitol without a dome is no capitol at all. Better to look towards eternal Rome, mother of our culture. Therefore, our architects quickly substituted Corinthian for Doric (without passing through the Ionic) with a dome rather like that of the Palais de Justice at Brussels. However, the two hemicycles—Chamber and Senate—were too reminiscent of the theatres at Delphi and Epidaurus, and looked rather austere, cold, and false when it came to adding the rostrums, whose existence in such a place were a vital democratic necessity. A new national architect, succeeding two national architects who were already discredited and fallen into disgrace as a result of the intrigues of a great many other national architects, took his inspiration from an English illustration of Shakespeare's *Julius Caesar*, and drew a plan of a hemicycle in the Roman style with columns above, which was for a while approved by the Council of Ministers. But then they remembered that the country was a great producer of mahogany, and that our mahogany, a deep warm red in colour, ought to be copiously used in a work of such size, to face the walls and make panelling, rostrums, benches, doors, presidential throne, etc., in both hemicycles. And since the Romans never used wood in this fashion, a fifth project for the Capitol arose, based on the neo-Gothic style of the Budapest Parliament. But as the Austro-Hungarian empire was at war with Latinity, these plans too were rejected, and someone remembered the genius Herrera and the imposing bulk of the Escorial.

"Not to be thought of," put in the Head of State. "When you say Escorial you say Philip the Second. And anyone saying Philip the Second here says: burned Indians, negroes in chains, heroic chiefs tortured, princes on the gridiron, tribunals of the Inquisition . . ."

Project 15 was rejected because, in its eagerness to use some national marble recently discovered near Nueva Córdoba, the architect had conceived something too like Milan Cathedral, and such an ecclesiastical flavour would have disgusted the masons and freethinkers and other people whose criticisms carried weight. Project 17 was no more nor less than a pretty outrageous copy of the Parisian Opéra.

"Parliament is not a theatre," said the Head of State, throwing the plans down on the Council table.

"Sometimes . . ." murmured Doctor Peralta behind him.

At last, after a great deal of cavilling, discussing, considering, and reconsidering, Project 31 was accepted as offering the simplest solution: a replica of the Washington Capitol, using national woods and national marbles for the inside—but if the latter should not prove as good as they were thought to be, marbles bought from Carrara would be put in their place, while for the public they would remain "national marbles."

The work began on the day of the Centenary of Independence, with the laying of the First Stone and the obligatory speeches, using all suitable rhetoric fortissimo. But one problem remained: under the dome there ought to be a statue of the Republic. All the nation's sculptors offered to make one. But the Head of State knew that none of them could measure up to such a task.

"What a pity Gérome is dead!" he said, thinking of his gladiators and his retiarius. "There was a man for you!"

"Rodin is alive," observed Doctor Peralta.

"No. Rodin, no . . . A great sculptor—who could doubt it?—when he sticks to reality. But if he fires off a second Balzac, we're completely buggered. If we reject him they'll make fun of us *over there*; and if we accept him we shall have to leave the country."

"You could always ban press comments."

"That would be against my principles. You know that. Bullets and machetes for bastards. But complete liberty of criticism, polemics, discussion, and controversy concerning art, literature, schools of poetry, classical philosophy, the enigma of the universe, the secret of the pyramids, the origin of American Man, the concept of Beauty, and everything else in that line ... that's culture."

"In Guatemala, our friend Estrada Cabrera founded a cult of Minerva, with a temple and everything."

"A fine enterprise by a great ruler ..."

"... who has already been in power for eighteen years ..."

"... for that very reason. But it seems that his statue of Pallas Athena is nothing very wonderful."

In his perplexity the Head of State wrote to Ofelia, who had now returned to Paris before spending several months on Andalusian ranches, as she had now suddenly become as enthusiastic about bulls, cloaks, and *cante jondo* as she had formerly been about Bayreuth or Stratford-on-Avon. Not very fond of writing letters, which revealed her fantastic ideas of spelling, the Infanta simply replied with a cable: ANTOINE BOURDELLE.

"Never heard of him," said Doctor Peralta.

"Nor have I," said the Head of State. "He must be one of her bohemian friends."

His doubts led him to write to the Distinguished Academician for more information. And he received by return of post some photos of reliefs carried out by this artist at the Théâtre des Champs-Elysées in 1913. One was an allegory of music and displeased Peralta outright by two false, confused, distorted figures, who seemed to have been forcibly crushed into a rectangular space: a nymph doubled over her violin in an impossible attempt to use her bow with an arm that passed above her head, and a bestial, twisted satyr, more entomological than Hellene, playing on an enormous pipe, far from suggestive of rustic melody, and much more like part of a 30-30 machine gun. And with the photos came a number of the *Gazette des Beaux Arts*, where an article by the famous critic Paul Jamot, underlined in red pencil, said that the sculptor didn't treat his figures in the archaic style, but with *a coarseness evocative of Germanic taste* [*sic*].

"Germanic! Germanic! So this is what Ofelia recommends us at this moment! It seems to me she's becoming imbecilic from going to so many bullfights. She hasn't a trace of political sense." Then, suddenly thinking of the phonetic aspect of the problem: "Besides, he's impossible because of his surname. *Bourdelle*. Just think what that sounds like in Spanish."

"I should say so!" said Peralta. "First they'd call him *Booo-uuurdeye*. Until they were told the correct pronunciation!"

"And then, what jokes from my friends. They would simply be handed them on a plate: the Capitol is a    ; the Republic is a . . . ; my government is a . . . Unthinkable!"

"The best thing we can do is trust ourselves to Fellino," suggested Peralta.

And the Italian marble worker, provider of innumerable angels, crosses, and family vaults for cemeteries, and of very satisfactory eponymous statues for many of our towns, whether heroic or religious, warmly recommended a Milanese artist whose works had won prizes in Florence and Rome, and who was especially famous for his ideas for monuments, municipal fountains, civic sanctuaries, equestrian figures, and (in general) every form of official, serious and solemn art, with historically exact uniforms when necessary, and who treated nudes with dignity where nudity was needed for some allegory expressed in a form intelligible to all, neither antiquated nor too modern in artistic style—for the question of modernism in the plastic arts was much discussed at that time. Aldo Nardini—that was the sculptor's name—sent a model, which was immediately approved by the Council of Ministers: in it the Republic was represented by a huge woman, her stalwart body dressed in the Greek style, leaning on a spear—symbol of vigilance—with a noble, earnest face, bearing a resemblance to the famous Juno in the Vatican, and two enormous breasts, one covered, the other bare—symbols of fecundity and abundance.

"Not a work of genius, but it will please everyone," concluded the Head of State. "Have it carried out."

Several months passed by in executing and casting the statue, with paragraphs in the press about the progress of the work, until one morning a ship from Genoa entered the bay of Puerto Araguato with the Immense Woman on board. An expectant crowd collected on the quay to witness her arrival. But there was some disappointment on learning that the statue would not emerge complete, already upright, as she would be seen in the Capitol, but would have to be carried out in pieces and put together in her eventual position. However, the sight was well worth watching. The cranes and grappling irons were raised up, the cables descended into the hold, and all at once in the midst of applause the Head appeared from the shadows and was transported through the air, followed by different pieces of her anatomy. Left Foot, with its corresponding piece of Leg and Drapery—Right Arm, with a piece of the shaft of the spear in her hand; Fertile Belly, with the vital axis well grooved in the bronze; Covered Breast, followed by Right Foot and Left Arm, before the ascent of the gigantic Phrygian Cap, which was to crown the Republic. But at this moment the twelve o'clock sirens went, the cranes stopped work, and the dockers went to have their dinner, though the crowds didn't disperse. And there was no doubt that something big must still remain in the profundities of the ship. At two o'clock the men returned to the job, and amidst applause and exclamations the Bare Breast of the Great Figure rose out of the hold and descended to earth with solemn slowness. Then all the pieces were removed in lorries to a goods train on whose planks and wagons the Giantess was laid, one piece on each wagon, presenting a disconcerting vision of a form which, although already that of a human body, had its parts displayed in a horizontal series and never achieved a significant totality. First wagon: Phyrgian Cap; second: Shoulder and Covered Breast; third: Head; fourth: Shoulder and Bare Breast; fifth: Fertile Belly ... And now, in anarchic file, came the thighs, arms, feet shod in sandals something between the Hellenic and the Creole, three pieces of spear, with a locomotive in front and a locomotive behind, because the weight was great and the mechanics were afraid this enormous load of bronze might get stuck on its way up Las Cumbres, where the recent rains had already caused some landslips on the line.

But the Republic finally arrived at her Capitol, and this was how, instead of possessing a monument by Bourdelle, the nation saw a statue by the Milanese Nardini erected, whose serene and serious face vanished forever from public view, because owing to the excessive height of the figure her head was lost in the upper part of a dome whose circular colonnade was visited only when it was cleaned twice a year by workmen—acrobats of scaffolding, too concerned with keeping the balance needed for their vertiginous task to be able to stop and appreciate the merits of a work of art.

# 11

THE CAPITOL WAS GROWING. ITS STILL SHAPELESS white mass, caged in scaffolding, was rising above the city roofs, sending up columns, spreading its wings, although its construction was suddenly delayed by contingencies of wages and cash. Of course, this was not due to the country's economy, for it had never known better days, but to the fact that the cost of materials increased from month to month, the price of tools and machinery, of freight and transport, constantly breaking the limits of an ever-rising initial estimate—sufficiently encumbered, what was more, by the rake-offs promised to many ministers and high officials of the Commission for the Promotion of Public Decoration, not to mention two cheques, one considerable and the other more modest, more than once handed to Doctor Peralta secretly by the Office of Public Works. All at once work stopped, an arcade remained without any arches, a porch without a pediment, the chisels of the engravers of acanthus leaves and astragals were silent, and a new assignment of credits became necessary, an increase on the duty on Swedish matches, foreign liquor, or profits on horseraces, to finance the work. And then it happened that in periods of inactivity the central zone of the capital was transformed into a sort of Roman forum, an esplanade from Baalbek, a terrace from Persepolis, while the moon shone down on this strange, chaotic landscape of marbles, half-finished metopes, truncated pillars, blocks of stone between cement and sand—the ruins, the dead remains, of what had never been. And as—though roofless still—the two hemicycles of Chamber and Senate were already rising by stages within this area of expectant building, its empty space was made use of during the pauses in the work by the University's Faculty of Humanities and by the promoter of a skating rink. Thus, there were nights when one could hear the laments of Ajax, the cries of Oedipus the incestuous parricide in the north hemicycle, used by students as the Theatre of Antique Drama, while, on an echoing wooden floor in the southern hemicycle, young women could be seen circling to the strains of Waldteufel's most famous waltz, who rather than renounce fashion for sport had succeeded in fastening their Louis XV heels onto roller skates. In some intermediate spaces, a travelling Dupuytren Museum might be installed, or Great Panopticon of the Discovery of America and the Torture of the Indians, an exhibition of animals, the pillar of someone fasting, while up above, on wires fixed to columns without cornices, several tightrope walkers with pink tights and balancing poles, floodlit as they travelled from capital to capital, passed obliviously over the circulating skaters and the tragedies of Sophocles below, hourly expecting to be expelled by the army of workmen who periodically returned to their abandoned task to continue the almost liturgical elevation of the Civic Temple towards the lantern at the top.

These alternations between building and stoppage were still going on when one morning, with a jubilant air, Doctor Peralta entered the Head of State's private apartments, where the Mayorala Elmira was still in her underclothes:

"A miracle, Señor! A miracle! German submarines have just sunk a North American ship, the *Vigilentia*! All the gringos in the crew went to the bottom! Not one was saved!" (He was laughing.) "Not one, my President! Not one! They were

all done for. And although the news isn't official, it's known
that this will bring the United States into the war. Yes, really:
they'll come into the war!"

And they were both so pleased that without waiting for
anything more they took the Hermès case and filled their
glasses with Santa Inés. ("So I'm to be treated like dirt, am
I?" said the Mayorala, hastily bringing up a tooth glass.) It
was some time since the Head of State had been so delighted,
because the European war had become a stationary war of
trenches, positions, resistance, and slow struggles to win a
height, a copse, the ruins of a fort already ten times ruined,
a war of minimal advances and retreats, but with countless
dead, and therefore monotonous—in fact: boring. For anyone looking at it from here it lacked interest as a spectacle.
People no longer moved little flags over maps of distant lands
to mark victories or defeats, because there were no dramatic
victories or defeats, and whenever a real battle took place
it was always in the same area of the Argonne or Verdun,
between places with unknown names, barely a centimetre
apart on the 1:1000 maps that were still on display, dusty and
ignored, in newspaper offices. Certainly the country was enjoying astonishing prosperity. But the increasing cost of living kept the poor in the same misery as before—breakfast of
baked banana, yams at midday, crusts and tapioca after the
day's work, with some dried goat's meat or cow dead of foot-
and-mouth disease on Sundays and birthdays—in spite of
wages appearing to be good. As a result of this state of things,
students, intellectuals, and professional agitators—that filthy
intelligentsia who always destroy one's patience—had gradually combined together to make an opposition movement.
And just when he was counting on peace and quiet, the Head
of State was surprised by a proliferation of hostile forces invading the city, manifested here, there, where least expected,

to trouble his mind and interrupt his sleep. When he thought he had been quite forgotten, the hand of Doctor Luis Leoncio Martínez reappeared in proclamations arriving in envelopes with different postmarks, and denouncing events—this was the serious part of it—known only to a few people connected with the intimate life of the Presidential Palace. It had been discovered too late (that cretin the Chief of Police we waste money on never knew!) that a professor of modern history at the University had given lectures on the Mexican Revolution, speaking about the strength of its proletariat, peasants' leagues, the Syndicate of Tenant Farmers of Vera Cruz, agrarianism, the socialist government of Carrillo Puerto in Yucatán, and the articles written by the gringo adventurer John Reed—about everything, in fact, that had ruined, sunk, and impoverished the magnificent estates of Don Porfirio, humanist and civiliser, who instead of reposing in a huge national pantheon was buried, a victim of ingratitude, in a sad corner of the cemetery at Montparnasse. And as a last straw our Secret Service had failed to catch some anarchists, probably from Barcelona, who came out at night like elusive ghosts and chalked the letters R.A.S. on the walls, which appeared to stand for *Revolution of Anarchists and Syndicalists*, sometimes accompanied by phrases like "Property is theft" and other well-worn formulae taken seriously only in our imitative and backward America.

Now, with this splendid sinking of the *Vigilentia*, the United States would come into the war, and we should come into the war ourselves: patriotic feelings would be galvanised, and since a state of war necessarily implies a permanent state of emergency, we should round up, to the tune of the National Anthem, the "Marseillaise," "God Save the King," "God Save the Tsar," and "The Star-Spangled Banner," the most formidable cast of oppositionists, conspirators, and suspicious ideologues—all pro-German—that had ever been seen in the country.

Meanwhile the Head of State drank rum on fast days and sent for the Ambassador of the United States to inform him that the republic would stand beside her Great Sister of the North in these days of trial; then, after holding a rapid session of the Council of Ministers, he urgently summoned the two Chambers, appeared before them, and the text of a declaration of war against the Central Powers was approved by acclamation, with applause for every "considering that" and "whereas" serving to justify it.

And that same day, the war began with an operation as excellently profitable as it was speedy in execution: at exactly five o'clock in the afternoon the military authorities from Puerto Araguato went on board four German ships—the *Lübeck*, the *Grane*, the *Schwert*, and the *Cuxhaven*, which were moored to the quay awaiting orders from their government—took possession of them, and seized their crews. Delighted to see that the war was over for them, the sailors welcomed the port authorities with cheers and marched gaily off to their place of internment, boisterously greeting passers-by on the way. One Nietzschean officer who shouted "We'll die rather than hand over our ship!" was thrown overboard with an insult obviously meaning something like "son of a whore" in the Teuton tongue. And the captives were taken to a farm surrounded by a lot of land, where they slung their hammocks from trees and at once began gathering herbs and parasitic plants. Next morning they used some wood given them by orders from above to build pretty chalets in the Rhenish style, while others planted gladioli and rolled the ground to make tennis courts. Three weeks later the farm had become a model estate. There was a library, with the poems of Heinrich Heine and even of the socialist Dehmel. Of course it lacked women, but many of them had no need of them, being homosexual on the whole, and as for the unyielding few, they got permission to visit the brothel of La Ramona every Friday, under military escort. And as they were very musical, they made an orchestra from the instruments they had brought on board ship, and began to play the lesser works of Haydn, Mendelssohn, and Raff, his *Cavatina* in particular. Sometimes a poisonous reptile, rattlesnake, coral, or mapanare would join the concert; but it was always seen in time by the cellist, who looked at the ground more than the other musicians, and the serpent died at a single blow accurately given on its spine by the stick of the bow—*col legno* as it is technically called. And the purser of the *Lübeck* would often sing in his charming tenor voice, well accompanied by the orchestra:

> *Winterstürme wichen*
> *dem Wonnemond*
> *in milden lichte*
> *leuchtet der Lenz.*

The second action in this war had as its objective the confiscation of the Little German Train—the Head of State directed this operation in person, at the head of the sappers of the Second Tactical Regiment. When H-day dawned, the two terminal stations were occupied—the one above and the one at the bottom— as well as all the intermediate stops, signal boxes, and controls of points, etc. And as journeys remained suspended pending a fresh order, the President had the chance to realise an old dream: that of playing with the Little Train to his heart's content, putting Peralta, black in the face with dust, in the coal tender. Once he'd grasped the mechanism, the engine advanced, reversed, went in and out of the repairing shed, and revolved again and again on the

turntables; whistled, spouted steam from all its valves and
ballbearings, emitted even more steam, came, went, and
stopped to take a cargo on board: bundles of sugar cane,
barrels, a basket of squid, pots of areca nuts, empty cages,
a double bass, hens, and one or two negro drummers. And
when the Head of State had mastered the whole technique
of stoking the engine, driving, accelerating, keeping up the
speed, and braking in such a way as to stop the train with
the carriages opposite the platform, the entire Cabinet was
invited to take a first trip to the Olmedo Colony, with pies
and tamales served in the carriages, and enough champagne
to drink the health of the First Mechanic of the Nation. And
the President found his artefact so amusing that for several
days he quite forgot the European war, and stopped reading
the foreign papers regularly brought him by Doctor Peralta—
among them a piquant French magazine called *Regiment*, full
of nudes amongst uniforms.

Meanwhile, "La Madelon" and "Roses of Picardy" had
been succeeded by "Over There," a tune that invaded the
country with astonishing speed. Beginning with the pianolas
of Puerto Araguato, it had travelled along the Great Eastern
Railway, from gramophone to gramophone, taking possession of pianos in music schools, pianos in middle-class drawing rooms, cinema pianos, café pianos, nuns' pianos, tarts'
pianos, before reaching its most sonorous expression in
the Sunday concerts in Central Park. *Over there, over there,
over there . . .*

Huge posters representing a North American soldier
charging an invisible enemy with his bayonet and shouting
"Come on!" invited the public to buy war bonds, and met
with such a good response in the country that a little later
Ambassador Ariel solemnly handed President Woodrow
Wilson the sum of a million dollars, collected in less than

twenty-five days. The cinemas showed documentaries glori-
fying General Pershing—the man who had sent a scandalous
"punitive expedition" to Mexico a short while ago. Over there,
over there, over there. Now, as well as "Over There," came
Sousa's noisy marches with bass tubas and flourishes on the
piccolo. A young officer, warmly supported by the government ("War stimulates male energy," said the Head of State:
"War is to man what childbirth is to woman"), took upon
himself the task of raising the National Legion of Volunteers
to go and fight in France—under his command, of course.
Armed warfare was full of dangers, naturally, but much that
was enjoyable went with it. In proof of this, one need only
read an article by Maurice Barrès, often reprinted in the local
press: "Good humour reigns in the trenches. Of course, on
rainy nights it's not like being in a luxury restaurant ... But
I know a place where there's a labyrinth of eight kilometres
of very well kept trenches, connected by paths called names
like the Champs-Elysées or the Rue Monsieur-le-Prince. I
know an underground shelter where one officer has installed
a crimson velvet armchair, and a table with a vase of roses
and old Strasbourg china. The trenches are furnished with
objects found among the ruins of bombarded villages. Gaiety reigns in the trenches" [sic]. Such literature was synchro-
nised with pictures of Bengal lancers, handsome bersaglieri,
and cossacks—recently become republicans—who were now
hurling themselves with fresh energy against a Germany
whose starving population had nothing to eat but bread made
of straw and sawdust; all this, opportunely reinforced by a
portrait of Ofelia dressed as a Red Cross nurse, looking more
Creole than ever as she bandaged the forehead of a wounded
Englishman, played a part in raising an army of 250 young
men eager to see the Eiffel Tower, the Moulin Rouge, and
Maxim's restaurant.

"Now the people *over there* will realise we've got guts," said Peralta.

But there was some disappointment among the public when they heard, weeks later, that as soon as the volunteers from their country arrived *over there* they had been dispersed among different French units, and that the young officer, deprived of the command of his men, had returned in a state of furious indignation, declaring—after taking a close look at the situation—that the Allies would lose this war, even with North American help, because there was nothing to be seen but mismanagement and chaos. But what interested people most was not whether the Allies would win or lose the war, but that it should last as long as possible. Given three, four, or five years more war we should become a great nation. From the six o'clock Mass to the evening rosary, from the bells of daybreak to the ringing of the angelus, everyone was praying for peace, of course, but with the almost universal gesture, difficult for foreigners to understand, of placing their middle fingers on top of their forefingers. When all was said and done, we were not responsible for what was happening in Europe. We weren't guilty at all. The Old Continent had been at fault in setting itself up as an example of wisdom. And if our country was enjoying an unexpected period of progress and plenty today, it was proof that the Almighty—as the Archbishop had said in an eloquent sermon—favoured those who were out of sympathy with empty philosophies leaving dust and ashes in the soul, and with certain social doctrines as wicked as they were corrupt and foreign to our character, but who had known how to safeguard the religious and patriarchal traditions of the nation. As he said this the prelate made a gesture embracing both the Holy Ghost swinging above his head and the Head of State, who happened to be present in the Cathedral that morning.

The construction of the Capitol was almost complete. Already enclosed between the walls of a palace too narrow to shelter her, the Giantess, the Titaness, the Immense Woman, a combination of Juno, Pomona, Minerva, and the Republic, had grown bigger day by day as the building went up around her. Every morning she seemed larger, like those jungle plants that shoot up amazingly during the night, trying to reach a dawn hidden from them by the trees above. As if oppressed, crushed by the surrounding stones, she looked twice as thickset, corpulent, and tall—particularly tall—as she did when she had been set up piecemeal in an open space. The cupola had already closed over her head topped by its noble lantern—imitated from the Invalides in Paris—which, now that its beacon was lit, dominated the city nights, cruelly reducing the Cathedral towers to dwarfish proportions and interrupting the dialogue they used to carry on with the distant cone of the Tutelary Volcano, according to a poem by one of our great writers of the last century.

The work was nearly finished, but it seemed improbable that the building could be inaugurated, as had been hoped, on the date of the Centenary of Independence, which was already fast approaching. On the day when this problem was broached at a stormy meeting of the Cabinet, the Head of State became suddenly enraged and violently dismissed the Minister of Works, threatening the others with exile or prison if the Capitol wasn't finished, painted, gleaming and burnished, complete with gardens, in time for a date that could not be postponed.

And now the work took on Egyptian dimensions. Hundreds of peasants were rounded up with machetes, yoked to carts and drays, lodged in huts and summoned to do alternate shifts of work by bugle calls; with their help, columns and obelisks were erected, gods and warriors, dancers, muses,

and kings arose, hoplites and horsemen equipped with helmets and breastplates were elevated to the highest friezes.
Everything needing polishing was polished, what had to be
gilded was gilded, what had to be painted was painted. The
work went on at night by the light of spotlights and reflectors.
Hammering continued so incessantly that for weeks it was
like living in a blacksmith's forge, among drills and anvils,
while the last paving stones were being laid on the steps of
the staircase of honour. And one afternoon the Royal Palms
entered the city, lying horizontally on lorries and wagons with
their leaves sweeping the pavements and raising dust from
the streets, to be planted in deep pits filled with black earth,
grit, and manure. Behind—like Macbeth's forest—appeared
small pines, clipped box trees and arecas, brought from all
sorts of places, ready to be transplanted and staked by hundreds of men, waiting watering can in hand, though it was far
from certain, truth to tell, if their leaves would be green in
time for the Great Day.

"Any leaves that wither must be painted the night before,"
said the Head of State. Meanwhile, with their eyes fixed on
calendars and watches, impatient and sleepless, the architects
and overseers urged on the workers with the shouts and attitudes of slave drivers, until the building was quite complete,
even to the sumptuous final touch of inserting a great diamond from Tiffany in the middle of a star of reddish green
marble at the feet of Aldo Nardini's statue, to mark the zero
point of all the roads of the Republic—the place where, ide-
ally, all the projected means of communication from the far-
thest limits of the country would meet in the capital.

And at last on the Thursday of the Centenary of Independence, the capital awoke to find itself brilliant and shining,
covered in flags, shields, emblems, allegories, and cardboard
horses representing famous battles. A salvo of a hundred

guns went off at dawn, rockets were fired from the roofs, there was a grand military parade and band, many bands, of the regiments of town and provinces, who, when the official procession was over, went on playing all day in the public parks and kiosks at street corners, sending the scores around by messenger—as there were very few copies of some—and choosing mainly national airs and patriotic marches, though they also included some *pièces de résistance* to show what they could do, carefully chosen by the Head of State with the help of the Director of the National Conservatoire. No German music, of course, least of all Wagner, who seemed to have been excluded forever from symphony concerts in Paris after Saint-Saëns had implacably described him as the sinister and abominable incarnation of the German spirit. As to Beethoven, it was best to forget about him for the present—although there were some who maintained that the Germany of his day wasn't the same as Von Hindenburg's, after all. So they marched from square to kiosks, from parks to summer houses, to the overtures of *Zampa* and *Guillaume Tell*, and to tunes from Massenet's *Scènes Alsaciennes*, Paladilhe's *Patria*, and Rubinstein's *Toreador and the Andalusian Girl*—they were short of Russian composers in their repertory—and to Victorin Joncière's *Serenade*—a serenade that dropped its "Hungarian" because we were at war with the Central Powers, just as Berlioz's *Hungarian March*, with its tremendous drumbeats, figured under the simple title of *March*.

A day of general enthusiasm, a day of jugs full of aguardiente, and veal cooking on the grill, free sweetcorn, barrels of beer, toys for poor children, ribbons and bows, choirs singing in the National Pantheon, salves in the churches, dancing in houses and tearooms, alleys and brothels, with every pianola, piano, gramophone, street musician, and maraca player combining full-tilt in a general haphazard concert, while waiting

for the inauguration ceremony of the Capitol, within whose
Large Hemicycle were gathered the entire government, heads
of the Armed Forces, Diplomatic Corps, and an elegant
crowd, rigorously filtered, surrounded and observed by a
whole legion of agents of our Intelligence Service, who were
dressed for the occasion in dinner jackets too like one another not to look like uniforms. And then the soirée began
with all solemnity, pomp and show, epaulettes, gold braid and
decorations—the Order of Isabella the Catholic, of Carlos III,
of Gustavus Adolphus, the Sovereign Order of the Knights of
Malta, Legions of Honour, Honi-soit-qui-mal-y-pense, garters and crosses, and even the exotic insignia of the Dragon of
Annam and of the Waterlily and the Arcade, recently granted
to our high officials. After listening to the National Anthem,
the Head of State walked to the rostrum—he certainly appeared surprisingly confident and in command of himself
that afternoon—wearing all the emblems of his high rank. He
began his speech slowly as usual, using the theatrical gestures
common to a good lawyer and a good orator, sketching an exact and moderate outline of our history from the Conquest to
Independence. And those who were ironically expecting his
customary verbal flourishes, elaborate epithets, and striking
vocatives were surprised to hear him pass from this sober historical narrative to the arid world of statistics, and presenting
from the precise viewpoint of an economist a clear and convincing picture of national prosperity, coinciding as it did—
and here his tone became more emotional—with the greatest
attempt to destroy Graeco-Latin Culture that had been made
in any epoch of human evolution. But that great culture
would be saved. Before long, victory for our Spiritual Parents would ensure the permanence of values that, threatened
*over there*, would rise again on this side of the ocean, more
splendid than ever. And contemplating, and inviting others

to contemplate, this superb building wherein we now were, this crystallisation in stone, marble, and bronze of the classical orders of Graeco-Latin architecture—Vitruvius, Vignola, Bramante—the Head of State speeded his rhythm and raised his pitch, while his gestures became wider as he suddenly returned to the prolix, ornate, and overcharged style that had been so often made fun of by his enemies. And closing an invocation to Her who, as the Guide of all Reason and all Intelligence, must rule over the republic itself and thus over this recently built Civic Temple, the inspired voice exclaimed: "O Archagetis, ideal incarnate in the masterpieces of men of genius, I would rather be the least in your mansion than the first elsewhere! Yes: I will attach myself to the stylobate of your temple; I will forget every discipline except yours; I will be a stylite on your columns and my cell shall be placed upon your architrave. And—something more difficult!—for your sake I will if I can become *intolerant and partial* ... (The crowd was tense with expectation.) *I shall be unjust to everything that does not concern you; I shall make myself the slave of the last of your sons.* The present inhabitants of the land you gave to Erectheus shall be exalted and flattered by me. I will endeavour to love even their defects, and I will convince myself—O Hippias!—that they are descendants of the horsemen who are celebrating their eternal festival in the marble of your frieze." (Here he gestured towards the roof.)

The Head of State seemed to have come to the end of his speech. The audience gave him a long standing ovation. But Peralta, sitting in the secretary's place opposite the audience, the better to keep an eye on the Diplomatic Corps, had noticed the French Ambassador nudging the British Ambassador at the name of *Archagetis*. At *stylobate*, the British Ambassador's elbow had nudged the Italian Ambassador in the ribs; from *stylite* to *architrave*, from *Erectheus* to *Hippias* a series of nudges had passed from ambassador to business representative, from councillor to cultural attaché, as far as the lean rib cage of the Japanese Commercial Attaché, who didn't understand the language and was therefore half asleep. The impact nearly knocked him over, just as in physics the last ball of the apparatus is hurled in the air when the action of a first ball of the same weight communicates its energy to six identical intermediate balls. One or two laughs were stifled behind the many handkerchiefs mopping up non-existent sweat—because it was not a warm night and the winds were from the north, cooled by the snows of the Tutelary Volcano. At this moment the Head of State silenced the audience with a simple gesture and said that he was particularly pleased by this applause, since it was directed at the famous writer Ernest Renan, whose *Prayer on the Acropolis* included the fine paragraph he had just quoted, because it seemed to him to correspond in every way with his profoundest spiritual desires and the solemnity of the occasion.

There was more applause, louder and more prolonged than before—as though some desire for forgiveness lay behind it—during which Peralta left his seat, and going up to the French Ambassador, said to him with sly coarseness:

"*Il vous a bien eu, hein? Pas si con que ça, le vieux!*"

"*Pas si con que ça, en effet,*" replied the other, taken by surprise and suddenly worried by the idea that his thoughtless response might be reported to the Quai d'Orsay, which was in no mood for jokes these days and had had the brilliant ideas of sending Alexis Leger to China and appointing Paul Claudel Minister to Rio de Janeiro, so as to raise the lamentable intellectual level of French representatives in Asia and Latin America.

But this was the signal for the assembly to break up; people abandoned their seats in haste, descended the stairs, and made for the doors in an avalanche, pushing with their elbows so as to get as quickly as possible to a gigantic buffet whose tables displayed enormous silver dishes laden with as many good things imported from New York and Paris as could be added to the national delicacies: pheasants decorated with their feathers, truffled quails, suckling pigs stuffed with galantine and pistachios, highly seasoned tamales and turkeys with cranberry sauce, Saint Honoré à la crème and maize cream in glasses, marrons glacés and tamarind pies, national savouries next to black and red caviar piled onto elephants sculpted in ice, the whole spread being surmounted in the middle and at the ends by architectonic cakes made of meringue and almond paste representing the Capitol, without a single column missing, and all the statues and obelisks in marzipan. All this was admired and enjoyed, washed down by wine and liqueurs, brandy and tequila; and fresh bottles of champagne were taken from coolers full of crushed ice tinted pink to enhance their gold-covered corks.

And everyone drank toasts standing around the huge statue of the Republic, while an orchestra, hoisted up inside the cupola, launched into Cuban *danzóns* and Creole bambas, interspersed between the "Beautiful Ohio" waltz or the syncopation of "Pretty Baby." And then fireworks were let off, setting the sky on fire, falling in torrents and cascades of stars and lights on the roofs and terraces of the town.

And at two in the morning—according to the Head of Protocol no official soirée could go on after this hour—Peralta and the Head of State returned to the palace, exhausted but happy, longing to take off their evening clothes and drink something stronger and more to their taste than what the party provided. The Mayorala Elmira was waiting for them in the presidential apartments, dressed in her petticoat, but with her bosom muffled against the cold mountain air creeping through the Venetian blinds. And as the secretary had been as good as his word and brought her some of what had been served at the buffet that night, despite her doubts as to whether she would find it to her liking, the zamba eagerly took them out of their hamper, one by one, with the mistrustful caution of a bomb-disposal expert examining the suspicious contents of an anarchist's case. She found a derogatory definition for them all; the Burgundian snails were "slugs"; the caviar, "buckshot in oil"; the truffles, "chips of charcoal"; the halva, "nougat trying to be like *turrón* from Jijona."

The President had already drunk a lot and was asking for more; he didn't feel ready for sleep, while Peralta never tired of praising his brilliant use of the quotation from Ernest Renan.

"Don't they say I'm an affected and ridiculous speaker?" remarked the President. "But I'm really sorry our friend the Academician wasn't there. Because he would certainly have fallen into the trap too."

"The thing is that that passage seemed to have been written expressly for the inauguration of our Capitol," said Peralta, "and with such appropriate threats against the bastards of the opposition."

The Head of State was looking out the window at the confused panorama of scaffolding and building, which would soon be covered with workmen. Far away, the Tutelary Volcano had hardly emerged from its veils of mist in the belated dawn. After drinking a sixth large beer from the neck of the bottle, the Mayorala pulled her camp bed into the doorway and threw herself down to sleep, as always, with a sawn-off shotgun in reach of her hand. Peralta, who was rather drunk, drowsed off on the leather sofa, with its wide back and deep cushions, standing opposite the somewhat Renaissance-style fireplace—with Louis XII's porcupine at the top—where, for lack of the fire that was never lit, red electric lightbulbs winked amongst false logs.

"The ceremony was a success, a real success," the Head of State kept repeating, listening to the discreet summons to matins from the Cathedral—the bell had been muted because the neighbours wouldn't get up as early as usual and had asked that it should sound less loudly than before. And he went on pacing around the room, from chair to chair, having a last drink, which always turned into a penultimate drink. A man accustomed to short nights and long siestas, whose spartan audiences lasting into the small hours were the torment of his colleagues, he couldn't make up his mind to rest a few hours in his hammock tonight—a long net hammock like the one in Paris—before he took the bath that the Mayorala Elmira would prepare for him as usual, scented with English bath salts and the water at blood heat. He was delighted by the Capitol affair. Now photographs of the building would be sent to our embassies and published in the European and continental papers—paying for the space according to the columns occupied and tariff per centimetre, as he always did when he wanted to control the captions under a picture. Thus the world would hear how greatly increased in importance this town had become, which at the beginning of the century had been hardly more than a village surrounded by a wasteland full of snakes, bare hills, thorny scrub, water tanks breeding mosquitoes, and cattle driven along the main streets with shouts and whistles.

He was happy with such thoughts as these, and hardly had daylight dawned when he became aware of distant reveilles from the barracks, and the first trams carrying people with baskets, knapsacks, and crates to the marketplace, where caged birds were already fidgeting and turtles munching lettuces in their boxes. The Head of State looked at his agenda.

Today was free from councils, audiences, and other worries. So maybe he would change the order of his habits: he would have a bath first and then a sleep till the middle of the morning. But he lounged in an armchair and ate liqueur chocolates, in no hurry to make up his mind.

"Whatever you like," murmured the Mayorala as if talking in her sleep.

"A bit later, my dear. Don't trouble."

He felt himself possessed of the same strength and sovereignty as the volcano, which had now emerged from its trammelling clouds and stood revealed among craggy spurs of blue quartz. "A success! . . . a success," he went on repeating to himself. "As for the rest . . ."

A tremendous explosion shook the palace. All the windows of the façade broke at once; several candelabra fell from ceilings; bottles, vases, ornamental pottery, and plates were shattered, and a few pictures came away from the walls. A large high-explosive bomb had just gone off in the presidential bathroom, spreading heavy fumes smelling of bitter almonds. Ashy pale from the effort to appear calm, the Head of State looked at his watch: "Half past six . . . my regular bath time . . . Congratulations, gentlemen; but I wasn't there today." And while guards, footmen, and maidservants came running with all speed and noise and the Mayorala shouted for more, he added, pointing towards the town: "This is what I get for being too lenient."

# 12

*... there is something like a very powerful and clever deceiver who uses all his skill to keep me constantly deceived ...*                    —DESCARTES

MINISTERS WERE DRAGGED OUT OF BED BY TELEPHONE calls from Doctor Peralta—they had been sleeping off the official dinner, prolonged when they got home by large doses of digestive drinks, yellow liqueurs, green benedictines, and purple cherry brandy—and summoned to an urgent council meeting at 8:30 in the morning, where there would be plenty of coffee trays to help those who were still drowsy shake off the effect of their drinks. When they arrived—chewing peppermint, sweating out aspirin, and clearing their eyes with lotion—the Mayorala Elmira took them to the President's bathroom, where they were shocked at the sight of broken porcelain, shattered mirrors, debris of bottles, and soap dishes in a pool of eau de Cologne, a bidet with its taps wrenched from their sockets, spouting out uncontrollable fountains of water, and even the ceiling smashed by the explosion.

"Horrible ... Terrifying ... Inconceivable ... And to think how nearly ..."

"I've refrained from going in," declared the Head of State somewhat dramatically, when everyone was seated, "because I'm afraid of my own anger."

There was a long pause, charged with menacing possibilities. Then, in a calmer tone:

"Gentlemen, let us get to work." The secretary opened the meeting by describing what had happened, the exact time, circumstances, etc. Captain Valverde, Chief of the Judicial Police, had already begun his investigations. Because of the inauguration of the Capitol, the presidential guard had yesterday been transferred to the Great Hemicycle, and it was true that the palace itself had had insufficient attention, the key posts being left to soldiers who were inexperienced in such duties. However, no one except the domestic, personal, and confidential staff had entered the building after the changing of the guard.

"Apart from that," observed the President, "the bomb which exploded here was not one that could have been brought in someone's pocket. It must have been under the bathtub itself for many hours, with its mechanism set to go off at the appointed time. This wasn't the work of some amateur using nitrobenzene, gunpowder, or picric acid; the bomb was made by someone who knew his job. The expert says that the smell of bitter almonds, which is still noticeable, is a sign of technical skill."

These were the possible hypotheses: the RAS (Revolution of Anarchists and Syndicalists), who had for months past been scrawling their initials on the walls of the city with invisible hands; or perhaps Doctor Luis Leoncio Martínez's supporters might be more active than was realised—they had been agitating lately with some skill, it must be admitted, and gaining followers in the city and provinces; students, possibly, because students always got mixed up in rioting and bloody-mindedness (and why shouldn't we close the University of San Lucas this very day?); Russian nihilists ("rubbish," murmured the President); members of Samuel Gompers'

American Federation of Labor ("that's absurd") who had recently carried on revolutionary activities in the north of Mexico.

"And then there's Red Literature," said the Minister of Education.

"That's it: Red Literature," said the others as one man. But the Chief of the Judicial Police saw no relation between that morning's incident and the circulation of books such as are published by the Biblioteca Barbadillo, called *The Pleasures of the Caesars*, which he had been shown recently, containing reproductions of Roman cameos wherein the Emperor Octavian was to be seen laying hands—and how!—on his daughter Julia, while in another Nero appeared doing things he couldn't describe here out of respect for the company.

"That's not what we're talking about; pornography does no harm to anyone, after all," said the Minister for Education. "We mean books on anarchism, socialism, communism, workmen's Internationals, revolution—*Red Books*: that's what they're called everywhere."

"Don't let's digress, gentlemen; don't let's digress," said the Chief of Police, somewhat peevishly. The problem was simpler. As everyone knew, certain printed leaflets were in circulation, full of insults against the government, and written in an unmistakably Creole style—calumnies, of course, but the sort of calumny in common use among some sectors of the opposition. Not nihilist, nor anarcho-syndicalist, nor of the "as the gentleman says, but I don't understand English" description. Our enemies were, quite simply, politicians in disguise, who were trying every way they knew to stir up feelings and overthrow the government. They've been watching us, they are all around; and now, with last night's business, they have declared open war. And now that it was war, we would reply with war, he said, laying his pistol on the table.

"But if there is to be war, we must know where the enemy is," remarked the President.

"Leave that to me. I know where to begin. I've already got some names on my list. I'll read them if you like . . ."

"Better not, Captain. I'm quite capable of being too lenient to some. I trust you entirely. Carry on. At once and forcibly. We understand one another."

"A mistake would be disastrous, however," put in Peralta.

"*Errare humanum est*," concluded the Head of State in *Petit Larousse* Latin. And to cheer up his ministers, who were still looking worn out with anxiety and their late night, he sent for some bottles of cognac: "Just this once," he said, filling a glass.

"You've got every justification," chorused the rest.

The masons and plumbers were beginning to arrive to repair the bathroom, bringing tiles, blow lamps, and tools.

"Anyway, look into this business of Red Literature," said the Head of State to the captain, but in the tone of someone who doesn't consider the matter of great importance.

"Don't worry, Señor. I have people trained for that sort of thing," replied the other, taking his leave with the praiseworthy haste of someone who is eager to get to work.

"We shall pull in a fine haul of pro-Germans today," said Peralta.

The people of the capital were treated to a strange and unexpected performance at about two in the afternoon that day. It was the hour when employees went back to their offices, the hour of dessert in restaurants, or of drinking under the awnings of cafés—the Tortoni, the Granja, or the Marquise de Sevigné—installed as a great novelty in imitation of what one saw in Paris, so the streets were full of people. And in these crowded streets there suddenly appeared, preceded by small cars—Fords, naturally—with their sirens screaming, some Black Marias, like cages on wheels, with fierce-looking policemen standing on the back steps, rifle in hand. It was soon learnt that these sinister vehicles, recently acquired by the government, were being used as substitutes for the earlier prison cars—"bird cages" as they were called—hitherto used to pick up drunks, thieves, and homosexuals. At the same time, unusual activity was noticed among the city police. Motorcycles going to and fro. Sudden appearances, now here, now there, of detectives, quickly spotted as such by their obvious attempts at "not attracting attention," and dressed in a commerical traveller style mixed with that of Nick Carter, which left no room for doubt. And all the time those sirens went on calling to one another, stridently, disturbingly, from district to district, over the roofs and terraces, causing a panic among the pigeons fluttering between the modern buildings.

"Something's up," people said in surprise. "Something's happening."

And a great deal was happening, a great deal was in fact happening that day, which was becoming more and more overcast, with warm drizzle falling, hour by hour. At half past two in the afternoon the Vice-Chancellor of the University was explaining in a lecture the nominalism and voluntarism of William of Occam when the police burst into his classroom and took him and all his pupils prisoners for holding a demonstration. Continuing their task of subjugating the Faculty of Humanities, they carried off eight more professors with kicks and shoves towards the new prison cars. Tired of hearing him call upon their century-old rights and autonomy, Captain Valverde threw the Chancellor into the fountain in the central court, along with his mortarboard and gown— attributes he had tried to use to gain the "invaders" respect.

At three o'clock, under orders from Lieutenant Calvo, the chosen expert, the authorities occupied several bookshops where cheap editions were on sale of such books as *Red Week in Barcelona* (a tract about the anarchist Ferrer), *The Knight of the Red House*, *The Red Lily*, *Red Dawn* (Pîo Baroja), *The Red Virgin* (a biography of Louise Michel), *Le Rouge et le Noir*, *The Scarlet Letter* (by Nathaniel Hawthorne)—all examples, according to the expert, of *red literature*, revolutionary propaganda, to a large extent responsible for such incidents as had happened at the palace last night. The books were thrown into lorries and dispatched on their way to the rubbish incinerator, built a short while before on the outskirts of the town.

"Take *Little Red Riding Hood* while you're about it," shouted one of the booksellers, beside himself with rage.

"You're under arrest, you joker," said Lieutenant Calvo, handing him over to one of his agents.

Then—it was about five—they began on private houses: police rained from heaven, ran over roofs, jumped onto patios, entered kitchens, broke down doors, crept under beds, searched wardrobes, turned drawers upside down, and opened trunks, while women wept, children screamed, and old women cursed, a patriarch raged from his wheelchair, and a consumptive, near to death, declared that the Head of State was the son of a drunk and that his late wife Doña Hermenegilda, so often described as a saint, had worn herself out accommodating the organ of a young officer of hussars, famous for his exceptional proportions.

So night fell, amidst confused rumours of arrests, detentions, disappearance of "subversive elements," German spies, and pro-German socialists, yet the pulse of the city's normal activities seemed unchanged. The advertisements for Vino Mariani, Gyraldose, and Urodonal turned on their lights, bells rang in the cinemas, while—in cafés and bars—people vainly turned the pages of the evening papers, which mentioned everything except what they were looking for. The Black

Marias seemed to be taking a rest from their rounds. As it was a Thursday, the Fire Brigade Band played the march called "Sambre et Meuse," the ballet from *Samson and Delilah*, and several bullfight *pasodobles* in the bandstand in Central Park. The streets in the red light district—San Isidro, la Chayota, el Mangue, Economia, and San Juan de Letrán—filled with clients. But on the stroke of eleven there was a sudden, violent invasion of brothels, gambling dens, bars, and halls where people danced to violin and guitar. Everyone who couldn't prove that he was a public employee or a soldier was piled into military lorries—sometimes without his clothes—and carried off to the old Central Prison, whose cells, corridors, and courtyards were already crammed with people.

And when dawn came, Terror reigned in the city. The arrests continued. The Black Marias went their rounds again. But in spite of the terror, when the Mayorala Elmira was cleaning the little library of the Council Chamber that afternoon, she found, behind a copy of Cesar Cantú's *Universal History*, a suspicious-looking tin of animal crackers, which turned out to be a crude home-made bomb. It was defused in time by one of the palace guards, apprentice to an expert.

"We'll have to tighten the pressure," commented Peralta.

With age and the hardening of his arteries, the Head of State's eyes—he would never wear spectacles, as he didn't need them for reading—had acquired the strange defect of eliminating the third dimension. He saw things, whether near or far, as flat images without relief, like the stained glass in Gothic windows. So every morning, just as if they were figures in a Gothic window, he looked at the Men of Regulation Colours—this one in blue and black, the next in white and gold, and the third in a buff-coloured tunic—who told him about the work they had carried out the day before, their night spent in police stations and prisons, barracks and

cellars extracting words, names, addresses, and information
from people who didn't want to speak. And their accounts of
ducking and racking, hanging and violence, their catalogue
of pincers, truncheons, braziers, and even corncobs—these
were for women—called up visions from hagiography, the
downfall of the damned, illustrations of torture, all transferred to a large stained-glass window opening onto the remote splendour of the Tutelary Volcano. With a "Thank you,
gentlemen," the first stained-glass window broke, eliminating
the blues, whites, and yellows of the original image, while
in at the other door to take their place in the second window came the Listening and Looking men, the Watchers, the
Hearers, the Hypocrites, the masters in maieutics, virtuosos
in heuristics, who not only brought information extracted by
skill, snatched in flight, half understood, of some guilty remark picked up at a diplomatic reception, a bar counter, in the
warmth of a bedroom—they were everywhere, they entered
without being seen, Guests of Glass one day, Guests of Stone
if more acceptable, insinuating, snooping, often charming—
but were in fact Watchers of the Watchful, Observers of the
Cunning, recorders of everything invented, plotted, and
schemed, even by the collaborators, familiars, and associates
of the Head of State himself, thanks to his Exalted Protection. As he listened to these people of his, who had their eyes
to the keyhole and their curiosity on the alert, he realised
(sometimes with annoyance, sometimes with amusement)
what diverse and picturesque transactions were going on behind his back: there was the business of a bridge built over a
river that wasn't shown on any map; the business of the Municipal Library without any books; the business of the stud
animals from Normandy that had never crossed the ocean;
the business of the toys and alphabets for kindergartens that
didn't exist; the business of the Peasant Women's Maternity

Homes, to which peasant women naturally never went, since
for centuries they had been in the habit of giving birth on a
broken stool, pulling on a rope hanging from the ceiling with
their husband's hat on their head so that they should get a
boy; the business of the kilometre stones that were still only
painted boards; the business of pornographic films sold in
Quaker Oats tins; the business of the Chinese Charade ("*jeux
des trente-six bêtes*," as it was called by Baron Drummond,
who introduced the Cantonese lottery of numbered animals
to America), managed by the brigade of the National Police
for the Repression of Illicit Games; the business of Erectyl,
a Korean liquor containing mandragora root, the "stallion
liana" from Santo Domingo, powdered tortoiseshell and extract of Spanish fly; the business of the slot machines—three
bells, three plums, or three cherries gave you the jackpot—
owned by the Chief of the Secret Service; the business of birth
certificates *ad perpetuam memoriam* for those "*interdits de sé-
jour*" and Frenchmen from Cayenne wanting to become our
compatriots; the business of consultations with astrologers,
fortune-tellers, palmists, card readers, horoscopes by correspondence, Hindu mystics—forbidden by law—who all had
understandings with the Minister of the Interior; the business of the Verascopes of Love, tolerated in fairs and amusement parks, and owned by Captain Valverde; the business of
Catalan postcards—less refined than the French, said those
in the know—run by Captain Calvo; the business of "Lucky
Sheets for Newly-weds" ("*Draps bénis pour jeunes mariés*"
[*sic*]), manufactured in the Marais in Paris and designed for
the trousseau of every Christian bride.

Between amusement and annoyance—but more amused
than annoyed—the Head of State contemplated this panorama
of swindling and gangsterism every morning, reflecting that
the least he could do was reward the fidelity and zeal of those

who served him with the currency of folklore. Because he was not, and had never been, a man for small transactions, owner of companies managed by stealth, he was Master of Bread and Fish, of Corn and Herds, of Ice and Springs, of Fluid and the Wheel, beneath a multiple identity of symbols, syndicates, trade names, and always anonymous societies immune from failure or setbacks. Thus the Head of State contemplated his early-morning windows, but observed that, in spite of the terror unleashed by the first bomb in the palace, there was *something*, something that his men had been unable to grasp, something that slipped from their fingers, that neither prison nor torture nor a state of siege could put a stop to; *something* that was moving in the subsoil, underground, that arose from urban catacombs not previously known to exist; something new in the country, with unpredictable manifestations, mysterious mechanisms, which the President could not explain. It was as if the atmosphere had been changed by the addition of some impalpable pollen or hidden ferment, an elusive, slippery, occult but manifest force, silent although throbbingly alive with a circulation of clandestine leaflets, manifestos, proclamations, pamphlets small enough to go in the pocket sent forth by ghostly printers ("And are you incapable of finding something so difficult to conceal, so noisy, as a printing press?" the Head of State would shout, on his angrier mornings). These didn't insult him in the Creole argot of the tenement house, with its simple-minded puns and jokes as formerly, but described him as *Dictator* (a word that wounded him more than the most obscene epithet or untranslatable nickname, because it was annoyingly current abroad—especially in France) and revealed to the public in plain and cutting language many things about him—actions, business matters, decisions, and *eliminations*—that should never have been known.

"But who, who, who publishes these leaflets, libels and infamous calumnies?" the Head of State would cry aloud every morning to his usual stained-glass windows of sweating, twitching faces, distressed by their inability to answer. Those in the regulation colours of blue, white, and yellow stammered something or other; the pale Maieutic Brotherhood hinted at and contradicted one another, proceeding by elimination although obviously disorientated. They tightened their noose around the printed matter and searched for guilt between the lines. It wasn't the anarchists: they had all been taken; it wasn't Luis Leoncio Martínez's followers, who were all shut up in different prisons; nor was it the timid oppositionists of other factions, who were thoroughly taped and watched, and hadn't the technical means to keep an underground printing press functioning so continuously and exasperatingly.

And so, by dint of subjecting conjectures and hypotheses to the calculation of probabilities, and by joining the loose letters together like the pieces of a jigsaw puzzle, they arrived at the word C-O-M-M-U-N-I-S-M, the last to come to mind.

But the fact was—as the Head of State remarked when he was alone with Peralta—we were a very imaginative people, like all Latin Americans. It was enough for something to travel about the world—whether a fashion, a product, a doctrine, an idea, a style of painting, writing, poetry, or of foolish talk— for us to welcome it with enthusiasm. This was just as true of Italian Futurism as it was of the *Juvencia del Abate Soury*; or of Theosophy as of dancing marathons; of the philosophy of Krause as of table-turning. And now this exotic, impossible Russian communism, condemned by all honest men ever since the infamous Treaty of Brest-Litovsk, was stretching its tentacles towards America. Luckily this doctrine without a future and so alien to our customs had few supporters—or at least their activities had not been obvious hitherto—but

as soon as they thought of it as a possible motive, there rose
to the minds of those present the despised figure of a young
man called Álvarez or Álvaro or Álvarado—Peralta wasn't
sure which—better known as the Student ever since he had
said in a particularly aggressive speech: "You mustn't think of
me as a student, but as any student, the Student," and who had
played a prominent part in recent university agitations. One
informer had heard him talking approvingly of this fellow
Lenin who had overthrown Kerensky in Russia and established a regime there in which riches, land, cattle, silver plate,
and women were all shared.

"Well, you must look for him," said the President. "Maybe
we'll get something out of him." But the usual morning
stained-glass window at once became a picture of conster-
nation. There was no conceivable way of seizing the Student. And as he had seemed too harmless even to be kept
under observation—he was more interested in poetry than
politics—the Security Experts couldn't agree about his physical appearance, height, physiognomy, or degree of corpu-
lence. Some said he had green eyes, others that they were
chestnut; some that he was of athletic build, others that he
was weak and sickly; he was twenty-three years old according
to the university registers; his mother was dead; his father was
a schoolmaster who had been killed in the Nueva Córdoba
massacre. He should be in the city, however; but when the police broke into his hideout all they found was a rumpled bed
with indications of recent occupation, a half-empty bottle of
beer, burned papers, cigar ends, and a book lying on the floor:
Volume I of *Das Kapital* by Karl Marx, bought—as could be
seen by the shop stamp—in the Atenea bookshop, kept by
Valentin Jiménez, now in prison for selling red books.

"That's it!" cried the Head of State when he heard. "The
cretins were busy confiscating *Le Rouge et le Noir* and *The*

*Knight of the Red House*, but left the most dangerous books in the shop windows."

And as the Distinguished Academician had sometimes talked to him in Paris about the "Marxist danger" or "Marxist literature," he instructed Peralta ("he's much more intelligent than these bloody detectives, including present company") to bring him all the literature of this type he could find in the city . . .

Two hours later, a number of volumes were ranged on the table of the presidential study: Marx's *The Class Struggle in France (1848–1850)*, Louis Bonaparte's *18 Brumaire*, and *The Civil War in France (1871)*.

"Bah! All that's prehistory," said the Head of State, pushing the books away contemptuously. Marx-Engels: *Critique of the Gotha and Erfürt Programmes.* "This seems to savour of a pamphlet against the European nobility. Because Gotha, as you know, is a sort of annual telephone book of princes, dukes, counts, and marquises." Engels: *Ludwig Feuerbach and the End of Classical German Philosophy.* "I don't think that's likely to pervert our tram conductors." Marx: *Value, Price, and Profit.* And the President read aloud: "The determination of the values of commodities according to the relative amount of work incorporated in them is totally different from the tautological method of determining values of commodities by the value of the work and the wages." . . . "Do you understand any of it? Nor do I." . . . Marx. *Contribution to the Critique of Political Economy.* He skimmed through the book as far as the appendix, which provoked his hilarity: "With poems in English, poems in Latin, and poems in Greek. Let's see if they can indoctrinate the Mayorala Elmira with this." ("You always think I'm stupider than I really am," she said, piqued.) And he laughed again when he picked up another volume: "Ah! Here's the famous *Kapital* . . . Let's have a look:

"The first metamorphosis of one commodity, its trans-formation from a commodity into money, is therefore also invariably the second metamorphosis of some other com-modity, the retransformation of the latter from money into a commodity ... M–C, a purchase, is at the same time C–M, a sale; the concluding metamorphosis of one commodity is the first metamorphosis of another. With regard to our weaver, the life of his commodity ends with the Bible into which he has reconverted his two pounds. But suppose the seller of the Bible turns the two pounds set free by the weaver into brandy, M–C, the concluding phase of C–M–C (linen, money, Bi-ble) is also C–M, the first phase of C–M–C (Bible, money, brandy) ...

"The only thing I find comprehensible here is the brandy," said the Head of State, in high good humour.

"And what does this whacking great German tome cost?"

"Twenty-two pesos, Señor."

"Then let them sell it, let them sell it; let them go on selling it. There aren't twenty-two people in the whole country who would pay twenty-two pesos for a book as heavy as lead ... –M–C, M–C–M ... I never could get on with equations."

"But look at this, on the other hand," said Peralta, taking a thin pamphlet out of his pocket: *Breeding Rhode Island Red Poultry.*

"What's this got to do with the other?" asked the Presi-dent. "We've never been able to acclimatise American poultry here. Neither Nat Pinkertons, with feathers on their legs; nor Leghorns, though in the north they lay more eggs than there are days in the year; but here, I don't know why, they shut up their arses and only lay four a week; as for those plump Rhode Island Reds, as soon as they get here they're devoured by lice."

"Open this little book, President. And take a good look," Marx-Engels: *Manifesto of the Communist Party.*

"Ah, hell! this is quite another thing!"

And frowning suspiciously, he read aloud: "A spectre is haunting Europe—the spectre of communism. All the powers of old Europe have entered into a holy alliance to exorcise this spectre: the Pope, Tsar, Metternich and Guizot, French radicals and German police spies."

There was a silence. Then: "As usual: hieroglyphics or prehistory. The Holy Alliance (wasn't that after the fall of Napoleon?), the Pope who never bothered anyone, Metternich and Guizot (does anyone in this country remember that gentlemen called Metternich and Guizot ever existed?), the Tsar of Russia (which one? Even I can't tell). Prehistory, pure prehistory."

However, when, turning several pages together, he came to the last lines of the pamphlet disguised as a guide to poultry-keeping, he paused deep in thought at a sentence he found there: "In short, the Communists everywhere support every revolutionary movement against the existing social and political order of things."

There was an even longer pause. Then, at last: "The same anarchism as ever: bombs in Paris, bombs in Madrid; attempts to assassinate kings and queens; anarcho-syndicalism, communism, R.S.A., C–M–C, M–C–M, P.O.S.D.R., and Y.M.C.A. Alphabetic chaos, proliferation of initials, a sign of the decadence of the age. However, this business of breeding Rhode Island Reds. It's ingenious. Order everyone found carrying this avicultural literature to be picked up and imprisoned. And also ... But—what's going on?"

It was three o'clock in the afternoon. The clapper of the Cathedral bell began its solemn, measured strokes. And as if some gigantic hammer, progenitor of bell-children or children-bells, were striking the first bell created by some enormous liturgical bronze-worker, the sharp but never timid bells of the Hermitage of the Dove replied from up aloft on the snow-covered slopes of the Tutelary Volcano; then their voices were taken up by the soprano of San Vicente of Rio-Frio, the baritone of the Little Sisters of Tarbes, the coloratura of the carillon of the Jesuits, the contralto of San Dionisio, the basso profundo of San Juan de Letrán, the silvery music of the Divine Shepherdess, setting alight a festival of chimes and peals, of calling and ringing, rejoicing and gladness, while from their ropes were hanging, rising and sinking, striding, dancing in the air, bell ringers and acolytes, agile seminarists and dexterous capuchins, who kicked themselves off the ground and swung themselves aloft again in time to the tumult pouring from the great resonant shafts of the church towers. And the concert spread from north to south, and from east to west, involving the city in a prodigious polyphony of swinging, throbbing, and percussion, while factory sirens, motor horns, frying pans hit with spoons, saucepans, tins, everything that could make a noise, resounded, set up a deafening din, above narrow old alleys and wide new asphalt streets. Now railway engines whistled, fire-engine sirens wailed, trams set their copper bells quivering.

"The war is over!" cried the Foreign Secretary, entering without waiting to be announced, and seizing the bottle of Santa Inés, which the Head of State and his secretary had left on the book table, after uncorking it in complete confidence that they were unobserved. "The war is over. Civilisation has triumphed over Barbarism, Latinity over Germanism. A victory which is our victory too!"

"Then we're buggered," said the President softly. "Yes, now we're properly buggered."

Children, let out of class, ran shouting and singing out of school. The gay girls of the Calles de La Chayota, Economia, or San Isidro rushed into the street wearing Lorraine headdresses, or black Alsatian bows in their hair. "The war is over . . . the war is over."

Artisans, bricklayers, piano tuners, pawnbrokers, brakesmen, hawkers of mangoes and tamarinds, maize millers, athletes in picture shirts, ice-cream sellers, organ grinders with monkeys dressed as Italians, street cleaners, professors with starched shirt fronts, sugar refiners, naturists, Theosophists, spiritualists, laboratory workers, homosexuals with carnations in their mouths, students of folklore, bookish men, gamblers, men in cap and gown, all streamed past shouting as one man: "The war is over! The war is over!"

Newspaper boys appeared crying a special edition with 64-point type: "The war is over! The war is over!"

Students, knowing that the police would have the good sense to leave them alone at such a time of rejoicing, ran into the streets in a dense crowd, those from the University of San Lucas carrying a wooden platform on their shoulders, on which a mechanical mule wearing a pointed helmet and with a German flag on its back was kicked into space and beaten each time by a blow from the sword of a dummy in tricolor and gold, representing Marshal Joffre. And the procession following behind sang:

*The Kaiser cuts capers*
*And Joffre calls the tune.*

This animated allegory went around the town to Central Park more than once with their Joffre in red trousers. They stopped in front of the Presidential Palace. Then they followed the Boulevard of the Republic to the upper town, just as the priests of the Divine Shepherdess were bringing out another platform supporting the Virgin in a great glittering cloak, victoriously mounted on a green dragon twisted in its death agony—it had been taken from the altar of Saint George—from whose demonic head hung a cardboard notice bearing the word *WAR* written in thick indian ink letters. And this time women were singing the old village song:

*Santa Maria*
*Save us from evil*
*Protect us, Señora*
*From this terrible devil.*

Then the others returned through the Calle del Comercio with their mule and marshal moved by wires, playing on maracas and firing off rockets:

*The Kaiser cuts capers*
*And Joffre calls the tune.*

The retinue of the Divine Shepherdess entered the Calle de los Plateros and climbed the steps to the Boulevard Auguste Comte:

*To kill the Devil*
*The Virgin seized a blade*
*On all fours the monster*
*Lay down in the glade.*

"We're done for," said the Head of State, watching all this with a far from happy expression.

"But, President, it's the triumph of Reason, the triumph of Descartes."

"Look here, Peralta: this means that the bottom will at once fall out of our market for sugar, bananas, coffee, chewing gum and gutta-percha. The days of the Fat Kine are numbered. And people will say that my rule had nothing to do with the country's prosperity."

*The Kaiser cuts capers*
*And Joffre calls the tune.*

"Give orders for a grand official banquet to celebrate the victory of Sainte Geneviève over the Huns, of Joan of Arc over Clausewitz, of the Divine Shepherdess over International Communism. Now the storks can come back from Hansi to the roofs of Colmar, and Déroulède's glorious bugle will sound. Descartes won the war, but we must mop up the mess" ...

*Santa Maria*
*Save us from evil ... "All the same, there is a way of get-*
*ting a last cut from the conflict. Now, while people still*
*have cash, we'll open a large fund for the Reconstruction*
*of the Devastated Regions of France. Send Ofelia a cable.*
*Tell her to come as soon as possible. We can still make use*
*of her Red Cross nurse's outfit." Indifferent to what was*
*happening in the street, and out of sympathy with the*
*general pandemonium, but a prey to nostalgia and secret*
*anxiety, the Head of State wound up the long-horned*
*gramophone sleeping in a corner of his study and listened*
*to a record of Fortugé's:*

*Lorsque la nuit tombe sur Paris*
*La belle église de Notre-Dâââââme*
*Semble monter au Paradis*
*Pour lui conter son état d'âââme.*

# 13

THE CAMPAIGN TO COLLECT FUNDS FOR THE Reconstruction of Regions Devastated by the War was a magnificent success; besides procuring marginal benefits as plentiful as they were uncontrollable, it re-established the prestige of the country and its intelligent government in a Europe too absorbed in the problems of peace to remember small, local exotic events taking place in the now-blurred distance of a period before a certain historic August which had turned the world upside down.

In her Red Cross nurse's uniform, Ofelia travelled from city to city, from meeting to meeting, with an exhibition of prints, drawings, posters, and eloquent photographs showing scenes of destruction, dead villages, mine craters, severely damaged cathedrals, and crosses stretching to the horizon. "*We ask you for schools for the children of these men*" was inscribed on the desolate view of a military cemetery. "*Give me back my home*" was at the feet of a Christ pierced with bullets.

Meanwhile, this exaggerated stimulation of an already inflated prosperity swelled the tide of speculation and extravagance, nor did those whom fortune favoured pay any attention to the gloomy forecasts of some economists—puritan killjoys whose sibylline calculations were out of tune with the confident tones of those singing the praises of a myth that was renewed every day. For they were living in a fable. Without being aware of it, people were taking part in a huge conjuring

display, where all values were upset, ideas inverted, appearances changed, roads deviated, and disguise and metamorphosis created a perpetual state of illusion, transformations
and topsyturvydom, through the vertiginous effect of a currency that changed its appearance, weight, and value between
night and morning without ever leaving the purse—or rather,
the bank account—of its owner. Everything was upside down.
The poor lived in Foundation Palaces, dating from the days of
Orellana and Pizarro—but now given over to filth and rats—
while their masters inhabited houses belonging to no tradition, native, baroque, or Jesuitic, but theatrically got up in
Mediaeval, Renaissance, or Hollywood-Andalusian colour
schemes, and without the smallest connection with the country's history, or else in large buildings aping the Second Empire style of the Boulevard Haussman. The new Central Post
Office had a superb Big Ben. The new main Police Station
was a temple from Luxor in eau-de-nil. The country house
of the Chancellor of the Exchequer was a pretty miniature
Schönbrunn. The President of the Chamber kept his mistress in a little Abbaye de Cluny, swathed in imported ivy.
Fortunes were made and lost every night at Basque pelota
courts and English greyhound races. People dined at the Villa
d'Este or La Troika (a nightclub recently opened by the first
White Russians arrived here via Constantinople) while only
in Chinese eating houses could one eat the national dishes,
now scorned as something connected with rope soled shoes
and ballads sung by the blind—Cantonese kitchen boys thus
becoming conservers of the National Culinary Arts. The musical successes of the day were "Caravan," "Egyptland," "Japanese Sandman," "Chinatown, My Chinatown," and above all
"Hindustan," to be seen on the music stand of every piano,
bound in a cover showing an elephant and a mahout silhouetted in black against a crimson sun. Women who profiteered

from the boom didn't know where to go to show off their tiaras, pendants, and necklaces, and their dresses from Worth, Doucet, and Callot. And by the same token the Head of State remembered his long-cherished but now realisable desire to install an Opera House inside the Opera-City, the Capital of Fiction, and offer his compatriots a spectacle like those to be seen in Buenos Aires and Rio de Janeiro—towns that had always kept their eyes on the arts and refinements of the Old World. Adolfo Bracale was entrusted with the task of giving the National Theatre "the best staging in the world." Impresario of American touring companies, animated by such a passion for lyric drama that he had taken *Simon Boccanegra*, *Manon*, and *Lucia de Lammermoor* to the Chilean nitre works, banana growers' haciendas, southern ports, and rubber plantations in Manaus, crossing deserts, travelling up rivers, visiting the West Indian islands great and small with his cast, wardrobe, and scenery, he was a man capable of taking the baton if the principal conductor fell ill of malaria, or of putting on *Madame Butterfly* with an orchestra of a piano, seven violins, flute, saxophone, ophicleide, two cellos, and a double bass, if nothing better could be found.

So, one fine morning, the train from Puerto Araguato entered the capital's station bringing antique temples, alchemist's retorts, a Scottish cemetery, several Japanese houses, the Castle of Elsinore, the platform of Sant'Angelo, monasteries, grottoes, and dungeons, all folded or rolled in pieces to be put together with expanding forests and fabric cloisters, filling so many cases that two trains were hardly enough to take the lot. And finally, when evening came, a third convoy—that of the ultra-modern dining car with its menu in French—arrived at the Terminal Station, glittering with celebrities who stepped onto the platform among magnesium flashes and a profusion of flowers, complete with officials, applause according to their fame, and mandoline music by the Italian Colony. Chief among them was the great Enrico Caruso, wearing a double-breasted waistcoat, diamond tiepin, pale grey hat, and platinum cuff links. Amiable, verbose, and cheerful, but bewildered by so much solicitous flattery, he forgot where he was, greeted a lance-corporal as "General" and the Head Porter as "Excellency," ignored the real minister but embraced a melomaniac who looked like a minister, distributed autographs by the dozen, kissed children, and seemed happy in surroundings reminiscent of some small Neapolitan piazza on a day of revelry. The next to appear was Titta Ruffo, scowling dramatically, robust of figure, roaring like a lion, and dressed in a light Palm Beach suit; it seemed impossible that a man of such athletic stamp could come to terms with the tormented fragility of Hamlet as displayed on the hoardings, a part he was to play in a few days' time. Now Lucrecia Bori descended from the train, all teeth and coloratura, already assuming the role of Rosina in her Spanish hat and skirt; then Gabriella Bezanzoni, the contralto, with a knife in her garter, her expensive elegance contrasting cruelly with the feebleness of some pale North American ballerinas carrying their ballet shoes in oil-cloth bags, who got out of the presidential coach behind her. Riccardo Stracciari, wearing kid gloves and the frock coat of a close relative at an important funeral, replied to journalists' questions in an affected voice. The tall, thin Mansueto, looking like a shady schoolmaster, had thought it amusing to disembark with Don Basilio's shovel hat under his arm; and lastly came Nicoletti-Korman, whom we were to see bare-chested, Chaliapinesque and blaspheming in Boito's *Mefistofele*.

The tailors of the capital worked day and night, snipping for all they were worth at cloth for tailcoats and piqué waistcoats, while the dressmakers ran from fitting to fitting to put finishing touches or slight alterations to this and that, let out skirts, lower necklines, readjust some thin woman's dress to her taste, stretch seams for some fat woman, let out an expectant mother's waistband, modernise and adapt out-of-date fashions in line with the latest models. The chorus was organised from students and members of glee clubs; the best musicians in the country were united into an orchestra under the direction of an atrociously bad-tempered Bolognese who, without pausing in a passage he was conducting, would shout instructions like: "Sustain that note, you bastard," or "Crotchets, you brute" . . . "*Dolce ma non pederasta*" (this was for the prelude to *La Traviata*), "*Allegro con coglioni*" (this for the overture to *Carmen*), declaring all the time—and in this he imitated his maestro Toscanini—that it was better to live among pimps and prostitutes than with musicians, although as a matter of fact as soon as the rehearsal was over he wrapped his neck in towels and went with them to the Roma, a popular and lively bar, to drink several glasses of Santa Inés rum diluted with Fernet Branca.

While waiting for the season to begin, a party was given every night in honour of the singers from La Scala and the Metropolitan, who always declared that they "weren't in voice" before finally singing some romance from Piedigrotta's repertory or else Tosti's "Vorrei morire." And meanwhile, in spite of hammering, grumbling, oaths, accidents, damage to scenery, trapdoors that failed to work, lost spears, broken accessories, a distaff left behind in Italy, inadequate spotlights, vapours from the underworld that never emerged at the right time, an invasion of rats in the dressing rooms, dysentery, spring colics, the soprano's allergy to certain flowers, a quarrel between Mansueto and Nicoletti over a mulatto, contracts broken and signed again, the leader of the orchestra punching the second bassoon, an infinite number of complaints, several attacks of lost voice, two boils due to the climate, mosquitoes, stained costumes, tropical rains, one hernia, more losses of voice, bruises and swellings—such an impressive and memorable *Faust* was mounted that its marvellous qualities at once passed into the verses of Gaucho singers, to the amazement of those who hadn't heard it. Afterwards came a magnificent *Carmen* with Bezanzoni and Caruso, although in the smugglers' act, because the pistols had been lost on the journey, the chorus was armed with Winchester rifles, but this was noticed only by the cognoscenti. Then there was a *Barber of Seville* wherein Mansueto's Don Basilio was so truculent and comic that his performance excelled Titta Ruffo's Figaro in brilliance and conception. Maria Barrientos' *Traviata* reduced the audience to a frenzy of delight: the *brindisi* had to be sung three times, the applause being so great as to prevent carrying on with the score; the great scene between the elder Germont and Violetta produced discreet tears, and at the end so many flowers were thrown onto the stage that when the performers made their bow they trod on a carpet of roses, carnations, and tuberoses.

The season continued triumphantly with *La Favorita*, Flotow's *Marta* (one of Caruso's greatest successes), *Hamlet* by Ambroise Thomas, *Rigoletto*, and *La Sonnambula*. The Head of State was happy. The opera had transformed the capital. After performances the smart cafés were full of expensively dressed people, glittering with jewels, and stared at from the street by crowds who were amazed to see here, within reach, as it were, a luxurious world hitherto only imagined through the media of romantic novels, films in a millionaire's setting, or the covers of *Vanity Fair* in the magazine kiosks, and to find so many of our own women suddenly taking to fashion and finery in an ambience reminiscent of John Singer Sargent or Jean-Gabriel Domergue.

"We're winning, Peralta; we're winning them around,"
said the President, looking at the sumptuous auditorium,
where nothing was talked about in the intervals except rac-
conto, portamento, fiato, tessitura, and arioso.

All went well until the first night of *Tosca*, when something very unusual happened: at the end of the second act,
when Floria buried her knife in Scarpia's chest, a torrent of
applause exploded from the upper seats and persisted for so
long that the orchestra had to stop playing. As nothing had
been sung at this moment of the action to justify such enthusiasm, Maria Jeritza didn't know what to do—she was making
her début that night—except move the candlesticks to right
and left of the corpse of a Titta Ruffo who was as stupefied
as she was. Finally a shout from above of: "Death to the *sbir-
ros*! Down with Valverde!" gave a meaning to this thunderous
applause and caused Tosca to leave the stage, the curtain to
descend rapidly, and the orchestra to remain dumb with bewilderment, while the police broke in among the gods and arrested everyone who hadn't time to escape down the staircase.
Next day Giordano's *Andrea Chénier* was given in a theatre
surrounded by troops and under military occupation by officers in full dress uniform, strategically placed in stalls and
galleries. Even so, during the Revolutionary Tribunal a cry of
"Viva Robespierre!" went up from some situation unknown.

From now on every opera was the occasion for ovations,
murmurs, hissing, and exclamations that had nothing to
do with the quality of the music or aptness of the interpretation. Outlaws, regicides, rebel troubadors, and Hernanis
were always applauded; informers, governors, Uskoks, stool
pigeons, and Spolettas were hissed. The Head of State thought
it advisable to cancel Giordano's *Siberia*, and now awaited
with irritation and impatience the performance of *Aida* that
was to close the season. For this, unheard-of scenic effects

were projected. The New York firm of Leady had provided the straight trumpets for the triumphal march. Camels and elephants from a recently arrived circus would figure in the procession, followed by fifty horsemen from the third battalion of Hussars, dressed as Egyptians and carefully made up, unless their natural complexions gave them a sufficiently Nubian or Ethiopian appearance. And no performance ever began so brilliantly as to scenery, production, the action of the chorus, and the skill of the orchestra, which had enormously improved during the last few weeks under the direction of an energetic and confident conductor. The clothes and décor were praised; "Ritorna vincitor" was encored as expected, and the second act opened in an atmosphere of tension, anticipation of pleasure, and general appreciation of scenery, singers, and production as the action approached the concerted paroxysm of the return of Radames. The famous theme of the march was hummed by the entire audience. And the great final scene arrived, with two hundred persons assembled between columns and palm trees, Horus and Anubis and the Nile as background—a Nile picked out with electric lights—when suddenly there was a terrific explosion in the orchestra pit under the footlights, sending cymbals, violin cases, tympani and kettle drums flying in a sudden cloud of white smoke. A second bomb exploded beneath the double basses, causing the musicians to clamber onto the stage and try to escape through the pit and boxes, increasing the panic in the audience, who rushed helter-skelter towards the exits, jumping over stalls, pushing, screaming, trampling on anyone who fell down in the mad rush, while the flies collapsed on the heads of Pharaoh's guards, priests, archers, captives in chains, and soldiers of the third battalion of Hussars as they ran, fought, and struggled to get to the doors into the street, among fallen obelisks, sphinxes, and broken scenery.

"The Hymn! The Hymn!" yelled the Head of State to the Bolognese conductor, who had remained on the rostrum, pale and vociferating as he tried to control his disbanded orchestra. But as only seven or eight musicians were left, the only response to his cries of "The Hymn! Quick! The Hymn!" came from an almost inaudible wail of four violins, a clarinet, oboe, and cello.

While the public gathered in the square outside, trying to pluck up their courage, and those who had been bruised or kicked (none were really wounded) were carried from the theatre in the arms of the police, the Head of State found out that the explosions had come not from bombs but large petards emitting noise and smoke.

"The performance must go on," he said to Adolfo Bracale, who had bravely accompanied him on this tour of inspection, followed by the electricians. But it was impossible; the theatre was full of the smell of gunpowder, the scenery was ruined, the parchment of the drums had burst, the double basses were in splinters, the curtain wouldn't come down, several members of the chorus had been hurt in the rush, the horses of the triumphal procession were kicking and biting, and Amonasro had lost his voice. The victim of a nervous crisis, Amneris had shut herself in her dressing room and was shouting that this was what came of singing in a country of savages. As for Caruso-Radames, he had disappeared. As someone remembered having seen him go out at a back door, they hunted for him in vain in bars and cafés near the building. Nor had he returned to his hotel. He might have been hurt, hit, or perhaps he was lying in a faint in some dark corner. The impresario was anxiously looking for him when a short circuit left the theatre without lights.

The Head of State returned to the palace, followed by his ministers and generals. His silence at such a time expressed a rage that went far beyond mere rage. An inner rage, shut in upon itself, a violent nervous crisis expressed in a terrible fixed stare, unaware of the faces confronting him, an apocalyptic stare apparently directed at distant visions in which tempests, screams, and retribution figured. He was in this state of intolerable tension when the telephone rang in the Council Chamber. His Excellency the Italian Minister was calling. He informed them that Enrico Caruso had been arrested in the street by a policeman for wearing fancy dress when it was not carnival time, and women's clothes moreover, and with ochre-coloured make-up and painted eyes and mouth—such were the details of the accusation; this made him subject to the Law of Repression of Scandalous Behaviour and Defence of Civic Morality, whose Article 132 anticipated thirty days' imprisonment for an attempt on decent living, and unbecoming behaviour in public, with increased punishment if it were accompanied by manifest evidence of homosexuality in personal attire and appearance, which in the present case was plainly shown by a coiffure of horizontal strands brought down over the forehead, ornamental rings in the ears, fancy bracelets, and around the neck several chains adorned with scarabs, amulets, charms, and stones of colours that—according to the police report—were a sure indication of being "queer."

"This to happen, in a civilised country!" cried the Head of State, passing from his dramatically silent rage to verbal explosion, at the same time throwing books, paperweights, and inkpots onto the carpet. But he did what was necessary. And it was Doctor Peralta who rescued Enrico Caruso from confinement; the singer arrived, much amused and still dressed as Radames, saying that it was nothing, and that he and his ambassador wished to recommend the policeman who had arrested him—"a good chap, splendid fellow, only doing his

duty"—to the President's indulgence ("he was merely carrying out the law, he had never seen an ancient Egyptian in
the streets of the capital"), and everything came to an end in
the light of dawn with drinks and Havana cigars—long, thick
cigars such as the singer liked best, whose trademark was the
blond, blue-eyed head of Fonseca.

The Tutelary Volcano emerged from its cold mists, the
Mayorala Elmira brought sandwiches and fruit juice, and before he left, Adolfo Bracale announced that the opera season
would definitely close with Verdi's *Un ballo in maschera* that
night—*Aida* was out of the question after the disaster.

"A masked ball is what I shall give those brutes who go
planting petards," said the Head of State to Doctor Peralta
before going to bed.

And now there began to arise above the city a round
building—round as a bullring, round as the Coliseum in
Rome, round as a circus for contortionists and lion tamers:
it was the Model Prison, based on the most modern ideas
of penitentiary construction invented by North American
architects, who were masters of that art. Accustomed to the
slow progress of stone buildings—the sawing-up of stone
provided a lesson in stereotomy, demonstrating theorems
with hammer and chisel—and the very long time needed to
produce their main bulk and details, the Head of State had
now discovered the magic of building in concrete. Gravel
and sand rotated in enormous grey iron cocktail shakers,
plates of cement miraculously hardened and tightened over
a metal skeleton; the city witnessed the marvel of a building
that started by being liquid, a soup full of gravel and pebbles,
before it rose with astonishing verticality, placing walls on
walls, floors on floors, cornices on cornices, until—in a matter of days—it reached the sky with a flagstaff or a gilt statue
with winged ankles. And since the Head of State had fallen in

love with the speed of concrete, with the fidelity of concrete
and the docility of concrete, he had entrusted concrete with
the task of closing the gigantic circle of the Model Prison (on
the Hill of La Cruz above the cupola of the Capitol, above the
spire of the Sacred Heart) before he started a political operation on a large scale. Day and night, by the light of reflectors
when darkness or fog made them necessary, work continued on this exemplary building, whose concentric walls had
the euclidean beauty of a series of orbits whose radii grew
progressively smaller, enclosing one another, until reaching
the axis of a central patio, whence watch could be kept on
all the cells and corridors. When the work was finished and
nothing was left to do but bring the aluminium bathtubs, and
armchairs with buckles and straps destined for some of the
underground rooms (these figured on the plans as "technical
annexes"), photographs of this beautiful building were sent
to several international reviews of architecture, and it was
much praised for its functional qualities as well as for solving
the difficulty of harmonizing something necessarily grim in
appearance with the beauty of the surrounding landscape.
Here could be seen an evident and perhaps unique attempt
to humanise—the aim of architecture being to help man to
live—the conceptual and organic vision of a penitentiary establishment, thus making it tolerable to the delinquent, who
after all (as modern psychologists had shown) was a sick man,
an antisocial being, usually the product of his environment
and victim of heredity, whose behaviour had been distorted
by certain things that were just beginning to be called "com-
plexes," "inhibitions," etc., etc. The days of Venetian prisons
and the dungeons of the Inquisition were over, or of the fortresses of Ceuta or Cádiz—so similar to those of La Guayra,
Havana, or San Juan de Ulúa—or of the penitentiaries named
in the classic songs of Bruant. In the matter of imprisonment

we had outdistanced Europe—a logical state of things, since as members of the Continent-of-the-Future we must make a start somewhere.

But while the finishing touches were being put to the Model Prison, the country was falling sick of a crisis; most disappointingly threatening to the fertility of an exceptionally rich if virgin soil, giving fabulous promise of productivity under cultivation, age-old humus, a boundless supply of wood (forests covering an area as large as the whole of Belgium), and rich underground seams of invaluable minerals. We had them all: space, land, fruit, nickel, iron. We were a privileged country in the World of the Future. Such was the report of the Ministry of Agriculture and Public Works. To realise the splendour of our earthly benefits we had only to follow the convincing picture given by statistics, organograms, columns of figures, weekly balance sheets, expert comments, futurological equations enhanced by the eloquent presence of a well-placed letter from the Greek alphabet. But though these memoranda and bound reports were brought to him every day after the unfortunate opera season was over, and considered retrospectively in financial terms, the Head of State realised that, as a background to these orchestral preludes and tenor cadenzas, the sugar supply of the republic had suffered an alarming drop compared with rubber and slate in world markets. Our sugar was fetching 23 centavos a pound when Nicoletti-Korman, a magnificent devil, was sending up prayers to the Golden Calf. With the North American anthem in the first act of *Madame Butterfly*, it fell to 17.20. It was quoted at 11.35 during *Thaïs*—"*Alexandria, terrible cité*," sang Titta Ruffo. On the disastrous day of *Rigoletto*—and hunchbacks are supposed to bring good luck—it fell to 8.40. The cheating at cards in the fourth act of *Manon* hastened the collapse, which with the catastrophe of *Aida* left us at 5.22.

And when carnival time came, sugar—by far the most important substance in the whole of agricultural Latin America—
had slumped, with warehouses full of unsold sacks, to 2.15
a pound.

And suddenly one morning, as if nothing had happened,
the recently founded Banco International announced that it
was suspending payments until further notice. The Banco Español, the Banco Miranon, the Banco Comercial y Agricola,
and the Banco de la Construccion shut down their guichets
with a sharp click, while the Banco Nacional and the Clearing
House filled the newspapers with communiqués and information, promises, calls for confidence and calm, in order to
stem a panic that had started from small savings books registering minimal family accounts and ascended to the realms
of high finance. The situation was described as "accidental
and temporary" in the newspapers, and a cabinet meeting
was called to consider it. The government asked for calm,
confidence, and patriotism. No queuing or disturbances.
A moratorium—a word unknown to the public, but whose
sound had for some of them a disagreeable relationship with
death and wills—was proposed as a certain means of straightening out the confusion in a few weeks; this brought relief
to the minds of many, and as it was carnival time, the Festival of Masks opened in a clamour of processions, Chinese
trumpeters, and negro drummers, with fancy-dress parades
including cars decked with much ingenuity, such as the "Venetian Bucentaur," which won a special prize although it had
been tremendously difficult to get it as far as the judges' dais,
since its prow crowded with female doges dressed in sequins
was too high to get under the telephone wires. All this revelry had come at a fortunate time, because it had always been
important to the life of the country, and people forgot their
troubles and dangers when absorbed in this multitudinous

catharsis. At this time funerals were without mourners, telephones without operators, bakers had no flour, and babies at
the breast no milk. People were dancing, singing, joining processions, abandoning themselves without regard to discipline
or timetables, commitments or promises, to satisfying the
desires they had accumulated during months of repression.
A lot of women were naked under their dominoes. Everyone
did as they liked under the protection of hood, veil, or tawdry
mask. People sang and danced in the parks, on terraces roofed
with vines; cafés were taken by storm. They fornicated on the
upper floors of the National Observatory, under the arches of
bridges, in halls decorated with holy images and in suburban
shrubberies, and even installed themselves in church porches
to drink sugar-cane spirit, tequila, and aguardiente. These
were days when dusk merged into dawn and dawn into dusk,
when the traditional fraternities used heron feathers and
raffia to polish up their magic chains, diabolical costumes,
cardboard sharks, serpents worked by a spring, hawk-men,
carnival dragons, grotesques, old figures inherited from Africa or from rituals whose original purpose was lost in ab-
original darkness. What with dancing and paper streamers,
competitions, beauty queens, gilt cardboard crowns, giants
and monstrous heads, turbans and stilts, a long week went
by in pleasure, swaggering, musical rhythms, drunkenness,
and hangovers. But suddenly, in the middle of this tumultu-
ous jollity, one or two harlequins with their faces covered in
black stockings fired at the police; one or two gypsies from
the cast of *Carmen*, who had failed to return the Winchesters
borrowed from the smugglers' scene, seized the rifles and re-
volvers from the Santa Barbara barracks and loaded them
into Red Cross ambulances; members of the Pompadour processions, dressed in salmon pink, with their wigs pulled down
over their eyes, threw a bomb into the police station of the

Fifth District, setting free more than forty political prisoners. In the police station of the Second District, some of our Indians, apparently high on mescal but disguised as Red Indians from North America in imitation of Vitagraph films they had seen, cleared a secret arsenal of its hand grenades and then disappeared among the crowd; three anarchist leaders were rescued from their cells by false agents from the Secret Services; a snowstorm of proclamations and manifestos fell from the spire of the Sacred Heart and the cupola of the Capitol, calling for a revolutionary rising. But now, to the report of rockets and firecrackers from the familiar troupes of clowns, reports with a sharper repercussion were added. The harmless bottles of ethyl chloride intended to be pushed down the front of women's dresses were replaced by tear-gas bombs, an amazing invention being used for the first time by the police; the cavalry charged at random against strolling players and allegorical groups; the screeching of carnival whistles and cardboard trumpets was transformed into the cries of the trampled and wounded, and fancy dress gave way in panic to military uniforms. A whole rainbow of different colours became neutralised into the twofold range of indigo and buff. A violent presidential decree suspended the carnival there and then, and the Model Prison quickly filled with masks. There were the yells and gasps of the dying, tightening of garrottes, dentists' drills boring into sound teeth, beating with sticks and whips, kicking in the balls, men hung up by their heels and wrists or revolving on cartwheels for days on end, naked women pursued through the corridors, thrown to the ground with legs apart and violated, their breasts burned, their flesh penetrated with red-hot irons. There were fictitious shootings and real shootings; blood and lead from Mausers spattered the newly built walls, still smelling of mortar; and there were defenestrations, strappados, piercing with nails, and people herded to the great Olympic Stadium, where there was more room to machine-gun a crowd together—thus avoiding the loss of time involved in forming shooting parties; and there were those who were shut in great rectangular boxes filled with cement and the blocks so formed were lined up against one wall of the prison, in such numbers that the neighbours thought they must contain stones for enlarging the building ... (And many years passed before it was discovered that each of these blocks contained a body in fancy dress and mask, moulded by the hard material surrounding it—a perfect record of a human anatomy within a solid substance.)

# FIVE

*. . . I am, I exist, that is certain. But . . . for how long?*
—DESCARTES

# 14

AY . . . BEE . . . CEE . . . DEE . . . AY . . . THE ALPHABET resounded strangely, very strangely, in the classrooms of the North American Methodist Colleges and Augustinian Lycées now open in our principal cities, arousing serious doubts concerning the efficiency and modernity—especially the modernity—of the teaching given to children by the Salesian fathers and French Marists, the Dominican and Ursuline nuns, or the Little Sisters of Tarbes. Now one could hear: "This is a pencil, this is a dog, this is a girl," where formerly the classical declensions of *Rosa, Rosae, Rosa, Rosam* had flourished, obliterating the memory of the inevitable jokes at Aunt Jemima's expense, a short while earlier, when they had moved on to adjectives of the first category with *Nigra, Nigrae, Nigra, Nigram*. The Cid, Roland, Saint Louis, the Catholic Queen, and Henry IV emigrated from the history books along with sword, horn, centenarian oak, pawned jewels, chicken stew, and all the rest, to be advantageously replaced by Benjamin Franklin, with his lightning conductor and *Poor Richard's Almanac*; Washington at Mount Vernon, surrounded by good negroes whom he treated like members of his family; Jefferson and Independence Hall in Philadelphia; Lincoln's Gettysburg Address; the migration to the west and the dramatic death of General Custer in the Battle of the Little Bighorn against the barbarian hordes of Sitting Bull. As soon as they were weaned by their Indian wet nurses who sang them nursery rhymes and taught them, like Pythagoras, that it was bad to poke the fire with a knife, children were guided to where the little Mozart lay in the Pantheon of Infant Prodigies, next to Daniel Webster because of his early battle against a malignant growth—which, as it was God's creation, had a right to life just as the slaves in *Uncle Tom's Cabin* had a right to life. Rapidly moving on from *L'Illustration*, *Lectures pour tous*, *Collier's*, and *The Saturday Evening Post*—with attractive covers by Norman Korwin—they began to tell the truth (bitter truths, maybe, but now it was possible to speak plainly, and history was history) about the recent war.

Without "Over There" and General Pershing, France would have been lost. Britain had fought half-heartedly, without conviction: the "Tommies" belonged to folklore, Marble Arch, and tea served in the trenches to turbaned sepoys and Scots with bagpipes. Italy was a country of bad soldiers with cock feathers in their hats, and only one battle: Caporetto. As for Russia: the monk Rasputin, the Tsarevich, haemophilia, Madame Virúbova, mystical orgies, inspired idiots, *Resurrection*, Yasnaya Polyana, and the unstable, tortured Slav soul, always oscillating between the angelic and infernal abysses, had collectively borne fruit in a deluded reformer—a man of the Kremlin like Ivan the Terrible—the ephemeral Marxist Paraclete, whose days were already counted, weighed, divided by the onslaught of the forces of Denikin, Wrangel, Kolchak, and the Franco-British armies of the Baltic, who would quickly achieve the ruin of a system already doomed to disaster. For (as the Evangelists said in a verse of the Bible as emphatic as it is difficult to find amongst so many pages printed in two columns on India paper) there would always be both rich and poor in the world—and as for the camel and the eye of the needle, we know that a rather low and narrow Door of the Needle existed in Jerusalem, through which intelligent camels could always pass if they bent their knees a little. It had been proved that Europeans were incapable of living in peace, and President Wilson had been obliged to cross the Atlantic to put some order into their affairs. But this would be the last time. We would never again trouble to devote our youthful energies to defend a culture whose axis of gravitation—as it was time to say openly—had been displaced in the direction of America, North America, of course, while awaiting the time when we of the south finally succeeded in freeing ourselves from the evil traditions that kept us living in the past. The world had entered the technical age, and Spain had bequeathed us a language incapable of developing a technical vocabulary. The future belonged to Inventors, not Humanists. And Spaniards had not invented a thing for centuries. The internal combustion engine, the telephone, electric light, the phonograph, on the other hand . . .

If, by some whim of the All-Powerful, Columbus' caravels had crossed with the *Mayflower* and stopped at the island of Manhattan, while the English Puritans had hit on Paraguay, New York would today be rather like Illescas or Castilleja de la Cuesta, whereas Asunción would astonish the whole world with its skyscrapers, Times Square, Brooklyn Bridge, and all the rest of it. Europe was the world of the past. A good world in which to float in a gondola, dream among Roman remains, look at stained-glass windows, visit museums, and spend pleasant, instructive holidays but a world whose decadence was being speeded up by an increasing amorality manifest in everything to do with sex, with women who were ready to go to bed with anyone, with those "horrid French customs" brought back by young North American soldiers and sometimes alluded to in a hushed and shocked voice (though the mother of a family ought to know everything) by the chaste "Daughters of the Revolution." The triumph of

Latinity—as Latin American papers persisted in calling the European war—had had the most disastrous consequences for Latinity in our countries, by renewing the Quarrel of the Investitures,* and by the multiple influences of the north. Bookshops formerly selling the works of Anatole France and Romain Rolland—nor must the legendary success of Barbusse's *Le Feu* be forgotten—now displayed *The Prisoner of Zenda, Scaramouche, Ben-Hur, Monsieur Beaucaire,* and the novels of Elinor Glyn, in gaudy coloured wrappers suggesting that they would appeal to readers who wanted to keep up to date with the latest literary movements. And in contrast to a feeble European cinema without any outstanding stars—they all seemed to have fallen in battle—the magnificent artistry of the miracle-working David Griffith, mover of multitudes and explorer of Time, was showing us images such as we had never before seen (much more impressive than any erudite evocation), interpreting the Birth of a Nation, the Tragedy of Golgotha, the Massacre of Saint Bartholomew, and even the world of Babylon—although Doctor Peralta, who was an addict of Mallet's handbooks and Reinach's *Apollo*, declared that the enormous Elephant Gods appearing in Griffith's Babylon had never been seen there, and irreverently described them as the "visions of a gringo with a hangover."

Aware that she was losing ground in these spheres, France arranged to send us a short official tour—a three-day convention, while the Head of State was resting at Bellamar from the disappointments of his operatic venture—including Sarah Bernhardt, plastered with powder and paint, gravitating on the axis of her one leg, bewigged like one of Toulouse-Lautrec's clowns, but still sustained by her desperate

---

* Between the popes and the emperors (1074–1122), and ending in the separation of spiritual and temporal powers.

determination to rise superior to her own decline, and declaiming the most pathetic alexandrines from *Phèdre*, or the
dying tirades of an almost octogenarian Aiglon, in a quaver-
ing voice of approaching doom—while having to be carried
in someone's arms, lean on the furniture, sit on a throne, lie
prostrate, or be conveyed in King Titurel's litter. Next, to be
greeted by the cheerful indifference of a public enthralled by
dazzling young actresses from Hollywood, Italy sent us El-
eanora Duse, fantastically attired in a braided and frogged
hussar's jacket and high black hat as one of Heine's grena-
diers, bringing with her the ruins and broken columns of *La
Città Morta* by D'Annunzio, an author the young had suddenly tired of, after years of enthusiasm for *La figlia di Iorio*.
All this belonged to the past, and as things of the past do, it
seemed to them to smell of funereal flowers. Perhaps this was
why there was an increase in the sales of North American reviews, or periodicals like *The New York Times*, whose Sunday
magazine provided information about new music, extraordinary painting, and eccentric literary movements going on
in Paris (despite what was said, they seemed to be having a
minor renaissance there). *L'Illustration* and *Lectures pour tous*
ignored these developments, or if they alluded to them at all
it was only to trounce them in the name of "order, proportion,
and moderation," so that to find out about these surprising
innovations—the poetry of someone called Apollinaire, for
instance, who died on the very day of the Armistice   people
had to go to New York publications.

"Young people always like newfangled things," said the
Head of State. But he didn't know that these verses without
rhyme or punctuation, these sonatas full of dissonances,
amounted, interestingly enough, to formidable criticisms
of our country. One morning, the news spread quickly that
the *New York Times* expert on Latin American affairs had

published a long editorial, ruthlessly analysing our financial ruin, alluding to repression by the police and torture, going into the mystery of some disappearances, denouncing assassinations that no one here knew about, and reminding its readers that the Head of State—who was put in the same category as Rosas, Doctor Francia (permanent Dictator of Paraguay), Porfirio Díaz, Estrada Cabrera of Guatemala, and Juan Vicente Gómez of Venezuela, not to mention all the Louis of France and Catherines of Russia—had been nearly twenty years in power.

Orders were given for the issue to be instantly suppressed—there were no copies left on kiosks and bookstalls, except three found by Doctor Peralta on a vegetable stall, whose owner regularly bought this paper to wrap up his cabbages, greens, and yams in its 120 pages.

"We ought to ban the paper from coming into the country," said the secretary, noticing the anger on the Head of State's face as he read it.

"A Yankee paper. A major scandal. They'll soon be dumping the whole of Randolph Hearst's chain on us." There was a pause. "Besides, the printed word slips in everywhere. You can put a political enemy in prison. But you can't stop the circulation of a foreign paper even if it tells lies about your mother. One copy is enough. It arrives by air, is hidden in travellers' briefcases, diplomatic bags or ladies' petticoats, and passes from hand to hand, across frontiers, rivers, and mountain ranges." There was another silence, rather longer than the last. "It was a bad day when I signed the order for English to be taught in schools. Now everyone here can say 'Son of a bitch.'" There was a third silence, even longer than the second, broken by Peralta, who had just re-read the editorial:

"It alludes here to Article 39 of the 1910 Constitution." And, quoting by heart, as if it were part of a betrothal ceremony: "*Presidential elections will take place not less than three months before the current six-year period has expired.*" There was a fourth silence, longer than the third.

"But who the hell told them that we had elections of any description here?" burst out the Head of State suddenly.

"Yes, but the 1910 Constitution says ..."

"It says what you've said, but it also says that those elections aren't held if the nation happens to be in a state of armed conflict or war declared against a foreign power."

"Exactly. But who are we fighting, except those shits in the interior?"

The Head of State looked at his secretary with an expression of sly solemnity. "We're still at war with Hungary."

"So we are!"

"I've not signed a peace treaty with Hungary, nor do I intend to at present, because it's in utter chaos. The Ambassador hasn't received his salary for months and has had to pawn his wife's jewels. If his country goes on like that we shall soon see him playing the violin in some gypsy cabaret. It's bloody well all up with them! But we're at war with Hungary. And when there's a war there are no elections. To hold elections now would be to violate the Constitution. Quite simply."

"Ah, my President! There's nobody like you!" said Doctor Peralta, bringing up the Hermès case to celebrate this unforeseen prolongation of the world war. This business about war with Hungary smacked of a marvellous cocktail of cumbias and czardas, bambas and friskas, creole serenades and Liszt Rhapsodies, all dominated by the oneiric voice of the soprano who inhabited the looking-glass of Jules Verne's *Castle of the Carpathians*—just as the Mayorala Elmira was now inhabiting the mirrors of this audience chamber, busily looking for wine glasses.

*The New York Times* published three more articles on the

country's economic and political situation, and these were widely circulated in spite of Peralta's vigilance in buying up all copies of the paper as soon as they arrived at the bookshops, including the American Book Shops. But the fact was that an office as clandestine as it was active—and obviously run by supporters of Doctor Leoncio Martinez—secretly translated the articles, had hundreds of copies made by a machine, and distributed them by post in envelopes of various sizes, very often fraudulently stamped with the trademarks and patent names of well-known industrial and commercial businesses, so that they were circulated like innocent advertisements. Meanwhile our own press, although censored and prevented from broaching the numerous subjects it was thought desirable to suppress, devoted itself with increasing skill— inspired by old supplements of *Le Petit Journal* and New York tabloids—to exploiting the sensationalism of any horrific incidents or unusual developments. Suddenly the Crime of the Calle Hermosilla or the Trial of the Parricide Sisters filled whole pages with headlines stretching across six columns and lasted for several weeks. And they were a blood-curdling and monstrous procession, making magnificent use of adjectives, subtle euphemisms for the scabrous, sly metaphors for the sexual, osteological nomenclature, terms from legal anthropometry, the language of necrophily and the dissecting room. There was the case of "The Man Buried Alive at Bayarta," "The Child Born with the Head of a Cavy," "A Troglodyte Village in the Middle of the Twentieth Century," "A Doctor's Honour Cleared," "The Sextuplets of Puerto Negro," "He Killed His Mother Without Cause," "Sadism in Seaport Taverns Must Be Suppressed," "Savage Shooting Affray at Birthday Party," "Old Man Devoured by Ants," "Den of Sodomy Discovered," "Recrudescence of White Slavery," "Woman Quartered at Crossroads"—all this sort of stuff being mixed with matters of permanent interest, historical or human content, such as the Queen's Necklace, the death of the Prince Imperial at the hands of Zulus, the drowned continent of Atlantis, the story of Abelard and Héloïse, subjected to necessary euphemisms when it came to the action of Canon Fulbert, whom certain blackguards identified—so eager were they not to miss a trick—with the Chief of the Judicial Police.

In the midst of homicides, crimes of passion, and unheard-of events, the season of the Nativity came around, and in a strange guise, for it was the first time that it was transformed into Christmas. Charming family traditions were quickly forgotten: no cribs were constructed by sticking together pieces of paper, with manger, Virgin, Saint Joseph, ass, ox, and shepherds—more numerous if the house was a richer one—who came to adore the chubby, angelic Child, lying on a bed of guava leaves, which were changed every day to give more fragrance to the scene. Families no longer worked hard at re-painting and varnishing the figures of saints from last year, glueing together those that were broken, and fixing the Angel of the Annunciation to his gold wire under the silver star on the ceiling. Strange things happened this year: a forest like that which advanced on Dunsinane marched up to the capital from the Atlantic ports: they were thousands of fir trees from Canada and the United States, bringing their exotic aroma to the rich quarters of the city, where they were set up and festively decorated with glass balls, garlands of gold tinsel, small twisted candles, and paper bells covered with cotton-wool snow. Peculiar deer with branched horns appeared, never seen before in the country and known as "reindeer," pulling sledges laden with parcels. And at the doors of toyshops stood bearded old men dressed in red, called Santa Claus—or *Santicloses* by the populace. The traditional Nativity of yesteryear, of all time, was supplanted in a single day by

the Nordic Christmas. This year no parties of revellers singing carols to tambourines went out into the street and called
on the neighbours with their normal "Rat-a-plan ... Who is
it? ... Men of peace," their singers reeling through the streets
from all the aguardiente, etc., they had been given as a reward for the happy news that the Messiah had become flesh
once again, and was alive among us. These old-fashioned
songs were supplanted in respectable houses by music boxes
playing such tunes as "Silent Night" or "Twinkle, Twinkle,
Little Star."

Alarmed by this sudden transformation of Christmas,
priests (in their Midnight Mass sermons to which few listened) denounced Santa Claus as a heretic invention, an introduction of Saxon customs, which, like decorating a fir tree,
could only represent a revival of German paganism—dating
from a period when (while we were listening to the divine
voices of Ambrosian plainsong and witnessing the splendid
ritual of the Sacrament) they were still hairy savages living in
forests, just as Julius Caesar had found them, wearing rough,
horned helmets, drinking mead, and worshipping the Holly
and the Mistletoe. Besides, no lives of the saints referred to
this "Santicló" who brought toys to children *three days before*
the Three Magi had done the same thing—as had always happened here. Spanish shopkeepers, whose dolls in Toledan,
Valencian, and Galician dress, little kitchens with earthenware cooking pots, and rocking horses had still not been unloaded in Puerto Araguato, protested against the unpatriotic
competition, which had filled their windows ever since December 20 with mechanical objects, Red Indian feather head
dresses, ouija boards to play at spiritualism—I ask you!—and
cowboy outfits—Texan hat, sheriff's star, studded belt, and
two pistols in a fringed case.

Some said that Santicló was really Saint Nicholas. But

people who understood hagiography declared that neither Saint Nicholas of Mira, patron saint of Russia, nor Saint Nicholas the Great, the first pope of that name, had had anything to do with selling toys. And someone finally asked ironically, in an article overlooked by the censor, if this Santicló in his species of Phrygian cap, dressed all in red, in spite of the white trimmings, might not be a *Red* in the most dangerous sense of the word. However, the journalist and his attempt at a joke came to a bad end, because when Holy Week came around he was still shut up with pimps and sodomites in Gallery 13 of the Model Prison. And if this last Christmas had been strange, Holy Week was stranger still, because instead of evoking the Story of the Cross, the length and breadth of the country witnessed the Story of the Strike.

It all began on Ash Wednesday, in the quietest way imaginable, when some hands in the American Refinery unexpectedly stopped work and refused to accept vouchers exchangeable for goods instead of wages. The movement quickly spread to all sugar mills. The rural police, the mounted police, and the provincial garrisons were all mobilised; but there was nothing they could do against men who were not demonstrating nor rioting, who were not creating a public disturbance, but who remained quietly in the doorways of their houses, refusing to work, singing to the accompaniment of lutes or guitars:

*I'm not cutting cane,*
*The wind can lay it low,*
*Or else the women*
*As they go to and fro.*

That strike was defeated. But on Easter Saturday the miners of Nueva Córdoba began one of their own, as a protest against arbitrary dismissal, and this was promptly followed by that of the stevedores of Puerto Araguato and the dockers of Puerto Negro.

Like the rashes of those tropical diseases that break out unexpectedly and redden first one shoulder before moving on to the right thigh and the left hip, the evening before they reach the chest, by way of those parts of the human body where the Cabbalists located the centres of Splendour, Triumph, Love, Justice, and Stability, the red eruptions suddenly appeared without warning on the map of the republic, here, there, in the north, in the south, where the fruit of the cacao was ripening, mounds of coal were steaming, bananas were growing, tobacco plants were coming into leaf, or rocks were waiting to be blown up with dynamite. Nothing could halt the epidemic; threats and edicts from the authorities, proclamations, troops with machetes or bayonets; people had become aware of the tremendous strength of inertia, folded arms and silent resistance, and when they were herded to their farms and factories with kicks, they went determined to do their work badly, to produce very little, using every trick like causing a mechanical fault, paralysing the cranes, or filing through the links in chains, when they didn't throw handfuls of sand into the axle of the principal wheel in the conduit of a pump. It was said that the Student—that same "student" who was beginning to be someone to reckon with, incessantly active though invisible, on the move and ubiquitous, working underground but manifestly, travelling from the plains to the mountains, from the fishing ports to the sawmills of the Torrid Zone—was the instigator and originator of the whole business. And it was obvious now that he wasn't alone in these multiple, combined activities; there were many, many more who adopted his tactics and ingenuity and used the same system.

"They work in *cells*," said Doctor Peralta, trying to

explain everything by a term the Head of State didn't fully understand.

"As for cells, there's the Model Prison," he replied. "And there aren't enough to take so many." (He tried to laugh.) "I've become the foremost hotelkeeper in the republic." And he impatiently turned the pages of *Anti-Dühring* and the *Critique of the Gotha and Erfürt Programmes*, which were still lying on the table. "There's nothing here about cells. Nor in the *Manifesto*. The only clear statement is this on the last page but one: '*The Communists everywhere support every revolutionary movement against the existing social and political order.*' "

At about this time Doctor Peralta brought the President a strange periodical that had arrived by ordinary mail. It was a curious publication, the like of which had never been seen in the country: printed on India paper, consisting of eight pages in 16mo, small and light, no bulkier than an ordinary letter. Its title was simply: *Liberation*. Well produced, however, with four columns to a page but as perfectly legible as a dictionary. This "Number 1, Year 1" began with an editorial severely attacking the regime, without unnecessary adjectives, but as sharp as the crack of a whip and written in clear and concise prose.

"This is something new," murmured the Head of State, finding its contents much more upsetting than the exaggerated and outrageously Creole insults commonly fired at him by the supporters of Luis Leoncio Martínez. Afterwards came a full report on the most recent brutalities committed by the police, with the names of the victims and agents. Next, a thorough analysis of the recent strikes, drawing practical conclusions from their successes and mistakes. And in the middle pages came the worst of all—a detailed list with dates and numbers, undoubtedly obtained from highly secret documents, of the most private business carried out by the

President, his ministers, generals, and followers in the last few months.

"There's a Judas among us," cried the Head of State in a furious rage.

"But ... who published this?" asked Doctor Peralta in a puzzled tone.

"No need to ask. Read the sentence at the end of this number: '*Workers of the world unite!*' "

"Damn it, that's the end of the *Manifesto!*"

"What it means is that this unsigned pamphlet is really signed."

Before ten o'clock it turned out that thousands of people had received this clandestine pamphlet in their morning mail. Typographical experts, summoned to a cabinet meeting to examine the situation, gave their opinion that it could only have been produced outside the country, judging by the type used, the style of composition, and the origin—German, apparently—of the India paper, which wasn't available in the city at present. Perhaps the printing press was in some frontier town. Censorship was therefore imposed on all correspondence from neighbouring countries. But on the following Tuesday, soon after waking up, the Head of State received Number 2 of *Liberation* on his breakfast tray, brought to him by the Mayorala Elmira. Internal censorship was next imposed on all distribution offices. But this didn't prevent the appearance of Number 3, without help from the post office—in a wrapper but with no stamp—in the letter boxes of ministries, public offices, businesses, and private houses, not to mention copies passed from pocket to pocket or drawer to drawer, slipped under doors, thrown onto balconies, or left on flat roofs and windowsills by mysterious hands. All the printing presses in the republic were put under military guard. There was a detective in every newspaper office, and behind every linotype and every machine turning out proofs. But nothing could prevent Numbers 4, 5, 6, and 7 of *Liberation* from appearing. The clandestine printing press, the ghostly, invisible, silent press, went on working with exasperating efficiency. It was like some central laboratory, a gnomes' forge, perhaps here in this quarter of the town, or perhaps in that, farther away, but producing without noise or fuss those accursed little 16mo pages, which kept the Head of State awake every night.

It was about now that, during one cabinet meeting, the Minister of the Interior uttered for the first time a threatening and sinister phrase: "Moscow Gold."

"What Moscow Gold, what on earth do you mean by Moscow Gold?" roared the President. "The Bolsheviks haven't any; they're all dropping dead, and you think they have gold to spare for ..." (He picked up a recent number of *Illustration* from Paris.) "Look. Look at these photos. Mountains of corpses on the shores of the Dnieper and the Volga. Children nothing but bones and eyes. People starving as they did in the year 1000. Cholera. Typhus. Grand duchesses begging in the streets. Endless, hopeless poverty."

The Minister insisted. All this was quite true. But those Bolsheviks were selling the treasures of Potemkin and Catherine the Great, crowns from the Kremlin, jewels confiscated from princes and boyars, the pictures from the Hermitage, so as to pay for international revolution, the only thing that could save communism from disaster.

"Read, read Kerensky's articles in the North American press." Moscow Gold was no fiction. Moscow Gold was the only thing that could explain the existence of something like *Liberation* in this country (Number 8 had just appeared), with its expensive paper, its presses hidden in some cave or in one of the undiscovered passages that—according to some historians—the Spanish Conquistadors had made underneath what was today the capital of the republic, to connect three fortresses, now in ruins.

And when, a few nights later, another petard exploded in the palace—although it did little damage, as it had been put in a storeroom full of useless furniture—the Head of State became convinced of the reality of Moscow Gold. The caricatures in *Le Rire*, showing a bear throwing bombs with fuses alight onto the map of Europe, were not foolish fantasies by humorists, nor was the picture of the Red Octopus, stretching its tentacles to every corner of the globe from the onion domes of Saint Basil. One of those tentacles had entered our country.

"We must take emergency measures," murmured Peralta.

"And what is left for us to do?" replied the President, as if suddenly exhausted, suddenly missing the Arc de Triomphe, which if it stood here instead of this useless Volcano would have led him under its high vault into the delicious peace, smelling of wine and wood, of Monsieur Musard's Bois-Charbons.

In times of agitation and anxiety he used to yearn for the Land of Intelligence, where even in the Métro one could read an alexandrine worthy of Racine:

*Le train ne peut partir que les portes fermées . . .*

A country where, as the Distinguished Academician (now so far away) would sometimes remark, *Athalie*'s Azarias, reincarnated in the person of the Station Master of the Pigalle Station, might have said, "*en un lieu / souterrain par nos pères creusé*" (*Athalie*, Act 5) as the train set off for L'Etoile:

*J'en fait devant moi fermer toutes les portes* (Act 3).

# 15

*I do not think that fear or terror can be praiseworthy
or useful . . .*                    —DESCARTES

ONE MORNING THE NEWS WENT AROUND THAT A
dead and putrefied horse, with a blown-up stomach, had
turned up in the city's chief reservoir of drinking water, and
that as a result anyone who had drunk from the taps connected with the Municipal Aqueduct—and it was now eleven
o'clock—was threatened with typhus. But when the Minister
of Health went in person to investigate the situation, he found
that the only thing floating in the famous Almond Basin, pride
of national hydraulic engineering, was a black wooden horse
with silver hooves: a famous model from the harness maker's,
"The Andalusian Horse," stolen thence during the night by
sinister jokers. As soon as calm was restored, a fierce and
blazing red fire—too red—broke out in a tobacco warehouse
in the suburbs. And when a lot of wailing fire engines had
been mobilised, the firemen found themselves faced with a
large flare of Bengal lights, set going in some inexplicable way
and bringing their display to an end with a cheerful explosion
of rockets. Next day, several newspapers published in all good
faith the announcement of the death (with corresponding
*requiescat in pace*) of some officials who were actually enjoying the best of health. This was the beginning of a period of

mystification, of unpleasant jokes, spreading of rumours to
create a climate of disturbance, anxiety, mistrust, and uneasiness throughout the country. Skulls were received by post; funeral wreaths arrived at houses where no one had died; the
telephone rang in the middle of the night to say that the master of the house, who was away, had died of a heart attack in
a brothel. And there was a flood of anonymous correspondence, sometimes made from letters cut from newspapers,
with threats of imprisonment or assault, accusations—nearly
always truthful—of homosexuality or adultery, false reports
of risings in the provinces, disagreement in the Military High
Command, imminent strikes, failure of insurance companies,
and preparations to ration essential foods. They were pitched
in a minor key, promoted gatherings, processions, protests,
arguments with the police, and spread false news of profitable exchanges—old casseroles for sewing-machines, tools
for Swiss watches, wheelbarrows for bicycles—in shops with
a wealthy clientele or a recently opened American grocery.
Workers were advertised for at magnificent wages in factories
long since closed down.

"Don't eat meat of animals with foot-and mouth-disease,"
warned a handbill circulated at midday. "The National Bank
is suspending transactions," announced another at dusk, and
next morning people rushed to the guichets. And life went
on in the midst of disorder, with incorrect information, street
notices altered, the crossing of wires, where the telephone
from the morgue was mysteriously connected with the Head
of State's office, and the number of a brothel rang the papal
nuncio very early in the morning. Someone who ordered a
Steinway piano from New York found a decapitated donkey
inside it; someone who bought a record of Tito Schipa, a tenor
much admired because he sang in Spanish, heard a stream of
abuse of the government as soon as the needle was placed on

the disk although it bore the trademark of His Master's Voice. All these escapades, growing more and more audacious, were the work of activists who started panics in cinemas with explosions of magnesium, carried off tramway rails, and cut electric wires—leaving half the town without light, the better to throw stones at the windows of business houses.

There was a whole underground army, mobile, intelligent, full of bright ideas and treachery, operating everywhere to disorganise the structure of society, disconnect administrative arrangements, keep the authorities in a perennial state of shock, and above all to stimulate an increasing climate of alarm. No one trusted anyone any longer. And the police were impotent in spite of their numbers being continually augmented by agents, detectives, informers, and spies, and they kept on making false moves without ever catching the people really responsible for this or that incident. Two bombs had exploded in the palace, although visitors were all searched when they entered the building and all parcels from outside were examined. And since someone had to be accused, yet none of them liked to admit their bewilderment, they tried to find valid reasons for being sure that the promoter of everything, the mastermind behind these fiendish activities and mysterious devices, was the Student. But the editorials of *Liberation*—never signed, of course—stated that the strange events disturbing the citizens were not due to Communist action:

"We do not make use of jokes and mystifications to further our struggle." And then in a more characteristically Latin American tone: "True revolutionaries don't come from brothels and gambling dives." And next to this as usual was a collection of Marxist ideas printed inside a frame: "Humanity only sets itself problems that can be solved, because if they are carefully studied it is found that the problem arises only where material conditions for solving it exist" (*Introduction to a Critique of Political Economy*).

"I'm beginning to believe," said the President, much disturbed, "that that little bastard is telling the truth. He's got other aims in view. He's deluded. But sincere. He wouldn't waste time telephoning to say I died like Félix Faure last night."

"But the bombs?" said Peralta.

"Yes, the bombs," said the Head of State, once more undecided. "Communists, like anarchists, put bombs anywhere they can. One only has to see the pictures in the international press. All the same ..."

"The trouble is that people think the Student is responsible for everything that's happening here," remarked the secretary. "And so he's becoming a sort of myth: something like Robin Hood but who owns Gyges' ring. And our poor population is charmed by such stories."

And he was quite right, for the novels of Ponson du Terrail, and also Les Misérables, had had an extremely wide appeal throughout the country, with their characters who changed name, age, and appearance and always deceived their pursuers. Gaston Leroux had shown a criminal's powers of mimicry in his often translated and much read Mystery of the Yellow Room. So it was against a background of classic rebels, historical outlaws, impossible to catch and always on the side of justice, that the image of the Student was evoked among little groups of farmworkers, in tenement-house gatherings, in the coplas sung softly in the back rooms of village shops (although in fact these people had very little idea what communism was), as a sort of fighter for reform, defender of the poor, enemy of the rich, scourge of corruption, saver of a nation alienated by capitalism, a descendant of the popular leaders in our wars of independence, whose generous and just deeds lived on in people's memories. The fame of his ubiquity, above all, increased day by day: he was the genius of unpredictable journeys, who made fun of police cordons, customs officers, and sentinels, and flew from the mines in the north to the dockyards of La Verónica, from forest to cistus-covered highlands. And the legend of the Student, greatly enriched by stories of laudable deeds, whispered news, and ballads that passed from mouth to mouth, slipped through windows so narrow that it seemed like magic; he ran over the roofs, jumped from terrace to terrace, now disguised as a protestant pastor, now as a Franciscan capuchin, pretended to be blind one day, acted the policeman another—farmhand, miner, muleteer, doctor with his black bag, English tourist, wandering harpist, loader of crates. And while the forces of State Security were hunting for him, clattering about on their motorcycles and besieging whole suburbs, the hunted man was probably sitting on a seat in Central Park, wearing an old man's wig, a white beard, and black spectacles, with his nose buried in the daily paper, while a few of his followers—if they really were his followers—began singing far away amongst the agaves and prickly pears, the nets and seaweed, the mountain wheatfields and threshing floors among the clouds, a copla very popular in Mexico some years ago:

> *We farmworkers—or so they say—*
> *Are just a lot of twisters*
> *Because we have no wish to be*
> *The oxen of our masters.*

"I don't like myths," said the Head of State, faced with the increasing reality of the Student, whose imaginary—but unknown—profile crossed between the large window in his study and the earthly presence of the Tutelary Volcano every morning. "I don't like myths. Nothing can travel about so far and so fast in this continent as a myth."

"Certainly, that's true," observed the schoolmaster who often emerged in Peralta. "Montezuma was overthrown by the messianic Aztec myth of a-man-with-a-pale-skin-who-was-to-come-from-the-east. The Andes knew the myth of the Inca Paraclete, later incarnate in Tupac Amaru, who put up a good fight against the Spaniards. We had the myths of the Resurrection-of-the-Ancient-Gods, which gained us a Fantastic City in the jungles of Yucatán when Paris was celebrating the advent of the Century of Science and worshipping the Good Fairy Electricity. There was Auguste Comte's myth in the Brazilian style, with a mystical marriage between Batacada and Positivism. Myth of the gauchos being immune to bullets. Myth of that Haitan—I think he was called Mackandal—who could tranform himself into a butterfly, an iguana, a horse, or a dove. Myth of Emiliano Zapata, going up to heaven after his death on a black horse breathing out flames."

"And in Mexico too," observed the President, "our friend Porfirio Diaz was done for by the myth of 'effective suffrage, no re-election,' and the awakening of the Eagle and the Serpent, who had both been asleep for rather more than thirty years, luckily for their country. And now, here, everyone believes the Myth of the Student—the virtuous redeemer, spartan and omnipresent. We must deflate the Myth of the Student . . . And our bloody police, trained in the United States, are no fucking use; they don't know how to tie men up and beat and torture them, or drown them in the bathtub."

But Peralta was already opening the Hermès case to calm his master's rage, when the surprising, unhoped-for, and altogether astounding news arrived that the Student had been found in the least likely place and feebly allowed himself to be taken prisoner without resistance or glory at a customs office in the south, where the ingenuous police—but not as ingenuous as all that—had been surprised to find a cane cutter with uncalloused hands travelling in a cane cart. The photo of this individual, taken at the time, agreed with one on his student's record of entry to the University. And for almost two hours he had been shut up in a cell in the Model Prison, of course denying that he was the Student—didn't he like *cells*?

"For God's sake, don't do him any harm!" exclaimed the Head of State. "A good breakfast with corn griddle cakes, butter, cheeese, black beans, fried eggs, and even a long drink if he wants one. And afterwards bring him to my study. We'll have a man-to-man talk. And I give you my word I have no intention of using my powers against him. That way there will be less resistance."

The Head of State had set his scene very carefully. Dressed in an austere frock coat bound with silk—a pinkish grey tie, a decoration in the buttonhole—he was sitting with his back to the large plate-glass window giving onto the central courtyard of the palace, with his work table in front of him, so that the light would shine on his victim's face. In the middle of the table was a classical grey blotter bound in embossed leather; an inkpot—a napoleonic eagle on a pedestal of green marble; the obligatory leather cylinder full of well-sharpened pencils; a paperweight souvenir of Waterloo; a gold paper knife with the arms of the republic engraved on the handle, and files—a great many files in ostentatious disarray, with their papers turned out, here, there, as when someone is laboriously going through their documents. And here, on the right of the blotter, as if casually, lay a copy of the manual on breeding Rhode Island Reds in its yellow cover.

Doctor Peralta showed the Student into the room with the utmost courtesy, although the Head of State did not interrupt his apparent checking of numbers and ticking them with his fountain pen. Raising his occupied hand, he indicated an armchair to the visitor. And after clipping together a few pages he handed them to his secretary:

"There was an error of 320 pesos in the estimate for the viaduct. That won't do. Tell those gentlemen they had better see about getting one of those 'adding machines,' as they call them, from the United States."

Peralta left the room and there was a long silence. Corpulent, heavy-shouldered, his stature increased by the regal proportions of the presidential chair, the Head of State gazed at his adversary in some surprise. Where he had thought to find an athletic young man, his muscles hardened by playing fives at the University, with a tense defiant face, as if ready for battle, he was now looking at a thin, frail youth, halfway between adolescence and maturity, his hair rather ruffled, his face pale, but who was certainly confronting him almost without blinking, with very bright eyes, perhaps grey-green, perhaps grey-blue, and who in spite of a somewhat feminine sensibility expressed the force of character and determination of someone who can act when necessary with the toughness of a convinced believer.

So they both looked at each other, the Master, the Invested, Immovable Ruler, and the Weak, Invisible Utopian, across the trench dividing the generations, seeing each other in flesh and blood for the first time. Their mutual contemplation produced a lamentable effect on both. To the Inferior his Superior was an archetype, an exhibit in a historical museum, a figure created to take the centre of one of those posters (the products of very recent folklore) that illustrate the triad situated in a single body, of Power, Capitalism, and the Boss, an image as invariably printed on the retina as were, centuries earlier, those of Turlupin or the Matamoros of the Italian

Commedia dell'Arte. Today's protagonist of revolutionary allegories was this individual sitting in front of him in his frock
coat and striped trousers, with a pearl tiepin and expensive
scent, lacking only the emblem of a shiny top hat and a cigar
stuck between his fierce teeth to symbolise—sitting on sacks
of dollars that really existed, even if in the vaults of a Swiss
bank—the Spirit of the Bourgeoisie.

To the Superior, his Inferior was a character from folklore, whom he was measuring, weighing up, and analysing,
while conscious of surprise at having to attend to someone
so unimportant. The man in front of him was something like
a Latin American version of the classical student in Russian
novels, full of dreams and theories, more of a nihilist than
a politician, proletarian out of sense of duty, who lived in a
garret, under-nourished, badly dressed, falling asleep among
his books, roused to bitterness by the mediocrity of his existence. They had both had the same origins. But while the
Superior, a pragmatist who thoroughly understood his environment, had taken with impatient haste the upward path,
which was today bordered with statues and busts of himself,
his Inferior had fallen into the trap of a new form of Mes-
sianism, whose fatal progress would carry him to the Siberias
of the Tropics, to the indignities of Bertillon's tests, or to the
denouement—a theme for the articles of journalists in the far
future—of disappearing-without-trace, leaving the relatives
of this weak, insubstantial figure to take flowers on assumed
anniversaries and lay them on aimless tombs, engraved with
names, but with the sadness, worse even than that of an occupied coffin, of an empty grave.

And in a silence barely broken by the whistle of a bird
frisking among the areca palms on the patio, there took place
a dialogue between voices that never emerged from lips. Each
was looking at the other: *He doesn't realise to what extent he's*

*playing a part / he seems more like a provincial poet than any-*
*thing else / he's absolutely "taken up a position" / one of those*
*who win prizes in Flower Festivals / flashy clothes / suit from*
*the Quality Shop / face like a bottom / cheeks like a girl / comes*
*out paler in photos: as he gets older he returns to his origins /*
*hair uncombed, tie crooked, to give himself some style / smells*
*like a tart, with all that Cologne / he needs size, strength to*
*make something of him / there's a repulsive quality in his ex-*
*pression / he thinks he's Masaniello / I thought he was older /*
*I wonder if it's hate or fear he's looking at me with / his hands*
*are trembling: alcohol / he's got a pianist's hands, but he ought*
*to clean his nails / the classical Tyrant / the Archangel we all*
*were once / a vicious, obscene man: it's all in his appearance /*
*the face of a boy who hasn't screwed many women: intellectual*
*lightweight / not even a monster: a petty tyrant giving himself*
*airs / those weak ones are the worst / all this is pure theatre: this*
*way of receiving me, the light on my face, that book on the ta-*
*ble / capable of anything: he's got nothing to lose / don't look at*
*me like that, I won't lower my eyes / although he may be brave,*
*he wouldn't resist torture / I wonder if I could stand torture:*
*some people can't / I believe he's afraid / ... torture ... / if they*
*put him under a certain amount of pressure / they'll try to get*
*names out of me / why such a long wait? A good fright to start*
*with / his hand's going to the bell: he's going to ring / no: I gave*
*my word / I don't know if I could resist / talk to him first / it's*
*horrible thinking of that, of that, of that ... / one mustn't make*
*martyrs, one mustn't make martyrs of these people: avoid it if*
*possible / he gave me his word; but his word isn't worth a fuck /*
*everyone knows that He is here now, and that I've given my*
*word / he's going to ring: I shall be handcuffed / others, tougher*
*than this one, have been persuaded / when will he decide to*
*speak? / let him go, and have him followed: he must go some-*
*where / why doesn't the bugger speak to me? Why can't he open*

*his mouth? / He's sweating! Now I'm sweating and I've no hand-*
*kerchief, I've no handkerchief; not in that pocket either ... /*
*He's afraid / he's smiling / he wants to suggest something: some*
*beastliness / I'll offer him a drink / I'm sure he's going to offer*
*me a drink / he won't accept it, so as to pride himself on his*
*virtue / if only he'd offer me a drink: I'd feel better / I don't want*
*to risk a refusal / come on, go on, that's it, risk it; it'll be a bottle*
*from that case; everyone knows what's inside it / however, yes:*
I tell you ... I repeat ... *But he doesn't seem to have heard me:*
*that lorry / now it's the tram / I don't understand his expres-*
*sion / I don't think he understood my expression / we've stared*
*at each other quite long enough; now for the book, so that he*
*can see ...*

The Head of State picked up the book on breeding Rhode
Island Red poultry. He opened it and, pushing back his spectacles, began to read in a markedly sarcastic tone: "A spectre
was haunting Europe: the spectre of communism."

And the other went on, with even more marked sarcasm:
"All the old European powers combined together to pursue
this spectre: The Pope and Wilson, Clemenceau and Lloyd
George."

"Metternich and Guizot," corrected the President.

"I see you know the classics," said the Student.

"I know more about poultry breeding. Don't forget I'm a
son of the soil. Perhaps that's why ..." And he stopped, per-
plexed as to the style he ought to adopt in this dialogue. Ornate language, like that of the "Prayer on the Acropolis," would
never do; a young man of the coming generation would find
it ridiculous, nor must he fall into the opposite extreme of the
rough vocabulary that coarsened his intimate conversations
with Doctor Peralta and the Mayorala Elmira, though giving
them a certain jauntiness. He therefore opted for a deliberate,
humanistic tone, without the familiar form we always used,

a tone that by its remoteness from that world of drink and confidences immediately created a distance greater than that set by the table separating them. Like an actor very much in command of his gestures and talking between his teeth like Lucien Guitry, he addressed the boy in front of him as if he were a character in a tragedy, about to be overwhelmed by the inscrutable designs of Fate:

"Why do you* detest me so much?"

His formal manner of speech sufficiently conveyed his verbal strategy to the Student / *he approaches me in the style of Voltaire when he tells us he "had the honour to go off" with an Indian woman in a loincloth . . . /*, who replied in the meekest and most peaceable voice that his terrified throat could produce:

"I do not detest you, Señor."

"But actions speak louder than words," said the Powerful One without raising the pitch. "Bombs aren't thrown against the palace servants. Therefore there is hatred, anger in you."

"Nothing against you, Señor."

"But . . . those bombs?"

"I didn't plant them, Señor. I don't understand anything about explosives."

"Well, it wasn't you,† then? But your followers planted them, your friends and accomplices / *he suddenly thought the word* accomplice *was vulgar and belonged to the vocabulary of police reports* / your co-religionists, your helpers, those on your side." / *careful: I've dropped into flowery language again.*

"We don't plant bombs, Señor."

The Head of State began to grow impatient. The fable of the Wolf and the Lamb was being played out between them.

---

* *Usted*, the polite form, is used.
† *Tú* (familiar form, rectified to *usted*).

"But . . . who planted them, then? Who? Will you tell me?"

"Others, not one of us. We've too often seen the failure of anarchists' attempts to change the world. Ravachol and Caserio are just as futile with their deliberate self-immolation as Bakunin and Kropotkin with their doctrines."

"Don't try and come over me with your pointless discussions and sophistries from the Council of Nicaea / *as if mine were different!* / it all amounts to the same thing, in fact. Even supposing you and your friends didn't explode a bomb in my bath, you applauded it."

"On the contrary, Señor. The worst that could happen to us now is that someone should kill *you*. I have a comrade, a practising Catholic—there's nothing to be done about it—who prays and makes vows to the Divine Shepherdess to preserve your precious life for us."

The Head of State got to his feet, moved by astonishment and rage mixed.

"My precious existence? You've got a nerve and no mistake! And *nerve* is a euphemism." / *Now he's beginning to call me "tú."* /

"We need you, Señor."

The Powerful, Enormous man burst out laughing.

"That's really great! So now I'm a Marxist, Communist, Menshevik, and revolutionary, and the same mother bore all these, who are all the same and all after the same ends: to be installed in the Kremlin, the Elysée, Buckingham Palace, or to sit on this chair (and he thumped the back of the presidential chair), enjoy life, fill one's purse with money, and fuck all the rest. The Tsar's ambassador who stayed here with us, waiting and hoping that all that business would come to grief, told me that Lenin's wife used to wear the jewels, necklaces, and crowns of the Empress Alexandra."

"It's splendid that you think that way, and make up such

stories, Señor. It's better we shouldn't understand each other at all than only half understand each other. Those who half understand us fight us more effectively than those who take us for visionaries."

"However, if I were in fact to die tomorrow . . ."

"It would be lamentable for us, Señor. Because a military junta would seize power, and everything would go on just the same or worse under the government of someone like Walter Hoffmann, God rest his soul."

"Well, what *do* you want, then?"

In a slightly raised voice but not speeded up at all, the young man said, "That you should be overthrown *by a popular uprising.*"

"And afterwards? You would come and occupy my place, isn't that certain?"

"I have never desired anything of the sort."

"Have you got a candidate, then?"

"The word *candidate* doesn't figure in our vocabulary, Señor."

The Head of State shrugged his shoulders. "Tarradiddles! Because, in fact, someone, someone must take power. There must be a Man, always a Man, at the head of a government. Look at Lenin in Russia. Ah! I know! Luis Leoncio Martínez, your professor at the University."

"He's a cretin. He can go to hell with his Puranas, his Camille Flammarion and Leon Tolstoy" (and he laughed). " 'Return to the Earth' indeed! Whose earth? The United Fruit Company's?"

The Head of State was beginning to be irritated and impatient at the turn taken by the conversation.

"Then you mean to introduce socialism here?"

"We're looking for a way."

"The Russian way?"

"It may not be the same. Here we are in a different latitude. It's both easier and more difficult."

The President was pacing up and down his study and apparently talking to himself:

"Oh boys, boys, boys! If socialism was introduced here, in forty-eight hours you would have North American marines landing at Puerto Araguato."

"It's very probable, Señor."

"And then?" (in a protective, amiable tone) "I envy you. At your age I thought about the same sort of things. But ... now? Look here: they burned Joan of Arc at nineteen because if she had reached thirty she would have gone to bed with the King of France, and then she would have got as much by negotiating with the English and not had to die at the stake for it. You've got your idols. Good. I respect them. But don't forget that the gringos are the Romans of America. And you can't do a thing against Rome. And less, with the rabble" (an intimate tone, now). "You can talk to me in absolute confidence as if to an older brother. I have political experience, which none of you have. I can explain why some things are possible and others not. All I want to do is understand. Let us understand each other ... Trust me ... Tell me ..."

"I'm not quite mad!" said the young man, suddenly laughing, and beginning to pace the room in the opposite direction to his interlocutor, in such a way that when one of them had his back to the fire of imitation logs the other was against the corbel supporting a mirror between two doors, which made the room look larger. Suddenly the President made a gesture of depression, in the style of a good actor:

"One never stops learning lessons in this life. Hearing you talk today, I suddenly realised that I'm the First Prisoner of the Nation. Yes. Don't smile. I live here surrounded by ministers, officials, generals, and doctors, all bent double with obsequiousness and bowing, who do nothing but hide the truth from me. They only let me see a world of appearances. I live in Plato's cave. You know about Plato's cave? Of course! Stupid of me to ask … And suddenly you arrive, full of faith, impetuosity, fresh blood, and the phrase of the French poet comes alive for me: 'I learn more from a young friend than an old master.' Ah, if I could count on the sincerity of men like you! I should make fewer mistakes! Now listen: you see one eager to take the conversation into a new climate. For instance, look here: I realise that we've been too—what shall I say?—rigorous in dealing with the problems of the University. How would you like it if we considered them now, face to face, and if you left here within an hour with a solution satisfactory to your people? It depends on you: what do you think?"

The young man walked from the fireplace to the mirror.

"Comedian!"

The President was taking irritated strides between the mirror and the fireplace, his former composure rapidly disappearing.

"Look here! If you've read Alfred de Vigny, so have I. Don't try playing the part of Pius VII before Napoleon. Because before you'd said 'Tragedian!' you know what would happen." And he took his Browning out of the left inside pocket of his frock coat and laid it on the table with the barrel pointing at the young man.

"So the war is to go on?"

"It'll go on, with me—or without me."

"You persist in your utopias, your socialisms, although they've failed everywhere?"

"That's my affair—and a lot more besides."

"The Mexican Revolution was a failure."

"And taught us a lot, for that very reason."

"The Russian Revolution has failed."

"That's not yet been proved."

The Head of State was playing with his pistol, ostentatiously filling and emptying it of its five bullets.

"Kill me and have done with it," said the Student.

"No," said the President, taking up his pistol again. "Not here in the palace. It would dirty the carpet." There is a silence. The hummingbirds are twittering in the patio. Two pairs of eyes avoid each other by looking at the walls. (*How long is this going on? ... That picture wants straightening ... A situation with no way out.*) At last, as if it cost him an effort, the President spoke:

"All right. As you don't want to come to an understanding with me, I give you three days to leave the country. Ask Peralta for anything you want. You can go where you like. Paris, for instance. I'll give instructions for you to get a month's allowance extra, unconditionally. You won't have to go to our embassy. Your friends won't be surprised to see you go, because they'll know that you're *finished* as a revolutionary here ... No! Wait a moment! Don't be melodramatic! I'm not trying to buy you off: I'm offering you the Paris of women and Maxim's restaurant, as I would one of our social climbers. I'm offering you the Paris of the Sorbonne, of Bergson, of Paul Rivet, who seems to know a lot about us, and certainly published the other day a magnificent piece of research into a mummy I presented to the Trocadero Palace. The rest is your affair. Salute Racine from me when you visit Saint-Etienne-du-Mont; and Voltaire and Rousseau in the Panthéon. Or if you want to make your Prayer on the Acropolis in the Bolshevik manner, you've got the Mur des Fédérés at Père Lachaise ... There's something for all tastes ... you can choose." (And he repeated "You can choose" several times in an increasingly ambiguous tone of voice.)

"I've got nothing to do in Paris," said the Student, after a marked pause.

"I leave it to you. Stay here, then. But from Tuesday" (the day after tomorrow) "I shall give orders for you to be killed without hesitation, wherever you are found."

"My death would be the worst possible publicity for you."

"My boy, the law of flight is a universally accepted lie. Like saying that a fugitive committed suicide, or that a man hanged himself in his cell because they forgot to take away his shoelaces. And that happens in the most civilised countries, where they have spendid leagues of human rights and other equally respectable institutions to safeguard the Liberty and Dignity of the Individual. Ah! And I warn you that anyone who has sheltered you will fall with you, their family and all. Understand?"

"May I go now?"

"Go to hell! And prepare your epitaph: *Here lies one who died because he was stupid.*" The Student got up. The Head of State made a gesture of dismissal, not wanting to risk holding out his hand for fear of a snub.

"You don't know how sorry I am. Such an estimable young man. The worst of it is that I envy you: if I were your age I should be with your lot. But you don't know what it's like governing these countries. You don't know what it's like cultivating the soil with human material that ..." The Head of State's reflection vanished in an avalanche of broken glass. The mirror, the shelves, pictures, and fireplace had come crashing down in a confusion of plaster, broken laths, gilt woodwork, splinters, and paper, with a thunderous, ear-splitting noise, which seemed to reverberate in the chest and stomach. The President, very pale, brushing away the powdered plaster that whitened his frock coat, gazed at the destruction. The Student had fallen on the floor. Now he was feeling himself all over and looking for blood on his hands. His face, first, because women were important to him.

"Nothing. We've escaped death this time," said the President.

"And did you think I was idiotic enough to throw bombs at myself?" said the other, getting up.

"Yes, I believe you now. But that changes nothing. What I said before; that's all."

The room was filling with people: servants, officials, police, the Mayorala Elmira, the secretaries.

"Go out this way," said the Head of State, taking the Student to a little room next door, decorated in pink with elegantly licentious engravings on the wall and a wide sofa covered in cushions, connected with the street by a spiral staircase, the subject of much gossip in the town.

"Is this how the girls come in?"

"At my age, I can still hold their interest. You've realised that." And putting his hand on the young man's shoulder: "To you I must seem a sort of Caligula, don't I?"

"More like Caligula's horse," replied the other, driven to some unheard-of insolence, before dashing down the stairs with the speed of a squirrel.

The Head of State was so dumbfounded that when Doctor Peralta appeared, all he could say was:

"Open up downstairs. And let him go free."

"They've just brought the first-aid chest, Señor."

"I don't think I need it. I'm quite all right. All right. All right." And he felt his body, from chest to knees, but his fingers found neither pain nor moisture.

# 16

*. . . there is greater honour and safety in resistance than in flight.* —DESCARTES

IN MARCH OF THAT YEAR IT WAS NECESSARY TO extend the Moratorium, because the result of an official decision not to extend it had been that all those who normally operated it had prolonged, stretched, and extended it to the limits of the calendar. Bad faith, trickery, and cunning combined with insolvency, all sheltered under the magic, healing, and somewhat sepulchral word *Moratorium*. No one paid for anything. The inhabitants of labourers' quarters and tenements received rent collectors with blows from sticks and stones, and loosed the dogs at them to drive the message home. Merchants from the Canary Islands, Syrian pedlars, and dealers on credit were accused of being anarchists by housewives sure that the police were close at hand, should they insist on presenting a long-due account for lace or lingerie. Things were bought on credit and pawned the same day, cash taken from here to stop a deficiency there, and people had recourse to bullies and moneylenders, were perpetually shuffling papers or attaching signatures and bribes to the margin of denunciations, and lived by expedients and miracles, by lotteries and borrowing, while there were so many dud cheques in circulation that even those who still had a reputation for wealth had to pay cash for everything. The result of all this was that the

new town decreased—that is the word: *decreased*—as rapidly
as it had increased. What had been large grew smaller, flatter,
contracted, as if returning to the clay of its foundations. Suddenly exuding poverty, the city's ambitious skyscrapers—now
more like fogscrapers than skyscrapers—looked smaller as
their topmost storeys were deserted, abandoned by companies that had gone bust, and made opaque and gloomy by
stains of damp, the sadness of dirty windows, loneliness of
statues grown leprous in a few weeks. Unpainted, uncared
for, these buildings combined to make a sort of urban grisaille
that degraded, crippled, and decomposed the modern part of
the town, swathing it in the decay of what had already been
old at the beginning of the century. The porches of the Stock
Exchange, half asleep and almost deserted, had been transformed into a market for the sale of singing birds, parrots,
and turtles, with stalls of salad vegetables and sweet corn,
workshops for cobblers and knife grinders, sellers of prayers
and amulets and booths where one could consult healers using mountain herbs. ("For you with sugar in your blood, an
infusion of purple basil is good; for you, for your asthma, cigars of double bellflower; for you, for the discharge from your
member, coconut milk with hollands; and for you, neighbour,
for delayed monthly, balsam tea with two leaves of lentisk, applied here—excuse me—between your legs . . .")

"The merchants of the temple," sighed the Head of State,
in biblical mood.

"In spite of the Treaty of Versailles, things are going badly
in Europe," said Doctor Peralta by way of consolation, dreaming of another good long, enjoyable war, perhaps nearer than
people thought. "With his Fourteen Points, Wilson has annoyed everyone."

Countless notices of clearance sales and liquidations
sang the requiem of business firms. Abandoned by their

contractors, buildings that had not passed the stage of their milk teeth (with incipient walls not yet as high as a man) were to be seen everywhere, ruins of the unborn, presences of what had never existed, permanent beginnings, with roofless drawing rooms, staircases leading nowhere, involuntarily Pompeian columns, while vast urbanisations and building lots in the outskirts had been re-conquered by the plants descending from the mountains—plants returning to the capital with their bells and festive plumes; and behind them shrubs, and behind the shrubs trees and tree ferns, all the seedling vegetation of Quick Advance and Quick Growth, shading the small stones amongst which exiled snakes were now returning to spawn. Meanwhile, the hills surrounding the city had been overspread with a rash of shacks made of corrugated iron, tarred cloth, packing-cases, or newspapers pasted together, supported on wooden props, and placed on such impossibly steep slopes that the early spring rains were tilting their floors and tumbling whole families into the river bed. These were the Squalor towns, the Hunger towns, the Shanty towns, from which every night the spectator could contemplate the paradisal view of the town with all its lights—shops selling silver and cut glass, specialist philatelists, and wine shops with their vintage bottles, where there were still people who planned tombolas in aid of the Preservation of Colonial Churches, or elected a beauty queen to represent us (Creole, but not too dark-skinned) in the International Contest of Coral Gables, whence came the waltz "On Miami Shore," now all the rage.

That year the sugar mills had closed down earlier than usual. Left to their fate, the wounds in the trunks of the rubber trees in the southern jungles healed over. There were more strikes in the north, rioting in the sawmills of Ciudad Urrutia, bloody clashes between miners and the army in Nueva Córdoba. Several armed bands, under hitherto unknown ringleaders, roamed the mountains of the south, burning farms, sacking warehouses, attacking barracks, and for two or three days taking possession of villages where they made the mayor, merchants, and notables dance to their tune, firing at the ground to increase their animation. The authorities of some provinces were powerless against the rebels, who—as had been observed more than once in the history of the country—awoke from their meek, resigned slumber of thirty years' duration to pass suddenly, when least expected, to a violence thought by our sociologists to be foreign to the congenital good nature so characteristic of the national temperament. Peasants suffering from malaria and bilharzia, sandal-shod, and hollow-eyed with disease, now rode on wretched flea-bitten nags, covered with sores and spavins, against the magnificent shining Kentucky-bred horses of the Rural Police. There were battles between catapults and Mausers, or the knives and goads of farmhands against well-sharpened regulation machetes. In the bigger villages they fought with tiles, bricks, stones, and sometimes dynamite, against bullets.

All these events kept the Head of State confined within an island, an island with lookout posts and windows, many gates, and a symmetrical arrangement of palm trees which was the Presidential Palace—where he received so many confused, contradictory, false or true reports, optimistic or tinged with gloom, that it was impossible to gather a clear, general, and chronological picture of what was happening. Anyone wanting to minimise the severity of a defeat denied its importance and spoke of a meeting between bandits and cattle rustlers, when they had really clashed with a strong popular force; anyone wanting to justify his impotence exaggerated the size of the hostile forces; anyone wanting to conceal his complete lack of information sidetracked the facts.

"You remind me of those European generals," said the Head of State angrily, "who, having lost a battle, speak of 'strategic withdrawal' or 'straightening the line,' elegant ways of admitting that they've received a thorough thrashing."

And governors and garrison commanders fell from grace, as did leaders in uniform or in panama hats; so that there was a continual shuffle and re-shuffle of dismissals, replacements, substitutions, responsibility taken away and given back again, unwelcome tasks entrusted to those who preferred to remain at home, renunciations exacted by telegram, summonses to ex-colleagues out of a job, patriotic speeches, and exhortations to national concord. And the island of the palace became more isolated day by day, with its ever-closer concentration of government servants, who felt themselves protected and defended, as it were, between these walls of good Colonial masonry, against hostile forces which like a swell caused by distant hurricanes (for their course was just as unpredictable) pounded against sentry boxes, loopholes, and parapets, where the bluish metal of long weapons gleamed at all hours of the day. And there were sandbags—a precaution that is never unnecessary—on the flat roofs of the building. There was a smell of criminal assault in the air. A door suddenly banging in the wind, the brutal starting up of a motorcycle, a flash of lightning from a dry sky, without the warning of rain—as so often happened during these months—produced a sudden scare, and the Mayorala Elmira's "Don't be so stupid!" echoed through the vastness of the well-guarded corridors like the repeated leitmotiv in a Wagnerian opera.

"Be tough with them, President, be tough. You must be tougher," said Peralta when some unpleasant incident occurred to darken a new day. But the worst of it was that, though he might have been tough previously, it had now become difficult, because beside the island of the palace another

island—extremely close yet inaccessible—had sprung up in
the city: a yellow island, overcharged with mouldings and
ornament, Californian plateresque in style, in the shape of a
block almost next door, which grew and grew steadily. In it
were to be found the cool shadows of the Hotel Cleveland,
the grocery smelling of maple syrup, the half-asleep Clearing House, Sloppy Joe's Bar, and various curio and souvenir
shops, which for lack of local handicrafts—our people were
very musical but deficient in plastic feeling—sold ponchos
from Oaxaca, Cuban rattles, shrunken heads, half nutshells
containing fleas dressed for weddings and funerals, gaudy
buttons and other things not produced in the region, as
well as bogus archaeological finds. And the centre of this island was the American Club—where, according to reliable
information—as well as poker parties, meetings of Daughters of the Revolution, sessions of Masons wearing Turkish
fezes, celebrations of Independence Day, Thanksgiving, July
4, and Halloween—with firecrackers and children carrying
illuminated pumpkins—serious discussions took place about
the national crisis, disorder and bankruptcy, reaching the incredible conclusion that, for lack of anyone better, the Man
needed at this moment—their last hope as it were—might
well be Luis Leoncio Martínez, defeated at Nueva Córdoba
it was true, but suddenly and astonishingly approved by the
North American Department of State.

"Although it was all very hush hush, Ariel knows that
he spent several days in Washington," commented Peralta,
"which only shows yet once again that in politics no enemy
is ever dead."

The Head of State reflected out loud: "And those were
the people, *those*, whose interests I always made a point of
defending; *they* got anything they wanted out of me, and
now they accuse me of everything that has gone wrong in the

country. They won't admit that the crisis is nothing to do with us: it's general, it's universal. Let them take a look at Europe, where all they've done is turn the map upside down, ruin currencies, create artificial nationalities—chaos, I tell you, absolute chaos. And now they're trying to interfere in our troubles by means of this idiotic professor."

"They think a change—it's the everlasting Myth of Change—will straighten out our problems. Perhaps they think we're moth-eaten, a bit *vieux-jeu*," groaned Peralta, while the President was revolving in his mind an idea that had for several days perturbed him:

"What an imbecile I was not to polish off the Student when I had him in front of me as plain as I see you now. And with my Browning on the table. A mere gesture. And for the benefit of the public; *he tried to attack me and I defended myself*. The Mayorala Elmira could have fired a shot at the right-hand shoulder of my frock coat suspended from a coat hanger, and I would have put it on afterwards. And a good photo of the young man stretched on the carpet, the unfortunate victim of my legitimate instinct of self-preservation. Plain as a pikestaff. All clear. And the first applause would have come from the American Club."

"It wouldn't have improved the situation at all."

"But the Student is still here: he hasn't gone. Our police are just as unable to get him today as they were yesterday. And he's still publishing his pamphlets on India paper."

"Principally read by the members of the American Club. Because the public it's intended for are almost illiterate. His ideas are too complicated for our people in sandals and overalls."

"They don't understand our young man's ideas, but they believe in him."

"Bah! In an abstract way. He's someone-who-will-put-things-to-rights. The Myth of Change again! But he's lacking flesh and blood, an image, palpability. For our peasants, Saint Speed (unknown to the calendar of saints) has more solidarity and is someone they can turn to when they want something, just as they pray to a picture printed in Paris, showing the Miracle worker, unknown to the Church, brandishing a sword with the word *Hodie*, only they pronounce it *Jode*, engraved in the steel."

"And you think Leoncio has more popular appeal than the Student?"

"Not at all. But it's just because the gringos are afraid of the Student—and especially of the ideas he represents—that they support the man from Nueva Córdoba. They care very little about the individual. But he's come to personify a type of *democracy* that they invoke every time they want to change something in Latin America."

"A matter of vocabulary."

"Everyone has their own; they talk about Defender of Democracy, we about Defender of the Established Order."

The Head of State began thinking aloud again: "Perhaps we could twang the string of national honour: the unforgivable interference of Yankees in the interior affairs of our country. Our people loathe gringos."

"Our people do—yes; but our bourgeoisie always gets along with them. To our wealthy people *Gringo* is a synonym for Order, Technique, and Progress. Those sons of the family who aren't educated by the Jesuits of Belén are at Cornell or Troy, if not West Point. We're being invaded—and you know it—by Methodists, Baptists, Jehovah's Witnesses, and Christian Scientists. North American Bibles are part of the furniture of our rich houses, like Mary Pickford's photo in a silver frame rubber-stamped with her familiar 'Sincerely yours.' "

"We're losing all our character: we've got too far away from Mother Spain."

"We shan't do any good by bemoaning that. You've got

plenty of guts and I've fought bulls myself in better days. Generals like Ataúlfo Galván and Walter Hoffmann were the real danger, with some of the army behind them. At least we haven't got to keep our eye on the barracks."

"That's true enough: I can count on the army. Without the smallest doubt."

"And the Yankees know that, President; that's one thing the Yankees know."

Just then music from stringed instruments struck up from behind the flamboyant trees in Central Park, slow, sweet, and smoothly bowed.

"There they go!" cried the Head of State. "Elmirita says they're bringing a coffin. Shut that window, Peralta."

And the secretary shut the window, suddenly shocked by this contact with the everyday Business of Death, the only thriving business, managed in these times of crisis by clever men, connoisseurs of a safe clientèle moved by ancestral and scatalogical emotions towards that Sleep-Which-Has-No-Awakening. Throughout the country, by a fusion of traditions wherein Extremadurans—our first Conquistador had come from Cáceres, like Pizarro—had combined with Indians, funeral ceremonies were complicated, ostentatious, and prolonged. When someone died in a village, the neighbours invaded the house and turned the wake into a collective activity with widespread repercussions, a gathering of men in doorways, on patios and pavements, against a dramatic background of weeping, wailing, and fainting women; and the whole night was punctuated by servings of black coffee, cups of chocolate, strong wine, and brandy, with much histrionic and emotional embracing, speeches and lamenting around the coffin, and exaggerated reconciliations between relations who had been at daggers drawn and passed years without meeting, before coming together on this solemn occasion. Afterwards came mourning, half-mourning, quarter-mourning, and then permanent mourning, which in the case of a good-looking widow was observed until she married again. And this continued in the important modern capital, although the scenario was somewhat transformed. The corpses were no longer laid out and the wakes held in private houses, but in undertakers' establishments, which were becoming more numerous all the time—with a growing population, more deaths—and competing with one another in the sumptuous innovations they offered their clients. And, little by little, these funerals had multiplied in the middle of the town, spreading a taint of affliction around the Presidential Palace—with constant coming and going of coffins and flowers, movements of angels and crosses, horses draped in black, hearses with glass sides, arrival by night of stiff corpses wrapped in green sheets . . .

But the most extraordinary of all these establishments had just been set up nearby, next to the Ministry of the Interior and the dyeworks: this was an imitation of the *Deuil en vingt-quatre heures* to be seen in Paris behind the Madeleine, at the corner of the Rue Tronchet. The speciality of "Eternity" was that the families could choose a style of furnishing, decoration, and ambience in which to receive condolences at the foot of the coffin. There was a Colonial Room, an Imperial Room, a Spanish Renaissance Room, a Louis XV Room, an Escorial Room, a Gothic Room, a Byzantine Room, an Egyptian Room, a Rustic Room, a Masonic Room, a Spiritualist Room, a Rosicrucian Room, all with seats, emblems, ornaments, and symbols adjusted to the character of the funeral chapel. And if the users wished, they could benefit from a great innovation introduced from the United States: the wake could be accompanied by noble and serene music, devoid of contrasts in loudness or tempo—although not at all funereal—performed by quartets or small string orchestras with harmonium, perfumed with incense and hidden behind a trellis of evergreens or a hedge of wreaths on trestles. Their repertory was drawn from the "Méditation" from *Thaïs, Le cygne* by Saint-Saëns, Massenet's "Élégie," Schubert's "Ave Maria," as well as Gounod's, played and played again tirelessly from the arrival of the urn until its departure to the cemetery. When these melodies came creeping into the palace in the small hours, the Head of State, exasperated at hearing the same tune over and over again, repeated a hundred times— and louder when there were no cars circulating in Central Park—ordered all the windows to be shut, though he went on suffering torments from the themes reverberating inside his head. And he could get to sleep again only with the help of the Santa Inés rum in the Hermès case, which was always placed on the night table at the head of his hammock.

And since *that* had been going on for weeks and weeks, there came a morning when he felt deafened—but deafened by the silence, the unaccustomed silence. The windows had been opened early that morning by the Mayorala Elmira, but the light breeze coming into his room smelling of the verdurous dawn did not bring with it the "Élégie," *Le cygne*, the "Méditation," or the Ave Marias.

"Something strange is happening," he thought. And something strange, very strange indeed, was in fact happening: something never before seen or remembered—even by the oldest inhabitants with the longest memories. The capital was starting the day—that day—in silence, a silence that was not merely funereal, a silence of other eras, a silence of distant dawns, a silence of the days when goats grazed in the main streets of the town; a silence broken only by a far-off donkey's bray, the cough of someone with bronchitis, the wail of a child. No buses went by. There was no tinkling from trams. Milk floats weren't going their rounds. And what was stranger still, early businesses like the bakers and cafés hadn't opened their doors, and the shops still had their metal shutters down. The total absence of street cries—no "hot churros" nor "tamarinds for the liver," nor "fresh oysters from Chichiriviche," nor "good tamales," nor the fruit seller's bugle—seemed to announce events of extreme gravity, with that sense of contraction, that fearful expectation, latent and undefined, which is often felt—although the warning is never listened to—on the eve of great earthquakes or volcanic eruptions. (The trees in the Parícutin region *were afraid*, turned grey with silent terror, many weeks before the slow, inexorable advance of lava had bubbled with a dull sound around their roots.)

"But—what's happening? What is all this?" asked the Head of State, seeing Doctor Peralta enter his room followed by ministers and military officers, unceremoniously violating his privacy and over-riding protocol:

"General strike, Señor President."

"General strike? General strike?" he asked (asked himself, rather) as if stunned, not hearing what they said, nor what he said himself.

"General strike. Or, if you prefer: a *general standstill*. Everything is shut. No one has gone to work."

"And public servants?"

"There are no buses, trams, or trains."

"And there's not a soul in the streets," said the Mayorala Elmira, making her way between alpaca suits and military uniforms. The Head of State went onto the balcony. The palace dogs, led by the remains of the police force, were pissing around the fountain in the park. But dogs had no souls. They weren't people. And that undertaker's establishment without music . . .

He turned back to the others in the room with a face of thunder: "A general strike, is there? And you knew nothing about it?" The others began talking incoherently, tying themselves up in explanations, clarifications and excuses—"You remember I advised you," "You remember that at the last council meeting, I . . ." but they never succeeded in producing a single convincing argument. Hitherto, real strikes had been seen only in the interior of the republic, in Nueva Córdoba and the ports; calls for a standstill had had no more serious consequences here; it was true that during these last days papers and clandestine leaflets had been distributed; moreover it was the Student who had predicted strikes of farmworkers, porters, road men and so forth, and everyone knew that merchants, shop workers, and members of the middle classes had never listened to the Student's instructions and calls to action; men employed on regular work didn't feel that *Proletarians of the Whole World* referred to them, because they never thought of themselves as proletarians; "and I was away from the capital, and I had to take my family to Bellamar and I couldn't imagine it, all the same my daughter told me . . ." (*we don't care a fuck what your daughter told you*); besides, never, never, never in the history of the continent had a strike of white-collar workers been seen; that sort of hooliganism was confined to disreputable characters, so we didn't pay attention to all the rumours; my daughter told me that the nuns of Tarbes . . . (*stop bothering us with your daughter*); I always said that that campaign of rumours, false epidemics, the wooden horse in the aqueduct, threats of death, skulls sent through the post, in fact I always said that . . .

"And now we're on the subject of deaths," said Peralta, interrupting the confused sound of voices all talking together, "the Mayorala has just told me something most unexpected, most unusual: all the undertakers' staff has joined the movement. Not only the musicians of 'Eternity', but those who lay out the corpses, the drivers of hearses, gravediggers and sextons. Families have to keep watch at home over anyone who died last night, because no one will come and take charge of them."

"People who died last night didn't at least join the strike," said the Head of State, suddenly calming down. "What's more, we'll give them some company so that they shan't be bored in the Next World. They deserve a reward." There was an expectant silence. "Let's talk briefly and to the point. Ask Elmira to bring some coffee."

At about ten in the morning vehicles began driving rapidly through the streets—fire engines and motorcycles with sidecars, manned by police who yelled through leather megaphones and aluminium speaking trumpets, such as are used at sporting contests, to tell any tradesmen with ears to hear that anyone failing to open his shop before two o'clock, either with or without his workers, would be deprived of his licence and punished by fines and imprisonment; and that anyone of foreign origin—however long ago he might have been naturalised—would be expelled from the country. These warnings were repeated again and again until the Cathedral clock struck twelve:

"At least the bell ringer isn't on strike," observed the President.

"That's because an electric machine has been installed," explained Peralta, very quickly repenting of saying what might be interpreted as a joke. "We must wait."

The Mayorala brought bottles of cognac and earthenware jugs of Hollands, and Romeo and Juliet Havanas and Henry Clays.

At least once every half hour the Head of State took out his watch to see whether an hour had passed. One o'clock.

Two. A coffin emerged from "Eternity" carried on the shoulders of black-clad men—obviously members of the family—who set off on foot towards the cemetery. And at three the same silence as before reigned throughout the capital. Only a few Cantonese traders had opened their shops selling fans, screens, and ivory goods, for fear of being sent back to China, which was now in the hands of the Kuomintang and the Warlords.

Suddenly the President broke the long wait by saying curtly and firmly to the Commander-in-Chief of the army: "Machine-gun the closed shops." A click of the heels, and a salute.

A quarter of an hour later the first fusillade was heard, bullets against metal shutters, corrugated iron, signboards, and shop windows. Never had such a frivolous war been waged. Never had the infantry enjoyed themselves so much as on this moving shooting range, where without aiming, merely firing bullets in strips, they were bound to hit some target—a splendid battle with no danger of reply from enemy bullets. It was a massacre of wax people—wax brides with wax orange blossom; gentlemen in frock coats with wigs on their wax skulls; amazons playing golf and tennis, with very pale wax complexions; a maid, dressed in the French style and made of less pale wax; the footman, like our Sylvestre in Paris, but of darker wax than the maidservant; an acolyte, a mace bearer, a jockey, all represented by a shade of wax suitable to their occupations—and, of course, the Virgins and Saints, brought from the Saint Sulpice district, in their robes of polychrome plaster, with haloes and other attributes, offered for sale by traders in missals and articles of devotion. As well as the 30-30s, the army fired off their Mausers and even some old Lebel rifles, brought from the back regions of the Arsenal. And in this great battle-against-things, shop

windows disintegrated, dinner services set out as wedding
presents were sent flying, bottles of scent, Dresden and Mu-
rano vases and porcelain were splintered to bits, earthenware
casseroles, flagons, and pitchers broken, and bottles of spar-
kling wine liberated so much energy as they exploded that
they broke the bottles next to them. For several hours the
attack on toys went on, firing on babies' bottles, fusillade of
Buster Brown and Mutt and Jeff, defenestration of puppets,
massacre of Swiss cuckoo clocks, and a second decapitation
of Saint Dionysius, who saw the head he was already carrying
in his hands fall to the ground, struck in the middle of the
cheek by a large bore bullet.

But in spite of all this activity and travail, night fell
over the city without public illumination or spotlighting in
parks, and with bulbs in the advertisements and streetlamps
unlit—only a few gas jets still remained, and the lamps carried by watchmen in the poorer quarters—even the moon
was waning and overcast with clouds. It was a long, interminable night, a night of gloom weighing on a paralysed, silent
town, a town abandoned to senseless firing—a few intermittent bursts of which could still be heard here and there. During these hours of waiting, of not knowing what the morning
would bring, people realised that certain silences, silences not
leading to any sound of voice or meaningful phrase, could be
more agonizing than the clamour of a prophet or the delirium
of an inspired diviner.

However, there were many houses, silent houses with
the blinds drawn, ministers' or generals' houses, houses belonging to those in power or wearing soutanes, there were
attics, rooms beyond the patio, where someone would go by
with a lantern or an oil lamp, or candles held high, to conceal
things, take jewels out of trunks, lock boxes, dust suitcases,
sew banknotes (especially dollars) inside the linings, lapels,

and skirts of suits, coats, and capes, in preparation for some possibly necessary flight. In the morning the children would be sent to the Atlantic beaches (*they were anaemic; medical prescription*); many families would disperse into the provinces or towns of the interior (*sick grandmother; grandfather of ninety-seven*) or had gone to their ancestral homes (*my sister had a miscarriage; the other is queer in the head*) while they waited to see what was going to happen. Meanwhile, in kitchens whose only light came from cigars outlining a face with every puff, the men of the family, smoking more as they felt more conscious of danger, gathered around bottles of rum and whisky, groping for them in the dark to refill their glasses gropingly, and discussing the situation. A dull, infectious, increasing panic filled all the shadows and was brooded over in a thousand different ways, until the sweat of fear broke out on temples and napes of necks ...

The Great and Little Bears and other constellations were fading in the grey dawn, and still there was silence in the capital. The whole country was plunged in silence. The machine-gun fusillade had been useless. Slowly the sun invaded the streets, striking small flashes of light from the broken glass covering the pavements. And now, as a last straw, the Chief of Police found out that his men were panic-stricken. They hadn't seemed so timid and surly-looking when called upon to fight their way up streets, or assault barricades, during some clash between infantry and horsemen, or when marching shoulder to shoulder against a mob armed with sticks, belaying pins, metal pipes, or even firearms (generally old pistols, sporting rifles, or antique muskets); what terrified them was this silence, the solitude all around them, the emptiness of streets leading to the lower slopes of the surrounding mountains, where there wasn't a single passer-by as far as the eye could see. They would have been less afraid of an attack from an angry crowd than of solitary, isolated shots; these separate, single, carefully considered shots, taking careful aim, from a roof or a terrace, might leave a man stretched on the asphalt with a hole bored through his temple or brow as cleanly and surely as if drilled by a saddler's bit. The troops were in barracks; the infantry bivouacked on the patios and the sentries smoked in their sentry boxes. And there was nothing. Silence. A silence broken occasionally—very seldom—by the clamour of a motorcycle (they were always of the brand called Indian) accelerating as the terrified rider made his way to the palace with some disagreeable, laconic, and confidential message. There, some of them lying exhausted in armchairs or on divans, and those too soaked in liquor to drink more keeping awake with the help of tobacco and coffee, were the high officials and dignitaries of the nation, waxen-faced, their necks sweating, their coats off and braces dangling. In the middle of this general collapse, the Head of State was waiting, tense, motionless, dignified and frowning; he was waiting for the Mayorala Elmira, who had muffled herself in a lacy shawl and gone out to get some hot news, walking about in the streets, listening at doors, peering through shut windows, getting information from some unlikely passer-by—such as a drunk female crony and collector of gossip, tremulous with aguardiente. But now she came back, after having walked a long way and not heard anything of interest. Or rather, yes: one thing only. On all the walls and palings of the city, thousands of mysterious hands had written in pale chalk—white, blue, or pink—a single phrase, always the same: "Get out! Get out!"

After a brief pause the President rang a hand bell, as though in a parliamentary session. The others got up from where they were resting, straightening their ties, doing up buttons, and smoothing their hair in an attempt to regain a little composure.

"Excuse me—your fly," said Elmira to the Minister of Communications, who had left it undone.

"Gentlemen," said the Head of State. And there followed a good speech, dramatic but free of emotion or eloquence, a straightforward commentary on the Mayorala's narrative. If his compatriots thought it necessary for him to resign, if his most faithful colleagues (and he begged them to answer simply, frankly, and with equanimity) shared this judgement, he was determined to hand over power immediately to whomever was thought best fitted to assume it. "I await your reply, gentlemen." But the gentlemen did not reply. And after a few minutes of stupor and agonised consideration of the facts, they were left with the fear, overpowering fear, insuperable Blue Funk caused by the people's war cry. Suddenly, looking at one another, they were all thinking that the permanence, the rigour, and above all the Full Acceptance of Responsibility, the Full Acceptance of Guilt, of the Man who was awaiting the sound of their voices with growing impatience, was the only thing that could save them from the menace now haunting them. If the anger of the populace were unloosed, if the masses rushed into the streets, they would look for an abscess to lance, an object on which to rain their blows, a scapegoat, a Head to raise aloft on the point of a pike, while the rest of them might perhaps take different escape routes and manage to get away somehow or other. Otherwise, the general fury would reach them all equally, and for lack of the Body now standing before them their bodies would end up, dragged along, quartered, unidentifiable in the city drains—unless they had been hung up on a telegraph post with infamous placards pinned to their chests.

At last the President of the Senate spoke up and said what they all wanted him to say: That after so many sacrifices for the good of the nation (here came a list of some of them), at

a time when our country was threatened by dissolving forces
(here came imprecations against all socialists, Communists,
international crooks, the Student and his paper, the professor
of Nueva Córdoba and the party he created yesterday and gave
the pedantic name of Alpha-Omega—"he's the worst bugger
of the lot" remarked Peralta, and was immediately silenced
by a gesture of annoyance from his listener), in these critical
hours they were asking a supreme proof of self-sacrifice, etc.,
etc., on the part of the Head of State, because if in so serious a moment of peril he abandoned us, and deprived us of
the help of his lucidity and political sense (here came mention of his other qualities and virtues), our friendless country could only groan, like our Lord on the Cross: "*Eloi, Eloi,
lama sabachthani*."

The President, who had been listening to all this with
bent head and chin on his breast, now flung his arms apart
and straightened his whole body.

"Gentlemen, let us set to work. The Council is open."
There was long applause and each man took his place at the
long table running down the middle of the room next door,
which was hung with Gobelins.

At three o'clock that day a great many telephones began
ringing. At first there were a few only, intermittent and at
intervals. Then more numerous, with louder voices, impatiently shouting. A host of telephones. A vast chorus of telephones. A world of telephones. And calls from patio to patio,
voices running along roofs and terraces, crossing gaps, flying
from corner to corner. And windows began opening. And
doors began opening. And someone leans out, gesticulating.
And ten lean out, gesticulating. And people run out into the
streets; and some embrace and others laugh, some run, meet,
gather in groups, inflate their chests, form into a procession,
and another procession, and more processions appear at the

entries to streets, come down from the hills and up from the
depths of valleys, and coalesce into a crowd, an enormous
crowd, shouting: "Long live Liberty!"

Now everyone knows and is telling his neighbour: the
Head of State has just died. Of a heart attack say some. But
no; he was assassinated by conspirators. No, not that either:
he was shot by a sergeant affiliated with Alpha-Omega. No,
that wasn't right either: someone really in the know said that
he was killed by the Student, with the same Belgian pistol the
Man always had on his desk, and that he emptied the whole
lot of bullets—some said it contained six, others eight—into
his body. One of the palace servants had seen the whole thing,
and he said . . . But he's dead, all right. He's dead. That is the
great, beautiful, joyful, tremendous cause for jubilation. And
it seems that they are taking the Corpse—the enormous
Corpse—through the streets. The people living in the San
José district saw it being dragged along by a lorry, with the
skull bumping on the paving stones. Now everyone must go
to the centre of the town, singing in chorus the National Anthem, the Liberator's Anthem, the "Marseillaise" and the "Internationale," which unexpectedly came to mind.

But at this moment the armoured cars of the 4th Mo-
torised Division appear and open fire on the crowd. The men
of the palace garrison fire all together from behind the cover
given by the wide banisters of the upper terrace and sandbags brought days before. Grenades fall from the telephone
tower, leaving screaming gaps in the crowds holding a meeting below. Dozens of machine guns poke out from corners.
Closing the avenues, police and soldiers are now advancing
at a slow, measured tread in close files, letting off their rifles
at every three paces. The now-terrified people are running,
fleeing, leaving bodies and more bodies and yet more bodies
on the pavements, throwing down flags and placards, trying

to get inside houses by forcing shut doors, or jump into interior patios or lift the lids of sewers. And still the troops advance, slowly, very slowly, firing all the time, trampling on the wounded lying on the ground, or finishing off with bayonets or the butts of their rifles any who clutch at their boots and leggings. And at last, after the crowd has been reduced and dispersed, the streets are once again deserted. The fire brigades come out to put out a few fires. Here and there are heard the long, vicious, insistent sirens of ambulances. When night falls all the streets are patrolled by the army. And everyone—all those who had sung so many hymns and given cheers for this and that—had to face an appalling truth. The Head of State had assassinated himself; he had spread abroad the news of his death, so that crowds should throng the streets and be shot down with supreme ease.

And now, sitting on the presidential chair with all his supporters around him, he was celebrating the victory.

"You'll see, they'll open all the shops tomorrow and stop making such bloody nuisances of themselves."

Outside, the chorus of sirens was still going on.

"Bring some champagne, Elmira. The best: from that cupboard; you know where it is . . ."

An occasional single rifle shot could be heard, far away, and sounding feebler than the weapons of the army.

"There are still one or two fools left," said the President. "Gentlemen, once again, we have won."

So much had happened during the day, and public buildings were so deserted that nobody noticed one very strange thing: the sudden disappearance—by theft of course—of the Diamond from the Capitol; yes, of that enormous Tiffany diamond set in the heart of a star at the feet of the gigantic statue of the Republic, and marking the zero point—of convergence and departure—of all the major roads in the country.

# SIX

*... if the contest is too unequal, it is better to choose honourable resignation or abandon the game rather than expose oneself to certain death.*

—DESCARTES

# 17

WHEN I REMEMBER THAT DAY, IT SEEMS TO ME THAT
I lived through some sort of improbable carnival, whose
hours were fuller, more crowded than whole years—a confusion of images, descent into hell, mobs, aimless shouting,
figures revolving, masks, metamorphoses, mutations, din,
substitution of one thing by another, everything upside down,
owls hooting at midday, sunshine in shadow, appearance of
harpies, lambs biting, roars of the meek, fury of weaklings;
uproar where yesterday there was only whispering; and faces
that have stopped looking, and receding backs, and a decor
suddenly changed by the scene shifters of tragedies hatched
in secret, grown in shadow, born in my proximity, although,
deafened as I was by other choirs, I would not have heard the
sound of real choirs—choirs with few singers, but those few
possessing the voices of Great Singers . . .

And so I "opened my heart" to you—as they say here—
with the help of the wine of that triumphant night; at dawn,
after everyone left, I added a bottle of Armagnac, as we sat
there alone watching the peaks of the Tutelary Volcano turn
blue; *we must have a sort of Chamonix up there, and a skating
rink—skiing is marvellous exercise—and a cable railway to get
there, as they do in Switzerland;* two swings of the hammock
and it was three in the afternoon; thus, as an adolescent, you
opened your eyes on the operating theatre after being relieved
of an appendix full of seeds—they said at the time that the
appendicitis had been caused by eating guavas, whose pips

accumulated in that useless organ, left over from the prehistoric days when men were *vêtus de peaux de bêtes*, like those painted by Cormon, and fed on roots and stones of fruits; so you emerged from the chloroform dream, and that male nurse with the white cap and stethoscope around his neck was leaning over you: *have they taken it out already?*; but the nurse is Peralta in male nurse's clothes—*why?*—; and behind him—to my surprise—is Mr. Enoch Crowder, in his round spectacles, with his old puritan's face, but now instead of his frock coat, he has come dressed in tennis clothes, *here, to the Palace?*, striped flannel trousers, with YALE in red letters on his sweater and his racket in his hand; the United States Ambassador coming into your room like this, without asking for an interview, without a top hat or a stiff collar; *they aren't trying to annoy you, you idiot; I'm high on aguardiente, remember*; a half turn, a swing of the hammock, and leave me in peace to sleep; but now some words seem to be coming from a long way off, and swelling, getting louder as they approach, talking to me about a battleship; the *Minnesota* is in Puerto Araguato; a great big ship it is too, with its metal tower and its guns turning and taking aim by electricity, and by some strange chance navigating six miles off our coast for several weeks; they tell me (I'm understanding more and more) that they are going to land marines, that they are already landing; *coffee, damn it, coffee! where is the Mayorala?*; the marines, here; that's what they did in Veracruz; what they did in Haiti, hunting down the niggers; and in Nicaragua and in many other places, with bayonets ready for zambos and Latins; intervention, perhaps, as in Cuba with that General Wood, who was a worse thief than the mother who bore him; landing, intervention, General Pershing's "punitive" expedition, the man of "Over There" and "The Star-Spangled Banner" in the exhausted Europe of '17, who was made fun of and harassed in Sonora by a few guerrillas with cartridge belts around their chests; I'm laughing, but it isn't a joke—oh no; Mr. Enoch Crowder has come here like this, in tennis clothes, racket and all, because he's spent two days without once leaving the Country Club, deliberating in conference with the live wires of the Bank, Trade, and Industry; and it's these sons of bitches who are asking for the *Minnesota* to come here with her filthy marines; but the army, our army, won't allow such an affront to our national honour; only the army happens to have revolted at the present moment; soldiers have deserted their sentry boxes and machine-gun posts, saying that that business yesterday wasn't their fault; that they fired only because they were ordered to by their sergeants and lieutenants; and the sergeants and lieutenants have rebelled against their captains and generals, who have dug themselves into the tall building of the Hotel Waldorf, and go from the bar to the roof and from the roof to the bar, hoping that the marines will arrive and relieve them from being besieged by the crowd—the huge crowd yelling around the building and clamouring for their heads; the palace garrison has disappeared; not even a doorkeeper is left, nor a servant, nor a waiter; don't ask for your ministers; no one knows where your ministers are; *the telephone*: the telephones aren't working; *don't ask for coffee: much better have a glass of aguardiente*, says Peralta (but why the hell is he dressed as a male nurse, with that stethoscope, and that thermometer in the pocket of his overall?), *don't ask for coffee, the Mayorala's got other things to do*; but yes, now that I consider the question more thoroughly I agree with the captains and generals; let the marines land, let them land: we'll arrange about that afterwards—we'll negotiate, we'll talk—but for the moment, order, order is what we need . . .

"*You're crazy*," says the male nurse: "*what these people of the Bank and Business, and also this gentleman here, all want is for you to go to hell; they've had enough; you've been playing the devil with their patience for more than twenty years; they don't like you; no one likes you; if you're still alive it's because everyone thinks you're with the others in the Waldorf; they can't believe you could possibly be such a fool as to stay here alone, without companions or guards; it hasn't entered anyone's head; but when they do find out ... I don't like to think what'll happen! ... So let's bugger off. But—at once!"*

I begin to understand. I get up. I hunt for my slippers.

"*But, fuck it all, I've not resigned! I'm the President!*"

"*You think so?*" says the male nurse. "*Luis Leoncio is already in Nueva Córdoba. A procession of cars has gone to fetch him.*"

"*That cretin, with his Alpha-Omega?*"

"*He's the only man who can clear up the situation,*" says the tennis player.

"*But ...*"

"*For the present we're backing him.*"

"*So you're dropping me?*"

"*Our State Department knows what it's doing.*"

"*How can they take that professor seriously, a man who ...*"

The tennis player was showing signs of impatience: "*I've not come here to argue, but to face facts. Doctor Luis Leoncio has the support of the active forces in this country. A lot of young people with democratic ideals are supporting him.*"

"*I see: Belén, the Methodist colleges, and the Statue of Liberty.*"

"*Don't waste any more time, damn it: finish dressing!*"

"*Doctor Luis Leoncio has ideas, a plan,*" says the tennis player.

"*So has the Student,*" I say.

"*But that's a very different matter,*" says the tennis player, passing his racket from one hand to another.

"*You must know that it was really the Student who did you in,*" says the male nurse. "*The bombs, those macabre jokes and false rumours all came from Alpha-Omega. But the general strike was the Student's doing. A splendid piece of work, by the way. I wouldn't have thought him capable of it.*"

"*And are you going to tell me that all the tradesmen who refused to open their shops were Bolsheviks?*"

"*It was precisely because they were afraid of the Bolsheviks that they didn't open their shops. By joining the stoppage they were protecting their goods. And now they will lay them at the feet of the Caudillo of Nueva Córdoba, defender of order and prosperity, who will try to tame the Student—or something of the sort—and give some legality to his party. Because now there'll be political parties in the country.*"

"*The businessmen are managing things intelligently,*" said the tennis player; "*wise men.*"

Coming to my senses, I suddenly say that there's still time to do something: make peace with Hungary, which now has a stable government, restore constitutional guarantees, create a Ministry of Employment, remove press censorship, create a coalition cabinet until the forthcoming elections, to be supervised by a mixed commission, if that seems suitable.

"*Stop talking rubbish,*" says the male nurse. "*We've come to the crunch now. If we don't clear out quickly, the crowd will soon be here, and you can imagine what that means. They loathe your guts!*"

At that moment a strange figure loomed up in the passage leading to the patio; it was Aunt Jemima, Walter Hoffmann's grandmother, quietly making her way towards the main staircase, carrying on her head, as if it were a coffin, the grandfather clock from the dining room. "I've been in love with it for years," she said as she passed. Behind her came several shady characters—obviously her great-great-grandsons, carrying trays of silver, decanters, and table ornaments taken from the sideboards. This struck me as a final warning:

*"I shall take refuge in the United States Embassy."*

*"Out of the question!"* says the tennis player. *"There'd be a riot in front of the building. Demonstrations. Violence. An impossible situation. The only thing I can do is give you shelter in our consulate at Puerto Araguato. There you will be protected by our marines. My government consents to that."*

*"You'll take me in your car . . ."*

*"I'm sorry, but I can't expose myself to being fired at on the way. The Morejón woodcutters don't understand diplomatic car plates. And there are said to be armed bands in El Bajío."*

*"It's only that there are no trains . . . the strike,"* I say, in a voice that trembles because of saliva that refuses to be swallowed.

*"That's not my fault,"* says the tennis player. Peralta points to his clothes, his cap and stethoscope:

*"I've got an ambulance downstairs. There are no tolls on the road to the Olmedo Colony. And those Germans don't care a fuck for our politics."*

*"Good luck, Señor President,"* says the tennis player.

*"Son of a bitch,"* I say under my breath. But he hears me and says, in the manner of a comic clergyman:

*"Rahab, the woman of Jericho, was a bitch. And today she's reckoned among our Lord's ancestresses. Try reading the Bible on your way, Señor. It's a most comforting book and full of information. There's a lot about overturned thrones in it."* And he picked up his racket, one of those—I remember—that are carried in a trapezoid wooden frame, with four screws holding down the rim of the racket, and took himself off without more ado (I think he said, *"So long"*), and as casually as if he were returning to the American Club, with its deep armchairs, bourbon on the rocks, tickertape, and central heating.

"*Son of a bitch*," I say, and say again and again, because I
have no worse insults in my limited English vocabulary. Now
I look towards the gleaming peak of the Tutelary Volcano, no
longer white but a pale orange from the approach of dusk.
And I can't help my expression being saddened by the tender
melancholy of departure. But now the Mayorala arrives, ec-
centrically attired as a Nazarene Penitent, in a purple tunic,
yellow sash, sandals, a *rebozo* to match the tunic, and carrying
a bundle of clothes.

"She's coming with us," says Peralta. And she explains
with her special combination of mimicry and onomatopoeia:
"Everyone knows that when I was [*gesture of pouting out her
breasts and rounding her hips*] ... you me [*a faint whistle, and
one forefinger making a cross with the other*] and although
I'm not the same [*hands re-modelling a face that was now a
little coarsened*] you and I still go on [*now she joins her forefingers and rubs one against the other*]. And with them being so mad at me, if they caught me [*a whistle accompanied
by a hand clapped to her forehead, and her head falling on
her left shoulder with the mouth open*]. So that's why I ..."
(*loud whistle and arms imitating the movements of someone
running*).

"Besides, the Nazarene dress is a splendid idea," says Peralta. And suddenly I come to myself and remember the most
important thing of all:

"Money! Fuck! Money!"

The Mayorala shows me her bundle of clothes. "The cash
is in here." I open it, to make sure. Yes. Between petticoats and
blouses, there are the $200,000 of my private reserve, in four
bundles of fifty notes each, with portraits of Washington on
them, of course.

And now everything seems to speed up. Peralta is running; the Mayorala is running. A trunk appears. Without

thinking clearly what I'm doing I start putting things in it. Too many things. The blotting paper from my writing table, several medals and decorations, the book of our eleven constitutions, a photo of Ofelia with Gabriele D'Annunzio, that toy—a lizard made of rope—given me by my mother, that beautiful edition of *Les femmes savantes*, containing the lines that, at this moment of crisis, come absurdly to my memory, enlivened by a glass of rum: "*Guenille si l'on veut, ma guenille m'est chère.*"

"Don't put any more rubbish in the trunk," shouts the Mayorala.

"Two shirts, one pair of pants, that's enough," shouts Peralta.

"Two ties and three vests," shouts the Mayorala.

"And now put this waterproof cape right over yourself. Like the poor when they're ill and go to hospital," says Peralta.

"But quickly, for God's sake, quickly!" yells the Mayorala, her voice echoing through the vastness of the Deserted Palace. And they wrap my head in bandages and strips of sticking plaster. A little ketchup to look as if I'd bled. And I go downstairs. The first time in more than twenty years that I don't hear cries of "Attention!"; no one is there to salute me. Palomo, the porter's dog, comes and licks your sweaty hands. You'd like to take him with you.

"*Out of the question. No one has ever seen a dog in an ambulance.*"

And you lie on the stretcher for urgent cases, under the smell of macintosh, disguised as a wounded man—carnival is still going on, terrifying carnival, an apocalyptic transformation scene—and during the vicissitudes of the journey, you live through the hazards of the road you are travelling. Out through the back gate of the palace—former entrance for horse-drawn carriages. Turn to the right. Drive over asphalt.

Calle Beltrán: a short stretch of cobblestones. Left: smoothness of asphalt. Calle de los Plateros. Peralta in the driving seat—a bogus nurse-chauffeur of the Emergency Service—sets the siren going. I'm terrified, thinking we must be attracting attention: but no; it's exactly what we aren't doing. No one looks at the face of the man driving a wailing ambulance. They look at the siren; what's more, anyone who can help by doing so tries to clear the road. Right: more asphalt, the Boulevard del Brasil with its cafés—the Paris, the Tortoni, the Delmonico—sure to be shut because of the strike. Then we drive on and on: there seems to be no traffic on the roads. Peralta doesn't stop at crossroads. And there's a huge rut; there at the corner of the Gallo—the Ministry of Works gave sixty thousand pesos for it to be filled in and the drain put right, but it was never done. I know where we are, and suddenly, for that very reason, I feel afraid, terribly afraid. My flesh tightens over my bones; my thighs are trembling; my breathing has become irregular. Why are we driving so slowly? I know why. And now the male nurse with the stethoscope and smoked glasses is braking—his white cap is well pulled down right over his brows. There is a silence which opens my bladder—I can do nothing to stop it.

"*Excuse me: I've got a seriously wounded man here.*" Another silence, worse than the first. And then the Mayorala's voice: "*Please, Captain, let us by. Don't stop us, for his mama's sake... My brother... A bullet... In front of the palace.*"

The soldier's voice: "*Did they shoot your cunt of a mother too?*"

"*They shot her... [whistle] bang!... From the balcony... Now [*a long blood-curdling whistle on a downward note*]... they're dragging her away... And leaving bits of brains... [*a loud slap*]... at every corner.*"

Soldier: "*Thank God for that!*"

Peralta: "*May we please go by, Captain?*"
"*Go on!*"

And now the streets are of trodden earth. I seem to feel all through my body the ambulance wheels heeling over, falling, rising, staggering, between potholes full of water, whose stench of decay reaches me in my moving cell in spite of the wafts of chloroform pervading it.

"*I ought to have thought about that.*" A little beyond the Italian villas with their nacreous domes, cornucopias, box hedges, and vine arbors—miniature gardens of Aranjuez or Chantilly—we reach the suburbs of the Cerros, Yaguas, and Favelas; villages made of cardboard, dung, and tin cans, with paper walls, the tins rusty, cut up with scissors to cover the roofs—dwellings, if they deserve the name, that are ruined, knocked down and demolished by the rains every year, leaving the children paddling about like pigs, in puddles and mud.

"*I should have thought about that. A plan to build houses for poor families. There would still be time …*"

The Mayorala's voice: "*The road's clear.*" And the ambulance begins to climb, creaking, bumping, bouncing, turning, twisting but always climbing. I recognise the corners on the road. I know we have already reached the farm of El Rengo, from the smell of the brushwood fire burning esparto grass, something forbidden by law; now we are coming to the Little Spanish Castles, because there is the sound of a plank bridge beneath us. The zone of pine forests is beginning. Our road is edged with mulberry trees, whose shade attracts so many poisonous snakes.

I am so exhausted from fighting my terror that I fall asleep.

I open my eyes. We have passed in front of the Germans' Lutheran Church. I take off my bandages and sticking plaster. The ambulance doors open and I descend into the square with an air of calm dignity. But although a few people are about, no one looks at me. The Woglindes, Wellgundes, and Flosshildes go on with their milking. Too many curtains are drawn across windows. I expect human smiles and all I see is braces drawn tight over backs, and backsides with broad buttocks in leather breeches. Peralta talks to the pastor:

"The mechanics are on strike. So do what you like. We shan't interfere."

Followed by the Mayorala, who has just finished tying up my badly fastened suitcase with her sash, we go to the little brick station with its weathercock and imitation stork's nest occupied by a marbled bird lifting up a lobster-red foot. The Little Train is put away in its little hangar. There's enough coal in the tender. And the burnished engine, polished and shining like something just out of a luxury shoe shop, soon starts puffing out smoke. It is as if I could feel its impatient, vibrating life in the levers throbbing under my hands. All the houses in the Olmedo Colony have shut themselves into a darkness whose aim is to ignore me. I let in the steam: the connecting rods begin to move. And the Little German Train enters the curving track cut in the flank of the mountain. We pass the pines—leaving their scent behind—and descend steep slopes covered with cactus and agave, where the spikes of the asphodels are buzzing with bees and quivering in the sea breeze; then, from small to large, from grassy filaments to plumes, come the reeds, bamboos, shady banana trees, with their red fruit tasting of poverty; and then the ochre patches of bare earth—I don't see them, but guess at them from familiarity with the deep ruts in them—before arriving at the sandy plain, where we advance in a straight line as fast as possible, without signals or lights or level-crossing gates, until we stop in the tiny terminus of Puerto Araguato with a tremendous bump owing to tardy braking.

Several marines—white leggings and sweatshirts, rum drinkers' eyes—are drawn up on the two platforms. I discover that they have already occupied the power station, the vital points, bars and brothels of the town, after pissing on the Monument to the Heroes of Independence as they passed it. The North American Consul comes up to me, wearing creased trousers and a cowboy shirt of the sort that has little air holes in the armpits.

"Here I am; I've got the auto outside." And he drives us in a Pathfinder creaking in every joint to the building diplomatically representing his country: a wooden house, with columns and pediment, in a strictly Jeffersonian style, and a North American eagle with a shield on its breast displayed on the balcony.

"You've given me a fat lot of trouble," says the Consul, taking us to the kitchen. "I've got orders to put you on one of our cargo boats arriving here tomorrow, and send you to Nassau. If you're hungry, there are some packets of cornflakes, tins of Campbell's soup, and pork and beans. There's whisky in that cupboard. Help yourself, Mister President, because we know that if you don't get your booze you very soon go around the bend."

"A little more respect, please," I say in a stern tone.

"We're all equals here," says the Consul, going into an office full of bills and papers.

"The Hermès case, Peralta: I prefer our own."

The walls of the kitchen were decorated with cuttings from *Shadowland* and *Motion Pictures*: Theda Bara in *Cleopatra*: Nazimova in *Salomé*; Dempsey knocking out Georges Carpentier; a scene from *Male and Female* with Thomas Meigham and Gloria Swanson; Babe Ruth hitting a home run under the welcoming—almost presbyterian—eyes of an umpire dressed in dark blue.

We've eaten something, and are now sitting in the reception–waiting room–living room of the house, Peralta, the Mayorala, and I. After the tension of the last days, and the paroxysms of anxiety of the last few hours, I feel almost serene. My muscles relax. I begin fanning myself with a palm leaf, rocking myself in what the gringos call a rocking chair and we call, I've no idea why, a Viennese chair—I've never noticed any furniture of this description in Vienna. I look at my secretary:

"For the present, we must concentrate on saving our skins. *Guenille si l'on veut, ma guenille m'est chère.* Now the sea, Bermuda. And afterwards, Paris. In the end we'll get a bit of rest."

"Yes," replies Peralta.

"Our morning walks. Monsieur Musard's Bois-Charbons. Aux Glaces, the Rue Sainte-Apolline, the Chabanais."

"Yes," replies Peralta.

"Happiness prevails, I see," I say.

"Yes," replies Peralta with a gesture of displeasure and boredom.

"When one's luck is out, even dogs piss on one," says the Mayorala, with her usual philosophy, expressed in proverbs and sayings. And she flings herself down to sleep on a raffia ottoman. Close to the gramophone horn, on an antique corner cupboard, lies an old Bible, used by the Consul when some sailor who had lost his papers in a drinking bout could lay valid claim to having been born in Baltimore or Charleston only by swearing with one hand on the Scriptures. Knowing the habits of the members of certain North American sects at moments of crisis, I shut my eyes, opened the book at random, and, after describing three circles with the forefinger of my right hand, I let it fall on a page: "*Deliver me out of the mire, and let me not sink; let me be delivered from them that hate me, and out of the deep waters. Let not the water flood overflow me; neither let the deep swallow me up, and let not the pit shut her mouth on me*" (Psalm 69). I tried again: "*Cast me not off in the time of old age; forsake me not when my strength faileth. For mine enemies speak against me; and they that lay wait for my soul take counsel together*" (Psalm 71). A third time (Jeremiah 12): "*I have forsaken mine house, I have left mine heritage.*" "Fuck the book!" I exclaimed, shutting it so violently that a cloud of dust came out of the binding. And I lounged in the Viennese chair, which was ornamented with a blue ribbon passed through the holes in the wickerwork, and fell into a drowsy state not far from actual sleep. Confused noises. Reality becomes blurred and transformed into incoherent images. I'm asleep.

But I can't have slept long, because very soon—I think—a hand shook the rocking chair violently to waken me.

"Peralta," I said, "Peralta."

"No use calling him," said the Consul. "He's just decamped."

"It's true," said the Mayorala.

And I learned, in a state of such astonishment that I couldn't take in everything I was being told, that dozens of automobiles displaying the greenish-white emblems of Alpha-Omega were driving around the town, and that one of them—which appeared to be a grey Chevrolet—had come to fetch my secretary.

"They'll kill him!" I cried.

"I don't think so."

"But—this is insane! Didn't he resist? He was armed!"

The Consul looked at me sarcastically.

"They were some charming young men wearing greenish-white armlets and a badge—*Alpha* in silvery metal—on their lapels. They embraced Doctor Peralta, who seemed very pleased, and set off for the capital laughing and joking."

"And Peralta didn't explain anything? Didn't he leave me any message?"

"Yes: that I was to tell you he was sorry, but his country came first."

"It's true!" shouted the Mayorala, seeing my stupefied expression, as if it were necessary to shout or I wouldn't understand.

"*Tu quoque, fili mi . . .*"

"What *tu quoque*, and what the hell," said the gringo. "He was doing the dirty on you, that's all. You don't need Latin to see that. It's just politics, and happens everywhere."

"I thought the bastard was a traitor," muttered the Mayorala. "My aunt Candelaria, who knows a lot, saw it in the snails and by breathing into a plate of flour. And now I'm beginning to believe that those bombs that went off in the palace were brought by him in that French case of flasks. It was the only thing that wasn't searched at the door."

And there was the Hermès case, open, with its ten bottle tops in two rows of five. We took out the pigskin-covered flasks. That smell—it seems to me, but I'm not sure—is bitter almonds: the same smell left by the explosion.

"Maybe, maybe not," said the Consul. "It's pretty like the smell of old leather that has had a lot of rum spilled on it."

"The snails don't lie," murmured the Mayorala.

"Maybe yes, maybe not," repeated the Yankee.

Burdened by an enormous feeling of sadness, as of a father spat on, or a beaten cuckold, or King Lear thrown out by his daughters, I hugged my dear Elmira: "You're the only one I've got left."

"Better look out the window," said the Consul, "but be careful you're not seen."

# 18

*. . . it sometimes happens that after listening to a speech whose meaning we have perfectly understood, we cannot say in what language it was uttered.*

—DESCARTES

OUTSIDE, BEYOND THE GUARD OF EIGHT MARINES with rifles sloped from hip to shoulder, a slow and silent procession of people were passing and re-passing, but always looking towards the house. They knew I was there, and they went on walking around and around, like students on a Sunday walk, hoping that I would look out a window, open a door, or make my presence shown somehow or other.

"In the capital, they're looting the ministers' houses, hunting out police and informers, carrying off spies, burning secret archives. The people have opened the prisons and set free all political prisoners."

"The end of the world," said the Mayorala, looking panic-stricken.

"And when will they get me?" I said, with a forced smile.

"I don't think they'll jump over the wall," said the Yankee. "And they won't do that because the Student—the chap who started the strike—has distributed an intelligent manifesto to the public. Read that . . ."

But my hands were trembling too much, and my spectacles were misted with sweat.

"Better tell me."

"Well, to sum it up: he says they mustn't provoke our soldiers (no throwing stones or bottles, nor even insulting them); they mustn't attack our diplomatic representatives, nor our compatriots; in fact, nothing that could justify a major military action on our part. Up till now, there's been no *intervention*, only a *landing*. Question of subtle differences of meaning—*nuances*, as the French say. And the Student understands nuances. He says that the pleasure of hanging you from a telegraph pole isn't worth the risk of an *intervention*, which might very well turn into *occupation*."

"As in Haiti," I said.

"Exactly. That's what the Student doesn't want. He's intelligent, that boy!"

And I was thinking of the vertiginous transformation of roles that had taken place in the course of a few hours in the scenario of the revolt. Now it was the Student who had in a flash become the custodian of my threatened existence. And, while still remaining hidden, without replying to the calls from Alpha-Omega, who offered him guarantees and invited him to collaborate in the National Coalition Government, which Luis Leoncio Martínez was setting up in the palace, with the advice of Enoch Crowder and the help of those of the military leaders not implicated in the shooting of the day before yesterday, and one or two sergeants promoted to colonels, he remained faithful to his underground work as Invisible Man, and could still with one word control those who had collected in front of the Eagle-with-a-Shield-on-Its-Breast, and were beginning—by ones, twos and threes—to join their voices in a chorus of insults.

"So long as they don't go further than shouting," says the Consul. But I'm beginning to be afraid that they will in fact go further than shouting. And I suddenly see myself

in a looking-glass covered in fly shit, supported on a rickety bracket and covering one wall of the office; I'm a pitiful
sight; the dressing gown I was wearing when I left the palace is filthy; my shirt from New and Lingwood in London is
filthy and crumpled from so much coming and going, all the
starch of its collar melted by the sweat of fear; my pearl-grey
tie, very suitable to the Head of State, is stained with the saliva that has trickled from my mouth during my recent sleep.
And my striped trousers, suddenly detached from a stomach
dwindled in size in the last few hours, are slipping down over
my hips, giving me the look of the funny man in an English
music hall. And the Mayorala is replying with tremendously
obscene gestures, illustrating a large repertory of internal imprecations, to those people shouting outside. And all at once
I'm terrified.

"Why don't you take me on board the *Minnesota?*" I
entreat.

"You're just talking big," says the Yankee, in an unexpectedly joking tone, very unsuitable (truth to tell) to a diplomatic official. "I'm merely a simple consul, who believes he's
doing the correct thing in giving you shelter. If tomorrow
it suits my people to say I've made a mistake, I shall accept
that I've made a mistake, inform the press that I've made a
mistake, and say I'm sorry I made a mistake; then they'll send
me somewhere else, and no one will be any the wiser. On
board the *Minnesota*, on the other hand, you would be the
official protégé of our Great American Democracy" (he made
a comic military salute), "which can't at a moment like this
figure publicly as protecting the 'Butcher of Nueva Córdoba,'
who has once more been appearing from coast to coast in
Randolph Hearst's chain of periodicals, along with Monsieur
Garcin's photos and everything that cooked your goose when
they appeared in Paris. Besides, we don't know how long the

*Minnesota* will remain in these waters. Maybe a week; maybe a month; maybe years: just look at Haiti, where from *landing* to *intervention* and from *intervention* to *occupation—des nuances, des nuances, des nuances toujours*—one thing followed another. Don't get into a stew. Keep calm. I'll have you out of danger by tomorrow. Besides, I can't do anything else: I'm carrying out instructions."

I'm feeling swindled, made fun of, tricked.

"And I've always got on so well with all of you. You're indebted to me for so many favours!"

The Consul is smiling behind his tortoiseshell-rimmed spectacles: "And without that, how do you suppose you'd have kept in power so long? Favours, indeed? Now we shall receive them from the Professor of Theosophy."

"And why not from the Student while we're about it?" I said, to mortify him.

"That's difficult to bring off. He's a new species of man even within his species. A lot of his sort are appearing on the continent, although your generals and doctors try to ignore them."

"They loathe you North Americans."

"That can't be helped: our Bibles and their *Kapital* are hopelessly incompatible."

The row outside intensified. The Mayorala multiplied her dumb-show gestures in response to those who were insulting me. It would be easy enough to break through the guard of marines; easy enough to jump over the wall . . .

"Anyhow, I should be better off on board the *Minnesota*," I insisted.

"I don't think so," said the Yankee. And speaking between little hiccoughs of suppressed laughter he said:

"You've forgotten the Eighteenth Amendment to the United States Constitution. Ever since 1919—I'm quoting from memory—'the manufacture and consumption (I said: *consumption*) of all forms of alcoholic drink in the entire territory of the United States is forbidden.' The *Minnesota* is an integral part, in juridical and military terms, of the United States. All right for a man who drinks only ginger ale and Coca-Cola. But one doesn't wake up with trembling hands on drinks like those ..."

"But aren't we on United States territory here, too?" I said, pointing to the case left by Peralta, so it happened, just beneath an orographic and hydrographic map of the country.

"I can't prevent an invalid from bringing his medicines along. And as I've been *taken in*, over this whole affair, I can very well believe that this is chest mixture or Scott's Emulsion. On the *Minnesota* they'd throw *that* into the sea, in strict observance of the Eighteenth Amendment of our Constitution—although left to himself, the captain might be more of a drunk than the mother who bore him."

"They seem to be going away," said the Mayorala, with her nose glued to the shutters. I looked out: as if impelled by some event, people were making off in groups towards the Customs House, where some sort of movement of lorries and goods' trucks was going on.

"*The strike is over,*" I announced, deepening my voice without noticing it. "*The situation has been normalised.*"

"*There is order throughout the country,*" said the Consul, imitating me in a comic manner. And, regaining his good humour: "Come to Captain Nemo's cabin. You'll be better off there."

And letting me out of the house by a passage at the back, he took me to a long outhouse with its doors hanging from the hinges, and shut in by the water of the bay, which reached under cover as far as the extremity of a floor of wooden planks, smelling of the green slime of winkles, clams in shadow, stranded jellyfish, and rotting seaweed: with that penetrating odour of fermenting sourness, of sex and moss, dried fish scales, amber and saturated wood that is the smell of the sea at its work of destruction—a smell reminiscent of that of a wine press sleeping under its floor of grapes and nightly distilling its aftertaste of must. This was the boathouse where had been kept, only a short while ago, the elegant, light, pointed boats of the members of a yacht club that had come down in the world through the collapse of my currency. The boats themselves had vanished, and what in fact remained— the Consul's remarks had prepared me for this—indefinably reminded me by their Victorian style, like a copperplate engraving, a *ciné Lumière*, and a junk shop at the same time, of the illustrations to *Twenty Thousand Leagues under the Sea* in the Hetzel edition, with its title stamped in gilt on raspberry-coloured boards. Old armchairs, furniture suitable to Mr. Pickwick, with hunting horns hanging on the walls; etchings so encroached upon by fungi and saltpetre that their subject had disappeared beneath fungus and saltpetre, and fungus and saltpetre had become the only subject. And, looking at these unexpected objects filling the place—feeling somewhat strengthened personally by the unhoped-for disappearance of the people who had been insulting me a few minutes ago, and my legs cured of their trembling by the drinks I had swallowed—I am surprised by the value certain elements in my surroundings have suddenly acquired, by the new significance objects now possess, and by the way time is lengthened and expanded by immediate danger of death. An hour suddenly seems to last for two hours; each movement becomes a member of a hierarchy of successive movements, as in a military exercise; the sun moves more slowly or more quickly; a vast space yawns between ten o'clock and eleven; night is so far away that its arrival might perhaps be indefinitely delayed;

the advance of an insect over the cover of that book acquires enormous importance; the spiders' webs spread themselves out into works of art from the Sistine Chapel; the indifference of the seagulls, busy over their fishing as usual on a day like this, seems to me nothing short of indecent; the bell tolling once more from the hermitage in the mountains sounds disrespectful; I am deafened by the dripping of a tap, with its obsessional "never more, never more, never more." Yet, at the same time, this fantastic capacity to give sustained, acute, excessive attention to the appearances of things, to what is revealed, or grows bigger without changing shape, is as if contemplation were equivalent to clutching something, to saying: "I see, therefore I am." And since "I see" will have greater significance when I do see more, I am establishing the permanence of existence both within and outside myself.

Now the Consul is showing me a rare collection of root sculptures, sculpture roots, root forms, root objects—baroque roots of roots that are austere in their smoothness; complicated, intricate, or nobly geometrical; at times dancing, at times static, or totemic, or sexual, something between an animal and a theorem, a play of knots, a play of asymmetry, now alive, now fossilised—which the Yankee tells me he has collected on numerous expeditions along the shores of the continent. Roots torn up from remote soil, dragged along, cast up, and again transported by rivers in spate; roots sculpted by the water, hurled about, knocked over, polished, burnished, silvered, denuded of their silver, until from so many journeys, falls, collisions with rocks, battles with other pieces of wood on the move, they have finally lost their vegetable morphology, become separated from the tree mother, the genealogical tree, and acquired breast-like roundnesses, polyhedric arms, boars' heads or idols' faces, teeth, claws, tentacles, penises, and crowns, or are intimately connected in obscene imbrications, before being stranded, after a journey lasting centuries, on some beach forgotten by maps. That huge mandragora with its fierce thorns had been found by the Consul at the mouth of the Bio-Bio, close to the jagged rocks of Con-Con, rocking in a hammock of black waters. That other mandragora, contorted and acrobatic, with its fungus hat and bulging eyes— rather like the "root of life," which certain Asiatic peoples put in flasks of aguardiente—had been found near Tucupita in the estuary of the Orinoco. Others came from the island of Nevis, from Aruba, from the rocks like basalt menhirs that rise amidst thunderous marine gorges near Valparaiso. And it was enough to mention the name of a port to the collector for him to pass from the root found there to the invocation, evocation, presentation of images brought to life by the syllables making up its name, or the proliferative activity of the letters—so he said—a process such as was foreshadowed in the Hebrew Kabbalah. And merely by pronouncing the word *Valparaiso* there were plateaux of jurel fish lying on seaweed, a display of fruit in the church porch, the windows of inns showing the whole counter covered in apocalyptic spider crabs from Tierra del Fuego; and there were the German beer shops in the main street, where reddish-black sausages spotted with bacon fat lay beside warm strudels powdered with sugar; and there were the enormous public lifts, tirelessly moving parallel to each other, with orchestras of blind men playing polkas in the tunnels by which you reached them; and there were the pawnshops, with a broad-buckled belt, a reliquary made of shells, a scalpel with a jagged edge, a negro figure from Easter Island, slippers embroidered with *Souv* (for the left foot) and *Enir* (for the right), which, when put endways on to the passer-by, illustrated with amazing eloquence Kant's Paradox of the Looking-glass.

This other root—known as Leap-frog—looking like a

terrified flying lemur because it is running in the uttermost panic without moving, recalls Rio de Janeiro. The Itamaraty district, amongst municipal buildings crowded with acromegalic statues (always one and a half times or two and three quarter times as large as the real figure of the hero or important figure they are supposed to immortalise), has shops full of embalmed animals: boas gazing through glass marbles, armadillos, ounces, herons, monkeys, and even dusty, saddled horses, which appear to be standing waiting on their green wooden pedestals for a rider who never arrives—who is dead perhaps and has long been lying under a flamboyant Portuguese tomb. This other root, a sort of gnome whose stomach-head swings between feeble limbs—he is called "Humpty-Dumpty"—comes from Port-au-Prince, where in the district of La Frontière, between taverns built of planks and musty Voodoo charms, naked negresses lie in woven hammocks awaiting their visitors with supreme haughtiness, as if lost in their own thoughts, far away, and unconsciously imitating with a hand lying softly open over their stiff pubic curls the gesture of Manet's *Olympia*.

Next the Consul shows me "Erasmus of Rotterdam," a Veracruzan root in the style of Holbein and looking very much like a pensive humanist; "Pichrochole" and "Ragamuffin," bamboo roots with the aggressive appearance of German mercenaries, and bristling with nails; "Chimera," with a long beak and battlemented crest; "Kikimora," dishevelled and spurred, and those three shoots from a single stem known as the "Pieds-Nickelés" (familiar to me because I had subscribed for years to the Parisian paper *L'Épatant*—a fact not generally known); and a little farther back a Romanesque monstrosity of a Cuban mangrove, called the "Spanish Heretic," next to the liana ballerina "Anna Pavlova"; and the "Cyclops," who, with his red stone buried in his forehead, seems to be

watching over a wild world arranged on brackets, wherein
live the "Hydra of Larna," "Rackham's Witch," riding on a
broomstick that is part of herself, "The Silent Woman," seemingly cut from basalt of vegetable origin and (without direct
allusion to feminine forms) a figure of curves and turgidity, of
superimposed roundnesses, of flexions and hollows, arousing
unambiguous recollections in the hands raised to feel them.

The truth was that because of the eccentricity of his culture and his understanding of languages—unusual in a North
American—the Consul was beginning to figure as a dream
element in the real daytime nightmare now being experienced by eyes that were all too wide open—as I descended
into the depths of terror with the help of alcohol; although
I had hardly emerged from the vapour of one or two drinks
when the sweat of anxiety broke out on the nape of my neck,
my forehead, in my grey hairs, over a ground bass of hammering heartbeats so violent that I thought they were in the
armchair where I was sitting. And now the Yankee is sitting
in front of a harmonium in the corner, pulling out three stops,
pressing down the pedals, and he begins playing something
bearing a relation to the music that invaded my country many
years ago, although it's more angular and full of contrasts and
accents, of course, than such tunes as "Whispering" or "Three
o'Clock in the Morning," so often heard recently in the capital.
With his fingers still restlessly moving, marking time with his
head and releasing the notes with the casual automatism of
popular music:

"I'm a southerner . . . New Orleans. White enough to pass
as a white man, although my hair—well, my hair would be
too frizzy if it weren't for the pomades they make to deal with
that. (*B flat*, damn you!) I've 'crossed the line,' as we say there,
although in *sentimental* matters, as you might call them, I only
get on well with darkies. That way I take after my great-uncle

Gottschalk, a musician—you wouldn't know him—who, though preferred to Chopin by Théophile Gautier, adored by the same Lamartinian and philharmonic nymphs who went to bed with Franz Liszt, celebrated in Europe, favoured by royalty, friend of the Queen of Spain, ten times decorated, yet suddenly left all this (public, palaces, coaches, lackeys) to respond to the imperious, urgent call of negresses and mulattos waiting in the tropics to reclaim from him what was theirs by temporary right of conquest. And he followed them to Cuba, Puerto Rico, all the Antilles, rejuvenated, adventurous, liberated from protocol and honours, restored to the billing and cooing of early days, to his adolescent appetite, finally going to die in Brazil, where the Sacred Places of his peregrination also abounded—and how! '*Et les servantes de ta mère, grandes filles luisantes, remuaient leurs jambes chaudes près de toi qui tremblait . . . sa bouche avait le goût des pommes-roses, dans la rivière, avant midi.*' " (I don't know who wrote what he had just recited, but I do remember, yes, I remember that when my daughter, Ofelia, was learning the piano she played some charming Creole dances by that same Moreau Gottschalk, and that I was told how he once let loose on Havana a symphony he had written, including thunderous African drums among its instruments.)

The Consul goes on: "He was a friend, a very great friend of the amazing W. C. Handy, who wrote this 'Memphis Blues' I'm playing now." From there he passes to the "St. Louis Blues" by the same Handy, which has the effect of rousing the Mayorala and starting her off dancing—and probably very well, because she suits her steps and swaggering movements magnificently to the rhythms of music quite new to her.

"It's that they've got it in their blood," says the southerner. I look at his hands moving over the keys: it's a sort of dialogue—sometimes a battle—opposition and agreement between the female hand (the right) and the male hand (the left), which combine, complement each other, respond, but in a synchronisation that is situated both within and outside the rhythm. The Mayorala, as though under the spell of a novelty that she is absorbing through her skin, sits herself down on the harmonium stool, making sexy, enveloping and brazen movements with her shoulders, with one buttock unsupported because there isn't room for both in the space left by the Consul. He forgets his keys and presses his face to Elmira's neck, while she laughs as though being tickled, letting herself be sniffed with the delight of a Christian penetrating the perfumed ambit left by a censer.

> *Guidé par ton odeur vers de charmants climats*
> *Je vois un port rempli de voilures et de mâts*
> comes from the Consul.

"Leave Baudelaire alone!" I cry, jealous at this incursion into my own territory, first ploughed and tilled by me more than twenty years ago, and always yielding to my desires ever since, and which now that I had lost everything was all that I had left, the only plot ruled over by me in a country that was mine yesterday, mine from north to south, from ocean to ocean, and now reduced to a wretched shed made of rotten planks, filled with dead roots, a beggarly landing stage, where I must wait for tomorrow's launch—how far away, remote, unattainable that *tomorrow* seemed!—fated to be smuggled out of here like contraband goods, like a dead man's coffin in a rich hospital, from here, where I had been the master of men, destinies, and property. Hauling her up by one arm, I drag the Mayorala from where her sexual behaviour is exceeding what is admissible, and push her into an armchair in the corner of the room.

"That's better," says the gringo, laughing, "because *that*
is what sunk me in my career." This word *career*—diplomacy,
presumably—in the other man's mouth, in view of who he is
and where he is, is associated in my mind with the epithet of
"great nonsense" given by Don Quixote to a chivalrous romance badly represented by the figures in an altarpiece. For
every Latin American of my generation, a *career* is a sine-
cure involving little work and much pleasure, in embassies
surrounded by scenes from grand opera, Italian marbles and
the lights of Versailles, with violins on the platform, waltz-
ers in braided uniforms and low-cut dresses, solemn ush-
ers, chamberlains in knee-breeches, intrigues, soirées, love
affairs, alcoves, romance, the manners of the Marqués de
Bradomin and the wit of Talleyrand, prodigies of tact and
"savoir vivre," much too remote generally from the notions of
our own people, who never succeeded in absorbing the rules
of etiquette and who—through not asking, and not taking
advice—committed errors such as (it happened in my palace) arranging for the "Rondo alla turca" to be played when
Abdul-Amid's ambassador was presenting his credentials, or
Huerta's "Hymn of Riego" for one of Alfonso XIII's ministers.

"Everything went well with me," went on the southerner,
"until they found out in Paris that I went too often to a Marti-
niquan dance hall in the Rue Blomet. Since then, I have only
filled brilliant posts in North American diplomacy. Consul
in Aracajú, in Antigua, in Guanta, in Mollendo, in Jacmel,
and even in Manta, opposite the beaches of which sharks appear at noon every day with a punctuality comparable only to
that of the Apostles in Strasbourg Cathedral. And now I am
here, which is the devil's own hideout. And it's because they
knew" (he was looking at the Mayorala) "that I ... well, you
and I understand each other." He played an arpeggio. "If I
were to show myself as I now am at my birthplace I should be

lynched by the cowled members of the Ku Klux Klan; chaps with white souls and white robes, with that peculiar whiteness, very much ours, which was also Benjamin Franklin's, according to whom the negro was 'the animal who ate most and produced least'; the whiteness of Mount Vernon, where a slave owner used to philosophise about the equality of men before God; the whiteness of our Capitol, the temple where the hymn of the Gettysburg Address is sung—'government of the people, by the people, and for the people'—with a chorus of negro street sweepers, boot blacks, ash-can emptiers, and lavatory attendants; whiteness of our most illustrious White House, where the roundabout of uniforms, frock coats and top hats is organised, which in this Latin America of ours brings thieves and sons of bitches to the fore—present company not excepted—with each turn of the handle."

I remarked to the Consul that the epithet "son of a bitch" was rather strong in tone for someone who barely forty-eight hours ago was Head of State of a free and sovereign nation, which, as to heroic antecedents, great men, history, etc., etc.

"If my tongue was loosened, it was the fault of Santa Inés," said the Consul, filling my glass. "I had no desire to be offensive. Besides . . ."

"Look, look!" said the Mayorala in a tone that boded no good, inviting us by gestures to go close to a small window with broken panes giving onto the bay.

"Yes," said the gringo, "something is going on there on the wharf." He opened the exit hatches of the—hitherto nonexistent—racing launches. Over there, towards the end of the quay used by sugar boats, something strange was undoubtedly happening. A crowd had collected around one or two lorries—the same they had seen a little time ago, which were loaded with enormous objects, upright or horizontal, a bazaar of shapes laid crossways and in disorder, which . . .

"Take the binoculars," said the Consul to me. I looked. Singing and dancing tipsily, people were lowering from lorries and throwing into the sea, with roars of laughter and shouts, busts and heads and statues of me that had years ago been officially set up in schools, colleges, town halls, public offices, town and village squares, or one-horse dumps, where they had often kept company with some Lourdes Grotto or rusticised niche full of candles and tapers always kept lit in honour of our Divine Shepherdess. And there were marble figures, the work of local sculptors or pupils of the School of Fine Arts; and there were bronze busts, cast in Italy in the same foundry where Aldo Nardini's gigantic Republic had seen the light; standing statues—the full figure—in tailcoat with crosses and ribbon in relief, as general of the armies (with such an exaggerated kepi that my enemies used to say there was "a peak in advance and a peak in retreat"), and as Doctor Honoris Causa of the University of San Lucas (this had been in 1909) in cap and gown with a tassel falling over the left shoulder, as a Roman patrician, as a tribune making some sort of signal with his arm (inspired to some extent by the statue of Gambetta in Paris), as a thoughtful paterfamilias; a stern Mentor, as Cincinnatus crowned with laurels— now all these were lying prostrate, carried on stretchers, loaded onto carts and barrows, drawn by oxen, dragged along and thrown into the water, one after another, with crowbars and the rhythmic shoving of men and women together: "one . . . two . . . threeeee." Finally my equestrian statue appeared—the one I used to see every day from the palace balconies—lying on a railway truck, but now without its rider, because the rider had been torn down on the night of my flight, leaving only the bronze horse. And the horse, hoisted to an erect position by a crane and deprived of Him who used to control his bit from above, rose for a moment in one final heroic rearing movement before plunging into a sheet of foam.

"*Memento homo*," I said, leaving the rest unsaid, because the classical phrase had suddenly been supplanted in my mind by the recollection of a cruel joke the Student had made at my expense.

"Don't make fun of the text of the Requiem," said the Consul. "Now those statues of yours are resting at the bottom of the sea; they'll turn green with saltpetre, corals will cling to them, and sand cover them. And in the year 2500 or 3000 a dredger's scoop will come across them and bring them to light again. And people will ask, in the tone of Arvers' sonnet: 'And who was this man?' and very likely no one will be able to answer. It will happen just as it did to the Roman sculptures of the worst period that one sees in so many museums: all that's known about them is that they represent *A Gladiator*, *A Patrician*, or *A Centurion*. The names are lost. In your case they'll say: 'Bust, or statue, of *A Dictator*. There have been so many and there still will be in this hemisphere that his name isn't important.'" (He picked up a book lying on a table.) "Do you figure in *Pequeño Larousse*? No? ... Well, then, that's the end of you."

And that afternoon I wept. I wept because a dictionary—"*Je sême à tout vent*"—was unaware of my existence.

# SEVEN

*And deciding not to seek more knowledge than what I could find in myself . . .* —DESCARTES

# 19

SEIGNORIAL AND HARMONIOUS, SOLIDLY ESTABLISHED
within the circle of architectural blocks that surrounded the
triumphal square—as if armoured against some attack from
outside by a thick patina, growing darker every year, and variegated by mouldings and reliefs—the house in the Rue de
Tilsitt received him in the lap of her porch protected by high
black grilles, just as a mountain inn receives the alpinist who
has lost his way and knocks at the door after a hallucinatory
journey between avalanches and precipices. It was five o'clock
in the morning. Using his private key so as not to wake Sylvestre, the Head of State entered the hall and turned on the
light. Behind him came the Mayorala, who had been shivering and coughing all the way from the Gare Saint-Lazare,
in spite of the moth-eaten fur-lined coat she had bought in
Bermuda; she complained of fainting fits, a cold on her chest,
and aching bones, and asked for rum, a bed, and some balsam
of Tolu.

"Give her whatever Santa Inés is left and take her up the
back stairs to one of the rooms in the attic," said the *Ex* (he
called himself the *Ex* now, with irritable irony) to the cholo
Mendoza, who arrived with the luggage. Alone at last, he
looked around, noticing changes in decoration and furniture.
Where he had expected to find the mahogany table with Chinese vases on it, the marble flower in whose corolla visiting
cards used to be left, the water nymph swathed in her hair

who had as long as he could remember stood in front of crimson velvet hangings covered in daggers and swords, he now found himself faced by the nudity of walls painted a pale colour and with no decoration besides a few plaster arabesques, which with much thought might be seen as a very stylised representation of curving waves. As for the furniture, there was a long bench with cushions of a fiery colour that was perhaps the shade known as "tango," and standing on narrow pedestals were glass spheres, prisms, and rhombs, enclosing electric lightbulbs.

"It's not ugly; but what was here before was more distinguished-looking, more in keeping with the house," reflected the *Ex*.

He went up to the first floor, delightedly sniffing the aroma of the polished walnut stairs, whose very permanence helped to annihilate the long, infinitely long time that had passed. The pale yellow light of the rising sun was already beginning to appear through the drawing-room curtains. The President went to one of the windows and parted the brocade to look out into the Place de la Concorde. There, as magnificent and regal as ever, stood the Arc de Triomphe, with its open-mouthed Marseillaise, its vociferous Tyrtaeus in armour, and the old warrior in a helmet, followed by the boy hero with his little balls exposed to view. There, for all time, was represented the genius of Cartesian France, the only country capable of having created the anti-Cartesian world, imagined, given life, raised up and then broken by an improbable Corsican, a portentous foreigner, sexually bewitched by a mulatto from Martinique, who had lost his general's hat in a Muscovite fire after his armies, diluted with Poles and Mamelukes, had been thrashed by the guerrilla troops of the Cura Merino and the indomitable Juan Martín. But behind the man looking at this monument were some pictures that might have represented the spirit of Cartesian France more completely. He turned on the light and went up to them. And what met his eyes was so unexpected, so absurd, and so inconceivable that he sank into a chair, stupefied but trying to understand.

Instead of Jean-Paul Laurens' Merovingian Saint Radegonde with her pilgrims from Jerusalem there now stood three persons, if persons they could be called, their perfectly flat anatomy reduced to geometric planes, whose faces—assuming they were faces—were covered with masks. One of them wore a monk's hood and carried a musical score in his hand; the middle one, in a clown's hat, was blowing on something like a clarinet; the third, in harlequin checks, had a mandolin or guitar or lute, or heaven knows what, slung around his middle. And these three persons—if they really were persons—were there, motionless and grotesque, like creatures in a nightmare, gazing out—if that was what they were doing—with the air of people who are annoyed by the presence of an intruder. "What are you doing here?" they seemed to be saying. "What are you doing here?"

But this wasn't all: on the other wall instead of Elstir's delicate seascape there was something indescribable: a conjunction of lines—horizontal, vertical, and diagonal, in the colours of earth and sand—on which had been stuck a piece cut out of a newspaper (*Le Matin*), which the *Ex* tried to remove with his thumbnail, but without success, as the varnish resisted his efforts. Opposite, where Dumont's *Cardinals at Supper* used to hang, there was now something completely meaningless, which might perhaps be a pattern book of Ripolin paints, because it consisted of white, red, and green rectangles and circles, edged with thick black outlines. To the side, the place of Chocarne-Moreau's *Little Chimney Sweep* had been taken by a kind of crooked, hunch-backed, bandy

Eiffel Tower, apparently broken down the middle by a titanic sledgehammer fallen from the sky. Over there, between the two doors, some women—women?—whose legs and arms were made of something like sections of central-heating tubing. Where I had placed Bérard's *Fashionable Reception*, with its marvels of lace, décolletages, and figures silhouetted against the light, I was faced with an indescribable galimatias that, to crown all, displayed in clear round letters the title: *The Cacodylic Eye*. And there on a revolving pedestal of green marble stood a marble form, a formless form, without discernible meaning or purpose, with one ball—two—in its lower part, and a longer object above, which—forgive me the shocking idea—could only be taken for a not very realistic representation, much exaggerated in its proportions—and obscene of course—of what every virile male has where he has to have it.

"But what the hell is all this?"

"It's modern art, Señor President," murmured the cholo Mendoza softly; he had just left the Mayorala upstairs, wrapped in blankets, prostrate under a feather eiderdown.

And now the *Ex* hurried from room to room, finding everywhere the same pictorial transmutations, the same disasters: crazy, absurd, esoteric pictures, without any historical or legendary significance, without subject or message, dishes of fruit that weren't dishes of fruit, houses looking like polyhedrons, faces with a set square for a nose, women with their tits out of place—one up, one down—or with one pupil on their temple, and farther on, so confused that it looked as if they must be fornicating, two fractured anatomies entangled in their own outlines, lesbian perhaps, although to paint two people doing *that* (and he had a good collection of pornographic plates locked away) one needed skill in draughtsmanship, knowledge of perspective, and art in portraying entwined limbs, which these failed artists known as "modern" were very far from possessing, because they were incapable of drawing a nude perfectly, of planting a young Spartan in Thermopylae, of making a horse cantering that looked at all like a horse, of decorating—one may as well say at once—the ceilings of the Paris Opera House or of creating the illusion of a battle with Detaille's epic brio.

"I shall give orders for all this filth to be taken down!" cried the master of the house, suddenly becoming the Master of the House and seizing hold of the picture of the *Cacodylic Eye*.

"What d'you think of it?" said Ofelia, who had just come into the room dressed in a dark blue tailor-made, her hair rather wild, her mascara smudged, and very obviously under the influence of drink.

"My dear girl!" said the Head of State, crushing her in his arms so suddenly and fondly that his voice ended in a sob. "My girl! My own flesh and blood!"

"Darling little papa!" she said, weeping also.

"So sexy and so lovely!"

"And you, so strong and splendid!"

"Come and sit beside me ... I've got so much to talk to you about ... I've so much to tell you ..."

"It's only that ..." And over Ofelia's shoulder, on which an orchid smelling of tobacco had finally finished fading, the *Ex* saw appearing, like the grotesque figures in a Flemish kermess, dishevelled, painted faces, faces that had been up all night and were certainly drunk.

"Some friends of mine ... they shut the dance hall where we were having supper ... We've come to go on with the party." People, more people; unbuttoned, ungainly, slovenly people; rude, disrespectful, impudent people; people who made themselves at home—more than at home: as if in a brothel—sitting on the floor, fetching bottles from the pantry, rolling back the carpet so as to be able to dance on the waxed wooden boards, regardless of the harm they might do. Women with their skirts above their knees, with their hair in a fringe that was the mark of a whore *over there*; young pederasts, with checked shirts that looked as if made out of cook's aprons. And now the gramophone: "*Yes, we have no bananas*" (he had already endured this horror on board the boat throughout the whole Atlantic crossing), "*we have no bananas today.*" Ofelia was laughing with her friends, went away, turned, took records from the bookcase, came back with more drink, filled glasses, wound up the gramophone, and, as the *Ex* sat himself down resignedly on a divan, there was a dialogue of truncated scrappy sentences, never answered, and remarks that were left incompletely expressed between turns around the room: Ofelia hadn't gone to the Gare Saint-Lazare, because the marconigram announcing his arrival had arrived yesterday afternoon when she was at a vernissage; from there they'd gone to celebrate and it wasn't till now that she was given it by the concierge, who had only just got up: "But now we'll really be happy; you mustn't go back to that country of savages." ("St. Louis Blues" was starting on the gramophone, bringing painful memories: it was what the Consul had played that afternoon.)

"Listen: I've brought the Mayorala."

"And where is she?"

"Asleep upstairs."

"Frankly, I wouldn't have brought her,"

"She was the only person who didn't betray me *over there* . . . why, even Peralta!"

"I always felt in my bones that he was a skunk."

"Worse than that: a pocket Machiavelli."

"Not that even: but Machiavelli's pocket, perhaps."

(Again: *Yes, we have no bananas.*) "I wouldn't have brought the Mayorala: I can't imagine her in Paris: she'll be one more responsibility."

"We must talk about that, we've got lots to talk about."

"Tomorrow, tomorrow, tomorrow."

"But it already is *tomorrow*—it's day already." ("St. Louis Blues" again.)

"I say, are you going to leave all that filthy rubbish on the walls?"

"Oh, don't be such a back number, my old darling; this is the art of today; you'll soon get used to it."

"And what about my Jean-Paul Laurens, my *Wolf of Gubbio*, my seascapes?"

"I sold them at the Hôtel Drouot; of course, I only got a miserable sum for the lot: people aren't interested in that stuff now."

"Damn it all! You might have asked me first!"

"How could I ask you when the papers kept saying at the time that they'd shot you? I got the news at the Seville Feria." (*Yes, we have no bananas* once more.)

"And when they told you, did you cry much?"

"I cried and cried and cried."

"Of course, you wore a black mantilla."

"Wait, I must wind up the gramophone." ("*Yes, we have no ...*" rose in pitch from the depths where it had descended.)

"I say, are these people going to stay much longer?"

"If they want to stay, I won't chuck them out."

"It's just that we've so much to talk about."

"Tomorrow, tomorrow, tomorrow ..."

"But it's tomorrow already."

"If you're tired, why not go and have a sleep?" (A new record: *Je cherche après Titine, Titine, oh! ma Titine*: another obsessional tune from the boat.)

Now Ofelia left him alone on the divan and began dancing wildly with an Englishman with curly hair, whom she
introduced to me as she passed, but without letting go of him,
as Lord—I forget his name—whom she'd met in Capri and
who—so I was told by the cholo Mendoza, now sitting beside me—had got into a scrape with the French police for
using schoolboys from the Lycée Jeanson-de-Sailly in artistic scenic productions of one of Virgil's *Bucolics*, yes, the one
about Alexis, the shepherd boy; I know it, I know it. The *Ex*
looked at his daughter and at all the others with growing irritation: those two women dancing together cheek to cheek.
And those two men clutching each other around the waist.
And that other short-haired female kissing the skinny blonde
in a yellow shawl. And those stupid, incomprehensible paintings on the walls. And that obscene white sculpture, the marble phallus, surrounded by bottles of whisky with a horse on
the label—white, too, but which had at least come to signify
sterling worth. His face turned suddenly red in an access of
rage—Mendoza recognised the symptoms—he crossed the
room, lifted the sound box of the gramophone, threw several
records on the floor, and stamped them to pieces.

"Clear all this drunken rubbish out of here!" he shouted.
Standing protectively in front of the astonished few who remained, it was now Ofelia's turn to look at her father with
growing anger, like the chief of a tribe, measuring the strength
of the adversary before attacking. The "darling little papa"
was growing before her eyes—growing, blowing himself out,
turning into a giant, breaking the walls with his hands and
raising the roof with his shoulders. If he regained his old authority, and if she let him dominate her, order her about and
make decisions in a house where she had dispensed with his
presence very pleasantly for several years; if she didn't humble
his pride, and check his impulsive behaviour, he would end

up just as much of a tyrant *here* as he had been *there*—for he was accustomed to be a tyrant always.

"If you don't like my friends," she said, adopting the dry, cold tone that he had sometimes been afraid of, "if you don't like my friends, take your bags and go to the Crillon or the Ritz. They have good rooms. Room service and an elegant atmosphere."

"Sodom and Gomorrah!" yelled the Head of State.

"That's why they got rid of you; for talking drivel," said Ofelia.

"And who is this?" asked all the others.

"*Mon père, le Président,*" said Ofelia, suddenly solemn, as if to mitigate the brutality of her earlier remarks.

"*Vive le Président! Vive le Président!*" they all shouted together, while one imitated a clown's foolish antics, and sang the "Marseillaise."

"Go to bed, Papa."

The sunlight shone through the drawing-room curtains in spite of the electric light still on in the room. Morning had begun for the whole city.

"Let's go to Bois-Charbons," said the *Ex* to the cholo Mendoza.

"Bye-bye!" said Ofelia, and while the two men went down the great staircase, the others leant over the balustrade with masks on their faces, singing to the music of "Malbrough":

*L'vieux con s'en va-t-en guerre*
*Mironton, mironton, mirontaine.*
*L'vieux con s'en va-t-en guerre*
*Et n'en reviendra pas!*

"*Alors ... on a eu des malheurs, mon bon Monsieur?*" said Musard, looking more than ever like the moustachioed leader of the Arc de Triomphe, when he saw us arrive. (It was clear he had come across my portrait in some newspaper recently.)

"*Oh! Vous savez—les révolutions . . .*" I said.

"*Les révolutions, ça tourne toujours mal*," said the wine merchant, taking out a bottle. "*Voyez ce qui s'est passé en France avec Louis Seize.*" (I thought of the frontispiece of Michelet's *La Convention* in Nelson's edition, with Citizen Capet on the scaffold, very dignified, with his shirt open at the neck as if he were consulting an otolaryngologist.)

"*Ce sera pour la prochaine fois*," I said, raising my hand to my neck. Possibly realizing, rather late in the day, that his reference to Louis XVI had been slightly unfortunate, Monsieur Musard tried to mend matters:

"*Les révolutions, vous savez . . . Il paraît que sous l'Ancien Régime on était bien mieux. Ce sont nos quarante rois qui ont fait la grandeur de la France.*"

"This chap has been reading *Action Française*," said the cholo Mendoza.

"*He's treating us to a bit of Barrèsism*," I said.

"*Le Beaujolais nouveau est arrivé*," said Monsieur Musard, filling three glasses. "*C'est la maison qui règale.*"

I drank my wine with delight. From the back of the humble café came a pleasant smell of resinous wood, such as was sold in little bundles fastened with wire, to light coal fires with. There on the shelves, as if no time had passed, their shapes and labels unchanged, stood the bottles of Suze, Picon, Raphaël, and Dubonnet.

"What are you going to live on now?" I asked the cholo. "You're not an ambassador anymore."

"A man who thinks ahead is worth two. I've got more than enough money."

"Where did you get it from?"

"Thanks to me the population of our country has thirty

thousand new citizens, who don't figure in the census or know what our map looks like; forged passports and cards of citizenship for them ... Poor people without any country. Victims of the war. White Russians. Expatriates. *Heimatlos.* I was doing good. Besides, the transactions went through the diplomatic bag. I wouldn't have been the only one. I'm no saint. Other people use it for worse things." (He made the gesture of someone sniffing.) "*That business* is a great temptation, because now it brings in a lot. But it's dangerous. However, with the passports, I keep a duplicate of the Embassy stamps and seals. So the shop stays open ... discreetly, of course."

"Excellent: our compatriots deserve nothing better" (a sigh). "Oh well! It's difficult to serve one's country, old man!"

We returned to the Rue de Tilsitt. As I went in, out came a new porter, a war casualty, probably, because his left cuff was fastened with a safety pin to the shoulder of his blue jacket, and he wore a badge on his lapel. I had to explain that I was the master of the house before he let me pass, with theatrically embarrassed excuses. The drawing-room curtains were still drawn. Several of last night's revellers were asleep on the divan, in armchairs or on cushions scattered on the carpet. Stepping over their bodies—some of them interlaced or piled in heaps—I at last reached my bedroom. I took my hammock out of the cupboard and hung it on the two rings put there for it. On the Arc de Triomphe, Rude's Marseillaise was singing, as yesterday, as always.

But if the Marseillaise was still there, with her vociferous leader and the boy hero between sabres and palm trees, to me Paris seemed deserted. I realised this very afternoon when, after a long sleep, I tried to make a list of what could be rescued of my life in this city. Reynaldo Hahn didn't answer the telephone. Perhaps he'd gone to live in the suburbs. "*Abonné absent,*" said a female voice from the exchange.

The Distinguished Academician, always so understanding, to whom I wanted to confide my sadness and disappointments and whose advice I wanted to ask about—possibly—writing my memoirs, had died months ago in his flat on the Quai Voltaire, the victim of an incurable disease, after a mystical crisis that created a considerable stir in Catholic circles and caused him to spend whole days praying in the cold church of Saint-Roch, associated for me with a novel by Balzac I read as an adolescent in Surgidero de la Verónica. (I don't know why churches connected with Bossuet or Fénelon—in style, I mean, like Saint-Roch, Saint Sulpice, or the chapel at Versailles—fail to inspire me with devotion. To get the feel of a Christian church, I need it to be shadowy, enveloping, full of relics and marvellous images of decapitated saints, blood, sores, tears and sweat, lifelike wounds, jungles of tapers, silver limbs and gold viscera on the altar for ex-votos.) I knew that after Gabriele D'Annunzio had got caught in Fiume, he had retired—so they said—now a prince—so they said—to his Italian house, where with his back against a wall of rock he could see the prow of a battleship, raised up there in memory of some brave deed or other. I learned that Ofelia had told the truth and that Elstir's paintings had fallen out of public favour: his delicious seascapes could still be found in the less successful galleries, mixed up among any pictures containing waves, boats, sand, and foam that appealed to those who had made fortunes out of the war. Embittered by the fall in the price of his work, Elstir had retired angrily to his studio at Balbec, where he tried to achieve some sort of "modernity," which distorted but added nothing to his individual style, giving a sense of uneasy effort, as little appreciated by his admirers of yesterday as by those who were today following new currents. In music something similar was happening: nobody played Vinteuil's work anymore—least of all his Sonata—except schoolgirls, who put away his music in a drawer, after their piano lessons, and devoted themselves to the strange subtleties of "La cathédrale engloutie" or the "Pavane pour une infante défunte," unless they were indulging themselves with the vulgarities of Zez Confrey's "Kitten on the Keys." And the young, those "in the know"—of what?—the snobs, amazed by the Russian music brought over by Diaghilev, treated the fine maestro Juan Cristóbal as a "*vieille barbe*," and disowned him just as they used to disown *Rhinegold*. And worse, inconceivable things had happened: Anatole France, who could well have remained in the world of Thaïs and Jérôme Coignard, had irrelevantly declared himself a socialist at the last moment, proclaiming the necessity of a "universal revolution," including America—no less!—and giving large sums of money to that abominable periodical *L'Humanité*. Things were going very badly for others: the Comte de Argencourt, Belgian Chargé d'Affaires, formerly a ceremonious, stiff diplomatist in the grand style, had been seen by the cholo Mendoza a few days earlier opposite the puppet theatre in the Champs-Elysées, in a state of utter collapse, imbecile, with the face and expression of a smiling beggar, apparently about to stretch out his hand for alms ...

During these days, I didn't dare telephone Madame Verdurin, now a princess by marriage. I was afraid a princess—or someone with the presumptions of one—would scorn a man who was, after all, only a Latin American president thrown out of his palace. And I thought bitterly of the deplorable end of Estrada Cabrera; of many dictators dragged through the streets of their capitals; of those expelled and humiliated, like Porfirio Díaz, or of those who had gone to ground here in France, after a long stretch of power, like Guzmán Blanco; of Rosas of Argentina, whose daughter, tired of playing the part of unselfish virgin, or magnanimous intercessor against the cruelty of her terrible father, suddenly revealed herself as she really was at heart, and abandoned her stern parent when she got the chance, leaving him to die in melancholy solitude in the grey town of Southampton—he who had owned boundless pampas, rivers of silver, moons such as are seen only there, suns rising every day above horizons he had ruled over since he was in breeches, and watched the heads of his enemies go by, hawked as "good, cheap watermelons" in the carts of his rejoicing followers.

The days passed, and I hardly saw Ofelia, who was always involved in fun and games. The Mayorala, curled up into a ball under her feather eiderdown, refused to be attended by a French doctor and suffered the high fever of pleurisy without accepting any remedy but Santa Inés rum and balsam of Tolu—since none of the sort of herbal concoctions that performed miracles *over there* were to be had *here*. And I resumed my walks about Paris with the cholo Mendoza, going from Notre-Dame de Lorette to the Chope Danton, from an Avenue du Bois that hadn't been there before to Monsieur Musard's Bois-Charbons, without experiencing a single quiver of the city life, the air, the atmosphere that my nose and my memory sought in vain. The smell of petrol had taken the place of the country aroma—formerly everywhere, knowing no frontiers, belonging as much to the capital as to a hamlet—of horse dung. In the early morning one no longer heard the cries of the old-clothes man, the seller of watercress and birdseed, nor the rustic pipe of the scissors grinder. In the purlieus of the Place des Ternes, makers of porous jugs from Badajoz no longer arrived after a very long journey, with their donkeys decorated in the Extramaduran style. The only place that seemed permanent and unchanged was Aux Glaces at 25 Rue Saint-Apolline, where (among scagliola or mosaic tables, coloured glass windows, floral transfers on the long

backs of leather settees, a pianola with a loud tone, two waiters in white aprons with bottles on tray-covered trolleys—
like those on the Raphaeël labels) women were waiting for
me, who in spite of the passage of years, difference in generations, changes in personnel, a new hairdo, a certain delicate
restraint now being preferred to the opulence of the end of
the century, restored me to the early chapters of my history,
with its first pleasures and a thousand rejuvenating memories, and far-off events, whence—as in other Continental
countries—everything had been transformed, turned upside
down and perverted by the accelerated changes in ways of
life. Languages had been mixed together, values degraded,
adolescents corrupted, patriarchs insulted, palaces profaned,
and the just expelled . . .

Here, at Aux Glaces, I found the only permanence
that had always existed—despite larger breasts or smaller
breasts—here as *over there* I found presence and unique-
ness, dialectic of irreplaceable forms, a common language
of universal understanding. In the irreversible time of the
flesh it was possible to pass, according to period, from the
style of Bouguereau to that of a medieval Eve, from the décolletage of Boldini to the décolletage of Tintoretto, or, in-
versely, from Rubens' multitudinous buttocks and bellies to
the fragile, ambiguous appearance of a nymph by Puvis de
Chavannes; aesthetic fashions, variants and fluctuations of
taste all passed, lengthening silhouettes, playing with proportions, amplifying—while in other departments of life, too,
fashions were subject to perennial changes—yet never alter-
ing the fundamental reality of a nude. Here, looking at what
I am looking at, I feel I am witnessing the Arrest of Time,
somewhere outside the present epoch, maybe in the days of
sun clocks or sand clocks, and therefore liberated from everything that binds me to the dates of my own history. I am

less aware of being unseated from my bronze horses, thrown down from my pedestals; less of an exiled ruler, or actor in decline, and more identified with my own *ego*, still possessing eyes for looking, and impulses arising from the depths of a vitality that is deliciously stimulated by something worth looking at—riches definitely preferable (*I feel*, therefore I am) to those of a fictitious existence in the stupid ubiquity of a hundred statues in municipal parks, patios, and town halls.

When such serious reflections beset me in a place where I hadn't come for that purpose, and I took in the disparity between thought and situation, I burst out laughing, and made a remark to the cholo Mendoza that never failed to delight him: "Anything but 'To be or not to be' in a whorehouse." "That is the question," he replied (for he, too, fancied himself as well-read), making signs to an ample Leda, who knew she had been chosen beforehand, and so was awaiting her time without impatience, drinking some aperitif flavoured with aniseed at the next table, and counting on a client who had said nothing to her but was worth waiting for, because foreigners were generous clients and knew how to appreciate professional conscientiousness in work of every kind.

# 20

SUDDENLY CURED OF HER FEVER AND PAINS, THE
Mayorala had arisen from beneath her eiderdown, clamouring to know where she could find a church in which to
carry out her promise of dedicating prayers and candles to
the Virgin.

"Church, church," she cried to the concierge, who was
amazed to be approached by someone wearing three petticoats, one on top of another, for fear of the dew produced by
the unusually early summer sunshine.

"Church, church," she repeated, crossing herself, joining
her hands in a gesture of prayer, and displaying a rosary of
silver beads. The concierge, possibly understanding, signed
to her to go "there, turn left, turn right, and go straight on a
little way." And the Mayorala, life now restored to the strong
calves of her legs, had walked, walked, walked until she came
to an enormous church—it must be a church, although there
was no cross on it, because it had somewhat religious-looking
sculptures, such as Miguel Estatua used to make, at the top
of a façade with many columns—whence came organ music, murmured prayers, and where a priest was saying things
she didn't understand, but an altar is an altar everywhere, the
holy images had a familiar air and the smell of incense left no
room for doubt.

Her prayers said, she bought candles with some French
money the Head of State had given her when they arrived

at Cherbourg ("in case you get lost when you want to pee"), descended a few steps, and stopped in a very pretty flower market—although these carnations didn't have so much scent as the ones *over there*—stopping afterwards in amazement in front of a shop window where a solitary and magnificent mango was offered for sale, reclining on a bed of fine cotton wool. *There*, mangoes were sold in barrows decorated with palm leaves, "five for half a peso," and here it was lying in a box, like the gems displayed in French jewellers' shops in her country. The Mayorala boldly entered the store. From table to table, from counter to counter she went in delighted surprise; the yucca reached out brown arms to her as if calling her attention; green bananas were turning greener before her eyes, the rough peel of yams was developing pale blotches on its redness—more like coral than a subterranean fruit. And farther on she found the intense black of beans, the liturgical white of custard apples. And by means of her language of gestures and onomatopoeia, making signs, using her fingers, exclaiming, and grunting assent or negation, she had secured five of these, three of the others, ten of those, eight from this sack, fifteen from the box, and put the lot in one of the wide baskets sold there—which basket she proceeded to put on her head when the time came to pay, to the great astonishment of the cashier: "*Vous voulez un taxi, Mademoiselle?*" She understood not a word. She left the shop and took her bearings. On her way here the sun had been in her face. The sun hadn't yet got overhead and she wasn't hungry: therefore it must be ten or half past. So, to retrace her steps, she must walk with her shadow in front of her. The trouble was that these bloody streets turned, twisted, and changed direction, and her shadow—getting smaller all the time—crossed over from right to left and refused to remain in the desired position. Then she saw so many strange things to distract her: that

café full of Americans—you could tell them by their clothes;
the toyshop with a blue dwarf in it; that enormous column
with a tiny man on the top—a liberator, obviously; that park
full of statues with a grille. Here, with the trees on the left,
her shadow came back to its proper place. She walked and
walked, till she came to a vast square where there was a stone
standing, like those in some of the cemeteries *over there*, but
much bigger—and however had they managed to stand it upright? Now came an avenue, with some goats pulling little
carriages. There were stalls of sweets and toffees. And now
the basket was beginning to weigh more than she'd bargained
for, but suddenly—when the sun was directly overhead—she
saw far off at the top of the road that enormous, heavy, but
life-saving monument called the Arc de Triomphe or What-
Have-You. She walked faster. Home at last. She wanted to go
straight to the kitchen, but just then she was struck by a sharp
pain in the back. And her fever returned. She left the basket
in a corner of the room, took a glass of rum beaten up with
balsam of Tolu, and went back under her eiderdown, complaining bitterly of these countries with climates cold enough
to skin one alive.

And at about half past eleven next day, Ofelia was wo-
ken by unusually loud voices. The maid came in, looking and
sounding upset: "*Mademoiselle, pardonnez-moi, mais . . .*" The
cook wanted to see her; to see her immediately, she insisted.
There she was. Furious. And she came in, dishevelled—very
like a Fury, in fact—telling everyone whether half asleep or
not, who would listen, that this was impossible, it was intolerable, and she wouldn't stay another day in the house, she'd
hand back her apron. And she suited the action to the words,
taking it off and handing it over with an angry expression,
looking like some venerable master mason returning his
leather apron. It was intolerable: a short while ago a woman

had come down from the attic, wearing three skirts, gesticulating, dark-skinned—"*une peau de boudin, Mademoiselle*";
she had taken possession of her world of pots and pans, and
set about cooking extraordinary things—"*des mangeailles des
sauvages, Mademoiselle*"—dirtying everything, spilling oil,
throwing corncobs into corners, contaminating the casseroles
with mixtures of pimentos and cocoa, using a carpenter's
plane to slice plantains, cramming handfuls of fritters into
brown paper. And after preparing this unspeakable pigswill,
and leaving the kitchen poisoned with greasy vapours and
the stink of frying, she had carried off trays and soup bowls
to the little room that used to belong to Sylvestre, which out
of respect for the memory of that exemplary servant had remained exactly as he left it before he went away and died glo-
riously in battle on the plateau of Craonne, with the Croix de
Guerre on his breast and his photo published in *L'Illustration*
because of his heroic behaviour in the face of the enemy.

Beginning to understand the situation, Ofelia returned
her apron to the cook, wrapped herself in a dressing gown,
and went up to the attic.

The Head of State and the cholo Mendoza, their shirts
undone, hairy and unshaven—and looking as if they had
hangovers—were sitting at a long table, which was really a
door taken off its hinges and placed on two chairs. On several
trays and dishes, as if in some low restaurant in the tropics,
were laid out green avocados, red chillis, ochre and chocolate sauces from which emerged breasts and joints of turkey,
frosted over with grated onion. In a row on the carving board
there were little maize cakes and omelettes seasoned with
chillis, next to yellow tamales, wrapped in hot moist leaves
and exuding aromas suggestive of a country fiesta. There were
fried ripe bananas, plantains cut in fine slices by the carpenter's plane (those that had been crushed in handfuls). And

yam fritters and coconut cakes browned in the oven, and a punch bowl where, in a mixture of tequila and Spanish cider such as was drunk at weddings *over there*, there floated pine kernels, green lemons, mint, and orange blossom.

"Care to join us?" asked the cholo Mendoza.

"And who prepared all this?" asked Ofelia, still stupefied by her sudden awakening and the cook's protestations.

"Elmirita, servant of God and your honour," replied the mulatto, bowing with her legs crossed as girls are taught to do in French Dominican colleges.

Ofelia had been about to overturn the improvised table and put an end to the junketings, but now a maize tamale on the end of a fork approached her eyes and descended to her mouth. When it was opposite her nose, a sudden inner emotion, coming from a long way off, a fluttering in her entrails, weakened her knees and made her sit down on a chair. She bit into it, and all at once her body grew younger by thirty years. In white socks, and with her hair in curling papers, she was on the patio with the millstones and the tamarind tree. And from the tree dangled cinnamon-coloured parchment pods full of dark pulp, with a forgotten bittersweetness that made her mouth water. And there came back to her, too, the smell of fermented guavas—ambiguously combining pears and raspberries—from behind the fence where Jongolojongo the pig, with his long bristles and long snout, was grunting and rooting among broken tiles and rusty old tins. And the smells from the kitchen full of pots, vases, jugs, and black pottery, whence came the sounds of chewing, of the slow tread of boots on wet earth, of the pestle falling as rhythmically as a pendulum on the milky, fragrant, foaming mass of maize pulp. And Mayflower the cow, who had just calved, was calling to her little one to relieve her udders, and outside a street seller was crying molasses for sale; and the bell from the hermitage among the medlar and cherry trees; and this maize here (I'm seven years old, and already I look at myself in the mirror every morning to see if I've grown breasts in the night) entering my body at every pore. I'm seven years old:

> *Santa Maria,*
> *Save us from evil*
> *Protect us, Señora*
> *From this terrible devil*
> *And then everyone sang:*
> *To kill the devil*
> *The Virgin seized a blade*
> *On all fours the monster*
> *Lay down in a glade.*

"*Des mangeailles des sauvages*," said the cook, standing in the doorway with her arms akimbo.

"To hell with Brillat-Savarin!" cried Ofelia, her cheeks blazing from the cider mixed with tequila and pineapple juice, tasting this and that, plunging her spoon in the avocado salad and dipping a turkey joint into chilli sauce. And suddenly seized by an unexpected impulse of affection, she sat on her father's knees and kissed his cheeks, where once again she recaptured the smell of tobacco, aguardiente, French lotion (with some hint of mint, liquorice, and Mimi Pinson powder)—but less old, more virile, almost young—in a marvellous rediscovery of time past. For the first time since the days of the plateau of Craonne, they played the gramophone that had remained silent ever since Sylvestre's heroic death. They heard, in tones that grew deeper or almost died away when the mechanism ran down, several tunes collected by the cholo Mendoza: Lerdo de Tejado's "Faisan," "Alma campera," "El Tamborito," and "La Milonguita," flower of luxury and pleasure, men did you wrong and now you would give anything for a cotton dress; and listen to the story the old gravedigger told me one day: it was a lover whose sweetness cruel fate stole away; and goodbye lads, my lifelong friends; and every night he went to the cemetery to see the corpse of his beloved, and crowned her skull with orange blossom and covered her horrible mouth with kisses; and goodbye lads, my lifelong friends of happy days; and the day that you love me will be sunnier than June, with music by Beethoven singing from every flower; and again and again and again those happy festive days, and goodbye and goodbye, light of my nights, sang the soldier underneath the window ...

By now Elmirita and Ofelia had their arms around each other and were singing a duet, skilfully keeping to intervals of thirds and sixths, which the cholo accompanied with opportunely onomatopoeic flourishes on an imaginary guitar.

And when night fell, what with drinking, singing, and titbits of tomato and chilli sauce, the Head of State decided to instal himself finally in Sylvestre's rooms, entering and leaving by the back staircase: "I shall be more independent like that." Then Ofelia, down below, could go on having her parties of young people and live amongst those horrible pictures which so frayed his nerves—quite apart from the fact that he didn't understand them and never would. And the Mayorala would go on living here in the room next door, to keep him company and look after him. The Infanta agreed: Elmirita was a splendid girl, most unselfish and good, "Much more respectable and honourable than many of the friends of Madame What's-her-name, with her musical evenings, who doesn't want to clap eyes on you now that she's become a princess." But the zamba must be dressed differently. And Ofelia ran to her wardrobe to find her some clothes she no longer wore. Although full of praise for their quality, the Mayorala eyed them a little suspiciously: this one was cut so low as to be brazen; the slit skirt of the other seemed to her immodest. When she saw the lapels of a suit tailored by Redfern: "I don't wear men's clothes." To a black ensemble by Paquin she said, "Yes, perhaps it would do for a funeral." In the end she happily accepted a model of Paul Poiret's, partly inspired by Léon Bakst's designs for *Schéhérazade*, which reminded her of the flowered skirts and blouses of her own people. And that night they finally consecrated the new dwelling by fixing two rings in the walls, knotting cords to them, and hanging up the woven hammock for the Head of State to sleep in—"I beg your pardon: the *Ex*," corrected the Patriarch, enjoying his first swing in it.

The Mayorala soon became familiar with a large region of Paris centred around the Arc de Triomphe and with the river as its extreme frontier—a river she never crossed, because people who did a lot of ironing and cooking were in danger of catching a chill if they crossed a bridge. She had come across a church in the square where a bronze horseman, a very good poet who had been a friend of the Emperor Pedro of Brazil—so the cholo Mendoza had explained—seemed plunged in endless thought, and behind the church of Saint Honoré of somewhere or other was a superb fish market where they sold octopuses, prawns, and quahogs fairly like those she used to get *over there*, as well as clams identical with the ones from the beaches of La Verónica, which came out of the sand as though drawn by a magnet whenever they found out that a woman eager for a man had sat down on them. In a shop close by, earthenware pots and casseroles were sold, and by stealing bricks from a house being built—she carried them two at a time in the oilskin bag she used for lemons, garlic, and parsley—she had transformed the stove in the attic into a Creole range, feeding it with wood brought, tied up in wire, from Monsieur Musard's Bois-Charbons, where she went very often these days, having become much addicted to Muscadet and sweet Gaillac—wines that she used to say "toned up her system."

And she began to live there, under the slate roof, in a latitude and at times belonging to another region and another epoch.

The early morning was filled with the aroma of strong coffee, filtered through a woollen stocking and sweetened with cane syrup, which the zamba got near the Madeleine; she could always find her way there without getting lost, because she had proved that by going under the Arc de Triomphe exactly in the middle she could see the Standing Stone a long way off, and having reached it she turned left and found the building with many columns where she had given thanks for her recovery. Then followed a short rest on her hammock with a glass of aguardiente and a Romeo and Juliet cigar, and later still a cry of "Come along in" announced the appearance, on two broad mahogany tables supported on carpenter's trestles, of a country breakfast of eggs in peppery sauce, fried black beans, maize tortillas, pork, and white cheese pounded together in a mortar and served in any leaf available—so long as it was green—for lack of a banana leaf. After that came her morning siesta, interrupted when she was half asleep about eleven, by the cholo Mendoza, bringing the daily newspapers. But these papers hadn't seen the light in the small hours on Parisian printing presses. They were papers from overseas, had travelled a long way and were concerned with things other than current events. *Le Figaro*, *Le Journal*, and *Le Petit Parisien* never came up to this floor; they had been gradually supplanted by *El Mercurio*, *El Mundo*, and *Ultimas Noticias* from *over there*, or even by *El Faro* from Nueva Córdoba or *El Centinela* from Puerto Araguato. The Head of State was beginning to forget the names of politicians *over here*, and he cared very little what was happening in Europe—although the recent assassination of Matteotti had stimulated his admiration for Italian fascism, and that great man Mussolini who was going to put an end to international communism—he was interested only in what might be happening *over there*.

(Hailed as restorer and custodian of Liberty, after a triumphal entry riding on a black horse—but without boots, and in the white drill suit he had always worn in the University—Luis Leoncio had climbed the stairs of the Presidential Palace he had described in a recent manifesto as an "Augean stable" with the majestic step of an archon, his expression stern, his gestures few, and looking coldly—with some vague threat in his retinas—at those who were over-reaching themselves to congratulate him on his triumph. Much had been hoped of the Man who—after making a roll of public employees, thanks to a prompt North American loan—had undertaken in a monkish, frugal manner the enormous task of examining the national problems. For weeks and weeks he shut himself up in his study, silent and remote, poring over estimates, statistics, and political documents, preferring to get help from technical books, encyclopedias, reports, and memoranda, rather than consult experts trained to go into these questions in detail, and analyse a whole, in the Cartesian manner, into parts whose multiplicity was obscuring the vision of the whole itself. They awaited the results of his toil with unction and eager impatience. People walked through Central Park almost on tiptoe every evening, talking in low voices and pointing to the window where lights would be burning until the small hours, and behind which Something Important was being worked out. Everyone was waiting for the Wise Man of Nueva Córdoba to speak. It couldn't be long now. And at last he did speak, before an immense crowd gathered in the Olympic Stadium. And his speech was a torrential onslaught—without pause to take breath—as if a dictionary were unbound, let loose, with pages in confusion, words in revolt, a tumult of concepts and ideas, accelerated impact of figures, images and abstractions in a vertiginous flood of words launched to the four winds, and moving from Morgan's Bank to Plato's *Republic*, from the Logos to foot-and-mouth disease, from General Motors to Ramakrishna, coming at last to the conclusion—or at least some understood it thus—that from the Mystic Marriage between the Eagle and the Condor, and as a result of the fertilisation of our inexhaustible soil by foreign investment, our America would be transformed by the vigorous technology that would come to us from the north (and we were on the threshold of a century that would be the Century of Technology for our Young Continent), by the light of our own innate spirituality, a synthesis would be born of the Vedanta, the Popol Vuh, and the parables of Christ-the-first-socialist, the only true socialist, nothing to do with Moscow Gold or the Red Peril, or an exhausted, dying Europe, without sap or talent—and it would be as well for us to break finally with its useless teaching—whose hopeless decadence had been proclaimed not long ago by the German philosopher Oswald Spengler. The start of this new era, in which the thesis-antithesis of north-south was complemented by the telluric and the scientific, would be manifested in the creation of a New Humanity, the Alpha-Omega, the party of Hope, expressing the *sturm-und-drang*, the political pulse of new generations, marking the end of dictatorships in this continent, and establishing a true and authentic Democracy, where there would be freedom of syndical action, provided that it did not break the necessary harmony between Capital and Labour; the need for an opposition must be recognised, provided that it was a *co-operative opposition* (critical, yes, but always *constructive*); the right to strike was accepted, provided that the strikes didn't paralyse private enterprise or public services; and, finally, the Communist Party would be legalised, since it in fact existed in our country, provided that it did not obstruct the functioning of institutions nor stimulate class war.

And by the time the orator brought his speech to an end with "Long live our country!" he had uttered so many "buts," "howevers," "neverthelesses," "despite the sayings," and "provided thats" that his hearers were left with the impression that time had stood still, independently of the ticking of clocks, and that when the Austere Doctor stepped down from the rostrum he left behind him a total mental emptiness—blank brains and an agnostic trance in his listeners.

And in the ensuing months all was dismay and confusion. The Provisional President—not so provisional after all— could never come to any decision. Every suggestion made by his colleagues, every measure to be applied at once, seemed to him "premature," "inopportune," "hasty," because "we weren't ready," "it wasn't yet time for that," "the masses weren't mature enough," etc. And after a few months scepticism and shrugging of shoulders became the order of the day, and living for the day's pleasure, and renewed interest in lottery tickets and guitars and maracas on the part of those who had been too optimistic, while at the same time there was talk of "Discontent in the Army."

"A military coup on the way," prophesied the Head of State. "It wouldn't be anything new. As the proverb says: 'One stripe more on a tiger makes very little difference.' "

"But now they say that it's the *young officers* who are involved," remarked the cholo.

"Sub-machine guns instead of machetes," said the former holder of Power. "It's all the same."

But there was something new in the air: *Liberation*, now a legal newspaper, appeared every morning and contained eight pages—in spite of which, from time to time it would be unexpectedly suppressed by officious members of Alpha-Omega, who overturned crates, dispersed the galley proofs, and beat up the linotypists. People who couldn't possibly be suspected of Communist affiliation were working together on the paper at the time, and signing their names at the foot of their articles. The music publishing house of Francis Salabert in Paris had received an order for a thousand copies of the "Internationale," which was now being sung *over there* in a Spanish translation, recently published in Mexico by Diego Rivera in a review called *El Machete*.

And so the months passed, February papers being read in April, and those of October in December, while past events were talked of more and more and vanished individuals came to life. A Yesterday, unmistakably *yesterday* though present today, was living among us in flesh and blood that was in process of losing its fleshly nature, because it was obvious that the usually tall, strapping figure of the *Ex* was beginning to deteriorate, as it was also obvious that the passage of time was progressively speeding up, diminishing and narrowing the space between one Christmas and the next, between one military review of July 14 and the next military review of July 14, so that the huge flag fluttering beneath the Arc de Triomphe appeared to have been there ever since the last occasion. Chestnuts bloomed, chestnuts dropped their flowers, chestnuts bloomed again, as pages from the calendar were thrown into the wastepaper basket, and Monsieur le Président's tailor came again and again to the Rue de Tilsitt to alter his clothes to fit a dwindling anatomy, growing thinner day by day. His watch chain retreated visibly over a less prominent waistcoat, while his shoulders, formerly held up with inflexible rigidity, were now drooping over collarbones relieved of the extra flesh on his thorax—as the Mayorala noticed when at bath time she rubbed her President's chest with sponge and loofah. And since this progressive loss of flesh alarmed her and she didn't believe in medicine in bottles such as was sold here, she had dictated—stammered, rather—a letter to the cholo Mendoza, arranging that a certain Balbina, from the village of Palmar de Siquire, where there was no post office, should send her a parcel of healing herbs—to travel by donkey, mule, bicycle, bus, several trains, two boats, and another train, and be picked up today by Elmira at the Parcels Office in the Rue Etienne Marcel. Her Ex-President and Ex-Ambassador went with her because a great many forms had to be filled in and signed, and all this was for people who could read and write—and in French, which made it far worse.

With the package wrapped in a scarf, and all three wearing thick overcoats because it was a cold day, though the sun shone brightly from a cloudless sky, Elmira had her first sight of the towers of Notre-Dame. When she heard it was the Cathedral of Paris she insisted on going there to light a candle to the Virgin. She stopped still in amazement in front of the building.

"What I say is: we ought to do things like this in our country to attract tourists." The figures on the tympanum and lintels reminded her of the sculptures of Miguel Estatua, her fellow countryman from Nueva Córdoba.

"The zamba isn't being foolish," remarked the *Ex*, who hadn't hitherto noticed the stylistic resemblance between the two, especially in the devils' faces, the rearing horse, the horned demons, and all the infernal zoology of the Last Judgement. There followed an awestruck Penetration into the Nave—the nave alight with the whole gamut of colour from its windows, the figures of the visitors making dark silhouettes

against this brilliance, slight forms in this mid-afternoon of
fictitious spring. They sat down to rest between the two rose
windows in the transept. At the other end of the row of seats,
a young man in a long overcoat and warm muffler was gazing
at everything with deep and careful attention.

"A worshipper," said the Mayorala.

"An aesthete," said Mendoza.

"A student from the Beaux-Arts," said the Head of State.
And in a low voice, to entertain the zamba, he began telling her, like a grandfather to his grandchild, true stories of
things he had seen here: the archdeacon who was enamoured
of a gypsy who used to make a white nanny goat dance to a
tambourine (Elmira had seen gypsies like that when she was
a child, but they had made a bear dance); and the story of
the itinerant poet who egged on some beggars to attack the
church ("When there's rioting churches always get damaged,"
said Elmira, remembering a case that it would have been better to forget); and the story of a hunch-backed bell ringer,
who was also in love with the gypsy ("hunchbacks are very
amorous, and women notice this, but only want to touch the
hump because it brings good luck"); and the story of two skeletons that seemed to be embracing and perhaps were those
of Esmeralda and the bell ringer ("such cases have been seen,
so the old village sexton used to tell in his song; we've got a
record of it"). But now the organ began blaring a sudden outburst of music. They couldn't hear each other speak.

"Let's go," said the *Ex*, thinking of the delicious Alsace
wine they served at the café on the corner, where it would
certainly be warmer than here.

But the "worshipper"—as Elmira had called him—was
still sitting in his seat at the far end of the row, absorbed in daz-
zled contemplation. It was his first encounter with Gothic architecture. And the Gothic arches and stained-glass windows

rising on both sides were an unsuspected revelation to him;
beside this all other architecture seemed to him primitive,
rooted in the earth, chthonic, even when it was expressed in
terms conforming to the principles of Proportion, the Golden
Rules. This building, soaring upwards in exaltation of verticality, seemed to him to make even the pediments of the Parthenon dwindle, for they were merely a living, exalted version
of the sloping roof of the archaic dwelling, and its fluted column was a transcendent, glorified form of the roof tree—four
tree trunks, six or eight—which supported the lintels and ce-
darwood beams of the rustic doorways of peasants. In Greek
and Roman times this original relationship with the telluric
and vegetal was lost. From the hut of Eumeus the swineherd
to the temple of Phidias, the way was clear and open, through
a series of successive stylisations. Here, on the other hand,
architecture had become a matter of invention, ideas, pure
creation, materials had achieved unheard-of lightness—as if
stone were weightless—with a nervature owing nothing to
the structure of trees—and with the characteristic suns of the
prodigious rose windows: Northern Sun, Southern Sun. The
contemplator in the transept was caught between these two
suns, the fiery red of the sunset and the grave, mystical blue
symphony of the north window. On the north window the
Mother occupied the centre of a temporal court—to receive
Intercession, as it were—of prophets, kings, judges, and patriarchs. On the south—in the blood of sacrifice—the Sun ruled
over an ecclesiastical court of apostles, confessors, martyrs,
wise virgins and foolish virgins. The entire mystery of birth,
death, the eternal renaissance of life, and the changing seasons was to be found in the straight, imaginary, and invisible
line stretched between the two central circles of those immense sources of light, openings in a structural magnificat
rising from the ground, as if suspended weightlessly from its

bells and gargoyles. From the shadows, the organ pipes suddenly broke out into triumphal fanfares.

An atheist because his inner questionings did not seek
for replies on religious soil; a disbeliever because disbelief was
natural to his generation, and the way had been prepared by
the scientific spirit that came before; an enemy of the politics
and compromise that so often, in his world, took the Church
into the camp of his adversaries, and in the name of faith
maintained a false order that was self-destructive, the contemplator of the Sun Windows was nevertheless responsive
to the dynamic quality of the Gospels, and recognised that
their texts had, at one time, had the merit of causing a resounding devaluation of all the totems and inexorable spirits,
dark presences and zodiacal threats, of oracles, submissions
to the ides of March and inevitable fate. But if some new self-
awareness—putting the drama of life *within* instead of outside
himself—had induced man to analyse the values that led him
into primitive terrors, he had developed into an erring giant,
tyrannised by others like himself, who had become faithless
to their first vows and had created new totems, new destinies,
temples without altars and irreligious cults that it was necessary to destroy. Perhaps the days were close at hand when
the trumpets of the Apocalypse would sound, but this time it
would not be by the angels of the Last Judgement but by those
appearing before it. It was time to decide upon the protocols
of the future and to plan a Tribunal of Redistribution.

The young man looked at his watch. Four o'clock. The
train. He sank himself again into the total beauty of his surroundings, now that it was time to return to his own. "I don't
feel needed where everything is so perfect," he thought, as he
left Notre-Dame by the centre door—the door of the Resurrection of the Dead. There was still time to drink some of the
excellent Alsatian wine to be had in the café where he had left

his suitcase in the care of a waiter. He crossed the road and went into the bistro without noticing that three people—a woman and two men—sitting on a bench at the back were staring at him in amazement. Paying for his drink, the Student returned to the street and hailed a taxi.

"*A la garra del Norte, please.*"

His appointment was in the station buffet, where several delegates for the First World Conference against Colonial and Imperialist Politics were already gathered; it was to open next day, February 10, at Brussels, with Barbusse as president. Among them was the Cuban Julio Antonio Mella, whom he had met a few hours before, in company with Jawaharlal Nehru, delegate for the National Hindu Congress.

"The train has come in already," said someone, pointing to Platform 8. The three picked up their shabby cases and got into a second-class carriage. The Indian was sitting in a corner by the window studying some papers, while Mella was showing interest in the political situation of our country.

"We've just got rid of a dictator," said the Student. "But the struggle goes on, because our enemies are the same as before. The curtain has gone down on the first act, and very long it was. Now we're in the middle of the second, which, in spite of new scenery and lighting, is very like the first."

"We're just starting on what you've been through," said Mella. And he told him about the dictator recently in power in Cuba, whom he had defeated by means of a stubborn, prolonged, and successful hunger strike in prison, forcing his enemy to give him his liberty and then leaving for Mexico, where the fight was still going on ...

Gerardo Machado was much like our Head of State in physical appearance, political behaviour, and methods, but he was different because, being quite uncultured, he didn't build temples to Minerva like Estrada Cabrera (almost his contemporary) nor was he a francophile, as so many dictators and "educated tyrants" of the continent had been. To him, Supreme Wisdom was to be found in the north: "I'm an imperialist," he declared, looking enthusiastically towards Washington. "I'm not an intellectual, but I am a patriot." However, he showed unconscious humour when he informed the public one day in his newspapers that he was "studying the tragedies of Aeschylus."

"He's a good candidate to join the clan of the Atrides," said the Student.

"From what one can see he already belongs to the family," said Mella.

"He'll soon give orders for the confiscation of *red books*," said the Student.

"He's done it already," said the Cuban.

"One goes down here and another goes up there," said the Student.

"And that's a sight we've been seeing repeated for the last hundred years."

"Until the public gets tired of seeing the same thing."

"We must hope for the best."

Opening their leather wallets—both Mexican, with the Aztec calendar embossed on the outside—they exchanged the scripts of their reports and articles, to read on the journey. In his corner, Nehru, with several papers on his knees, seemed to be absorbed in his own thoughts, hidden behind wide-open eyes. There was a long silence. The train reached the frontier in the night—the twofold night—of the coal mines.

"Cool, cool," said Nehru, leaving the others uncertain whether he meant to say "cool" or "coal"—but it was indeed cold in this second-class carriage, excessively cold for these men from hot climates. And the Indian went on sleeping with his eyes open until the train got to Brussels.

# 21

*... those madmen try to make people believe they are
kings, but they are only poor men who dress their naked-
ness in gold and purple.* —DESCARTES

"EXILED..."

"Banished..."

"Or fled..."

"Escaped..."

"On the run..."

"What I know is that he was in a church," remarked the
Mayorala. "And Communists don't go to church, not even in
Holy Week." And they started on their conjectures again:

"Exiled..."

"Banished..."

"Escaped..."

"Repentant, perhaps..."

"Converted..."

"A spiritual crisis..."

"Had a fight with his friends..."

And for days and days nothing else was talked about in
the Rue de Tilsitt, while they waited for the newspapers from
*over there*—February numbers in April—to arrive on their

specially slow cargo boats, in tight rolls of seven numbers with a picture of the Tutelary Volcano on the stamps. Because, of course, the papers published here said nothing at all about the Student, an individual of no interest to them. And at last they received news, thanks to a copy of *El Faro* of Nueva Córdoba arriving in May, about the World Conference at Brussels, where the National League of Mexican Countrymen and the Anti-Imperialist League of the Americas (which had affiliations in our country) had both been represented.

"That explains it all," said the cholo Mendoza.

"What foolishness," murmured the *Ex*. "Imperialism is stronger than ever. That's why the man of the moment in Europe is Benito Mussolini."

And the chestnuts bloomed again, and conversations on the usual topics went on in the attic. They talked at enormous length, under the slate roof, about "the old days." The most trivial events, contemplated in perspective and seen from a distance, acquired significance, greater charm, strangeness, or transcendence. "Do you remember? Do you remember?" became a sacramental—almost daily—formula, evoking dead people and dead things that were explained by the often secret mechanisms of a resurrected past, taken out of its distant context and brought to these latitudes. All at once, refreshing his crowded memory, the patriarch began revealing the hitherto concealed background to certain strange events or tiny circumstances, which gave the clue to what might before have caused baffled questioning and a flavour of mystery. As a fakir or conjuror, grown old and retired from the stage, may enjoy revealing the technique of his tricks and miracles, the *Ex* remembered the business of issuing money without security, in order to boost the national finances; the gaming houses set up by the government, where marked cards were used (there was a North American press that manufactured them with such subtle indications on their backs that only experts could understand them), and where the stakes had to be made in dollars, pounds sterling, or—to get hidden reserves of cash out of people's houses—in old gold coins or silver Mexican pesos. Then there was the affair of the Diamond in the Capitol, that octagonal diamond of incomparable brilliance, officially bought and solemnly inserted in the floor at the foot of the statue of the Republic, to mark the zero point where all the roads of the nation met—a gem that was so expertly stolen one night that, according to the daily papers, the theft could be attributed only to some international gang, unless they were anarchists or Communists who were very proficient in such tasks. Elmira laughed when she heard this story: "He sent me there [*she pointed to the Patriarch*]: I put my friend Juliana up to occupying the night watchman, while I [*gesture*] with a chisel you can buy in the ironmonger's at Monserrate, and a hammer that I had hidden between my tits, lifted out the diamond and carried it to the palace in my mouth. My word! I could hardly breathe! And afterwards, what a hullabaloo! But . . . how we laughed! How we laughed!" And now her laughter was echoed by the Head of State's laughter, as he waved his hand towards a drawer in the cupboard.

"I've got it there. It brings me good luck. Besides, it's what the anarchists call *restitution*. And I, too, have a right to restitution."

"Bravo, my President!"

"My *Ex*, my dear boy; my *Ex*!"

The months passed while chestnuts were replaced by strawberries, and strawberries by chestnuts, leafy trees by bare trees, green leaves by rust-red leaves, and the Patriarch, all the time growing less interested in outside events, was gradually reducing, limiting and closing in the ambit of his existence. That Christmas was celebrated in the attic, with

our carols, with drum and tambourine, Christmas dinner
of suckling pig, with lettuce and radish salad, red wine, and
Spanish *turrón*—as we used to celebrate it *over there*. And
seeing the cloth spread and the table laid, the Head of State
began talking about Napoleon, who was rising in his estima-
tion every year; but tonight he was not remembering Jena,
Austerlitz, or Wagram, but was enjoying something he had
read in a book: that Bonaparte and Josephine used to eat at
Malmaison—he a Corsican, and she from Martinique—in
our fashion, just as Elmirita arranged things: all the dishes
spread out together, some cold, some hot, in reach of each
person's spoon and fork, without all that passing to and fro
of dishes which went on in the houses of *nouveaux riches*,
trying to behave like real princesses—and I know what I'm
talking about!—with long waits and delays and rows of dishes
that take your appetite away and scour your stomach with so
much useless ceremony. Here you could take the bottle and
fill your glass without someone muttering the date in your
ear—as if the date were so important, when what one wanted
above all in a wine was *cheerfulness*, which was nothing to do
with a few years more or less.

And when the Head of State was in this happy condition, he sometimes glanced towards the Arc de Triomphe
and declaimed in a deep voice the famous tirade of Flam-
beau in *L'Aiglon*: "*Nous qui marchions fourbus, blessés, crottés,
malades*," reciting with brio the last verse—a pretty revolting
one, it must be said—where we are offered the blood of a dead
horse to drink. But the cholo Mendoza noticed that as time
passed more and more gaps appeared in the *Ex's* recitations:
some alexandrines never got beyond eight syllables; Spain
and Austria were erased from the poetical map; the sabres,
tinder boxes, shakos, soldiers' songs, roasted crows, flags, and
bugles remembered by Napoleon's veteran on the march were

all reduced to a rhymed medley in the reciter's memory, on the pharmaceutical model of:

> *Nous qui pour notre toux n'ayant pas de jujube,*
> *Prenions des bains de pied d'un jour dans le Danube.*

And the cholo Mendoza ended by thinking that if this last rhyme remained alive in the Head of State's memory, it was because jujubes for the throat were first cousins to the liquorice pastilles he was so addicted to. And perhaps this mnemonic element was necessary, because it was clear that the mental mechanisms of someone who had plotted, calculated, and schemed throughout his very long career were beginning to become disorganised. On rainy days, for example, after announcing that nothing would induce him to go out, he was impelled by the absurd need to visit a distant bookshop and buy a work by Fustel de Coulanges or the twenty volumes of Thiers' *History of the Consulate and Empire*—which he never even glanced inside when he returned, wet and with a cold in the head, from his useless expedition. Always fond of opera, he took it into his head to put on evening dress and go to hear some sort of a *Manon* at the Opéra Comique, but was bewildered because he didn't see Mephistopheles in the act in Saint-Sulpice. The action of *Carmen* got entangled in his mind with that of the *Barbiere*, because they both took place in Seville; and he muddled up the end of *La Traviata* with that of *La Bohème*, because in both the heroine died in the arms of her lover.

In his conversation, too, he often made mistakes, such as saying that Plutarch's history was written in Latin, or that the virus of Spanish influenza was called the Peloponnese. Soon he began dictating a leader on the political situation in our country, but stopped astonished, when well into his discourse, because he realised he had nowhere to publish it. Talking for talking's sake, he appointed and sacked ministers, planned and decorated imaginary public buildings, and ended by laughing at himself when he returned to reality in front of a bottle of Monsieur Musard's Beaujolais nouveau. He had a surprising passion for visiting museums. He went to the Carnavalet to look at the toy guillotines. In the Louvre, in front of David's *Coronation*, he observed disconcerting parallels between Letitia Bonaparte and Colonel Hoffmann's Aunt Jemima. He visited the Musée Grévin to see if perhaps (one never knew) he might find a wax figure of himself in one of the rooms. And the cholo began to be alarmed by the Patriarch's eccentricities one May 5, when he awoke with the fixed intention—luckily half effaced at noon by news from the homeland—of sending an enormous sheaf of flowers to the Invalides because it was the anniversary of Napoleon's death on Saint Helena. Yet a certain majesty, a certain strength, gave dignity and style to the person of the old dictator. The dignity and style of despots who have come down in the world; of those whose will has for years and years been law in some part of the globe. It was enough for him to lie down in his hammock for that hammock to turn into a throne again. When he was swinging in it, with his legs over the edge—now this way, now that, by pulling the cord that controlled it—he became a giant, a horizontal immortal ignored by *Pequeño Larousse*. And then he would talk about *his armies*, *his* generals, *his* campaigns, like the one—do you remember?—against the traitor Ataúlfo Galván—and do you remember that night?—but no; it wasn't you—in the thunderstorm in the Cave of the Mummies.

And one morning he woke early talking of it, and suddenly wanted to visit the museum in the Trocadero. And he went with the cholo to that gloomy palace, built in a style compounded of Saragossa, Moorish, and the Baron de Hauss-mann, with its graceless arcades and false minarets; the cus-todian was dozing with his jacket unbuttoned in front of a huge Easter Island head. (The Patriarch's mind can't have been functioning very well that morning, as he asked the name of the sculptor of that object.) And they set off through the galleries, each longer than the last, each containing more canoes, totem birds, idols bristling with nails, dead gods of dead religions, dusty Eskimoes, Tibetan horns, and drums piled up in corners—broken drums, with loose cords, worm-eaten parchment, now silenced forever, after having pre-sided at scenes of revelry or sounded appeals for rain or calls to revolution.

And thus, going from bone sewing needles to the ritual masks of the New Hebrides, from negro amulets to gold breastplates, from shaman rattles to stone axes, the Head of State arrived at what he was looking for: that rectangular glass case in the middle of the room, mounted on a wooden base, where that mummy—"I've spoken to you about it so often"—was eternally sitting: the mummy found in the cave on the night of the thunderstorm.

A ruinous piece of human architecture, consisting of bones wrapped in shreds of material, its skin dry, full of holes, worm-eaten, supporting a skull bound with an embroidered fillet, a skull whose hollow eyes were endowed with a ter-rifying expression, whose hollow nose looked angry in spite of its absence, and with an enormous mouth battlemented with yellow teeth, as if immobilised for ever in a silent howl at the pain in the crossed shinbones, to which there still ad-hered rope-soled shoes a thousand years old, yet seeming new because of the permanence of their red, black, and yel-low threads.

And here this thing was still sitting—as it had been *over*

*there*—only a few paces from Rude's Marseillaise, like some gigantic fleshless foetus that had gone through all the stages of growth, maturity, decrepitude, and death, a thing that hardly could be called a thing, a ruined skeleton looking out through two hollow sockets beneath a repulsive mass of dark hair that fell in tattered locks on either side of the dried-up cheeks. And this exhumed king, judge, priest, or general was looking out angrily across countless centuries at those who had violated his grave.

He seemed to be looking at me, at me alone, as if to start a conversation, and I said something like: "Don't complain, you bastard, because I took you out of your mud and turned you into a person ... into a per—" Uneasiness, vertigo, collapse. Voices. People arriving... And I find myself in my hammock, where the cholo and the Mayorala have put me to bed. But my legs refuse to obey me. Here they are, where they ought to be, they are mine and yet they are alien to me, because they remain inert and refuse to move. The doctor: Doctor Fournier, much aged. His Legion of Honour. I remember. I lift my forefingers to my ears to show him that I can hear and understand.

"It's nothing to worry about," he says, taking a hypodermic syringe out of his bag. And the faces of Ofelia and Elmirita are going around and around my hammock, appearing, coming together, talking, and I'm asleep and I wake up. Again—or has he been here all the time?— here is Doctor Fournier with his hypodermic. And I'm awake. And I feel fine. I think of Monsieur Musard's Bois-Charbons. But they say no. Not yet. Very soon. But I can't be so well—although I feel pretty good when they rock me in the hammock—because Ofelia and Elmirita have filled my room with pictures of Virgins. There they are, in rows on the wall, surrounding me, watching over my sleep, present as soon as I open my eyes, the Virgin of Guadalupe, the Virgin del Cobre, the Virgin of Chiquinquirá, the Virgin of Regla, the Virgin of the Coromotos, the Virgin of the Valle, the Virgin of Altagracia, the Paraguayan Virgin of Caacupe, and three or four different pictures of the Divine Shepherdess of my own country, and naval Virgins and military Virgins, Virgins with white faces, Indian Virgins, black Virgins, virgins of all of us, Ineffable Intercessors, Señoras of help in all trouble, disaster, plague, helplessness, or misfortune—all are here with me, covered in gold, silver, and sequins, beneath flights of doves, the brightness of the Milky Way and the Music of the Spheres.

"God with me and I with Him," I murmur, remembering a simple prayer I learned as a child . . .

Convalescence. Elmirita brings me a meal of our own sort—pancake, tamale, stuffed pastries, double egg flip, custard powdered with cinnamon, the only things that seem to me to taste of anything. I'm beginning to walk fairly well, though now I need a stick. The doctor tells me that soon, perhaps tomorrow, he will let me take a short walk. Perhaps go and sit on a seat in the Avenue du Bois, near the beds of gladioli. Watch the dogs from the great houses romping on the lawns, under the vigilant eyes of the servants of the great houses. Then I'll go in a taxi—my body demands it—to the Bois-Charbons. And I suddenly think that it's some time, a long time, since I made love. The last time—when?—was with Elmirita. Now all I ask of her is that she lift her skirts a little—a thing she does with innocent simplicity. It does me good to contemplate, now and again, that firm flesh, well shadowed with hair, deep, generous: here is transcendent goodness. She has changed very little since the days of my triumphant maturity, and looking at her, I feel a renewal of desire to carry on this brute of a life. Because I'm not beaten yet, no. I take my daily walk now. A little farther from the house every day. And one day, I don't know why, I think of the cemetery of Montparnasse, where my double, Porfirio Díaz, is buried. (From here I can see through the window the house where his minister Limantour lived.) So we go to the cemetery—the cholo, Elmira, and I—where also lies Maupassant, whose stories are so much read and imitated in our countries. We buy some flowers near Joffin's marble works. And we are taken in tow by the porter, dressed in navy blue like the custodian of the Trocadero.

"*Cette tombe est très demandée*" [*sic*].

We pass in front of Baudelaire, whom they buried next to General Aupick—a sinister joke. And now we are with Don Porfirio. A sort of Gothic chapel has been raised above his remains—either a dwarf church or a huge dog kennel, grey, ogival—where, in an altar under the dedication to the Ineffable One of Tepeac, is a marble ark containing a small quantity of Mexican earth. And this mediaeval tomb, dated 1915, is presided over by the secular and mythical Eagle and Serpent of Anáhuac.

I think about death. About Baudelaire, so close, although I can't remember those lines of his—my memory is failing badly—which speak of old bones and a deep grave for a body more than dead, dead among the dead. When my time comes, I would like them to bury me here. I tried to make some macabre joke, suitable to our surroundings, to show the others that I wasn't afraid of Death. But nothing occurred to me. We returned to the Rue de Tilsitt in silence. And that evening I lost the use of my legs again. And cramp in my left arm. And those sudden cold sweats in the nape of my neck and on my forehead. And that painful bar across my chest at times, but seeming much more as if it were on my flesh—outside—than beneath it. Doctor Fournier wants them to put me to bed. He says a hammock isn't a bed; that it's folklore, belonging to

Indians and Fenimore Cooper. The bloody conceit of these
people. They would like to put me in a Louis XIII bedroom,
so that I can suffocate under a canopy, or in one of those beds
like those at Malmaison, which were so narrow and short that
I wondered how Napoleon and Josephine could ever make
love in them. In the end they left me to rock in my hammock,
which moulds itself to the weight of my body—my body that
now seems to be full of buckshot. I go to sleep. When I wake,
the cholo tells me that Ofelia and Elmirita have gone to the
Sacré-Coeur to make vows for my speedy—"and certain"—he
added, recovery. Early in the morning they dressed themselves as penitents—or *promesas*, as they say *over there*—in
violet dresses, with sandals, but no hat or scarf in spite of the
rain, with an orange cord round the waist, and they went up
the hill to Montmartre, prostrating themselves on the seats of
the funicular before going on their knees, tapers in hand, up
the stairs to the chief altar of the church. I go back to sleep.
(When they came out of the sanctuary at Montmartre, the
Mayorala insisted on putting some flowers at the feet of a
saint on the right, who was alone and unprotected and must
be very full of compassion, because he had been put in a place
apart, very visible, chained to his post, reliving his martyrdom. She kneels on the wet asphalt . . . She prays . . . But Ofelia
brutally forces her to get up, and drags her away from her
devotions after reading the inscription at the saint's feet: "To
the Chevalier de la Barre, executed at the age of 19 years, on
July 1, 1766, for failing to salute a procession." Elmirita doesn't
understand how a monument to a heretic can be put up so
close to a church. Ofelia decides it would be too tiring to enter
into explanations that the zamba would in any case not understand, because to her the words "free thinker" savour of an
anarchist sect or something of the sort.)

I wake up. And Ofelia is leaning over me, in her penitent's

dress, and Elmirita in hers, but pouting out her breasts in an automatic gesture very typical of her, forgetting the garment she is wearing. And now a new figure, a nun of Saint Vincent de Paul—but a real one this time—who injects my right arm with a needle. Her head-dress is starched, her collar is starched, her apron is starched; her blue dress, the blue of washed-out indigo, reminds me of the North American overalls worn by all the workmen in my country. Candles, such as they've lit in front of the Virgins in my room; candles, just lit and beginning to sweat their wax; little red candles of altar lamps, floating in a cup of oil. Candles that will soon be put around me. I see it in those faces, yellow in the light of so many candles, leaning over my hammock and looking at me with forced smiles, while a pharmaceutical smell pervades everything. I sleep. I wake. There are times when I wake and don't know whether it's day or night. An effort. To my right I hear ticking. What time is it? Quarter past six. Perhaps not. Perhaps it's quarter past seven. More likely. Quarter past eight. This alarm clock would be a marvel of Swiss watchmaking but its hands are so slim that one can hardly see them. Quarter past nine. That's not right either. My spectacles. Quarter past ten. That's it. I think so, because—as I notice now—daylight is shining on the pieces of stuff the Mayorala has fixed up to muffle the light that pours into this attic from the skylight in the roof. I think about death, as I do whenever I wake. But I'm not afraid of death. I shall accept it bravely, although I've realised for some time that death is neither a struggle nor conflict—mere literature—but a surrender of arms, acceptance of defeat, dreamlike desire to outwit pain that is always possible, always menacing, with its accompaniment of hypodermic needles, its Saint Sebastian martyrdom—the body pierced again and again—the smell of drugs in the nostrils, dry saliva and the sinister arrival of cylinders of oxygen, heralding the end as certainly as the oils of extreme unction. All I ask is to sleep without physical suffering—although it annoys me to think of the gang of bastards *over there* who will rejoice to hear of my death. Anyway, if I want to figure in history I must utter some phrase when the end comes. A phrase. I remember reading one in the pink pages of *Pequeño Larousse: "Acta est fabula."*

"What did he say?" asked the cholo Mendoza.

"Something about a fable," said Ofelia. "Aesop? La Fontaine? Samaniego?"

"He also spoke of a certificate."

"That's easy to understand," said the Mayorala. "He didn't want to be buried without a death certificate. Catalepsy . . ." (That was the greatest fear of all country people *over there.*) "In my village they buried a man as dead, and as he wasn't dead he woke in his coffin, and he managed to break the lid but he could only get one hand through the earth . . . And there was another case in La Verónica."

It was Sunday. Ofelia closed her father's eyes and covered him with a sheet that fell to the ground on both sides of the hammock like the tablecloth at a feast. Then she opened the drawer containing the Diamond from the Capitol.

"I'll keep it; it'll be safe. When they've re-established order in our unfortunate country, and the revolutionaries and Communists can't get hold of this jewel, I'll go myself and solemnly return it to its proper place at the foot of the statue of the Republic."

Meanwhile, until this was possible, the diamond was dropped into the Infanta's handbag, and there, amongst powder and lipsticks, it marked the zero point where all the roads in her distant country met. But now Ofelia seemed to be in a hurry:

"The cholo will see to the matter of the certificate. I don't understand anything about it. And don't announce his death until tomorrow. It's the Day of the Drags today. I must go and get dressed."

And soon there was an unusual noise of horses' hooves and wheels in front of the main gate of the house. Elmirita looked out the window: there was something like a coach there, with a roof and windows, drawn by four horses, and people perched inside, very like the mule-drawn bus that, when she was a small child and there were no trains, made the journey from Nueva Córdoba to Palmar de Siquire.

"How old-fashioned these people are," thought the zamba. And she saw Ofelia go out in a bright dress, open a white sunshade, and climb into the carriage. Whips were cracked and the horses trotted off amidst a great noise of laughter and jollity. One candle in a silver candlestick was burning on each side of the hammock where the body of the Head of State was resting. The nun from Saint Vincent de Paul was saying the rosary. Outside the little balls of the boy hero were turning gold in the sun.

"What indecency!" said Elmirita, shutting the window before proceeding to dress the dead man, whose corpse would be laid out downstairs in the great drawing room. On the back of a chair hung the last tailcoat he had ordered to be made on the eve of his illness: it was too big now for his thin body. But that would make it easier to get him into it—with the wide crimson band, which had been for so many long years the symbol of his Investiture and Power.

*The creeper grows no higher than the trees that support it.*
—DESCARTES, *DISCOURSE ON METHOD*

*1972*
*... stop a little while longer and consider this chaos ...*

—DESCARTES

## 22

GREY WITH HEAVY RAIN, NOT A LITTLE SNOW AND years of neglect, the small pantheon with two doric columns still stood in the cemetery of Montparnasse, not far from the tomb of Porfirio Díaz, and close to those of Baudelaire and General Aupick. Anyone gazing into the interior through the black grille protecting a door with glass panes set in gold-coloured metal would see a simple altar on which stood an image of the Divine Shepherdess—a copy of the image worshipped in her Sanctuary at Nueva Córdoba. At her feet, under a mystic garland of roses and cherubs, was a marble ark supported on four jaguars, in which a little of the earth of the Sacred Soil of the Homeland was kept.

What perhaps some people didn't know was that Ofelia, thinking that the Earth is all one and that the earth of the Earth is earth of the Earth everywhere—*memento homo, quia pulvis est et in pulverem reverteris*—had collected this sacred earth, guarded in perpetuity by the four symbolic jaguars, from a flower bed in the Luxembourg gardens.

*Havana–Paris.*
*1971–1973*

# THE NEVERSINK LIBRARY